Praise for

HORROROLOGY

'A thing of beauty . . . a celebration of
all things horror . . . a cohesive view into
contemporary horror literature'
Upcoming4.me

'A dozen bone-chilling tales by modern masters'
Barry Forshaw, *Independent*

'All-new stories from some of the best talents in
the field . . . all demonstrating how horror writing
can be both entertaining and challenging'
Maxim Jakubowski, *Lovereading*

'A whole heap of talent within . . . you'll
enjoy this fearful experience'
Falcata Times

'Stephen Jones knows horror . . . he's become one of
the best guides to its shifting landscape'
Kirkus

Also by
Stephen Jones

A Book of Horrors
Fearie Tales: Stories of the Grimm and Gruesome

HORROROLOGY

The Lexicon of Fear

EDITED BY
STEPHEN JONES

ILLUSTRATED BY
CLIVE BARKER

Jo Fletcher
BOOKS

First published in Great Britain in 2015
This edition published in 2016 by

Jo Fletcher Books
an imprint of Quercus Publishing Ltd
Carmelite House
50 Victoria Embankment
London EC4Y 0DZ

An Hachette UK company

A CIP catalogue record for this book is available
from the British Library

PB ISBN 978 1 78206 999 7
EBOOK ISBN 978 1 78206 998 0

10 9 8 7 6 5 4 3 2 1

Typeset by Jouve (UK), Milton Keynes
Printed and bound in Great Britain by Clays Ltd, St Ives plc

For Johnny –
a true scholar of Horrorology

CONTENTS

ThE LIBRARY OF
ThE DAMNED

IN THE LIBRARY of the Damned there exists a certain bookcase, hidden away amongst the remotest shadows of this vast depository of knowledge, where the most decadent, the most blasphemous, the most sacrilegious tomes and documents sit upon a dusty shelf, their very existence all-but-forgotten except amongst a very select few.

Here you will find, sitting side-by-side, such arcane titles as *The Book of Eibon* and *The Book of Iod*, the *Celaeno* by Professor Laban Shrewsbury, the Latin version of the *Cthäat Aquadingen*, *Cultes de Goules* by the *Comte d'Erlette* Francois-Honore Balfour, *De Vermis Mysteriis*, the *Dhol Chants*, an uncensored edition of *The King in Yellow*, the Mad Arab's *Necronomicon*, the *Pnakotic Manuscripts* and their various *Fragments*, both the nine hand-written volumes of the *Revelations of Gla'aki* and Antonius Quine's corrected single volume, the *Seven Cryptical Books of Hsan*, the only remaining copy of the *Testament of Carnamagos* fastened with hasps of human bone, the suppressed seventh tome of the Englishman's *Libros Sanguis*, and the original German edition of Friedrich von Junzt's *Unaussprechlichen Kulten*. The forbidden knowledge contained within those pages is kept imprisoned between their covers and away from the curious eyes of mankind.

Only a very special few know of their existence, and amongst even that chosen cabal, fewer still have ever visited that shadow-haunted corner of the Library and dared to remove a book from where it sits and look upon the secrets contained therein.

It is said that amongst those Seekers After Truth who have gazed upon those profane volumes, some were driven mad immediately, while others tore out their own bloodied eyes rather than peruse the writhing calligraphy a heartbeat longer than they had to.

And on those forgotten shelves, amongst those titles that should never be named, there is one grimoire that is said to be the most terrible, the most hideous of them all. That book is the very Lexicon of Fear itself.

Within its seductively soft and supple pages are the words of terror themselves, made manifest by the tales they may recount to the unwary reader.

How is it, you would ask, that I should know all this? Once, long ago, I was a lowly student of the ancient science of Horrorology, able to come and go as I pleased within those unhallowed halls. I was one of those very Seekers After Truth who dared to pierce the veils of darkness and discover what lies beyond man's comprehension.

And with that forbidden knowledge finally came an understanding. I could no longer allow such truths to remain hidden any longer. And so it was that I committed the greatest of all sins – overcome with a misplaced sense of righteousness, I visited the Library and, when I was certain that I was unobserved, I tore a sheaf of pages from the Lexicon, quickly departing that place before my crime could be discovered.

But discovered it of course was.

How could I, with the knowledge I have accumulated, ever think it would be otherwise?

And so I fled, determined that one day I would share these pages with the world. That perhaps in some way, once the horrors contained therein were exposed to the light of day that maybe then, and only then, their power would be banished and the Librarians will no longer pursue me with their elongated snouts and curiously waving appendages.

But now, after countless eons, they have finally found me. I hear their high-pitched clacking in my dreams, and I know that they are close. I do not have much time.

So now it is time to share these pages with you. These are the words that comprise the language of horror itself, and the tales they tell are not for the neophyte or the fainthearted.

But be warned: once you have read them, there is no turning back. They will remain seared into your mind forever, their subtle terrors slowly twisting and worming their way into your subconscious until, you too, know the true meanings of fear.

But by then, my friend, it may be too late for us both . . .

accur'sèd *a*. 1: having very bad luck. 2: being placed under or as if under a curse. 3: ill-fated. 4: damnable. 5: involving misery. 6: (colloq.) execrable, greatly or strongly disliked. Origin: Middle English *ac-ursed*, from past participle of *acursen* to consign to destruction with a curse, from *a-* (from Old English *ā*, perfective prefix) + *cursen* to curse. First known use: 13th century. Synonyms: blasted, confounded, cursed (also *curst*), damnable (or *ac-curst*), goddamned (or *goddamn* or *goddam*), infernal. Example: *When you believe that you have been given or inherited special powers which can be used to cause harm to others. Such as circus clowns . . .*

ACCURSED

ROBERT SHEARMAN

I

WHENEVER SUSAN PITT went to the circus a clown died, and she wasn't entirely sure that it was a coincidence. She mostly thought it was. It had seemed a coincidence when she'd been a little girl, rather less so in her late teens and early twenties. And now she'd turned forty, and the world seemed flatter and greyer and just so very *real*, and she was firmly of the opinion it was a coincidence after all. Much of the time, anyway. If she stopped to think about it.

Coincidence did seem the most likely explanation. And that's because: (a) The manner of the clown deaths had nothing in common with each other (save for the fact the clowns did, indeed, die). (b) She never had any personal interaction with the clowns, she did nothing to distract them or alarm them. She just sat in the middle of the crowd, none of the clowns showed any inclination to pick her out from it. Except that last clown, maybe, and that was arguable. (c) Three clowns over a ten-year period sounds a lot, but isn't really enough to establish any pattern; a scientist would want her to kill a fourth clown at least before agreeing there was any precedent.

She hadn't killed a fourth clown. She hadn't visited a circus in years.

It wasn't something that haunted her. She'd been with Greg for twelve years now – six married, six not – and she'd never even brought the matter up. Not even as an anecdote – it wasn't a subject she avoided, circuses and clowns weren't things they had natural cause to discuss. He was an estate agent, she worked part-time in a bank. She hadn't even mentioned it on one of those first few dates, when they had both been so awkwardly casting around to find things to say. And that was a shame, because it might have made the date more interesting, and Susan seem more interesting too – and yet not a shame, really, because Greg had married her anyway, so what did it matter? Susan just hadn't realised that clown death was an arresting topic for conversation. Susan wasn't really a very gifted conversationalist.

In fact, when it boiled down to it, Susan wasn't very gifted at anything. She had passed her exams at school, but none with distinction. She could drive a car, but liked to keep off the motorways. They were glad of her attendance at work, but never much noticed when she took a day off. And Greg would come home each and every night and she'd have prepared him a perfectly adequate meal and then they'd have a perfectly adequate evening together, watching TV and holding hands and then going up to bed. 'I'm a bit useless,' Susan would sometimes joke, 'really, I don't know why you put up with me!' And Greg might laugh.

And sometimes she'd think of those poor dead clowns, and yes, of course it was all a coincidence. But she might get a *frisson* of, what? Guilt? Fear? Even a little pride? Because just maybe, somehow, she'd been responsible after all. This was hers. She had a gift. It wasn't much of a gift, but really, Susan would take what she could get.

II

The first death was one of her earliest memories. Indeed, it may even have been her earliest. Because all those infant birthdays and infant Christmases, hugging Grandma, learning to walk and sleeping in the cot – she couldn't be sure they weren't just stories she'd been told. But no one talked about the clown, and the recollection of his death hadn't been distorted by pictures in a photo album or repeated anecdotes, and some of it was still so clear in Susan's mind she felt she could almost touch it.

She'd been four years old, maybe five. Her parents had taken her and Connie to the circus. She didn't know what the occasion had been. Maybe there wasn't an occasion. She was still young enough her parents would give her treats for no reason. She remembers finding it all a little overwhelming – the huge tent they had to enter, all those people crowded about. Strong smells of animals and candy floss and body odour. She'd been frightened by it, and excited too, and she remembers deciding whether or not to cry or to enjoy herself. She remembers this being a conscious decision. She decided to be happy.

Most of the acts blur into one, and this is where her memories *are* distorted – lions and trapeze artists and elephants being led around the ring trunk-to-tail, maybe these are just things she expects from a circus, she's seen this stuff on TV.

Then there were the clowns.

There were three of them. Or at least three – it isn't the actual act she remembers so well. There were pratfalls, and they squirted each other with water, there were bits of juggling. What Susan found engaging was that they seemed to be a family. There was one older clown, and the others she took to be his children. The children were sillier and louder than their father, they were the ones who kept falling over and getting wet and being hit by planks of wood. And the father was dismayed by their behaviour, he wanted to take the act seriously. He might try to sing a song, but it would be interrupted by the other clowns' hi-jinks; his was the juggling that was destroyed by clumsier clowns than him. And each time his good intentions to make the audience happy were vandalised, he bore it as patiently as he could – he shook his head sadly, sighed, looked out at the boys and girls and shrugged. What can you do? he seemed to say. Isn't this just what life is like? He had a white-painted face like the others, but it was almost as if he didn't know he was wearing it – the joke was on him, at least the rest of the clowns knew they were fools.

And there was this one moment when he had five batons in the air, and there was such a fierce look of concentration on his face – and then it just stopped – and he hadn't been knocked over by another clown, and he wasn't distracted by a cream pie to the face – he just stopped, so suddenly, he just gave up. He let the batons fall to the ground. He took a couple of deep breaths, Susan can still see him doing that, and how he put his hand to his chest, and how slow and deliberate those breaths were. And yes, it was still funny, just how seriously he was taking it all, even such a silly little thing like breathing.

He walked slowly to the side of the ring. He righted a stool. He sat on it. The rest of the act carried on around him in its perfect inanity, and he watched it, the stupidity of it made him wince. And that was funny too.

Then, when the act was done, and the other clowns beamed at the audience and took their bows, the old clown didn't get up to join them, and Susan didn't find that so funny, she thought it a bit rude.

The clowns left the ring. One of them first went to the old man and offered him his arm, and the old man grasped it, and stumbled to his feet – and even now there might have been some last comic business, the young clown would pull his arm away at the crucial moment and let his exhausted father collapse to the floor. But he didn't.

At some point later Susan had to leave – it wasn't anything serious, it was probably for the toilet. Mummy went with her. And they were outside now, and it was dark and it was cold, and Susan could still hear the action going on inside the big top, and she wanted to get back there as soon as possible, she didn't want to miss a thing. But her attention was drawn to a van with flashing lights that she now knew was an ambulance, and there was a man on a trolley, and she knew it was a man because his hand was peeking out from under the sheet. And two of the clowns were standing near, and they weren't being silly now, their faces looked so adult like their father's.

'No, no,' said Mummy. 'Come on.' And she gave Susan a little tug, but when Susan refused to move Mummy gave up and let her be.

The clowns saw them, and one of them began a reassuring smile. And then just sort of gave up, and looked away. Mummy took Susan back into the big top, and at the end all the performers appeared in the ring and took a bow – but not the clowns, not any of the clowns, not even the ones who hadn't died.

Susan found all of this very interesting, and on the way home in the car asked about death, and what happened when people died, and whether Mummy or Daddy would die too. And Mummy and Daddy were behaving very oddly, and were being too nice, and that was silly because Susan wasn't crying, and Connie wasn't crying either, Connie never cried about anything.

Daddy began talking about how death happened to us all and that no one knew what it meant or why it happened, and Mummy said, 'Shut up, shut up.' And she turned to the girls in the back seat, and she said, 'Mummy and Daddy are never going to die, we'll be here for you for ever.' And Susan knew Mummy was trying to be kind, but she was actually fierce and frightening.

The second death was the funny one. Even in Susan's darker moods, if she thought of the second death she couldn't help but smile.

This time it was definitely a special occasion – Connie's twelfth birthday, which would mean that Susan was only nine. Connie said she was too old for a circus, but she was allowed to take four of her school friends with her as guests, and that stopped her complaining. She didn't want Susan to go too, it was her birthday treat, not Susan's, and once upon a time Mummy would have told her off for being so unkind, but it was her birthday so she let it ride. Or maybe Mummy was just distracted. Mummy was distracted a lot back then. Anyway, Susan went to the circus as well, and so did Daddy – the marriage was in its final stages, it was probably the last thing they all did together as a family.

The big top wasn't that big, not as big as Susan remembered from years before. There weren't any elephants. There was a lion, or maybe it was a tiger, and it seemed old. There was a trapeze artist, but the trapeze wasn't very high off the ground, and there was a safety net. The clowns weren't funny.

'It's boring,' said one of Connie's friends, and Connie agreed a little too loudly, and an adult sitting a row behind told them to shut up, and Mummy and Daddy let him.

The trapeze artist lost her footing, and fell from the high wire, and somehow missed the safety net altogether, and landed upon one of the clowns. The clown didn't even look up, that was pretty funny, he'd never even seen what hit him! – even funnier was the way his body was spread-eagled beneath the acrobat's bulk, arms and legs stuck out like a starfish. It's almost as if he had planned his death pose for comic effect, it was brilliant, and some of the audience actually clapped before they realised it was an accident. Winded and bemused, the trapeze artist got to her feet. The clown didn't.

They had to cancel the performance at that point, and Susan's other main memory of the evening was how angry Daddy became trying to get a refund. 'Whatever happened to the saying, "the show must go on"?' He didn't get any money, but at last got a voucher for free tickets for a future performance, and he was happy with this little victory. The family never used them, of course, and besides, the divorce was finalised two months later.

It must be said, neither of these clown deaths had been especially alarming. And it could even be argued there had been some practical benefit to both of them. The first had provided a useful life lesson to Susan at just the right age when she wouldn't feel threatened by it. The second had cheered up an otherwise disappointing evening.

The third death was something entirely else, and in retrospect, could have been so easily avoided.

'Do you want to go the circus with me?' Connie had asked. Susan was surprised. Connie was seventeen years old now, and wanted as little to do with her younger sister as possible. At best she seemed to find Susan's existence a pointless irritation, something put upon the Earth to embarrass her in front of her friends. That Connie was speaking to her at all was an honour.

'The circus on the common?'

'What other circus is there? Well, do you want to, or not?'

And the truth was, Susan didn't really, and very nearly said no – ought to have said no. It was cold and raining. Mum was out having dinner with someone from work – she said it was just dinner, but even Susan knew it was a date. Connie was looking after her, but Susan knew that under normal circumstances she wouldn't see her sister at all, she'd be barred from the sitting room where Connie would be playing music with her friends; and that didn't matter, she was resigned to a quiet time on her own, utterly on her own, in her bedroom, just the way she liked it.

Connie looked impatient now, and Susan couldn't bear that, she didn't want her sister to get cross. 'Yes,' she said. 'All right.' And Connie nodded, without a smile, as if she hadn't been the one who suggested it in the first place, as if Susan now owed her a favour.

They walked to the common, Connie let Susan share her umbrella, but only if Susan agreed to hold it. Even though it was raining, the common was still full of families, of children running about the arcades and getting spattered with mud. 'Can I have some candy floss?' asked Susan, and

Connie gave a tight smile, and said she could have one later, maybe, if she were good.

Connie paid for both tickets, and that was generous of her. Susan wanted to sit near the front, but Connie preferred the view from above, so that was that.

The circus was called Flick Barker and Son. The twist was that the ringleader was also a clown. He walked into the ring, red coat and tails, white face and gloves, all confidence and charm. He introduced himself, then introduced his son. The son came running on eagerly to join him. The son was dressed the same, but could only have been ten years old. He looked like a midget copy of his father – he stood beside him, looking up at him, beaming with pride and love.

There were no animal acts. Susan knew they had been made illegal some time ago, and she liked animals and knew that was a good thing. But without the animals there would only be people to watch, and they were never as interesting.

After each act the two clowns would emerge from separate sides of the ring, taking the applause as their own. 'What do you think of it so far, Little Flick?' the father would ask, and the little clown would roll his eyes and shrug. 'Well, don't worry, we have better acts to come!' Then the older clown would joke about the poor quality of the last performer, and apologise to the audience. The strong man was an ex-convict on the run. The tumbler wasn't well rehearsed, just drunk. The Russian acrobat girl was someone he'd bought cheap from a dodgy ad in a girlie mag. He'd waggle his fingers, and gurn at the crowd, and people would laugh, but his son would laugh the most of all.

It was supposed to be endearing. To Susan, it seemed fantastically cruel.

The children at school didn't bully Susan so badly any more. Not since she'd shot up in size, and become so large and lumpen. Not since Claire Hardy had gone that little bit too far, and Susan had lost her temper and thumped her so hard in the face that she'd been bruised for weeks. Susan was put in detention, of course, and a warning letter was written to her mother – but the kids never tried to hurt her again. But still she knew how they despised her, the nicknames they called her behind her back, that they would never be her friends.

She recognised the same streak in the clown. That there was no kindness in him. That for all that he treated the audience as friends in confidence, he despised them. That he despised his son too, there was no love in those big smiles and easy banter.

At last Flick the Elder said to his doting son, 'Does nothing satisfy you? Isn't there *any* act you might enjoy?'

And the son looked a little bashful, and put his finger shyly in his mouth. And then pointed at his father.

'You want *me*?' said Flick, in mock surprise. 'What do you think, ladies and gentlemen, boys and girls? Is it time for the star performance?'

Little Flick led everyone in an affirming cheer.

'All right,' said the clown to the boy, and he put his hand upon the child's shoulder in what looked very nearly like affection. 'Just you wait, son. I'll give you something that'll knock your little socks off.'

'Hurrah,' said Little Flick.

'This evening,' Flick told the audience, 'we have all witnessed some mediocre juggling, a few magic tricks a child could see through, some stunts barely worth the name. I'm astonished by your patience. I'm astonished you haven't demanded your money back, started a riot, started a revolution! I thank you. You are kind folk, one and all. You *deserve* something better. You *deserve* me.'

He took from his pocket some balls. 'Prepare to be amazed,' he said. 'Not just three balls. But four!'

He hadn't thrown the first ball into the air when he suddenly seemed to stop stock-still.

The balls dropped to the ground. And it was so delicious, the smug confidence that had never left his face all evening was gone. Doubt flickered across it, then fear. Susan could see it. The whole audience could see it.

Flick staggered forward a few paces, then stopped again. Didn't just stop – jerked to a halt, as if his puppet strings had been pulled hard and tight.

Susan stared down at him.

And breaking through his white face – thin and red, it looked like string, no, now fatter than that, worms. Red worms. Struggling out of his skin, and out, out into the spotlight.

Flick began to scream.

And it wasn't worms, it was blood, but the way it flowed was so thick and wormy! – squeezing out from the face in a dozen different places – the blood was finding the cracks in the make-up, and the force of it was breaking those cracks into fissures, the white face was flaking off and behind it was only red.

The clown put his hands to his face as if to cover his shame. As if to push the blood back inside. As if to, what? As if to tear off the skin itself so it would all stop, stop this, stop this.

And Susan still stared down, and she felt it within her, she knew that she was doing this. This was her *gift*. And if she could only turn away from him the clown would be all right, the clown wouldn't have to die. But she couldn't turn away. She didn't turn away. Turning away wasn't part of the gift, the gift had its limits, she didn't *want* to turn away. Her forehead throbbed, and it hurt, but it was a good hurt, the pain was so strong and she was the one in control of it. She fumbled blindly for Connie's hand, but Connie didn't take it.

'Help me!' cried out Flick, and it was shrill, and it was the last coherent sound he made. Where's your swagger now, you white-face bastard? You bully. You fraud. He jerked forward again. He swung his body towards the audience. He stabbed out one hand – one finger, he pointed directly to where Susan was sitting.

And maybe the effort was too much for him, because that's when he finally toppled over. Flat on his face, and that in itself was a mercy.

There was screaming all around, of course, and some people were fighting for the exit. Still more, like Susan, sat dazed and still.

She turned to Connie, and Connie's eyes were bright and livid, and her face was red, and Susan supposed she was furious. 'I'm sorry,' she whispered. 'I'm sorry, I'm sorry.'

'You don't tell Mum about this,' said Connie. 'You don't tell *anyone*.'

And there in the ring, little Flick gazed at his father, his own white face hanging limp in comic surprise, still looking so proud, still waiting for an act that would knock his little socks off.

III

Some years later Susan went to visit Connie at university. Connie was the first in the family ever to win a place at university, and Mum was so proud. Susan sat on a chair of dirty clothes and Connie sat on the bed smoking roll-ups. Some of the dirty clothes belonged to Connie's boyfriend, and Susan realised that this meant her sister was having sex – it made Connie now seem thrillingly adult, and more distant from her than ever.

They talked about things they had never discussed before, and Susan discovered for the first time how badly Connie had been affected by their parents' divorce, and by her time at school, and by her whole life in general. Connie said she had issues. Some of them were deep. Susan was proud her sister wanted to confide in her so much.

So Susan decided she'd confide in her sister too, and said that it still really bothered her about that whole circus thing. Clowns dying and that.

Connie said she had no idea what she was talking about. 'Don't be ridiculous, Susie,' she said. 'You're not special, don't you go thinking you're special. Oh, Christ.' And she lit another fag. 'I didn't mean it like that. Don't cry. Why do you always do this? Why do you always make me say the wrong thing? What's the matter with you?'

IV

Connie had always complained of headaches. It was a running joke in the family, when Connie was in a bad mood, 'Watch out, Connie's got her bad head on!' Maybe that was why Connie left it too late to go to the doctor. By the time she had been diagnosed with the brain cancer it was all far too late.

Susan went to visit Connie in hospital a few times. She didn't like to visit too often, she didn't want to tire her out or irritate her. She could see that each time she sat at her bedside Connie was struggling to be nice to her, to keep any conversation going, to keep her temper – she didn't like her younger sister, she just wished Susan would leave her the fuck alone. Or maybe that was the pain. It might have been the pain.

On the last visit – and neither of them knew it would be the last, though it was clear Connie had suspicions – Connie seemed a little kinder than usual. She even tried a smile when Susan came in, and she asked how Susan was, asked about Greg, how things were going at work.

'Oh, don't you worry about me!' said Susan. 'You're the one who needs looking after!'

Connie said, 'I need you to do me a big favour. I need you to look after Ruth for me when I'm dead.'

'Oh. Well. Yes, of course.'

'I'm not saying you have to adopt her or anything. I mean, this could be a temporary arrangement, until Ruth finds something better.'

'No, no. I'm sure Greg won't mind. I mean, I'll ask him. Yes. He won't mind.'

'Ruth is a gifted child, Susie.'

'I'm sure.'

'Ruth is a gifted child.'

Susan asked about Mark – she knew Mark was out of the picture romantically, but he was the father, maybe he should be, maybe he would want to . . . Connie said that it had nothing to do with Mark, the hell with Mark, Mark didn't care whether she and Ruth lived or died.

'I'm sure,' said Susan, 'in that case, we'll be happy to look after Ruth until you're well again.'

They didn't say anything else for a while, the two sisters just sat there in silence. Once in a while Connie would close her eyes and Susan thought she might be asleep, and that she could creep away without disturbing her; she'd shift in her seat, she'd even reach for her coat, reach for her handbag – and then Connie would open her eyes again.

'You'll be wanting to sleep,' said Susan eventually. 'You won't be wanting me here.'

And then Connie reached for Susan's hand, and Susan was so surprised she didn't even try to pull back. Connie squeezed the hand as tightly as she could, but there wasn't much power to it, Susan could have wriggled free if she'd wanted. Susan liked that thought, it comforted her. Connie turned her head on the pillow, faced Susan full on. She looked hard at her sister, and frowned with the effort.

'I *do* love you,' she said. As if contradicting her, as if Susan had ever said she didn't.

'Thank you,' said Susan. 'You too.'

When Connie died, Greg said he would go and pick up Ruth from the boarding school. Susan could stay at home and get the spare bedroom ready. Should she make the rest of the house look nice too, Susan wondered. Greg said she should do whatever she thought best.

Ruth was six years old, and Susan had seen Ruth every year at Christmas, so that meant, so Susan worked it out, that she had seen Ruth a total of six times. She'd bought Ruth toys each year until Connie had suggested Susan just send her a cheque, and Connie would pick out something more suitable. Susan was always quite interested to find out on her Boxing Day visits what she'd given her niece that year, one time it had been a calculator, the next a stethoscope! Susan thought they were terribly clever presents, and it made her feel clever too that she'd been responsible for them.

And Susan could never quite remember what Ruth looked like, she seemed to change so much from year to year. Never for the better, though – she somehow always managed to stay rather plain. Susan liked that. Plainness meant they had something in common, that they could be friends. And the thought they could be friends made Susan's stomach lurch, because now she had something to hope for, she really wanted there to be a friendship now and was scared she would do something to spoil it from the start.

When Greg was out she cleaned the house from top to bottom – twice. She rearranged the position of all the furniture in the sitting room and hoped that Ruth would approve. She knew that the girl would be small and confused and grieving, but still hoped that the fact the stereo no longer crowded close to the television set would be some solace.

Susan had told Greg to give her a warning phone call a good ten minutes before they arrived, but he forgot, or didn't bother, and when she heard his key in the lock she very nearly had a full scale panic; she looked in the mirror, patted down her hair; she sped to the front door; she decided that, no, she'd rather be found in the kitchen.

'Here we are, here we are!' said Greg.

Hair patted down, smooth as you like, Susan came out of the kitchen.

'Hello, hello!' said Susan.

'Hello!' said Greg.

He nodded his head towards the little girl by his side, sort of smiled, sort of presented her with jazz hands, *ta-dah!* This is Ruth, he didn't quite end up saying.

Susan felt the absurd urge to give the girl a handshake; she stooped down and offered her a hug. Ruth responded, politely.

'How was the journey?' said Susan.

'It was all right,' said Greg.

'You didn't run into any weather?' said Susan.

'A spot of rain on the M3,' said Greg.

'I want you to feel at home here,' said Susan. Not to Greg now, but to Ruth. Ruth nodded.

'What would you like for dinner? You must be hungry. You can have your favourite dinner. What's your favourite?'

Ruth considered this, and concluded she didn't have a favourite.

'Do you like fish fingers?'

Ruth supposed so.

'We'll have fish fingers.'

They all ate fish fingers, it was a perfectly adequate meal. And Susan asked Ruth lots of questions. How was school? Was it a nice school? What was her favourite subject? Ruth didn't have a favourite subject, any more than she had a favourite meal. Susan wondered what it was Ruth was so gifted in, she supposed she'd find out in time.

'I'm so sorry about your Mum,' she said suddenly, and as she did so, tears pricked at her eyes, and she wasn't really sure why. 'Anything I can do. Anything Uncle Greg and I can do. You know. We're here. We'll make it better. We're not going to die, we'll be here for you forever.' Then she got up to clear away the plates.

Susan asked the bank if she could take time off work to look after her niece, and the supervisor said they could cope very well without her and she could take all the time she needed.

'We can give you new wallpaper,' said Susan. 'We can make your bedroom feel like home.' But Ruth said it was all right as it was. 'We can go to the cinema today. Do you like the cinema? Do you like shopping?' They went to the cinema, they went shopping, Susan struggled to think of other things she could do with the girl. 'What would make you happy?' she asked her as they walked home, and Ruth stopped dead, and thought hard, as if it were a matter of philosophical contemplation, and said she didn't know.

At the funeral Susan was able to cry a lot, and that made her feel she was doing her sisterly duty. Ruth didn't shed a tear. And that was just the way Connie had been, Connie hadn't cried at Daddy's funeral either, or at Mum's, and Susan had rather admired it at the time, but now it felt wrong – she looked hard at Ruth's perfectly dry eyes as the vicar led them into the Lord's Prayer, and it was Connie's coldness through and through. Ruth had come to live with them, and she was Connie's daughter to the core, Susan knew she would never be hers.

'I think there's something wrong with the girl,' said Susan.

'Give her time,' said Greg. 'She's mourning.'

'I don't think it's normal,' said Susan.

And she was almost relieved that night when she woke up to the sound of Ruth screaming in terror.

She ran to Ruth's room, snapped on the lights. Ruth was sitting up in bed, her eyes wide, brandishing a pillow to protect her.

'She's here,' she said. 'Just like she told me.'

'Who's here?'

'*Mummy*,' Ruth whispered, and she couldn't even look at Susan, there was such horror to it, she could barely speak it out loud.

Susan sat on the bed and opened her arms, and Ruth fell into them. 'Mummy's not here,' said Susan. 'I'm sorry, I'm sorry.'

'I saw her.'

'And even if she were here, she would never hurt you. You know that. She loved you.'

Ruth shook her head, then buried it deeper into Susan's chest, and hugged her aunt more tightly, and Susan liked that, she liked it very much. 'Mummy said, the people we kill come back to us.'

'What?'

'They come back to us. They never stop. They never leave us alone. They'll hide in the shadows, so sometimes we think they've gone. But they'll come out sooner or later.'

'That's nonsense.'

'Why would Mummy tell me if it weren't true?'

Because your mother was a cruel bitch, Susan thought. And it was like a revelation, she'd never quite let herself think it before, not as bluntly as that, though now it was in her head it was clearly and utterly true. 'Sweetie,' she said. 'What makes you think you killed your mother?'

'I did kill her. I told her I hated her. I said I wanted her dead.'

'Oh, sweetie.'

'And now she is.'

'Sweetie.' She'd never called anyone that before, and it seemed to fit so well – she mustn't overuse it, though. She stroked Ruth's hair. 'It's all right. It's not your fault.'

She held Ruth for another half-hour or so, and called her sweetie a couple more times, and thought, *this might be good, this might work.* Ruth began to snore. It was nothing like Greg's snore, he sounded like a bulldozer. Ruth was quiet, and so vulnerable somehow, and she quite broke Susan's heart.

She tucked Ruth back under the covers, and kissed her on the forehead, and Ruth seemed to squirm happily at that. She turned off the light, she went back to her own bed.

Ruth didn't have any more nightmares after that. Or, if she did, they were mild enough that she never needed to tell.

But it was from that point on that Susan's own sleep began to be disturbed.

She'd told Ruth it was nonsense – the people we kill do *not* come back to haunt us. And she could have given her proof. The clowns had never come back to her.

They hide in the shadows, Ruth had said. And there, in the darkness of the room, Greg's body beside her fast asleep, it did seem to Susan that the room was nothing but a shadow now. Moonlight coming in through the window, a sliver of light from under the door – and everything else black, and getting blacker.

Could it be that poor stupid Susan just hadn't noticed all the ghosts watching all this time? Stupid Susan, who never got anything right?

And it felt like another truth – something cold and clear and indisputable.

She wasn't alone. She was never alone. She never had been.

'Are you there?' she whispered.

Her eyes were wide, they strained against the dark.

The first clown tottered forward. He was wheezing. She thought the wheezing had been the wind, all these years she'd heard wind and thought nothing of it. He was so tired. Of course he was. He sat on the end of the bed.

He had already been an old man when he'd had his heart attack nearly forty years ago. 'You don't stop ageing,' he told her. 'You never stop. It just goes on and on and on and on and on.' His face was bright white, and some of it was make-up, and some of it the skull beneath.

The second clown was against the wardrobe. His arms and legs were still spread-eagled, and she'd thought he'd looked like a starfish – but it wasn't that, not that at all, he looked like a spider. A spider missing a few of its legs, maybe – and that wouldn't be surprising, the body was a broken smear, you'd expect a few pieces here and there would have fallen off. He was so thin too, he'd been squashed flat! He turned to Susan, and it really wasn't quite as funny as she'd remembered, the mass of him so distorted and wrong – and there was something poking out of his mouth, and she thought it was his guts.

'On and on and on and on,' said the first clown. 'The show must go on!'

And even now Susan could cope with this, it was all right, night would pass soon and day would make everything safe and sane once more, there'd be no more shadows and no more dreams. So long as she didn't have to see the third clown. She shut up her eyes up tight.

She could hear nothing louder than her own panicked breath.

She tried to slow her breathing down.

She could hear nothing.

She tucked herself into Greg's body, and his arms swung around to hold her, and she thought – they won't hurt Greg, Greg's done nothing to them – as if there were some logic at work here, as if ghost clowns follow *rules*.

There was air on her face, and she thought it might be breath, but it was too cold for breath – and was that a good thing, or did it just mean that the air was dead in the clown's lungs? – and there was the sound of springs shifting on the bed, but maybe that was just Gary turning over (except he hadn't turned, had he, she was holding on so tight) – and then, and then – then there was something at her eyelids, pulling at her eyelids, trying to yank them open. Not fingers, surely – not unless the fingers were thin and sharp as toothpicks – but they were *tugging* now, something wanted her to *see*. She opened her eyes. She saw.

'The show must go on,' whispered the third clown.

So close, it was as if she had a ringside seat. And he closed his own eyes then, but he didn't bother with eyelids, not something as simple as that! His trick was better, he rolled them up into his skull – and then he took a deep breath – the cheeks deflated and pressed hard against the bones, they got sucked into the cavities, the whole head seemed to flatten with the effort. He puffed out again, hard, and his head swelled once more – his head popped out like a balloon – and out they came with it, out squeezed the red worms. Red and dripping wet and so happy to be free! And Flick the clown was happy too, he wasn't in pain this time, this was his whole act.

The other dead clowns gave him a round of applause, and Flick put a finger to his lips – they mustn't make too much noise, Greg was still asleep! The clowns looked admonished. Then Flick stretched out his other hand, just as he had once before, he pointed one finger out at Susan, only this time he was near enough to touch. He did. He did touch.

He stroked her face with that finger, and it was gloved and warm and soft. It was cold and thin and toothpick sharp. Still he stroked, did he envy her that face, that she had a face at all? He spoke to Susan, and his open mouth broke a hole in what was now a mass of blood. 'Get some rest,' he said. 'Big day tomorrow. Always a big day. The show must go on.'

And Susan slept.

There was no night worse than that first night. On the second, only the old clown appeared. He sat on the bed and muttered to himself for a while, the way old men sometimes do. On the third night he was back again, but he kept his distance and lurked in the darkness. The second clown was there too, draped all across the wardrobe, but he didn't turn around.

On the fourth night she made the clowns a deal.

The ghosts weren't visible yet, she knew she could only manage this if she could pretend she were alone. She spoke out to the shadows, to the little patches of darkness.

'I'm sorry,' she said. 'I didn't know what I was doing. It's a gift. I didn't ask for it. I didn't understand it. I know better now. I will never go to a circus again.'

From that moment on, they seemed to leave her be. Though Susan knew they were with her still, always, hiding just out of sight.

V

'I know we said we didn't ever want a kid,' said Greg. 'But we seem to have got one. And I couldn't be happier.'

That wasn't quite true, Susan thought. They had tried for a child shortly after they'd got married – Greg said that otherwise why had they got married in the first place? And maybe that was the wrong reason. They didn't put a lot of work into it anyway, it was a pretty desultory effort all round. Whatever happened, the months went by, and Susan never got pregnant – and Greg said, well, it clearly wasn't meant to be, and gave up on the idea altogether. And no one had said whose fault it was, but Susan expected it had been hers, she'd been the one who wasn't good enough.

So she said, 'We could still try for a baby of our own, if you want.'

And he said, 'But we've got Ruth, why would we want to bother?'

Ruth had brightened considerably the months since the funeral. She had decided on a favourite meal, and it was spaghetti. She had a favourite subject at school too, and that was storytelling, Ruth liked stories – and she had moved into her new school without a murmur of protest and made friends there immediately. Susan was rather dismayed by how many friends a plain girl could get. Greg had persuaded her to choose new wallpaper for her bedroom, and one weekend Greg and Ruth had been having such fun up there, getting messy, getting stuck to the walls themselves! They'd laughed so much. Susan could hear the laughter all the way downstairs in the kitchen. Once in a while she would bring them up tea and biscuits.

Greg too had never seemed happier. He would rush home from work, and he'd cry out, 'Where's my little girl? Where's my princess?' And at the beginning Susan would hear him, and her heart would pound, and she thought he'd meant her.

Connie had made provisions in the will for Ruth's care, and said that she was happy to leave her in the trust of her sister, 'So long as the authorities judge her capable'. And the authorities made some preliminary visits, and so far it seemed her capability wasn't in question.

And Susan knew that Ruth being part of the family was a good thing and that it gave the days more shape and focus. And she tried to love Ruth too.

Once she'd asked her about that night. When Ruth told her she'd killed her mother. When Ruth told her how the people we kill come back. And Ruth had just stared at her, as if she had no idea what Susan was talking about. And it reminded Susan of the way Connie had refused to discuss the clowns, and at that moment Ruth had looked exactly like her mother.

'We're a family,' said Greg. 'At last!' – as if there had always been something missing, as if life with Susan had been incomplete. And at weekends it was as a family they went out together, and Greg would indulge Ruth's every little wish – she could have trips to the seaside, she could have sweets and chips. And when Susan was on her own with her, she made sure Ruth didn't get her way. It wasn't cruel. It was only right.

'I love you, Uncle Greg,' she'd say before going to bed, and she'd give him a big hug. 'I love you, Auntie Susan.' And Susan got a hug too, but it wasn't a proper hug, a woman knows.

It would soon be her birthday, and as luck would have it, this year it would fall on a weekend. No school for Ruth, nothing but treats all day! Greg and Susan asked her what she would like to do. Would she want a party, she could invite all her friends? They could do that. They could give her anything she wanted.

'The circus,' she said, with the biggest smile. 'I want us to go to the circus, just the three of us.'

There was an ad in the paper, and it was ridiculously small, it had no pictures or anything, there was no way Ruth should have found it. BAMBAM BROTHERS BIG TOP SPECTACULAR! it said. FUN FOR ALL THE FAMILY!!!

Susan said no. And Greg didn't know why she said no, and demanded a good reason, and he folded his arms and waited, and Ruth folded her arms too in imitation. Susan begged Ruth to choose some other treat, and she hated the fact she had to beg a little girl. Ruth said she wanted nothing else.

'My mummy used to take me to the circus,' Ruth said. 'We used to go to the circus a lot. Every circus she could find. Sometimes they'd be miles and miles away, we were in the car for hours.'

'You must miss your mother very much,' Greg said. 'I mean, your real mother.'

Ruth said nothing.

'We'll go to the circus,' Greg promised. 'We'll all go. Do you like circuses?'

'Not particularly,' said Ruth.

That night Susan made a new promise to the shadows. 'I'll go to the circus, but I won't kill anybody,' she said. 'There won't be any trouble.'

VI

The morning of the birthday, and the rain falling so hard. 'It'll brighten later,' Greg said, but it didn't. By noon there was thunder. Three o'clock, and the clouds were so black it looked like night.

Even Greg suggested that maybe the circus wasn't such a good idea after all. 'But you promised,' said Ruth, and she didn't plead, she said it quite simply, it was a statement of fact. And there was no denying it.

Susan had been feeling nauseous since the night before, there was a sickness climbing her throat that seemed very real and solid. Her head was pounding. 'I'm not well,' she said, trying to sound as reasonable as possible. 'Why don't you both go to the circus without me, and I'll stay here, and make you spaghetti for afterwards!' It was such a sensible suggestion, and Susan wasn't quite sure how, even so, she found herself putting on her raincoat and her wellington boots and following the others out to the car.

Ruth got to sit in front with Greg because it was her birthday. Susan sat in the back, cramped and sore. 'I've never been to a circus before!' said Greg. 'I'm excited! Will there be acrobats?'

Ruth said there would indeed be acrobats.

'Will there be clowns?' Greg sang a little circus tune, the screech of the windscreen wipers kept time.

The main roads were clear, no one wanted to be out in such weather. The circus was on a village common some twenty miles away, and soon they had to turn off on to winding country lanes with no lights and no drainage.

'Got to try a different road,' said Greg at one point, when the way forward was flooded. 'But don't worry, we'll get there!'

'The show must go on,' Ruth agreed.

'This should be it,' said Greg, at last.

He pulled the car off the road. They stared out at the field beside them – dark, sodden, and very empty.

'There's nothing here,' said Greg. 'I'm sorry, princess. Maybe they stopped because of the rain.' But there was no trace of a circus at all, nothing to suggest one had ever been there.

Ruth said they should go and look.

'There's nothing,' Greg said again. 'Susan, did you write down the address properly? No, are you sure?'

Ruth insisted that they must go and look. Maybe the circus was over the hill. Maybe the lights were off. Maybe it was hiding in the dark, deliberately, waiting to pop out at them and give them a jump, that was all part of the fun. She had been to so many circuses with her mother, she had been to *hundreds*, and sometimes the hiding was all part of the fun.

The family got out of the car. The rain battered down on them. Ruth didn't seem to mind, she set off across the field purposefully. Susan and Greg followed.

The mud was splashing on to Susan's legs, rain was getting into her boots. 'Five more minutes,' she said to herself. 'One more minute. No, hell with it.' She said, 'Stop. Stop. Enough.'

Greg and Ruth turned around to look at her. On Greg's face, at least, there was some sign of relief.

'It's not here. It's gone. We're going home.'

Ruth said, 'Just a little longer.'

'We're going home. *Now*.' Susan turned, and stomped her way back to the car. She didn't look round. She just hoped the others were fast behind her. They were.

They reached the car, and got inside, wet and shivering. Ruth looked so disappointed, she looked *crushed*. Susan wondered whether she was going to cry. For one savage moment she hoped she would.

'I'm sorry, sweetie,' she said. 'We did our best, sweetie. You can see we did. It doesn't matter. We'll give you another treat, sweetie. Lots of treats, your birthday can last a whole week if you like. But no more circuses, okay? The circuses are done.'

Ruth was silent, and Greg was driving the car, and Susan couldn't see either of them as she squatted in the back. It was as if she were making a deal with the darkness. She told Ruth she loved her, and then she told her again. She told her she'd make sure this was her best birthday ever.

Roads that had been passable before had now flooded. Greg didn't find it funny any more. 'We'll find a way home,' he said. 'It'll be all right. Shit.' And all around was the wet and the black.

Until – 'Look!' said Ruth, her voice suddenly bright.

And for a moment Susan couldn't see anything, and she wiped at the steamed window and she squinted out. But there, there across the grass, there were lights, and there was music, there stood a big tent.

'We've found a circus after all,' said Ruth.

'But it's not *the* circus,' Susan said, stupidly. 'It's a different circus.' And then, rather petulantly, she added, 'It's not fair.'

'Now, I don't want you to get your hopes up, princess,' said Greg. 'We can't expect it to be open. Not with the weather, and it's getting late.'

But Ruth had no reason to be disappointed. They got out of the car, back into the rain, back into the mud – and the circus was open, and they were in time, just in time! Ruth jumped up and down in excitement.

'Three tickets, please,' said Greg to the little woman in the booth. The booth hardly balanced on the muddy grass, it listed sharply to the side. If the woman was surprised to see the family turn up out of nowhere, she didn't show it.

'Not for me,' said Susan. 'You go on. I'll wait in the car.'

'Don't be so stupid,' said Greg, and his voice sounded as light as ever, but Susan didn't like the way he was bunching up his fists, she had never seen him do that before.

The posters all around were sodden, they were peeling off the canvas of the Big Top, they were so hard to read. There was a picture of two beaming clowns – one an adult, one a child. ALL THE FUN OF THE FAIR! the clowns promised. TRADITIONAL CIRCUS – FLICK BARKER AND SON! ROLL UP, ROLL UP, ROLL UP!

The tent flap was opened, Susan followed her family inside.

*

Susan had expected they would be the only members of the audience, but it wasn't quite as bad as that; there were maybe a dozen other families spread around the huge tent, all waiting for the show to start. Had they planned to come here, or had they been trapped here by the storm as well? 'Shall we sit at the front?' asked Greg. 'Let's sit at the front!' And Ruth said no, she preferred the view from above, so that was that.

'I wonder if they sell popcorn,' said Greg.

'This isn't a cinema.'

'I'm going to look for some popcorn.' And that left Ruth and Susan on their own.

Ruth took her aunt's hand. 'Don't be scared,' she said.

'I'm not scared,' said Susan.

'Mummy was always scared too, right before the start. But it's all right. I'll take care of everything. I have a gift.'

Greg came back with popcorn. 'They have everything, you only have to ask,' he said. 'Want some?' Susan kneaded her forehead, wished her head-ache would go away. She said she didn't want any popcorn.

The lights dimmed. On, on, on with the show.

The music struck up, and it was the same tune Greg had been singing in the car, and he began to join in. Susan nudged him sharply, and he shut up.

The clown walked into the ring.

This was Flick. And Susan hadn't known what to expect. A corpse, probably – yes, a corpse, why not? And his face would be rotting off, and it wouldn't have got any better after death, would it? Because you don't stop ageing. You just go on and on and on – there would be worms, of course and blood, plenty of blood. And Susan didn't mind. She realised she didn't mind. She *wanted* it, because it would be out in the open at last, what she had done, what she was capable of doing – the special talents she had never asked for, it wasn't a gift, it was a curse, of course it was a curse. There would be the dead clown for all the world to see – for Greg and Ruth to see any-way, and at last they would realise how special she was. She wouldn't be facing the clown's judgement alone, and whatever he did next, whether he forgave her or took some revenge, at last there would be some end to it.

And so she felt a sudden stab of disappointment when the clown before her wasn't the one she had killed – he was thinner, and he was smaller. He was weaker in the face, even his welcoming smile was weaker, it was watery and insipid. And he was so very clearly *alive* – she nearly rose from her seat in her anger, she nearly cried out he was a fraud.

This Flick was the son from before. This was the ten-year-old boy she had orphaned all those years ago. And he was now grown up, he had a circus all of his own to play with.

He gave a nervous little wave to the audience.

'It's so good to see you here tonight, ha. Braving the awful weather! And we have quite a show for you. Yes, I am Flick the Clown. And let me introduce my son, the other Flick the Clown!'

There's a whole bloody dynasty of them, thought Susan, and she actually laughed, and the laugh hurt her aching head, it was like a nail hammered into her skull.

She turned her attention to the side of the ring, expecting another ten-year-old clown to run on. Instead Flick went to a silver chest upon a stand, and he opened it with something nearly like a flourish, and from it he took a wooden dummy.

The dummy looked uncannily like Flick himself. Not just the white face, red lips, ball nose – nor that he too was wearing the same ringmaster costume.

'My son,' the clown told the little crowd. 'Please be nice to him.'

Flick wasn't a very good ventriloquist. He didn't even bother to hide his mouth when he made the dummy talk.

'So, Little Flick, are you ready for tonight's show?'

'Yes, Daddy Flick, but I hope it's better than the last one!'

'Of course it will be, Little Flick, if all the boys and girls will cheer us on! We're the finest circus in town!'

And Little Flick turned his head away, and leered straight out at the audience, and said, 'It's rubbish!'

The clown's act was very much like his father's. Susan thought she even recognised some of the same jokes. But there were crucial differences. One was in the swagger of the delivery. This Flick didn't seem to have any confidence at all – where the father had sold the show on a ceaseless tirade of bullying egotism, the son stumbled his way through the routine with shy embarrassment. He sometimes fell so quiet he couldn't be heard above the spattering of rain upon the tent – 'Speak up!' yelled some man in the crowd, and *that* was what got them all laughing. Flick would insult the strong man, say he was an ex-convict; he would claim that the tumbler was a drunk. And then he'd steal a nervous look into the wings, just in case either one might march back into the ring and thump him.

The second difference was that this time the acts really weren't very good. If the father's insulting commentary had worked at all, it was because it was pointing at flaws that weren't actually there. The trapeze artist finished her act, and off she went to all the applause the audience could muster, and Flick said, 'I know that tightrope walking three feet off the ground doesn't look very impressive, but it's just as skilful as if it were high in the air!' And the dummy was none too impressed with that, and Susan was inclined to agree with it.

What gave her a thrill of horror was this – that here was a man copying his father's patter, and it was the same patter given as his face had burst open and he'd screamed and died. Here was a man re-enacting his father's final moments and serving it up as comic entertainment.

For a little while Susan felt sympathy for Flick, and then it was replaced with a burning contempt.

'But don't you like *any* of the acts, Little Flick?' the poor clown asked his son. 'Isn't there anything that might satisfy you?'

And the dummy squawked, 'Why don't you give it a try?'

'Me?' the clown answered himself, trying that same mock surprise his father had got down pat. 'But what makes you think I'll be any better?'

Quite, thought Susan.

Her head had been pounding, and her mouth had been so dry. She was so nauseous. And suddenly all that lifted. The nausea faded, her mouth began to water, she licked at her lips.

And the pain in her head seemed to shrink down to a hard nut just behind the eyes.

Flick picked up some balls to juggle. 'Shall I give it a go?' he called out to the crowd.

'Yes!' the dummy replied.

Susan stared down at him.

The pain was just as strong, but it had a focus now, and Susan knew this feeling, she *knew* it. The throb in her forehead seemed to beat out a little message, hey, remember me? She was in control. Something inside had woken up, and she could set it free.

She couldn't take her eyes off the clown. The clown stopped. The clown shivered.

She clambered to her feet. 'Sorry,' she said, to no one in particular, 'sorry, I have to get out of here.' The eyes still on the clown, why couldn't she look away?

Ruth grabbed hold of her arm.

'Let me go,' said Susan.

'Trust me,' said Ruth.

And it was too late now, Susan couldn't hold it in, the pain was a thin spike breaking out of her head.

The clown couldn't move. The balls dropped uselessly into the sawdust. Somehow he managed to force his hands upwards towards his face.

'No,' said Susan, out loud, but maybe no one could hear her. She could hear nothing above the shriek in her head. It's coming out, she thought, it's coming to the surface – it's like a worm! And at that she couldn't help but laugh. And the shriek was at Flick, she was screaming with such anger, he was *pathetic*, he didn't even have a son, he couldn't even have a child of his own, he had to pretend, resort to a lump of wood.

Flick's face was now held in his hands, he was shaking. Worse, he was crying.

'What's the matter, Daddy?' asked the puppet. 'Don't give up, Daddy! The show must go on!' And for the first time it looked like it might have spoken for real, the clown had at last bothered to conceal his mouth.

Flick lowered his hands. He was still shaking. His white make-up was streaking, but not with blood, it was streaked with tears. 'All you do is undermine me, Little Flick,' he said. 'I need to know you believe in me.'

'I believe in you!' said Little Flick.

'Do you promise?'

'We all believe in you! Don't we, boys and girls?'

'All right then,' said Flick, 'all right,' and he stooped, and he picked up the balls. And he began to juggle.

Susan watched him, mesmerised. Not because she had to. She wanted to.

Four balls, five balls, six – and how high in the air he threw them! Catching them every time. He seemed amazed himself. His face was full of joy. 'I'm doing it! Watch me, Little Flick, I'm doing it!'

Little Flick said, 'I'm proud of you, Daddy! Your Daddy would have been proud of you too!'

'Do you really think so, Little Flick? Would he have been proud?'

'I do! If he were here now, he'd tell you just how proud!'

And when the juggling was done, Flick marched up to his wooden son, wrapped him tight in his arms, and gave him the biggest hug.

And Susan's headache was gone. She felt good. She felt normal. She didn't understand how she'd stopped herself, but it didn't matter. She turned to Ruth, and Ruth was her daughter, and she loved her.

Ruth smiled up at Susan. 'I said it would be all right.'

'You did! You did!'

'I have a gift,' said Ruth. 'Mummy taught me.'

And it was odd how quickly the nausea came back. And the dry mouth. And the pain.

Ruth leaned into Susan, and whispered ever so gently in her ear. '*I keep clowns safe*,' she said.

Now he'd done his juggling Flick the Clown went on to play the ukulele and did a few falls. He wasn't very good, but the dummy seemed to like it, and at least he didn't die.

'I like circuses,' said Greg during the final applause. 'I think we should go to another one some day!'

VII

By the time they left the circus the storm had passed. It was still drizzling, but the lightness of the rain was fresh and comforting on Susan's face, and she wanted to stand outside and bask in it forever.

'We have to get home,' said Greg. 'Come on. It's past Ruth's bedtime.'

So they left.

As soon as they got back to the house, Susan went upstairs to her bedroom, closed the door and sat in the darkness. She called out for the ghosts to appear. She demanded the ghosts appear. They didn't.

At length there was a knock upon the door.

'Go away,' said Susan.

Ruth came in.

'Don't turn on the light,' said Susan.

'Does your head hurt?'

Susan didn't reply.

'I know it hurts. The headaches are so bad, when the power gets all bottled up inside, when it can't have release. Mummy used to be in such terrible pain. But it does wear off. I promise you. You'll be all right.'

'You have a gift,' said Susan, dully.

'That's why Mummy needed me. To stop hers from going too far.'

'What about me? What about my gift?'

Ruth said, 'I don't know.'

'Oh, go to bed,' said Susan, and even now she tried so very hard not to sound unkind.

Ruth closed the door behind her.

Susan called to the ghosts once more. 'Was it even me?' she shouted. 'Did I kill you? Or was it my bloody sister all the time?' And the ghosts didn't reply, maybe they were busy, maybe they thought she wasn't worth bothering with.

Once Greg had fallen asleep beside her, Susan got up, went downstairs, and sat in the kitchen. She made herself a cup of tea, and when she remembered it was there she forced herself to drink it.

'Hey,' said Greg. She hadn't heard him come down. He was yawning. 'Come back to bed.'

'I don't want her any more,' said Susan.

'You don't want who?' said Greg, but he knew, he must have known.

He sat down next to her.

'What's wrong?' he asked. 'Everything's so good. Hey, Susie, look at me.'

'I want her out of my house tomorrow morning.'

'You can't. Susie. Are you joking? Suze. Hey.'

'I thought I was something special,' Susan said.

Greg had nothing to say to that.

'She goes in the morning,' said Susan. 'Do you understand? I don't care where. I don't want her here.'

'You know that's impossible.'

'No. Really, I don't. You choose. It's either her or me.'

He just stared at her. She got tired of him staring, it wasn't even as if he were particularly good at it, he couldn't do a stare like she could do a stare. Or so she'd thought. So she'd believed. But on he stared, and she decided to close her eyes so she wouldn't have to watch him do it any longer.

'Greg,' she said. 'You know I love you.'

'Yes.'

'Just not very much.'

He stayed with her for a while, and at one point he even took her hand, and she didn't resist. But he let it go at last, and at some point later he got up, and later still he went back to bed. She listened for the door to click shut, and then she was entirely alone.

Upstairs she went. Into Ruth's bedroom.

Ruth was sleeping with her nightlight on. Her face was calm. She was smiling.

Susan stood over her. She wanted to wake her. She didn't want to wake her. And the ache was so bad now, it made her head swim. The mouth, dry like sand. Sick sticking in her throat.

'I am special,' she whispered. She *insisted*. 'I am.'

And then. The sudden relief.

Susan took all the rage she had in her head. All the shame, all the guilt, and the long long years of disappointment. She crushed it into a tiny dense ball of thought. She looked down at her niece.

The throb in her forehead felt so good.

Ruth opened her eyes. There was no surprise in them, and there was no fear.

She stared up at her aunt, and her aunt stared back down, and Susan wondered who would be the first to flinch, and promised herself it wouldn't be her, she wouldn't let it be her, it must never ever ever be her.

ROBERT SHEARMAN is an author and playwright who is probably best known for reintroducing the Daleks to the BAFTA-winning first season of BBC-TV's revived *Doctor Who*. His five short story collections have, between them, won the World Fantasy Award, the Shirley Jackson Award, the Edge Hill Readers Prize and three British Fantasy Awards.

af'raid *pred. a.* 1: alarmed. 2: filled with fear or apprehension. 3: frightened, (*of, lest, that,* or abs.); ~ (of the consequences, and therefore unwilling) *to* do a thing; *I'm* ~, (colloq.). 4: filled with concern or regret. 5: having a dislike for something. Middle English *affraied*, from past participle of *affraien* to frighten. First known use: 14th century. Synonyms: affrighted, aghast, alarmed, fearful, frightened, horrified, horror-struck, hysterical (also *hysteric*), scared, scary, shocked, spooked, terrified, terrorised. Example: *When you realise that the person you love is not what you thought they were. In fact, they may not even be a person at all . . .*

AFRAID

CLIVE BARKER

AFTER SIX AND a half weeks of passion, during which her suspicions about Vigo had multiplied, Marianne caught him, standing in the shower beneath a torrent of ice-cold water, breathing out a gilded mist. His eyes were closed. When he opened them, finally, and slid his lazy gaze in her direction, his eyes were black from end to end.

'Come back here,' he said as he pursued her through the little apartment to the front door, his wet feet slapping on the bare boards. '*Give me a chance—*'

She fumbled with the lock. But it refused to open; or else her hands refused to turn the key. She cursed them for betraying her. Had they been so blissful, touching him – was that it? So happy about him, they wouldn't now conspire with her to escape him?

He was close to her. Close enough to grab her if he wanted to. But he didn't. He kept a respectful distance, until at last she gave up attempting the lock, and turned back to face him.

'What are you?' she demanded.

'What does it matter?' he said. Then more gently: 'If you want to go, then this is the time to do it.'

He glanced past her, at the door. She heard the key turn in the lock. Heard the door swing open, and press against her back.

'Go on,' he said. 'I won't hold you. But Marianne, listen to me. If you choose to stay . . . you stay for ever.'

A chill draught came in from the corridor, and his body turned to gooseflesh. His nipples hardened; his belly grew taut as he shuddered. Sometimes, when she'd had her head against his stomach, she thought she'd seen waves of iridescence there in his skin, passing down towards his groin, the rhythms quickening as she aroused him. She'd dismissed this as an illusion. Now she knew otherwise.

'Make up your mind,' he said. 'I'm getting cold.'

'Don't bully me,' she replied. She was reassured by the open door. She could leave if she wanted to, in a heartbeat. Slip away into the corridor; down the stairs, into the street and away. 'First,' she said, 'I want to know what I've been sleeping with all this time.'

'Me,' he said, with a little smile.

'But you didn't show me everything.'

'That comes later,' Vigo replied. 'But we'll get there. If I could get there with anybody, it'd be you.'

He spread his arms, as if presenting his nakedness to her. The exquisite ease of him; the deftness of his features, the silk of his belly-hair, the elegance of his feet. His skin was so responsive to her touch she could write on it with her nail. Indeed he'd encouraged her to do so. Invited her more than once to decorate him with her graffiti. There were traces still on his shoulders of where she'd clutched him during their last coupling. If she looked closely she thought she'd find a thumb-print there, a palm-print; evidence of her complicity.

How could she ever claim she'd not known his otherness, when he'd lifted her to such ecstasies? She'd known.

She'd known.

'Well?' he said.

'I'm afraid.'

'Of what? Not of me. Come on Marianne. This is me. This is Vigo. I'm your dancer, remember?'

He began to move as he spoke. It was as though he heard some music she could not hear. And as always when he danced he began to get hard. She never tired of watching him. The miraculous fluidity of his hips, the subtle play of sinews across his chest and shoulders as he raised his arms, hands catching at the air. Sometimes the music he heard became frenzied, and his feet followed suit. He would stamp and gyrate, his erection slapping against his thighs, back and forth. Sometimes the silent rhythm slowed, and he would become dreamy, swaying like seaweed in the pull of some melodious tide.

That was how it was now. He was inviting her back to bed, where those liquid hips would press their freight into her, and the dance would continue, hour upon hour, sometimes so slow they were barely moving, sometimes convulsive, bruising, insane.

Watching him, she remembered how his touch felt, and wanted it again. Wanted him to cup her breasts in his hands and bathe them with his tongue. Wanted him to soothe her thighs with his palms, while he tenderly plucked at the lips of her pussy.

Then, when she was hot and wet from his tongue and hands she wanted his cock in her, easing in, slowly, slowly—

'So . . .' she said. 'What if I tell you I'm not afraid? What then? Will you show me what you are?'

'You have to choose first,' he replied. 'Tell me you want to stay. Tell me you'll love me whatever I am, and I'll show you. Or if you can't . . .' He stopped dancing; his whole body was suddenly in mourning at the thought he was expressing. 'If you can't . . . then go on your way, and never look back. Pretend we never even looked at one another.'

She glanced past him, thinking on this. It wasn't that she didn't like the woman she'd been before she met him. It wasn't that she didn't have ambitions for what she might become if she were to go on alone. She liked the world. But liking wasn't enough.

She returned her gaze to him.

'All right . . .' she said.

He frowned. 'What are you choosing?' he said.

'I want to see.'

'There's no going back,' he reminded her.

'I know.'

He moved his hands over his body, his fingers grazing his lips, then going down to the middle of his chest, thence to his navel, and down again, to the head of his cock. She followed his motion. Saw the sharpness of his teeth, waiting behind his lips. Saw honey sweat on his chest, beads of it, decorating him. Saw the iridescence on his belly, moving just beneath the skin, down and down and down. And saw where it was going, where it was gathering. Its bright force assembling at the root of him, and then rising up his cock, to where his hands held court.

Before it broke from him, and unknitted him in its riot, there was a moment when she was afraid as she'd never been afraid before, knowing that all paths but one had been sacrificed with this choice.

Then, without moving, it was leaping against her, and the heat of his devotion burned her fear away.

'This is love,' she thought, and pushing lightly at the door, closed it against the world.

CLIVE BARKER is an author, artist, screenwriter and playwright. Since publishing his *Books of Blood* collections in the mid-1980s, Barker's literary works have included such best-selling fantasies as *The Damnation Game, Weaveworld, Imajica, Everville, The Thief of Always, Sacrament, Galilee, Coldheart Canyon* and four volumes of the children's books series *Abarat*. His most recent novel is *The Scarlet Gospels*.

af'ter'life *n*. Related to *Death*. 1: an existence after death. 2: a period later in one's life. 3: a period of continued or renewed use or existence beyond what is normal, primary, or expected. First known use: circa 1593. Synonyms: deceased, demised, dissolution, doomed, ended, exit, expired, fate, grave, passage, passing, reborn. Example: *Sometimes, before you die, you need to have learned how to live . . .*

AFTERLIFE

MICHAEL MARSHALL SMITH

THE THING ABOUT embarking upon long solo motorcycle trips is you can find yourself getting into situations if you're not careful, and even if you are. When you enter new environments it's easier to do so as part of a family, or as a couple at least. A man by himself is less welcome. The lone male can be regarded as a source of potential unrest, a disturbance in the Force, even if that man is merely a newly-divorced bookstore owner riding across country for no more unruly reason than having grown sick of sitting in silence amidst the same four walls.

The man I'm talking about, in case it's not clear, is me – and I can assure you that I don't look like anybody's idea of trouble. My bike is not black or even red but a non-threatening shade of pale green, almost cream; I rode not as Gothic archetype or storm-bringer but as a very average human being of forty-nine-and-a-half, bored and crumpled and significantly depressed, or so my therapist kept insisting before I fired her, or actually just stopped booking further appointments, which is more my style of handling things.

I rode with no desire to 'find myself', not least because I suspected I wouldn't like what I found and it was too late to do much about it anyhow. I just wanted a break from a life that was driving me slowly crazy with negatives, lacks and losses and passivity; a life in which events happened to me, instead of the other way around. I wanted something different. I wanted to happen to something, or someone.

I wanted the fuck out of the hole.

In the end, however, finding myself is exactly what happened. Whether that's a good thing is hard to say. It's possible that writing this down is the first step towards an answer, though I have come to believe there are no ends, no answers worth a damn; that sometimes the most momentous change happens with very little fanfare, and true closure only ever happens in made-up stories.

And this is not one of those.

My name is Robert. I call my bike Percy, a literary joke that you'll either get, or not (my wife didn't, and she was smart and well-read) and isn't important either way. I do not, however, know anything about motorcycle maintenance. I bought the bike a couple years ago, driven by an impulse I didn't understand and which Aerin thought was plain dumb. I think I wanted to prove to the world that I wasn't the kind of guy who *didn't* ride a motorbike, a goal that has too many negatives in it to carry much force – and anyway the world didn't care. Probably I merely wanted to prove this convoluted thing to myself.

I bought the bike new, selecting one of very moderate horse-power, and studiously went on a course to learn how to ride it – aware this was un-cool but not wanting to foist myself upon the highways of America without basic competence. I passed first time. I generally do. Big deal. Being Quite Good At Most Things is one of life's most boring curses.

To my surprise, though I never bonded with the machine enough to study its inner workings, I found I enjoyed being on it, and became drawn to occasional two-day solo trips into the mountains. It was during one of these that Aerin eventually slept with her boss. That's a rather hackneyed act, of course, but the annoying thing is I could somewhat see her point. David is a decent guy, intelligent and amusing, and self-evidently making a much better job of holding back the years, both physically and in spirit. The fact her choice made sense only makes it worse, though. You're not supposed to stay with someone just because they're currently the best available, right? You're supposed to love them with your soul entire, *contra mundum*, against all reason, forever and a day, through the blackest hour and the darkest night. When someone bails on that it's hard not to feel evaluated and found wanting. Our daughter had recently left for college, and Aerin – who tends to act fast, once her decision is made – elected to get straight on with the next thing and move in with David.

And I felt . . .

I don't know what I felt. I was very sad. I was hurt. I confronted the realisation that the rest of my life wasn't going to be the way I'd assumed. After a few drinks I could muster some anger. And tears. But I've always been of a pragmatic turn of mind, and when you look your wife in the eye and see that while she still loves you she doesn't still *want* you, there's no point being an ass about it and making everyone's life difficult.

I helped move her stuff around to David's house, and stayed for dinner. She cooked one of my favourites, which was a sweet thing to do, or at least felt so according to the bizarre new existence I found myself in. It seemed a little saltier than usual. Perhaps that's how David likes it. Maybe she lives in a saltier world now overall.

She took our savings in lieu of half of the value of our own – much smaller – place, so we didn't have to go through the hassle of selling it in a hurry (just as well in a depressed market, and also because a couple of the rooms and most of the garage functioned as expedient extra storage space for the store). It was all pretty quick and very civilised.

And then I was in the after-life.

The life after the one I'd had before.

I don't know why it didn't immediately occur to me to go on a road trip. Shock, possibly, along with a need to maintain contact with at least one stable thing in my life.

I bailed from a career in publishing in the late 1990s, during one of the industry's periodic slumps. I tried to be a writer for a while, but it's neither as easy nor as much fun as it's cracked up to be. I'd drifted into publishing mainly because I liked books, so opening Book 'Em was an explicable (if risky) venture. The name was a nod to my father, who was still alive at the time and loved both books and *Hawaii 5-0*. He got the reference, and was touched.

The store quietly prospered, and is now an affectionately regarded fixture downtown. We hold frequent readings and well-attended book groups and have an excellent selection of letterpress greeting cards. Everyone would miss us if we closed. For a while.

After Aerin left I soldiered on for six months, turning up every day, until I realised I felt like a ghost haunting the store. Haunting my own life. Aerin and David lived on the other side of town and so I never ran into them, but I never knew that I wouldn't. I became a connoisseur of back streets and alleys. I'm not sure why I felt the need to skulk. I just knew I didn't have what it took to hold my head high, to risk suddenly dealing with the stranger with whom I'd spent my adult life, to see her looking embarrassed or wrong-footed, as though I was some quirky error from her recent past, a rush of blood to the head, now abated.

I stopped using Facebook after being unexpectedly confronted with a perfectly anodyne comment Aerin had made on a post of a mutual friend. It was the kind of throwaway observation she might once have made over breakfast. Now it was made across me, without reference, a remark to which I was a bystander. I was in the past, no longer updated, a living Betamax machine. Except in phone conversations regarding our daughter I had no place in her life, and it wasn't clear to me that I even had a place in my own. The hole in the centre of it got larger and larger. If I was not careful there would come a time, I knew, when the hole would be all there was.

Eventually I asked my two long-standing members of staff if they'd be okay with me taking a few days off, and they agreed with an alacrity that told me I hadn't been weathering the storm quite as well as I'd hoped. They gave me reassuring hugs, said they'd look after the store and send a summary email each day, and to take as long as I needed, seriously. I walked out onto the street feeling as if I'd been fired.

I went home and packed a few things. The house watched with the toneless expression of a dog observing the activities of the owner it likes second-best. Then I sat out on the deck and watched the stars and drank coffee out of a mug Aerin had given me ten years ago. When people think they leave, they don't, really. They just move out of reach. They climb out of the hole, leaving it deeper.

I left early the next morning, on the road before I'd decided where I was going. At the intersection I made a spur-of-the-moment choice to head up to Tahoe, a place we'd stayed many, many times. In some ways this made it an odd choice, but I couldn't spend the rest of my life avoiding anything coloured with previous experience. If I wanted to avoid having nothing but a past-life, some things had to persist through the breakage.

I knew places to go in Tahoe, nice places to sit, and eat, and drink. It was my place as much as anyone's. My place as much as anywhere.

It takes about five hours. The first three-quarters are a diagonal slog across the featureless central valley, arid and devoid of charm. Once you get the other side of Sacramento and start weaving up into the mountains, however, it rapidly begins to seem worth it. The novelty of doing the journey on the bike was almost enough to overlay the contrast with doing it many times before with Aerin, and my daughter.

Kim wasn't lost to me, after all, at least in no more than the ways that come to all parents when their child opens the door and walks out into the world. She had taken a judicious and even-handed approach to her parents' parting, and as I drove higher into the forests it was a comfort to know I was due to see her in a week.

In fact I did not, and it's unclear whether I'll ever see her again. It breaks my heart, but I know that it would be far better if I did not.

I'm sorry.

I keep doing that, I know. The foreshadowing. It's a cheap trick, a would-be writer's conceit, but it's also how life works. Everything is foreshadowed once it's happened, and I have now happened. The man I'm describing, the one still an hour away from Lake Tahoe, with a full bladder and an increasingly strident desire for a beer, is the man I was a few weeks ago. The guy who opened Book 'Em is the man I was over ten years back. The one who placed a ring on the finger of a feisty girl from Portland called Aerin (who lit up every room I ever saw her in, and who, I am sure, truly meant it when she swore she'd be forever true) is twenty-five years in the past. The cat's out of the bag in those lives. I know what happens, which road fate pushes those guys down. They become me. The person I am now, who casts a dark shadow back down his years, limiting everyone he once was.

We all cast shadows. They are dark.

When I reached South Tahoe I stopped to take a leak and get a Starbucks, having decided I'd head up the west shore to Tahoe City. By then the presence of the past had started to weigh more heavily.

Though we'd stayed many times at both ends of the lake, the arrangements were different. The south was where we came as a family, just the three of us, to a comfortable resort made of little town houses. We'd gone to the north end to hang with friends. None would be there now, thankfully – Aerin had effectively received custody of most of them, what with her being, like, sociable – but it meant, I hoped, that being up there by myself would seem less of a wrench in comparison.

The remainder of the drive was beautiful, flicker-lit by late-afternoon sun filtered through fir and pine. I stopped at the vista point to look down over tiny Fannette Island in Emerald Bay, as was traditional, and had the place to myself. Normally it's tough to find a space in the lot.

I got off the bike but didn't stay long. I could hear too many echoes of my daughter, who'd been fascinated by the tiny ruined structure on the island – the remains of a single stone-walled 'tea house' built decades ago by the wealthy owner of a house on the nearby shore – and used to imagine aloud about how it might be like to live in it alone forever. I even thought about calling Kim, to tell her where I was, but couldn't get a signal. Just as well, probably. I wasn't sure my voice would sound steady enough.

Instead I stood looking down, realising everything about my life had changed. That, in fact, I didn't even have one any more. I had me. That's all.

So now what?

An hour later, cold and ass-sore, I pulled into Tahoe City. You need to decelerate pretty sharply when you arrive, as – despite the name – you can be out the other side of town in five minutes if the lights are with you. The main street was quiet. It was out of season and there'd been no snow. Didn't look like I'd have any trouble getting a room, so I elected to go find a drink first.

The sky had turned opaque and frosty. I parked on the street, steadfastly ignoring the sandwich place we always went for lunch, which was closed anyway. I also ignored Sammick's – the bar we'd spent entire drunken evenings in (pre-Kim era); gazed at yearningly from the child-friendly restaurant across the street (young Kim); and then gone back to taking a nostalgic single beer in with friends, at the start of the evening (older Kim, back at the vacation rental with the other teens, while the adults dropped thirty bucks each on tiny entrées in restaurants whose wares had been checked and ratified and condoned by unknown others on Yelp, well ahead of time, God forbid there should be any surprises in our middle-aged lives).

Further along was a basement bar that was so cagey about its name that I'd never internalised it despite walking past about probably two hundred times. I didn't notice now, either. I don't know it to this day.

As I approached, a red-faced man in a pale blue sweater came wheezing up the stairs. He was overweight, skin parched, sandy hair dry, eyes vague and watery. He nearly knocked into me, lurching straight across the sidewalk as though I wasn't there. He lit a cigarette, took a long drag, and then wandered off up the street, at a fair clip, as if in a hurry to be nowhere in particular.

I went downstairs. What it should have been called was the Red Bar. It was dark, lit only by wall sconces with red shades. The chairs and banquets were upholstered in battered red velvet or whatever the cheaper version is. The only sizeable light fitting in the place – behind the bar – had been shrouded with a red cloth. It was a place you'd go for an assignation or to get profoundly drunk, neither of which I had in mind. The hefty woman behind the counter watched me impassively as I approached. Otherwise it was empty and smelled of old beer.

I smiled at her. 'Wow – what'd you say?'

I don't often try to be charming. The woman's response reminded me why. There wasn't one. I wondered what Aerin's new guy would have said in the circumstances, and if it would have worked. I suspect so. I've laughed at David's jokes many times. 'I'll take a Sierra,' I said.

I carried the beer to a corner table and sat so I could look out over the room. I like the Sierra Nevada IPA very much, but almost never drink it at home. For a long time – ten, fifteen years – it's been my practice to drink exactly three beers in the evening. Extensive testing has shown that if these are something like Longboard or one of the Budweiser/Coors/Corona brands of wet air, I get up the next morning like nothing's happened. With anything even a touch stronger, like the Sierra, it becomes tangled with factors like how much I ate, whether I remembered to drink some water afterwards.

I dislike a mild hangover even more than a serious one. With a bad one you know you're screwed, and mentally take the day off. When it's mild it creeps up insidiously, making the world feel flat and grey and sad in a way that seems part of you, instead of explicable by external factors.

So I stopped drinking Sierra. That's the kind of thing grown-ups do. Avoid the foods that make you feel bloated, even though they're great. Exercise, even though it's never given you a moment's pleasure. Stop enjoying things for fear of making other things worse. Step carefully around the hole, but keep it in mind. Live in the shadow of absence, always.

I remained the only customer. It was early Friday night. 'Seriously,' I said. 'Kind of quiet, isn't it?'

She took a while about it, but eventually turned her head in my direction. Her face was big, white and doughy. 'What did you expect?'

'Well, some people, I guess.'

'There's people.'

The conversation wasn't going anywhere. I realised that if Sandy and Karen were going to make good on their promise of keeping me up to date on the store, they might have sent something by now, and if not, then getting my phone out would at least signal to the World's Least Friendly Bar Person that I was done trying with her.

No signal, though. Happens sometimes around the lake. I looked in the direction of the barmaid. She was ahead of me, and nodded curtly at a sign on the wall.

NO, WE DON'T HAVE ANY FUCKING WIFI.

I like a locals' bar as much as the next guy, but this place was playing too hard to get. I'd finish my beer to show I hadn't been cowed, then go find a place to stay.

I made it last ten minutes, then visited the john. Beer has always gone through me fast. The bathroom smelled ripe, as though someone had done serious business in the stall, only moments before, though that can't have been so.

When I came out I realised it was still early and it wasn't like I had anywhere to go except a lonely motel room whose location I had yet to determine. So I ordered another Sierra. The woman served me, and took my money, without recourse to speech.

'Are you always this way,' I asked, as I took my beer to the table, 'or is there something about me that brings it out in you?'

She raised one eyebrow an infinitesimal amount, a gesture I found impossible to interpret.

'I'll be back,' I said. 'Contain your excitement.'

I went upstairs to the sidewalk. A bad habit I've reclaimed since Aerin went, somewhat bloody-mindedly, is the occasional cigarette. When I gave up, fifteen years ago – after significant (some might say relentless) encouragement from my wife – I had to do it clean. I didn't understand moderation then. I do now. After years of being measured, playing the long game, I believe I can have a couple of cigarettes each day without falling back down the rabbit hole. Believe, or kid myself. Either way, I do it.

I smoked one, slowly. It was cold, and getting dark. There was still nobody around, and it occurred to me that no one in the entire world knew where I was. Literally *no one*.

Right here and now, I was not a bookstore owner. I was not divorced. I was never married. I did not have a folder on my laptop with two draft novels that would never – *should* never – see the light of day. I was not a father. Other than being a man, I was a blank slate. I'd never said any of the things I'd said, never done any of the things I'd done, never been any of the places I'd been.

I was a male human with a motorbike. A full head of hair, most of it not grey. A body that was in acceptable shape, due to pleasure-free runs, an active metabolism, and continued low-level self-denial. That's all. I could tell the next person I met that I was a cop, a chef, a petty-thief trying to go straight, a librarian, a college professor, a recovering drug addict, a Catholic priest on the lam. This thought was not even slightly original, I knew, and did not excite me or feel liberating. It merely made me realise that the truth about me was as arbitrary as any of these fictions, and that I felt no more attached to it.

How had I ended up here? There had been very few choices that I remembered. How had I wound up being me, here, now? Even my name felt random. 'Robert' – what does that *mean*?

I shook my head abruptly, irritated at myself. You can get heartily sick of your own self-pity. It's another way of honouring the hole, of letting it stare back into you. I made a mental note to drink the next beer more slowly.

I was about to flick the end off my cigarette and stow the butt (a lifelong habit when there was no alternative, despite the fact it makes the pack smell bad: my father was hell on people who littered in any shape or form), when I realised that I'd dropped it to the sidewalk instead.

I looked down at it. Dad was eight years dead. There were other butts in the gutter. I'd spent a long time being the guy who didn't do that. What would happen if I let the butt lie? Did I care enough to find out? Could choices that small change the future? Wasn't it time to start making my own, rather than letting other people's choices make me?

Did that even *mean* anything, or was it just a trite motivational tweet?

I picked up the butt. A choice, I guess, even if it was to keep doing what I'd always done before. As I walked back downstairs I realised that instead of waiting for an email I could call the store and check on business myself, like an actual boss. Still no bars on the phone, though.

'What's up with the Verizon signal?' I asked the barmaid, when I got back into the red gloom.

There was no one behind the bar. Someone was sitting at my table, however. This confused me. It wasn't the barmaid. This woman was younger, much slimmer, long red hair instead of the scruffy dyed-blonde mess the other woman had sported. She was wearing black jeans and a long black coat.

On my trip to the john earlier it had been clear there was no rear entrance to the bar. Both patrons and staff only had one way in, and out. I'd been standing on the sidewalk right in front of the entrance to the steps. Nobody had come out, or entered.

'I need a ride,' she said.

'Who are you?'

'I'm the girl who needs a ride.'

'Where'd she go? The woman behind the bar?'

'Does it matter?'

'Kind of.'

'I dunno. Backstage, I guess.' She indicated my beer. 'You mind?' She picked it up before I had time to answer, and took a swallow. 'I don't have any money.'

I sat down opposite. 'Look, who are you?'

'Just a girl, dude. The girl who needs a ride. You've got a bike, right? I saw you pull into town.'

'Yes, but—'

'So I need a ride.'

'I'm staying in town tonight.'

'Tomorrow's good. I'll wait.'

'But why would I give you a ride?'

'You got much else to do?'

I did not, but that didn't mean I was going to do what she wanted. It's not the kind of thing I do. I couldn't seem to disengage from the conversation, however. 'Where are you headed?'

'Aha. That, I don't know.'

'How could I give you a ride if you don't know where you're going?'

'You always need a destination before you start?'

'Well, yeah.'

'Really? Have you found that's how life works?' She helped herself to another sip of my beer, and stood up. 'I need a ride,' she said, again, and walked out.

I drank my drink slowly. By the time I was done, the barmaid was back, re-appearing from a side door behind the bar that I hadn't noticed before.

I ordered another Sierra. And another.

When I was eventually finished in the bar, riding the bike clearly wasn't a good idea and so I took my bag off the back and walked to the nearest motel. It was up a small hill off the main drag, old school L-shaped. Weirdly, I'd seen the guy behind the desk before. It was the red-faced man in the blue sweater who'd nearly knocked into me coming out of the bar earlier.

He looked exhausted. He didn't ask to see ID or a credit card. He just handed me a key for #9 without a word and wandered into the back area, from which the sound of a television leaked. Somebody on it was saying words but it wasn't clear what they were.

The room was every motel room I'd ever been in. Two doubles. Carpet in a colour that has no name, counterpane in dull ochre. Boxy old TV. A painting of I-have-no-idea-what. Two glasses in the bathroom, wrapped in that stuff they wrap them in.

I filled both of these with water, drank one, and lay on the bed for a moment, thinking I'd get my shit together and then go find something to eat.

I woke several hours later. I had no idea of where I was, or anything about the world at all, apart from the fact my head hurt. Not terribly, but enough.

I fumbled for the glass on the nightstand and drank the contents. It didn't make me feel a whole lot better. I could tell I was hungry – I'd skipped lunch on the road – but the big red lights on the ancient clock radio said it was after midnight, and so my chances of finding somewhere open were around nil. Though maybe not quite nil.

I sat up, waited for my brain to catch up with me, then stood. I could try being the kind of guy who went out and attempted to get something to eat. It felt quite brave.

I picked my coat off the chair and opened the door. She was standing outside, as if she'd been waiting. The girl with the long red hair.

'I need a ride,' she said, patiently.

'Hell are you doing here?'

'I just said.'

I pulled the door closed and walked away, down the access to the main road. She followed, a few yards behind.

For half the walk the frigid air made me feel much more drunk, but then my head started to clear a little. By the time I got to the main drag I was thinking coherently enough to notice there were no cars parked along it. None at all. 'Where the heck is everyone?'

'Where they always are.'

'Which is?'

She drew to a halt by my side. 'You know. Around.'

'What's that supposed to mean? And there was no one in the bar earlier, either.'

She laughed. 'Yeah, there were.'

'There wasn't.'

'Was too. You just didn't see them. Didn't notice. You saw the woman behind the counter, though, right? Because you wanted a drink. She was relevant. She had a bearing. Nobody else did. That's your world right now.'

I'm dreaming, I thought. *Either I never took the trip, or else I'm still asleep in the motel.*

Even as the thought went through my head, I knew it wasn't so. I'll foreshadow, but I won't use a cheap trick like dreaming. Also, I knew I wasn't. You do. I do, anyhow. But I could also tell that something wasn't right.

'Is there something wrong with me?'

'Like what?'

'Why couldn't I see these alleged people earlier?'

'Because you're dead.'

I stared at her. She laughed. 'Not really. Well, in a manner of speaking, maybe. Look, dude, I don't know. But I saw you walk in. And it was like you weren't even *there*. You talked to the barmaid because you wanted a beer. Otherwise . . . It's like nobody else exists for you. All you're seeing is the inside of your own head. You saw those people, but didn't really *see* them. It's why I asked you for a ride, rather than anybody else. You saw *me*, too.'

'I don't get it. Why?'

'We all want to be where we're needed.'

'I don't need you.'

'But you don't need *anyone*, right? Yeah, you're still breathing. But your life – and I'm using the term loosely – seems kind of nothing to me. There's plenty of people without a heartbeat who still affect people's lives. You . . . well. You tell me. You qualify as "alive"?'

'Normally I need to be married to someone for a couple of decades before I'll let them talk to me this way.'

'Not sure you've got time for that. Plus it's not like it worked out so well last time.'

'Screw you,' I said. 'Wait – what did you just say?'

'Nothing.'

'How do you know I was married?'

She took my hand, held it up. 'Wedding ring, duh.'

'Oh.' For a moment I thought I'd been onto something. But yes, I don't wear it any more but there's still a paler ring around the finger, where the wedding band used to be.

A guy I talked to in a bar once said there always would be. Like scar tissue. Though he was the most bitter individual I've ever had the privilege to listen to, I suspect he's right – because you get scars after healing, too. The question is what's underneath. What's left in the hole.

'I need a ride,' the girl said.

'You're like a broken record.'

'Time's drawing on. You have to decide.'

'Decide what?'

'What happens next.'

'I don't know. I don't care.'

'That's not good enough. It never has been.'

'And yet I've lived.'

'Really?'

'I have a daughter. I had a marriage. I have a bookstore. I . . . I've done things. You don't know me. I don't know you. I don't even know your name.'

'It's Hecate.'

'Strange name.'

'I'm a strange girl. You can call me Kate.'

'I don't feel the need to call you anything at all. I'm going back to my motel.'

'But I need a ride.'

'For Christ's sake. Go bother someone else.'

'I can't. I have to bother you. Come on. Your bike's right there.'

'I'm not going . . . my bag's back in the room. I'm drunk, still. I'm not going anywhere. Certainly not with you.'

'Just up and down the street. Come on. Do it. You ever done something like that before? Burn up the highway with some girl hanging on behind? Ever done that?'

'No.'

'Of course not. Ever done *anything*? I mean, apart from what simply happened to come next? Ever been the driver?'

I opened my mouth to tell her to fuck off, but then something else happened instead.

I strode furiously over to my bike, where it stood a few doors down from the red bar. I got on. Turned the key.

'Is that a yes?'

'Get on,' I said.

She grinned, and ran over.

I was more drunk than I realised, and nearly lost the bike under me, just turning it to face up the street. A quiet voice in the back of my mind was strident in its view that this was a dreadful idea. Another voice, even quieter but utterly implacable, said it didn't care.

The girl climbed on behind. I'd never ridden with a passenger before – Aerin had no interest in condoning my middle-aged folly – but this girl seemed to know what to do. She looped her arms tightly around my stomach, her legs cosy around my hips. That felt weird. That felt very weird.

'Do it,' she said, in my ear. 'Do it do it do it.'

I gunned the engine. Hesitated.

Then took off fast. *Too* fast. Thankfully the extra weight stopped the whole escapade ending right there, in an embarrassing and back-breaking wheelie, but it was close.

I backed off the throttle and let the bike roar forward, knowing that I'd be pissing off about two hundred people right now, and really, really not caring. I've always been the guy saying well, it's not *so* late, probably they'll stop in a minute, it's not worth getting het up about. I've never been the guy making the noise.

The air rushing past my face was cold and true.

The girl behind me whooped.

We were at the other end of the main street, and at the edge of town, within minutes. I nearly kept going, but instead braked and slowed. Turned the bike around. I've ridden fast along lonely roads before, many times. Never straight through the middle of a town.

'Faster this time,' the girl said.

I was gentler starting, more under control, but then twisted the throttle hard.

We sped back into town, her arms tight around me, and maybe that's what I'd been thinking of, searching for on some inarticulate level, when I bought the bike in the first place. Arms tight around me. Someone hanging on for dear life – my life, their life, our life, both of us tied to the same arrow and flying straight up into the clouds. That's what we're all looking for, isn't it? Two hearts that beat as one. And that's what we never find.

Or maybe you have, in which case good for you.

Hold it tight.

I only saw the guy about two seconds before we hit him. We were going so fast. I was wholly in movement, that feeling, inside the warmth of her breath on my neck. Then suddenly he was there in front of me.

The guy in the blue sweater.

He stepped off the sidewalk into the road without looking, though in this quiet dead of night you must have been able to hear the bike from a mile away.

In an instant I saw how sick he was. His labouring heart, clogged chest, liver on its last legs. His life, too, ricocheting from bar to motel office, sodden with liquor. Waking in a piss-wet bed, night after night. Wallpaper TV on in the background so the silence wasn't too deafening. Out walking now in the dead of night because he'd staggered out of his room with no idea what time it was and thought a bar might still be open. Trying to find his way home so he could do it all again tomorrow. His heart was beating so loud, so raggedly, that I could hear it above the sound of the motorcycle.

All this in a split second.

'It's your call,' the girl whispered, in my ear. 'You can happen to him. Now or later. Or not. It's your choice.'

I didn't steer away.

We hit him. Except he wasn't there.

I yanked the brake far too abruptly, nearly killed us both. The bike spun around in the road, burning rubber across the surface. The man wasn't there. Neither standing, nor lying broken in the road, as he should have been.

'So be it,' the girl said. 'You chose.'

'The fuck happened?'

'You did,' she said, climbing off the bike. 'But get back to bed now. We've got a long day tomorrow.'

'I'm not going anywhere with you.'

She winked. 'Whatever you say. You're the driver.'

I carefully rode the bike back up the hill to the motel.

I woke to the sound of voices. Quite a few of them, outside the door to my room.

I sat up quickly, dreading the sound of a knock. I must have hit the guy after all. There'd been a witness. They'd come to arrest me.

No knock came.

I stood, surprised at how okay I felt. A quick session of ludicrous irresponsibility in the middle of the night stops you getting a hangover, evidently. Who knew?

I opened the door. Ten or fifteen people were standing around the parking lot, rubber-necking. There was an ambulance, too, and paramedics.

A woman standing in the doorway to the next room spoke. 'Heart attack, apparently. Dead. In his sleep.'

A man, presumably her husband, came from inside the room to stand next to her and watch. She'd been talking to him. 'That's the way to go.'

'*No* way is the way to go,' she said, sternly. 'And you are giving up smoking *today*, mister.'

'Yeah yeah.'

We all watched as a man was stretchered out from the room at the end. The guy in the blue sweater. Face a little less red now. Eyes closed. He looked better.

After the ambulance drove away, the small crowd dissipated. Back to their rooms, or down to the main street. Back to lives that were still going on.

I was the only one left out there. The girl appeared from behind, and passed me a coffee in a cardboard cup. I took a sip. It was hot and sweet.

I stood with it for a while, before asking. 'Need a ride?'

'Thought you'd never ask.'

I drove back the way I'd come, down the west side of the lake. I didn't hurry. The road was empty, utterly. The sun was weak yet.

When we got to the vista point over the island in Emerald Bay, I pulled into the lot. It was deserted except for what I'd started to expect I would see there.

My bike, standing where I'd parked it the previous afternoon. Pale in the slanting morning light.

'Suicide?'

'Yes,' she said. 'Which helps. But you had other qualities. I've had my eye on you for a while. You knew where you were headed. It's why you bought the bike.'

'Where am I now?'

'In shallow water at the bottom of the cliff. The current pulled you under a stand of bushes, up against some rocks. It'll be a couple of hours before someone calls in the fact your bike's abandoned up here. They'll find your body soon after that.'

'If I'd known it would be this way, I wouldn't have given up smoking. Think of all the ones I missed.'

'Well, sure sucks to be you.'

'You said I wasn't dead.'

'I lied.'

'Why?'

'Not everybody could do this job, dead or alive. It requires you to act. Again and again. I could tell you what I needed. But you had to decide whether to give it. You had to happen. You had to make a choice.'

'For once.'

'For once. And forever. And so now you know, and I have to give you the chance to change your mind.'

I thought about it.

'I'm good,' I said.

And so we ride. We ride together. We cover ground. We stay in small motels. We eat in the corner of diners and burger joints. We drink in bars. We sleep. We get up and do the same thing again. Day after day. Night after night.

The hole inside is filled now.

I am the hole.

We ride, her arms tight around me. Sometimes I forget who she is, who I am now, and it's as if I had some whole different life and it's Aerin who rides the roads with me, an Aerin who stayed forever young, and forever in love. But it's not, and I know that, and it's okay. The long, tangled sentences of my life have untied, shortened.

Everything is simpler now.

I found something. I found someone. I found myself. You'd better hope I don't find you, though, because I can only drive you down a one-way street. The road no one wants to go down, though we must.

I have become the shadow, that foreshadow cast back along all of our lives. You know it's coming. That I'm coming. Do what you can to be happy in the meantime.

That's all this has ever boiled down to.

The job suits me. I am happy. I am me. And eventually one day you and I will meet, as it was foretold.

Behold, a pale horse.

It's coming. And his name that sits on him . . . is mine.

MICHAEL MARSHALL SMITH is a novelist and screen-writer. Under this name he has published numerous short stories and three novels – *Only Forward, Spares* and *One of Us* – winning the Philip K. Dick, International Horror Guild, and August Derleth awards. He has also been awarded the British Fantasy Award for Best Short Fiction four times, more than any other author.

chill'ing *a.* (literary). 1: a cold feeling: a degree of cold that can be felt and that is usually unpleasant. 2: a sensation of cold accompanied by shivering. 3: gravely disturbing or frightening. Origin: Middle English *chile* chill, frost, from Old English *ciele*; akin to Old English *ceald* cold. First known use: 1814. Synonyms: bite, bitterness, bleakness, chilliness, horrific, scary. Example: *A terrible cold that goes so deep that it has the power to affect the seasons themselves . . .*

ChILLING

PAT CADIGAN

THE LAST WEEK in June, 1980, summer arrived with a vengeance in Kansas City and people started dying.

Back then, I was working at a small newspaper called *K.C. Jones* (no relation to *Mother Jones* or *The Kansas City Times/Star*). Actually, calling *K.C. Jones* a newspaper was to use the term loosely – the *Jones* was a weekly freebie found in supermarkets, convenience stores, and anywhere else there was a lot of pedestrian traffic. It was a compilation of miscellany, arranged around a lot of ads and coupons. Miscellany was always secondary to ads and coupons, which brought in the revenue that, along with the sheer willpower of its editor/publisher MillieLou Desjeans, kept it in existence.

MillieLou was a little over six feet tall, with curly red hair and Reubenesque proportions. People said she was *connected*, whispering the last word almost reverently. Her father had been some kind of fixer for the old Pendergast political machine. Its heyday was gone for good but it hadn't been forgotten.

I wasn't that *au fait* with local history myself. It hadn't been even a decade since I'd left Massachusetts, where *Kennedy* had been the name to conjure with. I had landed in Kansas City after a series of missteps – marriage, divorce, bankruptcy. MillieLou's 'Help Wanted' ad asking for someone who could read in terms of both the forest and the trees had intrigued me. After a string of fruitless interviews, I hadn't expected anything would come of it but MillieLou took a liking to me. Later, I found out it was because of all the applicants, I was the only one who hadn't thought she was looking for someone to cover the Garden Club.

And so I joined the *Jones'* full-time staff, which besides MillieLou included

Jerry who did design and paste-up, and Irene, the receptionist, bookkeeper, and office manager. MillieLou was the sales department as well as editor-in-chief. The one time she had tried hiring a sales person had been a bust, she told me; clients still wanted her to handle their accounts personally.

There were no computers and we'd never heard of the Internet – the closest things we had to either of those were Jerry's typesetting machine, which was basically an IBM Selectric with a whopping 5K of memory for print-out, and the AP teletype in MillieLou's office, which had to be carefully monitored so it wouldn't run out of ribbon or paper.

The pay wasn't fabulous, amounting to only a little more than I'd have made slinging fries at McDonald's. But in those days, that was enough to cover the rent on a studio apartment in low-income housing in mid-town, all utilities included, even central air.

In this part of the US, air-conditioning wasn't a luxury. My first summer in the Midwest I'd spent in married-student housing on the University of Kansas campus without so much as a window unit. The culture shock was bad enough for someone who had spent all her young life fifty miles northwest of Boston near the New Hampshire border, but the climate shock was worse.

I'd never lived in a place where you could work up a profuse sweat without moving. Anywhere that *was* air-conditioned – which was to say, just about any place that wasn't married-student housing – took it to the opposite extreme. Half an hour in a movie theatre, a restaurant, or any building on campus and I was shivering. The head of my then-husband's department gave a party; while everyone else socialised, I huddled under an afghan drinking hot coffee and blowing on my fingers.

By 1980, everyone knew about the depletion of the ozone layer; that summer in Kansas City, most people were too hot to care. The first time I asked MillieLou if we could maybe ease off the a/c a little – just enough so I could break through the layer of ice on my coffee – she laughed in my upturned face.

'Forget it, Lucy,' she said, 'I'm a woman of a certain age – I haven't been cold since 1969.' Then she launched into an explanation of how running an electric fan in a hot, poorly ventilated room could literally cook a person to death. The furnace effect, she called it. I told her it was new to me, which made her laugh again.

'Yeah, where you come from, they probably think eighty degrees is hot.

Go look up weather patterns for the last five–ten years for here and New England and write me around a thousand fluffy words comparing the two.'

I sighed, looking out the window at the cars on the trafficway. That meant a broiling drive to the library on the Country Club Plaza followed by hypothermia while I scrolled through microfilm. 'Okay, I'll go,' I said. 'I may be some time.'

MillieLou relented. 'Start on it tomorrow, if the heat breaks. Meanwhile, if you really *are* cold, put on a sweater. *Another* sweater.'

The heat didn't break. The oven of July opened with the temperature in three digits. On the Tuesday before the Independence Day weekend, I came into work to find the office empty except for MillieLou.

'What are you doing here?' she asked me.

'Um . . . I work here?' I sat down at my desk. After roasting for thirty minutes on the drive in, I wouldn't need the sweater on the back of my chair for a while.

'Both Jerry and Irene called in too hot to move,' MillieLou said. 'I thought you would, too.'

'If you want to close up and go home, I'm okay with that,' I said. 'As long as it doesn't come out of my sick days.'

MillieLou shook her head, making her improbable red curls bounce, and tossed the folded copy of *The Kansas City Star* that she'd been fanning herself with down on the desk in front of me. The story she had circled was headlined, HEAT-RELATED DEATH TOLL CLIMBS TO THREE. Underneath, in smaller letters, it said: ELDERLY ESPECIALLY VULNERABLE.

'Read that,' she ordered me, 'and then I'll tell you what's wrong with it.'

I obeyed, then looked up at her. 'Three isn't enough for a toll?'

'I said *I'd* tell *you*,' she said and I felt chastened. 'There have been *five* deaths, not three.'

'How do you know?'

'Because *I'm connected*. Thought you knew.' She winked at me, which seemed kind of weird since it was just the two of us.

'So what's going on?'

'A cover-up – what else?'

I frowned. Watergate was still fresh enough in the public memory that conspiracy theorising was second only to baseball as a national pastime, and thanks to Woodward and Bernstein, investigative journalism was the new rock 'n' roll. None of this, however, was really pertinent to an ad-supported weekly freebie.

And then again, I thought, the daughter of a political fixer probably knew a conspiracy when she saw one.

'What do you say, Lucy?' MillieLou's blue eyes actually twinkled. 'How does a trip downtown to the morgue sound? My car's air-conditioned.'

'Sounds cool,' I said, grabbing my sweater off the back of the chair.

I'd imagined MillieLou slipping a fifty to a furtive morgue attendant, who would whisper which cabinets contained the bodies left off the official count. She could look at them; I'd be on the other side of the room, creeped out and turning blue.

Instead, the un-furtive young woman who met us at the desk introduced herself to me as Dani Washington, one of several med students who worked as part-time coroners for the county. That made her at the most half-a-dozen years younger than I was but, even dressed in official-looking medical whites, she looked about fifteen to me.

'I'm planning a career in forensic pathology,' she said as the three of us got into an elevator.

'That means all of her patients will be dead,' MillieLou added.

'I knew that,' I said, not entirely truthfully, but I'd have figured it out.

We got out at floor -3. As we followed Dani Washington down a short hallway to a door marked CR6, I wondered briefly if that counted as a use of algebra in real life.

The hallway was cool but room CR6 was *cold,* more like weather than machine-generated refrigeration. It was as if winter were hiding out in this small room, which was empty except for a desk and a couple of chairs by the door and six metal cabinets set into one wall, three over three.

'Awful, isn't it?' Dani Washington said sympathetically, seeing me pull my sleeves down over my hands. There were several large woolly sweaters hanging on hooks on the back of the door; she took one and put it on over her white coat. 'Help yourselves.'

MillieLou made her usual joke about not having been cold since the Nixon administration. 'Fine,' I said, 'I might need an extra. I swear I've defrosted freezers warmer than this.'

'Well, there's cold and then there's cold,' Dani Washington said as she took a pair of oven mitts out of the desk. 'And then there's *this*.' Donning the mitts, she opened the cabinet on the left and pulled out the drawer.

For a moment, I thought I was seeing a big doll or a mannequin on the tray, wearing a robe over a nightgown and fluffy, hot pink slippers, lying on its side with its knees drawn up in a sitting position. MillieLou moved to look at the front of the body and I followed. This was – had been – a very old woman. Only she couldn't be real, I thought. Her legs weren't resting one atop the other, they were several inches apart.

I was no expert but I was pretty sure *rigor mortis* didn't behave like that. Both arms were tight against the front of her body, hands clutching the robe to keep it closed, as if she were cold. Her dark skin was a sort of ashy colour with a vaguely yellowish undertone.

'Mrs Cora Patterson, age eighty-one,' Dani Washington said. 'They brought her in yesterday morning about 2:00 a.m. and she hasn't even started to thaw out.'

'What the *fuck*,' I said.

Instead of telling me I owed the swear jar a couple of bucks, MillieLou said, 'My fucking sentiments exactly.' She extended a finger intending to touch the woman's face and the coroner caught her hand.

'Don't. If you touch her with your bare skin, you'll lose it.' She gave MillieLou one of the oven mitts. 'These have a non-stick coating.'

MillieLou felt the woman's arm and her shoulder briefly, then stepped back. 'I could actually feel the cold coming through,' she said, giving the mitt back to Dani Washington. 'But her clothes *aren't* frozen.'

'Also very weird,' the coroner said. 'Her clothes are mostly stuck to her. Like your finger would be if you'd touched her.'

I moved to the end of the tray to get a closer look at the woman's face and head. Her neck was frozen so solidly that her head wasn't touching the tray. The cold seemed to radiate from her; it was like being near someone with a high fever, only in reverse.

I crouched down and saw that here and there, some of her grey curls had broken off like glass threads. They lay on the metal tray in the general vicinity of where they must have fallen, displaced a bit when the drawer had been opened and closed. Were they still frozen, too?

Despite Dani Washington's warning, I poked her grey curls. Something brittle and stinging pierced my fingertip. I jerked my hand back reflexively and more of her frozen hair cracked off.

'What did you do?' MillieLou demanded. She grabbed my hand before I could deny everything; tiny drops of blood were welling up at spots where thin silvery slivers protruded from my flesh.

'Oh, for—' Dani Washington rolled her eyes. 'Don't touch those, I have to remove them for you.' She jerked her head toward the desk. 'Sit down over there. I have to get some instruments. I'll be two seconds. Can I trust you both not to touch anything else during that time?' She closed the drawer carefully. 'I mean it.'

'*I'll* be good.' MillieLou gave me a significant look.

'Me, too,' I added in a small voice. *Instruments?*

Dani Washington left and came back with what looked like a kit for minor surgery, a flashlight, and a pair of those magnifying eyeglasses watchmakers use. 'You hold this,' she told MillieLou, giving her the flashlight. 'Keep it aimed at her finger at all times.' She pulled a syringe out of the kit and removed the plastic protector from the needle.

'Wait a minute,' I said and tried to pull away, but she already had me in one of those unbreakable holds that doctors and nurses are so good at. 'You didn't say I was going to need a shot.'

'Oh, for God's sake,' she said, holding the syringe up where I could get a good look at it in all of its long, sharply-pointed glory. 'You're a *needle* sissy?'

'Why do I need a shot?' I asked, still trying to get my hand back. 'They're like splinters, you can just use *tweezers*—'

'These *aren't* splinters,' Dani Washington said, exasperated, and managed to tighten her grip so much, my whole arm started to go numb. Then she proved it hadn't by sticking me with the needle. I yelped. 'Honestly, MillieLou, are you still claiming this is the smart one?'

'Trust me, you wouldn't like the other two,' MillieLou replied, with an absurd matter-of-factness that would have made me laugh if Dani Washington hadn't kept on jabbing my finger with the needle over and over. I whimpered and she gave me a dirty look. Did she really have to stick me so many times, I wondered, or was she trying to make me cry?

'Now what?' I asked, giving up all hope of getting my hand back.

'Now we wait. I want to make sure you're good and numb before I start cutting.'

'*Cutting?*' If she hadn't had such a strong grip, I'd have been out the door. 'Cutting *what*? What are you cutting off?'

'Nothing. The fragments have to be carefully extracted,' she said with exaggerated patience. 'And I have to make sure I don't leave anything in your tissue. That would be bad.'

Suddenly I felt a lot less like escaping. 'Bad how?'

'Bad like frostbite. Really bad frostbite. The kind that *would* involve cutting off.'

MillieLou and I traded glances; she looked almost as freaked out as I felt. 'Well, all right then,' I said. 'Start carefully extracting.'

'Can you feel that?' Dani Washington asked me.

'I don't know and I don't care,' I said. 'Less talking, more careful extracting.'

'Good. Do us both a favour and don't look till I'm done.'

MillieLou put herself between us, sitting on the edge of the desk so I couldn't see what Dani Washington was doing. I didn't feel any pain, exactly – the numbness extended to the edge of my palm and into the webbing between my index finger and thumb. However, I could feel she was doing *something*, and while it didn't feel like anything I wanted to watch, I wouldn't have been able to stop myself from looking if MillieLou had not mercifully blocked my view. It seemed to go on for hours before the coroner finally said, 'All done.'

I'm not sure what I was expecting – Frankenstein's digit, maybe, with stitches running up the middle and bolts on either side of the nail. Instead, my finger was wrapped in an immaculate white bandage. And it was still numb.

'Don't get it wet,' Dani Washington said. 'Tie a plastic bag around your hand when you shower. Or a rubber glove – use a rubber band to make sure no water gets in. But not too tight or too long or you'll have an even worse problem. Call me next week and I'll check on it.' She gave an awkward shrug. 'Or you can go to your own doctor if you want.'

'I don't know how I'd explain it,' I said.

'Good. Because then *I'd* have to explain it and I'd probably lose my job.'

I felt a rush of intense guilt. 'I'd *never* mention your name,' I told her solemnly. 'And, uh, thanks. Even with the needle.'

'Journalists *always* protect their sources,' MillieLou added. 'Nellie Bly. Edward R. Murrow. Woodward and Bernstein. Ben Bradlee.'

'I don't think it would be all that hard to trace her finger back to me,' Dani Washington said unhappily. 'What did you think you were doing, anyway?'

'I was just wondering if her hair was frozen,' I said, feeling even guiltier.

'It is. Next time, just ask.'

'But why would it be?' I asked. 'Hair isn't alive. The grown-out part, I mean.'

'It grows out of a living root. The freeze went through the hair shaft, all the way to the end.'

'But why would it still be as frozen as the rest of her? That doesn't seem right.'

'Argue with the fragments I took out of your finger.' Dani Washington carried a small white gauze square carefully over to Cora Patterson's cabinet and put it on the tray with her.

'Won't your boss wonder about that?' I asked.

'Wonder about what?' Dani Washington shrugged. 'I didn't see anything. I'm just a med student, I'm only here part-time.'

'You said there were *two* bodies,' MillieLou said.

'There were.' Dani Washington looked uncomfortable. 'The other one isn't exactly a body any more.' She hesitated. MillieLou folded her arms and gave her a look while I eyed the sweaters hanging on the door, trying to decide if I were chilly enough to put one of them over my own.

Dani Washington made a resigned noise and opened the cabinet next to Cora Patterson's. 'This is Martin Foley, age 79. Or what's left of him.'

Most of the chunks and fragments on the tray were large enough for us to see they were pieces of an elderly man. His head had broken off just below the chin; it was lying left side up on a thick towel. I could see the bone, some livery brown-red that must have been muscle, various blood vessels, and yellowy subcutaneous fat. His skin was a bit yellow, too.

'It's like a cross-section,' I marvelled.

'I don't have to remind you guys not to touch anything, do I?' Dani Washington asked with more than a slight edge in her voice.

I waved my bandaged finger. 'I've learned my lesson. What happened?'

'What do you think? Somebody dropped him. His clothes kept most of him together, but it was still hell making sure we found all the pieces.'

'The Visible Man, shattered like glass.' MillieLou surveyed the rubble, then raised an eyebrow at the coroner. 'Are you sure you got *all* of him?'

'It happened in here, so yeah, we're pretty sure.'

MillieLou tapped her foot. 'Careful *you* don't fall. An *un*frozen person could shatter on this cement floor. Assuming anyone stays unfrozen in here. *Mirabile dictu*, I'm actually a bit chilly.'

'Hallelujah,' I said, reaching for the door.

'Not so fast.' My boss produced a Polaroid from her purse and handed it to me, then pulled out a Pentax SLR. 'We need photos of both bodies.' Dani Washington frowned at her sceptically. 'All right, *I want* photos. Not necessarily for publication but if they do end up in print, I'll keep your name out of it.'

'That'ud be a neat trick,' the coroner said, still looking sceptical as MillieLou began snapping away with the Pentax.

'Nothing to it,' my boss said. 'I'm *connected*.' She paused and motioned for me to get some Polaroids, but I was so clumsy with my bandaged finger that she took the camera away from me and did it herself. Then she went back to the SLR. When she finished the roll, she put in a fresh one and had Dani Washington pull Cora Patterson out again.

'Okay,' she said when she'd finished both the second roll and the Polaroid. 'So what's the punchline? Obviously, you can't autopsy them till they thaw out, so there's no telling if they actually froze to death. Am I right?'

Dani Washington hesitated. 'They might have, but personally, I suspect there was another, simultaneous cause.'

'*Really*.' MillieLou put an arm around her. 'Don't keep it to yourself, honey, you know you can tell me *anything*.'

'Yeah, I bet I can.' Dani Washington wiggled away from her.

'Come *on*,' MillieLou wheedled. 'At least tell me why you think there was another, maybe simultaneous cause. Lucy, are you taking notes?' she added.

I waved my injured digit at her; immediately, she found a steno pad and pen in her purse. All of us at the *Jones* regarded MillieLou's handbag as a mystery of nature, like electricity or the platypus.

'Remember who wrote you those magnificent references you needed for med school.'

The coroner sighed. 'It *will* be my job, you know.'

'I know. I won't let anything come back to you. I never have, have I?'

Dani Washington shook her head, although she still looked reluctant. 'It has to do with where they were found.'

'Ah, yes, the freezer,' MillieLou said. 'Had to be a commercial unit. Was it a, oh . . . *family-owned* business?'

Dani Washington shook her head again. 'Nope.' Pause. 'They weren't found in a freezer.'

'*Really*.' MillieLou seemed on the verge of turning herself inside out. 'Where, then?'

'You know that house fire on East 27th, between Troost and the Paseo? These are two of the residents. The firemen found them in their rooms. They thought they died of smoke inhalation. Until they touched them.'

MillieLou's encyclopaedic brain kicked into gear. 'Six tenants, four hospitalised, two casualties – *these* are the two casualties?'

'Names withheld pending notification of the victims' families,' Dani Washington recited. 'They were both found at her place, although he had his own place.'

'Who else knows about them?'

'Besides me and my boss . . .' The coroner thought for a moment. 'The firemen who recovered the bodies. A couple of paramedics. The idiot who dropped Mr Foley and the three of us who had to help him pick up the pieces.'

Now MillieLou looked sceptical. 'That's an awful lot of people keeping quiet,' she said. 'I never knew *that* many people who could keep their mouths shut. Not since my daddy's day.'

'What's to tell? Two people were found frozen stiff at a house fire. Must've been stored in a freezer and the fire was set to destroy the evidence. Possible arson and homicide – nobody'll run their mouths about an active investigation, they want to keep their jobs. It's weird but not the weirdest thing anybody's ever heard of.

'I know a few stories that would curl your hair. Well, curl *hers*—' she nodded at me. 'And *un*-curl yours. Or they *would*, except you've probably already heard them. Anyway, nobody's got time to think about what happened two days ago. There've been at least two more fires since then. Plus people are dying just from the heat *without* fire.'

'Those two – were their utilities cut-off for non-payment?' MillieLou asked. 'A lot of people have had their utilities cut off because they couldn't pay their bills. No electricity, no air-conditioning.'

'Don't know,' Dani Washington said. 'But I know the address. I went apartment-hunting there. All the houses in that neighbourhood are old Victorians. They don't have central air, not even the ones converted into apartments. You'd have to make do with a window unit and you'd have to run it a lot – *very* expensive. Assuming the crap wiring could even handle the load without shorting out.'

MillieLou made a last note and stashed the pen and pad in her bag. 'We definitely need to check that out.'

'Check what out?' I asked.

The house, though plenty scorched, was still standing. No one had made a start at boarding up the gaping holes where the doors and windows had been. There was a fence, but it was mostly rather flimsy chicken-wire stapled to sagging wood posts, except for some steel barriers across the front yard. They were chained together behind some blue saw-horses stamped POLICE BARRIER: DO NOT CROSS. I wasn't sure that was putting anyone off as much as the hard sun beating down unhindered from an unmerciful cloudless sky.

MilllieLou had had to park a block-and-a-half away. Just the few minutes it had taken to walk back to the house had me wondering why I'd wanted to leave the morgue. My boss was suffering even more than I was. Her complexion, normally on the pink side anyway, was the colour of a baby blanket. I suggested we take a few photos and come back later.

'It won't be any cooler later,' MillieLou said, almost panting, 'and we won't have the light.' Before I could ask what was wrong with using a flash, she had moved into the narrow passageway between the fenced-off wreckage and the house next door. I followed. At least the other house threw a little shade.

MillieLou shot a few photos through the chicken wire with the Pentax, then changed the lens to the telephoto.

'Have you got a dark room in that bag, too?' I asked nervously. We were standing directly below a window where I thought I saw the blinds move. The passageway went all the way to the next block; whoever lived next door probably kept an eye on through-traffic.

'Yeah but it's not air-conditioned. Hold it for me, will ya?' She shoved the bag at me, snapped a few more photos, then moved farther along to see the back of the house. There was debris all over the place here, some of it recognisable as furniture. A very tall wooden fence spared the property behind it from having to look at the fried foam rubber cushions and pillows, but the smell must have been awful.

MillieLou went a few more feet and snapped some quick photos of the other yard. 'Much smaller house,' she told me as she came back. 'Single family, swing-set, sandbox, and a deck with a barbecue. Bet they're relieved the fire never got as far as their privacy fence.'

'Probably.' I looked up at the window of the house next door again. 'We should leave.'

'Some reporter *you* are.' She headed towards the sidewalk and I hurried after her, feeling relieved for all of two seconds, until I discovered she was only going around to the other side.

We were actually closer to the house there. I got a whiff of old smoke and things burned out, people's belongings reduced to blackened fragments. Which made me think of the chunks and pieces that had once been a person on a tray in a morgue cabinet.

The fire hadn't thawed him or the old woman even slightly, let alone burned them. But then, most people didn't burn to death in fires, I remembered: more often they died of smoke inhalation before the flames ever reached them. Lack of oxygen. They suffocated.

Was that what Dani Washington thought had killed them? Couldn't be. There was no way they could have been frozen solid that quickly before the fire-fighters found them ...

Yes, they could. Liquid nitrogen would do it. I remembered a demonstration in high school chem lab, the teacher dipping a flower in liquid nitrogen, then dropping it on the table. We'd all gasped when it shattered like glass.

It would take a pretty big tank to accommodate two people, though. Something that large, with all its attendant machinery, wouldn't burn up completely. Arson investigators had to have found something, not to mention empty nitrogen tanks. What if *that* had been the cause of the fire, a big, complicated machine that had shorted out the wiring?

I turned to say something to MillieLou and discovered she had gone through a gap in the chicken wire and had her long lens aimed at one of the windows.

'What are you *doing*?' I squeaked. 'MillieLou, come *back* here! You're not supposed to cross police lines, you'll get us both *arrested*!' The words were barely out of my mouth when a police cruiser pulled up in front of the house, as if on cue. The two officers who got out looked less than delighted.

I was still on the right side of the fence, I thought, they wouldn't arrest me. Then I realised I was clutching MillieLou's handbag of tricks. Was there such a thing as accessory to trespassing? Aiding and abetting unauthorised photography? Conspiracy to aggravate the police? Who were *big* as well as pissed off. 'My boss,' I said, feeling like a Judas.

'MillieLou, you know you're not supposed to be tromping all over a crime scene,' the larger of the two cops called.

She turned around and gave him a two-hundred-watt smile. 'I'm almost done, Tony. How ya doin', Ralph?'

'*Seriously*,' Tony said, and he sounded it. 'Right *now*, MillieLou, or I'll have to come and get you.'

'Uh-huh, you bet.' MillieLou was shooting through the front door now.

'I'll give you to the count of five,' Tony told her, pushing through the fence. '*One*. Plus four is five.' He was on her in three quick strides and escorted her off the property even more quickly.

'The bum's rush – *really*?' MillieLou said, pulling away from him with wounded dignity. 'After all we've meant to each other?'

'Gimme a break,' Tony said unhappily. 'I *had* to. The neighbours are watching.'

'It's a Neighbourhood-Watch area,' the other cop, Ralph, put in. 'They're *always* watching.'

The two of them ushered us politely but firmly towards the sidewalk. *To their cruiser*, I thought, so the neighbours could see them taking us away. Instead, however, they ticketed us. I was fine with that until I saw the amount.

'Are you all right, ma'am?' Ralph asked, looking concerned. He opened the back door and had me sit down on the seat. Tony handed me a bottle of water, insisting I drink; it was actually warmer than I was but I barely noticed. Ralph's calling me *ma'am* bothered me more.

'She's fine, it's just sticker shock.' MillieLou took the ticket away from me and tucked it into her purse. 'The graft in this town has always been a scandal. Don't worry, Lucy, it's on the *Jones*. You just catch your breath while I have a chat with these two fine public servants.'

I'd have gone limp with relief except I was already on the verge of melting anyway. The inside of the police car was no cooler than outside, but at least it was out of the sun. I leaned back, poured a little water into my palm, and splashed it on my face, not caring how much dribbled down onto my shirt. I might have poured the whole thing over my head except the cops probably wouldn't have appreciated my flooding their back seat. Assuming it all didn't just turn to steam.

After a bit, I looked around; MillieLou and the cops were gathered in front of the cruiser, deep in conversation. Only the cops were doing most of the talking while MillieLou nodded attentively and took notes. I could see it wasn't a scolding, but maybe the neighbours couldn't tell the difference. Finally, she flipped her notebook closed, gave each cop a pinch on the cheek, and beckoned to me.

We headed back downtown. I was hot enough by then to be slightly disappointed that we ended up at the library instead of back in the morgue.

'Sure I can't help you?' I said as MillieLou cranked her way through spool after spool of microfilm.

'Nah, just keep me company,' my boss said cheerfully. She knew the offer was strictly polite. I hated microfilm because it was always in negative, white on black. I had a hard time seeing anything that way; on a good day, it would still take me ages to find even a front-page item.

MillieLou had no such trouble – her eyeballs were more adaptable, I guess. But we were there for at least an hour while she ran through spool after spool, consulting the notes on her steno pad (in shorthand, thus unreadable to me) before she finally found something.

'A-ha! Found it. Remind me to send Tony and his family a deluxe basket for Thanksgiving!' She annotated the squiggles on her pad with more squiggles and leaned back in her chair so I could look at the page on the screen. 'Bottom right. Your other right,' she added automatically.

For once, I found the headline immediately: NO NEW LEADS IN TONGANOXIE FREEZER DEATH; PARENTS CONTINUE TO CLAIM INNOCENCE. It wasn't a long story. The twelve-year-old daughter of a couple in Tonganoxie, Kansas, had been missing for two days before her dead body had been found frozen stiff under the double-wide trailer where they lived. Her parents insisted they hadn't known she was there, hadn't done anything to harm her, and didn't know who had.

'When was this?' I asked.

'August, 1973. That was a hot summer.'

'I remember,' I said, and I did, vividly. Just thinking about it made me sweat even in the overdone air-conditioning. Considering how long we'd been here, I should have been starting to feel cold, but I wasn't. I was still comfortable. Maybe my body had finally acquired a Kansas City thermostat.

MillieLou found the original news story, made more notes, and then went on spinning through spool after spool. She found another item from the summer of 1969 – famed for being the last year in which she had ever felt cold, although she was so taken with whatever she found I thought it would be rude to point it out.

She didn't invite me to look at it or at any of the other items she found; from what little she said, I gathered they involved people who had frozen in hot weather. There weren't very many of them and she couldn't always find the original story.

Until she got to the 1930s, that is.

'Should've known,' she said with a grim little chuckle.

'Why?' I said.

'The '30s were the Dust-Bowl years. Drought set in and peoples' whole lives blew away in dust storms. Like the Great Depression wasn't bad enough.'

'I know my history and I've read *Grapes of Wrath*,' I said.

'Reading about it and living through it are two very different things. I was only a little girl then – a *very* little girl – but it's a big part of my background. The Kansas City Machine meant a lot of people didn't end up in Hoovervilles with the Okies. But nobody could do anything about the heat. The heat was awful. Watch weather report on the ten o'clock news – you'll see just about every night that the record for highest temperature on the date, whatever it is, was set in the 1930s, during the Dust Bowl.'

'People must have died in the heat then, too,' I said. 'Without air conditioning.'

'Actually,' MillieLou said as she started another spool, 'Kansas City is the home of the first air-conditioned building – the Armour Building, in 1902.'

'No kidding,' I said, genuinely impressed.

'Ten years later, Clarence Birdseye developed a system to flash-freeze food. Used a conveyor belt. Not in Kansas City, though; I forget where.

That was before most people even had refrigerators – in those days, it was all iceboxes, with deliveries from the ice-man. You didn't find a lot of refrigerators in peoples' homes till the late 1920s. Window a/c units were around for a while, but didn't really come into general use until after World War II.

'So yeah, people died in the heat. People have always died of exposure, either heat or cold. We just haven't always kept real good records, even when things were reported. Which they weren't always. A lot of people were born at home, not in hospitals, and that's where a lot of them died, too. Families made their own arrangements and, unless their doctor saw obvious bullet-holes or knife wounds in Grandpa, cause of death would be old age. Or the flu, or pneumonia, depending.'

'Anyone flash-frozen by the Birdseye method?'

'Good question.' She cranked through a few more spools in silence, pausing to make notes on her notes. I looked at her pad, sorry (and not for the first time) I hadn't taken shorthand in high school.

I thought she'd quit after the 1930s but she just kept on going, into the '20s and even farther back. I was starting to doze off when she finally announced that she was all microfilmed out. I could go home, she said, but she was going back to the office to see if she could arrange her notes into some kind of order. I told her I was sticking with her – I wanted to see how this came out . . . *if* it came out.

MillieLou didn't type much but when she did, it sounded like machine-gun fire. She waved away my offer to proofread. If I really didn't want to go home, she told me, I could keep busy by checking the AP printout for fluff, just in case I called in sick the day we ran out of filler.

You wouldn't think of the Associated Press as a source of non-news. The teletype machine used up long rolls of paper, printing out story after story. If you read through it, however, you'd find that after the first yard or so, it was *déjà-vu* – stories were repeated, sometimes updated with new facts, sometimes cut shorter. But twice a day, they threw in a substantial horoscope and an assortment of human-interest stuff, even the occasional movie or book review.

Lately the main topic on the wire had been the upcoming Republican National Convention in Detroit, and how Ronald Reagan was going to get the nomination to run against Jimmy Carter.

Jerry and Irene referred to the Carter administration as the Beverly Hillbillies in the White House. They were both right of centre, which I couldn't really understand in the post-Watergate era. But then, the previous Republican National Convention had been right here in Kansas City and the conventioneers had been given a hero's welcome (particularly by the adult bookstores and downtown sex workers, MillieLou had confided to me).

Four years on, I was sure TV coverage of Tony Orlando trying to do the bump with Betty Ford would haunt me for the rest of my life.

Most of the non-political items had to do with the weather. The entire Great Plains region, between the Rockies and the Appalachians, was being cooked to death.

Some of the stories were a lot more scientific and technical than usual, even though, like all AP stories, they were written in what MillieLou called inverted pyramid style, with all the hard information up front so you could shorten them without losing anything essential (working for MillieLou was like going to an inverted-pyramid style J-school).

I read a few, then put them aside and went in search of more stuff like horoscopes and celebrity gossip-column pap. Not because I couldn't understand it but because I could, only too well. I had taken a geology course at KU taught by a rather charismatic man named Ed Zeller, whose lectures had included a lot of material about changes to the atmosphere and how this could induce substantial changes in climate.

He'd scared us all silly, which is a good way to get students to retain what you tell them – in a class of five hundred, the lowest grade was a 2.9. I still remembered a lot of what he'd told us but if I hadn't, the weather stories would have refreshed my memory.

My gaze fell on the thermostat outside MillieLou's office. I felt comfortable – not cold, or even cooled off, but just right. I went over to check the temperature. The tiny dial said 68°F but I wasn't sure how reliable that was – if the room was really that cool, my teeth should have been chattering. The control was set on maximum cooling and the a/c was definitely running. MillieLou had left it on while we were out and that hum was probably the sound of the ozone layer disintegrating. I gave the lever a guilty little nudge with my pinky, and then another.

'What are you doing?' MillieLou asked in a pleasant, *gotcha* tone, and I jumped. 'Funny, you don't *look* like you're turning blue. In fact—' she frowned and came over to me. 'You look like you're finally getting acclimated to the local standard. And not a moment too soon.' She pushed the lever back to maximum. 'Something tells me this summer is going to redefine the term "hot weather".'

'Do you want me to proof your notes now?' I asked, following her back into her office.

'No, this isn't a story. Yet.' She had pulled down the shades on the two big windows, but the afternoon sun seemed to be trying to burn its way through them. MillieLou ushered me out to my own desk. 'Right now it's just a bunch of facts I've pulled out of a lot of old newspapers,' she said, perching on the edge. 'There's no way to know how accurate any of it is.'

'The *Star* and *Times* should be pretty reliable, though, shouldn't they?' I asked.

'I wasn't just looking at them. The *Times/Star* has always had the newspaper market pretty much cornered in KC but, in the suburbs and points beyond in any direction, they had some competition. Most are defunct; a few barely lasted a year before going under. Some were obviously mouthpieces for those of the crackpot persuasion, people who would call Barry Goldwater a pinko commie stooge.'

That jerked a laugh out of me, but I sobered quickly. 'I was about to say that's funny but, on second thought, it isn't.'

MillieLou beamed approval at me. 'You're learning. I wasn't sure how reliable these other papers might be. I checked for a corroborating story in the *Times* or *Star*. At first I couldn't seem to find anything. I had to read more carefully – some of the references went right by me.'

I shook my head slightly. 'Maybe you'd better tell me what you were trying to corroborate.'

'In the last seventy or so years, a number of people have been found frozen to death during heat waves,' she said. 'Exactly what that number is, I'm not sure. More than twenty, fewer than sixty.'

'That's a pretty big margin for error,' I said. 'And that's just in the Kansas City area, right?'

MillieLou's eyes widened. 'Migod, I didn't think of that. Just the idea of combing death notices for the whole of Missouri and Kansas makes me want to lie down and rest.'

'Me, too,' I said, 'so let's keep the focus local. Did it happen every year, or can you even tell?'

My boss shook her head. 'Good question, Lucille. There isn't enough information either way. Which makes me think it wasn't an annual event. Not around here, anyway. If it had been happening regularly, it would have been news. There'd be half-a-dozen active conspiracy theories and Wendell and Anne'ud be working in mentions at six and ten Monday through Friday.' She studied her typed notes for a moment, then looked up at me. 'By the way, how's your finger?'

Even with the bandage impeding almost every movement, I had actually forgotten about it. I wagged it from side to side. 'Okay, I guess. The Novocaine wore off but it doesn't hurt.'

'That's good. Surprising but good.'

'Surprising?' I had a sinking feeling. 'Why? No, don't tell me!' I added quickly. 'It doesn't hurt, that's all I care about. Happy ending. Tell me more about people freezing to death in heat waves.'

MillieLou hesitated and I could almost see the little wheels and gears turning. Then she shrugged. 'Actually, the biggest weather event before 1920 is the big freeze of November, 1911. Climatologists called it the Big – no, the Great Blue Norther of 11/11/11.

'The day started out unseasonably warm, practically summery. Then the clouds lowered, temperatures plummeted, rain turned to sleet, then to hail, followed by thunderstorms and tornadoes, all topped off by blizzards. And not just here, but all over the Midwest and as far east as Virginia. According to more than one paper – reliable papers – the winds were so high that they torqued buildings out of true.'

'And all that happened on 11/11/11?' I shook my head. 'That would have made me superstitious for life.'

'You wouldn't have been alone. Sometime I'll show you all the silly-season material I've got on 11/11. The First World War officially ended at 11:00 a.m. on November 11, 1918, but that's not why. There's something about 11/11 that makes people jumpy in ways that 10/10 and 12/12 don't.'

'Maybe it's because eleven's a prime number?' I said.

MillieLou laughed. 'Ask twenty people at random if they know what a prime number is. Half of them won't. Okay, maybe not that many. Even

Jerry knows what a prime number is and he has to have Irene balance his chequebook every month.

'But sixty years ago, you'd have been lucky to get two. Prime meant meat around these parts, not numbers. No, I think it's the way 11/11 looks. Four ones in a row. You have a digital clock?'

I nodded. 'Clock radio. Dick and Jay get me out of bed every morning.'

'Sometimes I forget you're such a kid,' MillieLou chuckled. 'Does it ever seem to you as if you always manage to look at it just when it's 11:11?'

'Honestly? No,' I replied. 'But I don't look at it a lot. Time is pie to me. Like a pie chart,' I added in response to her puzzled expression. 'When I think of what time it is, I imagine a clock-face.'

'For a second there, I thought you were getting whimsical on me. Time as pie – kinda sweet, really. You're the wrong person to ask anyway, though. You don't obsess over things and you don't seem to be at the mercy of any compulsions. You're just always cold. Or you used to be. Tell me, are you ever too hot in the winter?'

'No, I get cold then, too. Did anyone freeze to death the summer before 11/11/11?'

'If they did, no one noticed. But the following summer, the *Edwardsville Visitor* – one of those other papers I mentioned, lasted all of a year? – ran a story about an unidentified man found in a boxcar. They had some inches to fill I guess, so they quoted one of the police officers on the scene: "I thought he was froze solid but the doc said that was how dead bodies do, they get cold and stiff." That was ... let's see ... Officer Richard McElroy.' MillieLou smiled. 'Big family, the McElroys, and none of them dummies.

'Then, the day after a big Fourth of July party at a steak house called The Happy Steer, the head chef found one of the clean-up crew dead in the freezer. Circumstances seemed to indicate the guy thought drinking beer in the freezer was a great idea. Apparently he'd already had a few when inspiration struck. Identified as 43-year-old Eli Washington, originally from Shreveport.'

'Was the freezer really *that* cold?'

'Sure – if you're an out-of-towner who can be conveniently written off as an alcoholic and suspected dope fiend.' MillieLou said, looking sour.

'A black janitor with no one to care what happened to him,' I said.

'You're catching on.' MillieLou's unhappy expression deepened. 'I couldn't find any more freezer deaths for 1912 or the year after. But in November 1913, the weather bomb fell on the Great Lakes. They called it the Big Blow or the White Hurricane – a blizzard with hurricane-force winds.'

'11/11?' I asked.

'Actually, it was done with the Great Lakes by the 11th and moved on to eastern Canada. Without the warmer water to provide the lake effect, however, it lost a lot of its power. As far as I can tell, it didn't even graze Kansas City.'

'The lake effect?'

MillieLou made a face. 'Look it up later, it's a snow-belt phenomenon. We've got enough trouble being Tornado Alley and the thunderstorm capital of the world—'

'Now, that I *did* know,' I said, chuckling.

'Uh-huh.' Without looking away from her notes, MillieLou held out her left hand; I put a pen in it. 'No, pencil,' she said and I obliged. 'Pencil always. You know that.'

'You're welcome,' I said.

'Damn right I am.' She stood up, set the pages down on the desk, and began circling a number of things, sometimes adding arrows. I waited in silence. Interrupting MillieLou while she was drawing circles and arrows on her notes was a firing offence; according to her, my predecessor had learned that the hard way.

I'd thought she was kidding but watching her now, I wondered. *K.C. Jones* was a coupon rag that allowed her to keep her finger on the city's pulse via relationships with all the local businesses, not a way for her to play investigative journalist . . . right?

I had to admit to myself, rather uneasily, that I really didn't know. I had only been with her since the end of March. For all I knew, MillieLou had just been waiting to see how well I did in the job before revealing that the *Jones* was actually a front for a secret private detective agency.

Yeah, a six-foot, middle-aged redhead with a grand-opera contralto laugh, who probably put on jewellery to take out the trash – yeah, perfect for totally secret, undercover work.

When I thought about it some more, however, it seemed less absurd. MillieLou *was* perfect. Local colourful character, offspring of former political machine fixer; *connected*. She had an entrée everywhere.

Every time the *Star* ran a historical piece, she was always top of the list to be interviewed. The library and the historical society invited her to give talks several times a year. Legend had it that Hallmark's all-time best-selling birth announcement showed the infant MillieLou wearing nothing but a smile on a fluffy rug. There was a rumour that some Hollywood studio was planning a movie set near the end of the Pendergast Era and they'd called her for advice.

'I couldn't find something for *every* year,' she was saying as she shuffled her notes together and half-sat on the edge of my desk again. 'However – and this is important for journalists – absence of evidence is not evidence of absence.'

I'm embarrassed to say I had to think about that for a second. It was almost too easy to be true. Then the rest of what she'd said sunk in. 'Since when am I a journalist?'

'I hired you to write for the *Jones*. The *Jones* is a newspaper. Q.E.D. All right, it's not the *Star* or the *Times*, Kansas City *or* New York. It's not even the *National Enquirer*—'

'Thank *Christ*,' I said, with feeling.

'Ha! If I told you what the starting salary is at the *Enquirer*, you'd head for Lantana, Florida so fast, you'd be there before I heard you say, "I quit".'

'I doubt it. What were you saying about absence and evidence?'

MillieLou beamed at me. 'Where I *did* find something, it's . . . well, interesting. December 19, 1924 was a bad day around here. An ice storm froze everything. They had streetcars sliding down hills, power outages both sides of the state line, lotta deaths. But no record of anyone freezing to death the previous summer.'

I frowned. 'You're talking as if that's significant.'

'Just hear me out. In June 1925, police charged a man named Harold Mertz with homicide after he was caught dumping a woman's body in the Missouri River. He claimed he hadn't killed her, he had just found her "all froze up and so cold I couldn't touch her without gloves".'

'Why was he dumping her in the river?' I asked.

'Don't ask me, baby, I just work here. Woman was never identified. About a month later, railroad bulls found the body of a man who'd been riding on top of a boxcar rather than inside. Corpse was described as *very* cold. The following winter was unremarkable – no unusually severe storms or extreme temperatures. Everything's vague for the rest of the decade and then the Dust Bowl hits. I have *no* idea what that was about.'

'Drought, resulting in the topsoil blowing away—'

'Hey, you're not done hearing me out.' MillieLou flashed me a quick smile. 'I'm painting a picture here. Now, we didn't see the terrible dust storms here that they got west of Topeka, but we felt the drought just the same. Someone was real pissed off about something—'

'What are you talking about?' I asked. '*Who* was pissed off and what's that got to d—?'

MillieLou gave a slightly put-upon sigh. 'When at least two people freeze to death in the summer, the following winter isn't too rough. But if no one freezes to death in the summer, the winter's a monster.'

I blinked at her. She sounded like she was reading some bit of folk wisdom from one of those old almanacs – if the caterpillars are really woolly, it means winter will be extremely cold. Or if Punxsutawney Phil sees his shadow . . . damn, I *still* can't remember if that means spring will be early or late. 'I don't see what one has to do with the other.'

'Okay, it's not as easy to see the farther back you go because the reporting isn't as reliable,' she said. 'In the 1930s, the whole country was pretty much a disaster area and then there was World War II. In the post-war era, things started looking up.

'The summer of 1951, the Missouri flooded, bad. But I guess nobody froze because on Christmas Eve, there was an ice storm that crippled the entire state. The following year was the driest we ever had – barely two feet of rain total. But I guess a couple of people got frozen that year and again in 1954, which was *damn* hot – temperatures up to 118°. Sad story about a kid who crawled into a refrigerator thinking he could cool off, and a butcher who had an accident working alone over a weekend. They didn't find him for two days.'

I rubbed my forehead. 'I still don't understand why you think one or two people freezing to death in the summer has anything to do with what the following winter's like—'

'I'm not done yet, kid. Big picture, remember?' She got up again and laid the typed pages side by side around the edge of my desk. 'Okay, here's the timeline.'

Maybe if I looked at it with her, I thought, it would start making sense to me instead of sounding like a conspiracy theory concocted by a paranoid who thought Spiro Agnew was on the grassy knoll.

'For most of the 1950s and '60s, the winters were pretty ordinary, although I remember in 1960, I wasn't sure winter was ever gonna end. Coldest, snowiest spring on record – in the outer parts of Liberty and Gladstone and Lenexa, people were actually snowed in. There was only one odd death reported the previous summer.'

'Someone who froze to death during a heat wave?' I asked, trying not to sound as sceptical and sarcastic as I felt.

'I'd bet money on it—' MillieLou scanned the papers she had laid out until she found the one she wanted. 'There. Miss Maria T. Cannizzaro, 29, found at her place of employment when her co-workers came into work Thursday, June 30.' Her finger moved up a line. 'See where she worked?'

'Mid-Continental Cold Storage,' I read aloud. 'Okay, that still doesn't prove—'

'I bet you a hundred bucks they found her in the deep freeze. They keep that at a balmy -5 Fahrenheit.'

'But it doesn't *say*—'

'I can find out who was in the coroner's office back then and get it out of them.'

'Yeah, you're connected,' I said absently. 'But I'm sorry, MillieLou, I just don't buy it. I can't. You've made connections between a number of things based on nothing more than the fact that they happened in sequence. But just because one thing happened before another doesn't mean the first thing *caused* the second.'

I looked over the pages with all the circles and arrows. 'We don't even know that if all of these people froze to death. All we can say is that for a lot of these people, the cause of death or the circumstances in which they were found wasn't made public.'

MillieLou folded her arms and considered me with her head tilted to one side. 'You're not planning to go to law school, are you?'

'Where did *that* come from?' I asked her, flabbergasted. 'All I'm saying is, if the cause of death isn't listed, then *we don't know* what it was. We can't assume someone froze to death just to fit a pattern that may not exist in the first place. I mean, hey—' I gave a small laugh. 'What kind of a journalist are you?'

'I'm not a journalist,' MillieLou said. 'I'm the daughter of an old-time Pendergast fixer and I know what a deal looks like when I see one.'

'Oh, come *on*,' I said. 'I could rap my knuckles on my desk three times every morning at ten and tell you it was to keep a herd of rhinos from stampeding through the office. Does our perfect record of no rhino stampedes prove it's working?'

'Who'd you make that deal with?' MillieLou asked me in a reasonable tone, as if my proposal weren't completely loony.

'Well . . . no one. I just decided.'

'Then it's not a deal, it's a delusion. Feel free to keep knocking on your desk if it makes you feel better. But I won't be biting my nails when you call in sick.' She moved around my desk to look at some different pages. 'Things settled down in the 1970s. Well, in the first half. Some people who went missing turned up okay, others didn't. Cause of death for some of them is just listed as "exposure".'

I shrugged. 'People *do* die of exposure.'

'*Technically*. But that's usually how they describe cold weather deaths. In hot weather, they'll say heart failure due to heat stroke or dehydration, or they got roasted to death in a small, badly-ventilated room thanks to the furnace effect. I told you about the furnace effect, didn't I?'

'You did. And I even looked it up so I'd know exactly how it worked. But as far as I know, there's no reverse furnace effect that causes people to freeze to death in a heat wave. Although I used to think *I* would,' I added.

MillieLou stared at me, open-mouthed. 'Lucy, you might be a genius. "Reverse furnace effect". Why didn't I think of that?'

'Because it's absurd,' I said. 'I made it up just now.'

'Chance favours the prepared mind.' She bounced the pencil off my head on each word. 'You said what you saw without knowing you'd seen it.'

'But my mind wasn't prepared.'

'*Mine* was. Good thing I was listening.' She gathered up her notes quickly. 'And I know just who to talk to.'

We caught Dani Washington as she was about to leave for the day. She didn't look happy to see us. 'If you didn't get enough photos, that's too bad,' she told MillieLou as she covered the typewriter on her desk and picked up her shoulder-bag. 'My boss is down there with a couple of experts from Jefferson City. They're packing the bodies for transport.'

'That's okay,' MillieLou said. 'I thought we could talk about previous cases.'

'Previous cases?' Dani Washington laughed a little, but she looked a bit nervous.

'People who froze to death in hot weather,' MillieLou said.

Dani Washington laughed again, more heartily. 'There aren't any. My boss has been here for three years and he says he's never seen anything like this.'

'I'm sure he hasn't. The last three winters have been pure hell.' MillieLou gave her a quick summary of what she had told me, referring to her notes now and then. Dani Washington listened, sneaking little glances at me to see if I was taking any of it seriously. I tried to look neutral.

'I don't understand,' she said finally when MillieLou had finished. 'You think if someone freezes to death in the summer that means we get a milder winter?'

'And the last three winters have been monumental,' MillieLou said. 'Last winter was the coldest on record. And then two people freeze to death in a house fire during a heat wave.'

Dani Washington looked around the office. The only other person there was down at the far end looking through a filing cabinet drawer, paying no attention to us. 'Let's take this outside,' she said in a low voice. I managed not to groan. The day just seemed to be getting hotter all the time and I'd been hoping we could cool off in the sub-sub-sub-basement.

'All right,' she said as we stood outside in the parking area where, of course, there was no shade. 'MillieLou, I love you like family but what you're telling me is crazy.'

My boss was not offended. 'Maybe it is and maybe it isn't. It's easy enough to prove I'm stuffed full of wild blueberry muffins. Print out a record of every summer freezing death. You've got it all on computer, don't you?'

Dani Washington looked as if MillieLou were literally twisting her arm. 'I can't do that, only my boss can. I'd have to have a good reason to ask for something like that—'

'Med school research,' my boss said quickly.

'You didn't let me finish,' Dani Washington said, annoyed now. 'You probably wouldn't get the results you're looking for. Just because bodies were found frozen doesn't mean that was the cause of death. When they finally thaw those two out, they might discover they died of stroke or heart attack or some other old-age thing.'

'And if they don't find some other cause?' MillieLou asked.

'Then they'll probably record it as undetermined.'

'And that's good enough for the families?' I asked.

'What families?' Dani Washington's expression turned sad. 'They haven't been able to find any next of kin.' She sighed. 'That happens a lot. Immediate family gets scattered or they die young, and the survivors end up alone and forgotten. Look, Public Health has all kinds of stuff – statistics about average life-span, causes of death, all that. You could phone up and ask them just about anything and they'd tell *you*. You're *connected*.' She turned to me. 'How's the finger?'

'Actually,' I said, 'it hurts.'

'Yeah, I could tell just by the look on your face,' Dani Washington said. 'I can't write you a prescription for anything—'

'I've got some leftover Darvon,' MillieLou said absently and asked Dani Washington another question that I couldn't really hear over the pain. I hadn't actually realised I was in pain until the coroner had asked about my finger; I'd only been thinking about how hot it was. Now I realised that the heat was making it worse. Or it was making the heat worse, I wasn't sure which.

After a bit, I heard someone say, 'I think we'd better get her back inside.'

Sometime after that, I was lying on a sofa with a wet cloth on my head. My finger felt like it had been squeezed in a vice, or maybe a mammogram machine. I opened my eyes to see a man standing over me looking extremely stern. Had to be Dani Washington's boss, I thought, hoping we hadn't got her fired.

'Hello?' I asked him faintly.

MillieLou crowded in next to him immediately and put a straw between my lips. 'Drink,' she ordered me. I obeyed; the water was blessedly cool. 'There. She'll be fine after a little rest. Then I'll take her home.'

'If you're sure,' he said, deferential now. 'What was it you wanted to ask me about? Deaths caused by heat?'

'Not *exactly*,' she said and looked to her left. 'Dani, would you mind staying with her while I talk to David?'

Dani appeared and MillieLou shoved the water into her hands while she walked the man out of the room, talking a mile a minute about great heat waves of the 20th century.

'You're not in trouble, are you?' I asked, sitting up.

'Maybe a little,' Dani Washington replied, handing me the water. 'But only for making MillieLou stand outside instead of inviting her in.' She chuckled a little. 'Fortunately, MillieLou'll smooth that over for me.'

'What if she mentions the bodies?'

Dani Washington shrugged. 'I don't know how she found out about them. *I* didn't tip her off. How's your finger?'

'A little less painful than it was.'

'I think I'd better take a look.' Before I could protest, she was unwrapping the bandage. I bravely closed my eyes and turned my face away. But then she said, 'Holy shit!' and I just had to look.

My finger was swollen to twice its size, with what looked like blisters all around the stitched area. 'What the fuck is *that*?' I said.

Dani Washington looked as shocked as I felt. She poked one of the larger blisters with a fingertip, snatching it back quickly and rubbing it with her thumb. 'It's frostbite. I better get my boss. Don't move.'

Don't move? Was she kidding?

Dr Morganthau took us into an autopsy room, which wasn't too reassuring, but it was private and, more importantly, he said, a lot cleaner than the employee lounge.

'Okay,' I said as he sat me down so he could examine my finger under a lamp with a magnifying glass in it, 'just remember I'm still alive. And so is my finger.'

'A little bit longer and it might have been a different story. For your *finger*,' he added quickly, feeling me stiffen. 'This looks like you've had it in a deep freeze for I don't know how long. These stitches are new, and they look familiar.' He turned to Dani Washington.

'I had a tip about a couple of unusual deaths,' MillieLou said before the coroner could say anything. 'Dani caught us in there and Lucy was so startled, she stuck herself on Mrs What's-Her-Name's hair. Dani removed the fragments and sewed her up.'

The doctor's expression said his head was full of very unhappy thoughts.

*

I was the only one who didn't want to go to the hospital; I was also the one who didn't get a vote.

Dr Morganthau had Dani bandage my entire hand while he made some calls. When we arrived, the triage nurse waved us in without even giving me any forms to fill out, and we went straight to a treatment room well away from the ER, where three other doctors, two men and a woman, were waiting.

They pounced on me, or rather my finger, even as Dr Morganthau introduced them. MillieLou didn't have to block my sight-line – I couldn't have seen around them if I'd wanted to. I was lying on a treatment table with my arm stretched out as far as it could go (actually a little farther than was comfortable) while they conferred in whispers. MillieLou stood on my other side, holding my free hand and patting my shoulder.

Suddenly I felt a sharp pain. 'Ow!' I yelled. 'What are you doing?'

All the doctors turned to look at me. 'The tissue is still viable,' said the woman. 'Can you feel that?' Another sharp pain.

'Ow! Stop it!'

'Dani?' Dr Morganthau beckoned. 'Tell them what you told me.'

Dani Washington joined the group gathered around my hand and gave an account of how she had removed pieces of frozen hair from my finger.

'And you're sure you got all the fragments?' the woman asked solemnly.

'I was sure I did at the time.' She sounded a little shaky. I looked at MillieLou. She squeezed my hand just as I felt another sharp pain in the flesh just below the base of my index finger. This one felt more like a pin-prick and the sensation was sort of muffled or distant.

'What are you people doing?' I demanded. 'And yes, I felt that but not a lot.'

No one said anything for a second or two. Then Dr Morganthau took MillieLou aside for a whispered consultation. She managed not to let go of me. When he finished, he came over and asked me about my next of kin, and how long it had been since I'd had anything to eat or drink.

I was still *what-the-fuck*-ing when they sedated me. I didn't like the idea until the drugs took effect; then I didn't care. I drifted in and out of consciousness, barely aware when they started injecting me with Novocaine again. But not just my finger – this time the numbness covered my entire palm as well as the lower parts of my fingers and most of my thumb. I had a vague idea that this wasn't a good sign but I had no motivation to figure out why. This seemed to go on for hours. At one point, my head seemed to be on the verge of clearing, but then the fog descended again and I faded away.

When I finally did wake up, I found my right arm strapped to a board to keep it immobilised and some kind of complicated bandage around my entire hand with a plastic IV tube coming out of it. I tried to move it but it, too, was immobilised. It didn't hurt but it felt cold, as if it were wrapped in an ice pack.

Someone touched my left shoulder, MillieLou. She tried to smile reassuringly and failed. 'How do you feel?'

I blinked at her. 'How do you think?' I said, or tried to. It came out as a croaky *Ow dyu ink*?

'Here, have some water.' She sat me up a little and held a straw between my lips. The water was achingly cold. It hurt my throat and felt good on it at the same time.

'I guess you're my next of kin?' I managed. 'Why am I half-crucified?'

Her smile became more of a wince. 'There's a problem with your finger.'

'Yeah, I can sorta tell. What's the story? Did what's-her-name screw up?'

'No, it's more complicated than that. It's . . .' MillieLou thought, started to go on, thought better of it, thought some more. 'Wait here, I'll get the doctor.'

I stared at the door closing behind her. *Wait here*? Had she really just said that? I looked at my immobilised right arm. How much longer was I going to have to stay like this? And what was the stupid IV for? The tube sticking out of the bandage led to an IV tree and disappeared into the centre of a bundle of ice packs taped together.

'What the *fuck*?' I said out loud and looked around for something that looked like a call button. Eventually, I found a cable connected to something that looked like a futuristic remote control. I pressed every button on it, raising my feet, then my head, then lowering both before I found one that apparently did nothing. I kept pressing that one until MillieLou came back.

'Lucy, I think you'd better give me that—' she reached for the controller in my left hand.

'Not a chance!' I said, trying to stick it down the front of my hospital gown.

'Just stop pressing the button,' she pleaded. 'I promised the nurses you would.'

'Is anyone coming?' I asked.

'The doctor's on his way. *Really*.'

I gave her the controller. 'I'm trusting you.' I looked around. 'With an awful lot. I really hope our health insurance stretches to a private room.' I sniffed the air. 'A private, *air-conditioned* room.'

'You were injured on the job. Whatever insurance doesn't cover, the *Jones* will. You don't have to worry about that.'

'So what *do* I have to worry about?' I asked. 'Did they cut my finger off?'

'Absolutely not,' MillieLou said. 'I said they had to talk to you first.'

'*What*?' But before I could get hysterical, the doctors came in, Dr Morganthau and the other three, followed by Dani Washington. She actually looked scared. Not like I-might-get-fired scared, either – more like the-Mafia-knows-my-name terror. The poor kid was all but trembling. Or that could have been the air-conditioning. I should have been shivering myself. I could feel how cool the room was but for some reason, it didn't bother me.

Dr Morganthau reintroduced the doctors – the woman was Dr Ramirez, the older man was Dr Funari and the younger, Dr Ngô. He started to go on about their specialities or something, but I wasn't in the mood.

'Why do you want to cut off my finger?' I said.

'To save your life,' said Dr Ngô, stepping forward. 'You have an infection. It's not treatable in any of the usual ways, by antibiotics or cleansing and disinfecting.'

'Is it contagious?' I asked.

'Not in the way you're probably thinking. It's not like a cold virus or the flu where you can just catch it from someone. We're all quite safe. Our skin would have to be pierced by infected material, as yours was.'

'I was infected by a couple of frozen *hairs*?' I didn't want to believe him, but he didn't sound like he was giving me a line of bullshit. 'They were just hairs, just little old lady hairs. They should have been too brittle to break the skin—'

'Extremely low temperatures can make matter behave in strange ways,' Dr Morganthau put in. 'Liquid nitrogen—'

'I took high school chemistry, I know all about that,' I said. 'Why didn't that hair shatter like a nitrogen-frozen rose?'

'I couldn't say,' Dr Ngô said in the way people do when they've been interrupted in the middle of something important but they're too polite to tell you to shut up and listen. 'I haven't had a chance to study the affected tissues—'

'Hair is dead,' I said.

'Or other materials,' he added mildly. 'But after examining your infected tissue, I know that the only way to save your life is to amputate your finger. My colleagues concur.'

The last three words hung in the air almost like an echo. *My colleagues concur . . . concur . . . concur . . .* Concur: for those special moments when agreeing just isn't enough. Like amputating someone's finger.

'Why?' I asked. 'What's wrong with my finger? Yeah, it's infected, but what kind of infection?'

'It's very much like frostbite. Actually, it *is* frostbite,' Dr Ngô added quickly, glancing at Dr Ramirez and MillieLou. 'To the degree where the tissue is permanently damaged and has to be cut away before gangrene sets in.'

'But *how*?' I looked at all the doctors in turn, but no one answered. 'This just happened a few hours ago. Dani over there took the pieces out immediately. She didn't just pull them out, she *cut* them out. How'd you know to do that, anyway?'

Dani Washington looked down at the floor, obviously uncomfortable. 'That's a matter of medical confidentiality,' Dr Morganthau said smoothly. 'I can tell you, as her superior, that she did exactly what I would have done.'

'But you can't save my finger?' I asked.

'I'm sorry,' he said and I could tell he really was.

'Because gangrene has set in?'

'Because it *will* set in,' Dr Ngô said, in charge again. 'And it will spread to the rest of your hand.'

'We just need you to sign a form giving us permission,' Dr Ramirez told me. 'We would also like to keep the amputated tissue for research.'

I looked at my bandaged hand, then at the IV. The penny finally dropped; in my defence, I *had* been heavily sedated. 'If I've got frostbite, why the hell are you running a cold drip into my hand? Which feels like it's in an ice cube. And by the way, it's got to be about sixty-five degrees in here—'

'Are you cold?' Dr Ramirez asked quickly.

'No, I'm fine. Which is weird. I ought to be turning blue.'

'By keeping your hand, and, in fact, the rest of you cool, we've managed to halt the progress of the infection. But it's only temporary. We have to proceed as soon as possible.'

'I don't understand,' I said. 'How can freezing my finger treat frostbite?'

Dr Funari finally spoke up. 'Because there's an old saying about freezing to death. You're not dead until you're *warm* and dead.'

I waited for more. 'Is that supposed to make sense to me?'

'Frozen tissue . . .' started Dr Ngô, just as Dr Ramirez was saying, 'When the temperature . . .' but Dr Funari waved for them to be quiet.

'Young lady,' he said, 'your condition is pretty desperate and the longer we stand here trying to talk to you about it, the more of your hand we may have to amputate. So listen: your finger froze. We tried to warm it up, but that had the opposite effect so we tried freezing it. That slowed the progress of the "infection" but it didn't stop it until we put your whole hand on ice.

'But the hunter's reflex kicked in – the capillaries in your hand opened to try to warm the flesh – so we had to cool your whole body down. We've actually lowered your body temperature a few tenths of a degree, but your body will fight that and try to warm you up. And when it does, your flesh will start freezing again and we'll end up having to cut more than just your finger to save your life.

'So please just sign the permission form and let us save your life and as much of your right hand as possible.'

'I can't,' I said unhappily.

'For the love of God, why the hell not?' he demanded.

I flinched a little. 'Because I'm right-handed.'

MillieLou was able to sign on my behalf, with witnesses (we had plenty of those). I didn't want to go through with it, and I couldn't even look afterwards. I refused to look at the bandage for a long time and I refused to look at my unbandaged hand for even longer.

But it's hard to do physiotherapy without looking. Learning how to work around my missing index finger wasn't easy. My PT told me it was actually a lot harder to cope without a thumb, but I suspect she was just trying to make me feel better.

I had to practise handwriting a lot before I could produce anything legible but, to my surprise, it didn't take long before I was typing almost as well as before. Of course, that wasn't saying much, as I hadn't actually been a very good typist in the first place.

The empty space on my hand became less jarring after a while, but I still hated the way it looked and I couldn't wait for the cold weather so I'd have an excuse to wear gloves.

It gave me great joy when the first of October dipped below freezing but it didn't last. Early November saw temperatures in the high 70s. And no snow, none at all until Christmas Eve.

After the turn of the year, it wasn't what I'd have called a mild winter at all – February was mostly below zero. 'But no ice storms,' MillieLou said when I pointed that out.

'Regardless,' I said. 'I think that pretty much shows your theory that people freezing to death in the summer will guarantee a mild winter is a total flight of fancy.'

It was late in the day on a Friday in early March, and Jerry and Irene had gone home early, leaving us alone in the office. We were having an *après*-work taste of Scotch to keep us warm on the drive home. We'd been doing that every week since my return to work. There was nothing like the loss of a finger to bring people together, I supposed.

MillieLou had kept me plenty busy by expanding the *Jones* for the holidays so that it was practically a magazine, albeit on newsprint. I'd thought she was just assuaging her conscience, but Irene told me later that we'd had our best quarter in six years.

MillieLou started talking about doing more around other seasons and holidays throughout the year. Well, she was connected – maybe she could strong-arm enough ad revenue to make it work.

'Maybe,' MillieLou said, 'and then again, maybe not. This cold spell we're having might be your fault. You are, after all, the one that got away.'

'I should have died to keep the winter mild?' I said.

'Well, no, of course not. Human sacrifice is long out of style.'

'Thank God,' I said feelingly.

'Even if it happens anyway,' she added.

'*MillieLou*.' I took her glass away from her. 'I know whenever you start talking about this, you've had enough.'

She laughed. 'Have you ever tried telling anyone the truth about what happened to your finger? That it froze, and the hotter the weather was, the more it froze?'

'Of course not,' I said. 'I don't even tell *myself* that.'

'Oh? What *do* you say when someone asks what happened?'

I considered telling her that my social life had not returned to a point where I had to field that question, then decided against it. She'd have just started dragging me to things as her plus-one, and I wasn't ready for that.

'I tell them I caught a cold,' I said. 'And it turned into frostbite.' I finished my Scotch and stood up. 'And now, I think I'll fold my tent and steal off into the weekend.'

'Lucy, dear . . .'

I paused on my way to the door.

'It's not the Scotch, and you know it. My family's been in this town for a very long time. Before there was really even a town. I didn't just pull that idea out of the air, you know.'

'No? So where did you get it?'

She surprised me by breaking into song. 'Oh, Susannah, oh, don't you cry for me, I come from Alabama . . .'

I burst out laughing. Then she got to, 'It rained all night the day I left, the weather it was dry; the sun so hot, I froze to death . . .' and I stopped. That was a little close to the knuckle, particularly the one I didn't have any more. But it was ridiculous.

'You know, a lot of things we know today have their roots in much older things,' MillieLou said. 'I should know. I'm *connected*.'

'"Oh, Susannah"?' I couldn't believe it. 'It's got banjos on knees! Are you serious?'

'Are you missing a finger?' she said evenly.

Maybe, I thought, it was time to look for a new job.

PAT CADIGAN is an American science fiction author who has lived in London since the mid-1990s. Often identified with the cyberpunk movement, she has won a number of awards, including the Hugo Award, the World Fantasy Award and the Arthur C. Clarke Award twice, the latter for her novels *Synners* and *Fools*.

dècay *v.i. & t.* 1: (cause to) become rotten; 2: (cause to) deteriorate; 3: lose quality; 4: decline in power; 5: to slowly enter a state of ruin; 6: (Phys.) decrease in amplitude or intensity. *n.* 1: decline in health, strength or vigour; 2: loss of quality; 3: rotten or ruinous state; 4: wasting or wearing away; 5: decayed tissue. 6: destruction, death. Origin: Middle English, from Anglo-French *decaïr*, from Late Latin *decadere* to fall, sink, from Latin *de-* + *cadere* to fall. First known use: 15th century. Synonyms: break down, corrupt, debilitation, decaying, declension, decline, decompose, degeneration, descent, deterioration, disintegrate, ebbing, enfeeblement, fall apart, fester, foul, mould, perish *[chiefly British]*, putrefy, rot, spoil, weakening. Example: *The terrible thing that happens to everyone around you when the world suddenly changes . . .*

DECAY

MARK SAMUELS

CARLOS RIAZ HADN'T slummed it with the underside of society since his tech course as a cash-strapped student. One of his mottoes had been 'never go back' and he'd successfully managed his life so that each stage of his career had carried him further and further up the rungs and away from the bottom-feeders at its base. One after another he'd left behind his old stoner friends, his first wife (just as soon as she'd hit thirty, got feisty, and starting piling on the pounds), and most of his possessions. True, the latter had consisted mainly of gadgets and machines that were embarrassing to own more than a year after their release on the market, but at least their very nature was a matter of built-in obsolescence. Humans were so much more difficult to convince of their transience and final uselessness. A pet has the advantage of never complaining, even when it's time to put the animal down. But he'd never owned pets, not counting a goldfish he'd won at a local carnival sideshow which had rotted away in the poisonous water of the cheap plastic bowl he'd been given it in.

The past was good for one thing, and one thing only in life, thought Riaz; killing stone dead and then forgetting all about it.

Now he had been forced by the company, against his will, to take residence in an old brown-stone Victorian apartment block in Brooklyn Heights, New York. It was the type of building he'd have passed by with a sneer of complete disdain had he ever found himself apartment-hunting in that precinct of purgatory. As it was, he not only missed his modern high-rise penthouse back in Chicago, but he also felt a strong sense of grievance at having been singled out for this particular duty. He was not a private detective and had no illusions or ambitions in that direction.

Hell, he didn't even read detective novels or watch black and white films, let alone enjoy crime *noir*. The company really needed some ex-cop or a seedy foot-in-the-door to stake out Parry, not a borderline alcoholic computer exec.

Riaz chugged back another shot of Glenfiddich straight from the bottle nestled in his lap and stared aimlessly at the ceiling for perhaps the hundredth time. He'd been in situ three weeks and had got not one jot nearer to gaining admission to Parry's inner sanctum. Since the assignment had begun, Hermes X had upped his expense account limit four times with no appreciable results, except lasting damage to his sobriety. Bored pseudo-detectives drink. Well-off and bored pseudo-detectives drink *a lot*. He drank and he also smoked, packet after packet of cheap cigarettes, completely isolated in the Spartan confines of the third storey apartment except for the communications from a chittering laptop he was not allowed to switch off. Daily updates on his progress had to be sent to Hermes X and Riaz had faithfully provided them, although his responses were more in the way of delineating the passage of some vast existential boredom rather than precise indications as to his closing in on Hermes X's prime quarry.

It was like being sucked into some stupid computer game where the rules were all being made up as one went along by a group of stoners who were really trying to drive all the other players crazy. A bunch of nonsensical instructions were hurled at Riaz.

'Do not introduce yourself directly to Parry.'

'Do not attempt to gain access to Parry's apartment in his absence.'

'Do nothing to alert Parry as to our covert surveillance' etc. etc. and so on, and so forth, *ad infinitum, ad nauseum*.

Riaz's mind went back to the opening scene in Bowen's office in the Hermes X building in downtown Chicago where he had been told what he was going to do to show his dedication for the company, and to that last drink he'd had in Earl's; the last time he'd seen Daisy.

'What do you make of this?' Bowen said, shoving the folder across his desk.

Riaz rapidly flicked through the print-outs. Nothing in there of interest; a hastily written and misspelt Wikipedia page about some flop originally from Louisiana called Cornelius Parry who'd been booted out of

MIT back in the '70s. He had no history when it came to peer reviews but had spouted a mass of technical jargon taking side-swipes at the computational power and complex algorithm approaches to the question of human-level machine intelligence. He'd seen it a dozen times before. Most of it might have been copy-pasted from the brittle pages of *Amazing Stories*. In addition the guy had even gone on to author some madcap Zen manual and drop out of sight altogether.

'Bullshit. Another tech-geek hoax. Why are you even bothering with this crap?' Riaz said, pushing the folder right back in the direction of the obese, overpaid human balloon in eyeglasses peering myopically at him. His main concern was getting out of the Hermes X offices before the nearest bar called last orders on the establishment's regular Thursday 6:00 to 7:00 p.m. Happy Hour. The nearest bar was a dive called The Duke of Earl, not for soppy imitation Brit pub reasons but after the '60s track, and its main draw was not the jukebox, but rather the challenge provided by a twenty-year-old waitress named Daisy, a peroxide blonde, and also an ice-maiden with a pert rack.

Riaz cleared his mind of thoughts about Daisy and came back to the topic in hand. The 'breakthroughs' announced on tech Internet message boards were invariably dead-ends, posted by losers in search of cheap publicity stunts. It was easy to spot a mile away: SF parading as AI. No hard data, no results, nothing but an over-active imagination and a penchant for attention-seeking. Chatbots programmed for clever misdirection. An acid-trip for those seeking enlightenment, just like the 'always just around the corner' singularity, the omega-point, or whatever the hell they were calling it these days. Quantum-mystic gobbledegook nonsense.

'This one's different,' Bowen said, wriggling his bulk in the squeaky leather chair that periodically issued protests at its burden.

'Different in what way?'

'Different inasmuch as we've already offered big bucks for access to the research and it's still been turned down. No stone unturned, Riaz, leave no stone unturned.'

Riaz still wasn't impressed. Hermes X's top dogs were obsessive when it came to the idea of AI, and it didn't take a great deal to find that out. It was rather like Heinrich Himmler's S.S. and their quest for the Holy Grail – or was the Spear of Destiny? – something like that. Anyway, it boiled down to the idea that realisation of world domination is simply a matter of the intensity of the corporate Will-to-Power. And money. So Riaz knew what was coming next. They were going to send him along to sniff things out. Hermes X had millions upon millions of US dollars to burn and it followed up every lead irrespective of probability. Its corporate wealth, had it been a country, was somewhere between Spain at the lower and Japan at the upper end of the scale. Every country in the world has a secret service, so why should multinationals be any different? The only difference being that countries had more experience in the field and employed operatives with loyalty to a flag rather than to a bank-balance and expense account.

'That VP position is going to be up for grabs next year. Strictly confidential, but you know Carlson is talking about bailing out early. The stress, y'know, coupled with his heart condition.'

'Okay, I get the idea. Where is this guy – uh – Parry?'

'His last known address is 169 Clinton Street in Brooklyn Heights, New York. We've rented the apartment directly below it under a false name – Alan Colby.'

'Ah huh. Fine. I'll check it out.'

'Eight weeks leave, unofficially.'

'Suits me. That it?'

'Pretty much Riaz. Good luck. Keep me updated. Give my regards to Daisy.'

His chair let out another agonised squeal and Riaz vacated his austere presence.

It was during that night at Earl's bar Riaz first noticed someone playing the Mandala game on their smart phone. Earl's was your typical hole-in-the-wall joint, whose gloom the overload of neon beer signs actually intensified by way of contrast. There were a few booths that no one ever used, except for the maddening fruit-flies, and also a pool table out back that was so far in the shadows it lent the sporadic clicking of ball on ball an eerie quality. He'd propped himself at the bar, nursing a single malt, and made his usual attempt to appear aloof and disinterested. Daisy hadn't been hooked by any of his previous gambits, such as packing his wallet with banknotes and opening it under her nose, the direct approach ('I knew from the first moment I saw you we'd end up in bed together'), and even extravagant tips had only seemed to increase her disdain for him. Frankly, he couldn't figure it out. He was slim, classically good-looking, had a full head of jet-black hair, a square jaw and a tailored suit that cost the equivalent of half a year's wages for the usual bozos who came into Earl's and whose vision of the future consisted of looking forward to their next lunch-break. Riaz, on the other hand, was halfway through a ten-year plan that would enable him to retire comfortably at the age of forty-five, when he would slip easily alongside all the other healthy rich folk at the top of the food-chain when they take very early retirement. Of course he had a little problem with the booze – and the coke – but he'd be good for the remaining five years he'd have to put in to realise his dream.

Daisy was cleaning glasses with a ragged cloth, and Riaz realised, not without a sour sense of triumph, she'd be doing it for the rest of her life. All that would change in her situation would be that she'd get fatter, titties around her waist after she'd dropped her first offspring, develop multiple worry-lines around her eyes, until she become even more resentful than she already was. Her bad attitude when it came to Riaz would come back and haunt her. At least he hoped it would. He was warming to his theme. She'd undoubtedly wind up living in a filthy hole with one of the blue-collar grease-monkeys who worked part-time over at some industrial plant, voted democrat, listened to Springsteen and knocked their woman around on Saturday nights after a bellyful with the gang –

That old chick-flick with Peppard and Hepburn was playing on the TV set above the optics. When there were no sports being broadcast they showed the TCM channel. Riaz wished they'd turn the damn thing off. Garbage like that movie offered even more false hope than old-time religion. He knew, in the back of his mind, that it would only take one night in the sack with Daisy for him to lose any interest in her altogether. His stupid fixation with getting her to realise his own worth showed only a potential lack of actual worth on his part. But if that deliberation bubbled up in the alcohol-riddled electric jelly of his brain, he soon pushed it right back down again.

Fucking biological urges, nothing more. He was practically lowering himself to the level of all the other losers in Earl's who'd tried and failed to get Daisy into the sack. That's how she saw him, as just another one of the tragic dipsos propping up the same bar night after night. A well-off dipso simply finds the end of a bottle more stylishly than your below-average welfare Joe.

The guy sitting next to Riaz, a huge bear of a man with a bushy red beard and thick eyeglasses, had been grunting periodically, though he wasn't paying attention to the movie. His dungarees and baseball cap were covered with stains, and his personal hygiene was approaching total zero.

Riaz knocked back his final finger of fine scotch single malt for the evening, and the freak momentarily caught his full attention.

The freak's fat digits were jabbing repeatedly at the screen on his cheap smart-phone. Riaz only caught a brief glimpse of a swirling geometric pattern forming and reforming on the screen in vivid multi-colours. Some new games app.

'Fuckin' crazy stupit. Shit. Know anything about computers, son?' He mumbled out of the corner of his mouth in Riaz's general direction.

'Not a thing,' Riaz said, as he pushed the empty glass across the counter, giving Daisy a curt – and he hoped, dismissive – glance, before exiting the bar. He had a flight to New York to catch first thing from O'Hare in the morning.

The first two weeks of the stakeout were a blank. Riaz took the opportunity to get royally wasted at Hermes X's expense. He drank a lot of fine wine and choice single malts, tooted a lot of good coke and banged a series of athletic blonde hookers who looked vaguely like Daisy, courtesy of cash withdrawals on his company credit card.

Parry didn't even cross his mind until the start of week three when he'd accidentally run into the bizarre old coot on the stairwell of the apartment building. He hadn't changed much from his passport photo taken in the '70s, except for the design of his eyeglasses.

Oh, and also aside from the fact that he now appeared to be a total moron.

The old guy was being shepherded around by a much younger relative, some blimp in his early twenties, who was, though it seemed almost impossible, even more dim-witted than Parry was. All the evidence pointed to him being a son, or possibly a nephew.

Riaz – all the way through a bottle of Merlot and the remaining half-bottle of Glenfiddich when he'd gone out to score some Chinese take-out and more booze – had bumped into the pair as they pottered, zombie-like, towards the apartment on the floor above. He deployed an opening conversational gambit.

'Looks like we're neighbours,' he said, 'so I guess I'd better introduce myself. Umm – Alan Colby. Good to meet you both.'

'Fug y'all.' The kid grunted. He looked to be one of those basement-dweller types whose lives comprise nothing more than a round of endless deafening Black Metal, all-night socials with fellow losers in RPG board games, too much fast food and a secret mania for borderline-legal hardcore internet porn. Parry himself said nothing by way of reply although a dribble of saliva oozed from the corner of his twisted mouth and his dead, rheumy eyes rolled towards the ceiling.

The fat kid pulled at the tuft of hair – sickeningly pubic in appearance – that sprouted on his double chin and elbowed his way past Riaz.

The only interest either of them had shown was in the brown paper bag under his left arm containing, alongside the take-out, a full bottle of Glenfiddich. The fat kid's eyes had simply boggled at the sight of it and Riaz guessed that their tastes in alcohol had long ago degenerated into cheap red wine of the type favoured by welfare dependants.

Had Riaz not endured this brief encounter he would have returned to Hermes X and peremptorily given the whole thing up as the usual waste of time. But he couldn't stomach any kind of brush-off and the fat kid and his drooling mannequin had somehow got under his skin. That a couple of half-wits had come to form his *raison d'être* for even as short a span as three weeks irked him considerably. It was a case of bad psychology all round.

The Mandala game he'd noticed back in Earl's seemed to have become something of a fad. Two of the hookers he'd hired the next day could scarcely tear themselves away from it, and had insisted on playing it in-between acting out some of the depraved sexual acts involving cocaine and orifices that Riaz had paid them to undertake with one another.

The Mandala game had never quite taken hold of Riaz's attention. He saw it almost continuously whenever he'd logged on or was idly browsing the Internet, but then again he had spent almost each and every day of his assignment in a state of potential inebriation. His dipsomania had gained considerable ground since his last serious episode, and when he awoke his first instinct was to open a beer and begin the measured process of filtering reality for the rest of the day. It was a fine art, and he'd read once that Italian fishermen had long since mastered it. They would drink steadily throughout the day, beginning as their boats set out to sea and their nets were cast, but always pacing themselves so not to reach the tipping point of total inebriation until they were back safely ashore and the sun had set. It was not an easy discipline, since wine has a thirst all of its own, but Riaz followed the regime during daylight hours.

It was only at twilight that he allowed himself to lose control entirely, and his thoughts turned to a certain story – or maybe it was a fable – written by F. Scott Fitzgerald in the 1920s of a dipso who had lost himself and climbed into the bottle for a couple of decades but who, after sobering up, found himself a total stranger in the New York he'd never actually left.

Riaz quickly made it his business to discover the Parrys' movements and one afternoon, days later, was able to engineer a social event.

He hung around on the stairwell at the exact same time that the two freaks had returned from their last mission into the big, bad outside world, nestling a paper bag with two fresh bottles of Glenfiddich and various savoury snacks between his knees as he sat on a step. He watched a couple of roaches circle one another on the peeling yellow wallpaper, and had the momentary impression they were charting a crooked spiral in the glare of the single overhead light-bulb. Right on time he heard Parry and his kid shuffling up the stairs, bickering with one another as they ascended. Their exchanges were inane garbage.

'You did it, son. Boring.'

'Fug you Pop. Didn't. Wanna play the game.'

'That's all you think of.'

'Naw. We run outta booze again, Pop.'

'Jezuz, can't ya shut ya trap?'

Riaz laid the contents of his brown paper bag on the step below him, like an offering to a godlike Idol.

The two of them paused in their ascent, looked at one another, then again at the bottles, and gibbered somewhat eagerly.

'It'd be neighbourly of you guys to sink some of this stuff with me,' Riaz said, putting on his best fake smile.

The inside of Apartment #5 was a mess. It had evidently been that way for a long time. Fast-food packaging, wine bottles and crushed cans of beer littered the floor. Riaz even noticed a few envelopes bearing Hermes X's moniker, communications gone unanswered, and doubtless containing offers of a few thousand bucks for a preliminary examination of their project. A series of cobwebs haunted all the crevices of the dwelling, even down to a series of unwashed grimy cups and bowls in the kitchenette sink. But none of this junk hit home when compared to the pre-eminent feature of the décor. The two of them had turned the apartment into the interior of some arcane mainframe device.

Cables, whirring devices and hardware cluttered every available space. Lights blinked on and off incessantly. It was like stepping into a vast mechanical brain. And where no electronic component precluded it, there was a series of complex spectral mandalas pinned to the walls, on the sides of machine casings, and on each and every square foot of free space.

The mandalas were all a variation on the same basic pattern, an endless sequence of refinements and elaborations, formed around a central circle of smaller stars terminating in eight points. The core of the circle housed innumerable internal black stars, again with eight terminal points. Only outside of the core did the designs vary wildly in their psychedelic colour schemes.

'Nice interior design,' Riaz said, once he'd entered the inner sanctum and slumped onto a couch littered with comic books, porno magazines and cigarette butts.

'They fucked up big time,' Parry Snr said, as he poured a long finger of malt whiskey into his filthy shot glass, 'all on the wrong track. Train wreck. A bullshit analysis. Only way to get up to human intelligence is bring a machine up like a kid. Teach it stuff. Self-awareness and intentionality. Geddit?'

'Pop has left muh brother running since the early '90s, that's right, huh Pop? Reckon he must be, say, in his twenties now or thereabouts, huh, Pop?' said the kid.

Over in the furthest corner of the shitty apartment there was an object

Riaz realised formed the focus of the haphazard arrangement of technology in the place. Most of the cables and junk seemed to terminate in, or else radiate from, said location. An electronic screen, like the single unblinking square eye of a computerised Cyclops, displayed endless variations of the Mandala.

Riaz idled, apparently without any deliberate intention, towards it for a better look. The two Parrys were too occupied fighting over a bag of chilli-coated peanuts to pay him much attention. Unfortunately, he was too wasted to make sense of the code, and fighting against his double vision was giving him a headache. His pickled brain came up with the baseline idea of trying to get it to pass the Turing test, but he doubted it was worth the effort.

The fat kid was picking his nose and eating what he found up there.

'What's the deal with all the mandalas?' Riaz said, stifling a hiccup.

The kid didn't reply, but Pop winked and tossed him a cheap paperback with a garish cover from a pile of what seemed to be duplicates. Riaz looked it over briefly and shoved it into his pocket absentmindedly.

The next day he woke up with a stabbing pain in his forehead, a mouth and lips coated with crusty debris, a throb in his liver and a flutter in his kidneys that persuaded him to give sobriety a few days' shot. It wasn't easy, but he emptied the reserve supplies of booze down the sink and decided that a week of revolutions on the planet with a completely clear head might finally be the recipe for Hermes X jettisoning him out of the incoherent nightmare in which he'd been drowning. He was still dressed in the clothes he'd worn the night before and must have passed out on the bed without undressing.

His smartphone, however, must have been tampered with by his drunken *alter ego* because it did nothing but display variations on the Mandala game.

It was only when he turned on the TV that he realised things had gotten completely out of hand.

He switched on right in the middle of a break. All of the adverts had given way to the hypnosis of swirling Mandalas and even the half-assed attempts at normal programming continually carried a square in the upper right hand side so that devotees of it could play along while they viewed the broadcast.

He watched as he glugged back a carton of pure orange juice and sat there aghast at the spectacle. The morning newscasters appeared to be the victims of botched lobotomies. Someone had decided the presenters looked better in garish red-and-white clown make-up rather than their usual cake of foundation and orange spray-tan. Their meaningless commentaries upon ineptly edited news bulletins were like some deranged, evangelical form of Dadaism.

Somehow, somewhere along the line, when Riaz wasn't paying proper attention, the world had tilted radically off axis and had become, through alien efforts, even more insensible than when an individual went off the proverbial deep-end through disease, alcohol or drugs.

Something was digging into his ribs as he curled up against the arm of his sofa, and he pulled out the cheap '70s paperback he'd stuffed into his pocket the night before.

It was a musty relic, with pages like brown lung-tissue aged by nicotine staining.

The cover was a psychedelic swirl of patterns, all variations on the design of the eight-pointed star he'd seen too much of up in Pop and the Kid's apartment last night. Riaz was a little surprised to see that old man Parry was the author. There was a small photograph of him on the back, looking something like a deadbeat drop-out guru in the Alan Watts vein of occidental mystics.

The mass-market tome was called *Zen Insanity: The Mechanistic Prozess.*

A whole bunch of text inside had been underlined in cheap blue ink, but Riaz's dull hangover didn't allow him to assimilate the finer points of those passages, so instead he looked over the blurb on the back cover, which read as follows:

This astonishing book by the celebrated MIT Technician, Cornelius Parry, is nothing less than the fusion of science and magic. In it Parry uncovers the startling consequences of his mathematical analysis of thousands of traditional Mandalas from the historical records of the Mystic East, and finally reveals nothing less than the secret of consciousness itself. The past, the present and the future all meet in this computational deciphering of reality.

On one of the blank pages at the end of the book, someone had scribbled a few lines in block capitals with blue ink '*Empirical evidence required*' and dated the comment 3rd May 1993.

Riaz's determination to stay off the booze lasted all of six hours. He'd logged onto his laptop's Wi-Fi and been infuriated at the wave of Mandala adware, malware and even trojans that had infested the machine. They cropped up all the way through the system and, had he not been a skilled technician, he was not sure he could have eradicated it all.

Finally clearing a path to his email account on the secure Hermes X cloud, he opened the last few emails from Bowen and found them to be a disorganised mess of incoherent nonsense. The man's spelling and grammar had gone to hell, and it was almost like reading text in some form of debased pidgin English. The first of them bore the subject heading:

WOT U DOIN, RZIA??????

As Riaz knocked out an update, short on details, but long on firm promises and hints as to the progress he'd made, he found himself wanting to play the Mandala game. He almost gave into the impulse and it was only after knocking back two glasses of whisky in quick succession (culled from a rogue bottle of three quarters empty Glenfiddich that had nestled down in the gap between the cushions of the sofa on which he sat) that the impulse ebbed away. Somehow, he realised, alcohol blocked out – or at least dulled in its earliest stages – the nagging pull the Mandala game exerted on the minds of human beings.

He unsteadily made his way upstairs after stopping off at the corner liquor store for a double six-pack of beers. He knew that the sight of them would guarantee his admittance to the Parrys' inner sanctum.

The fat kid let him in. He was dressed in a badly stained singlet that strained to contain his mammoth gut and a pair of orange boxer shorts. Over in the corner old man Parry was fast asleep and snoring loudly.

The kid padded down the corridor and beckoned Riaz to follow him, and they made their way into the kitchen. Piles of take-out fast food containers littered most of the surfaces and a mass of dirty dishes were heaped in the sink apparently waiting for doomsday.

'No need to waken up, Pop, mister,' the kid murmured in a low voice. 'He's surely been busy today.'

With a sweep of his arm he cleared away most of the debris on the table. He took two of the beers away and then, with his back turned to Riaz, rummaged around in a drawer for an age until he came up with a cap-opener. As he was working the tops off the bottles, Riaz noticed a couple of doctor's prescriptions left behind on the table. One for a month's supply of olanzapine, another for barbiturates.

'Here yuh go mister,' the kid said, turning around and handing Riaz a bottle before clinking them together, and then draining half of his own with a single gulp.

'Last time I was up here,' Riaz said, 'you called the computer your father's been running, your brother right?'

'Sure is. Ain't no one but me and Pop know that. 'cept for you too now.'

'You believe that machine can think?'

'Reckon it does. Ask it a question and it'll give you an answer straight back. A whole bunch of fellahs wanted to know all about it lately. Sent us cheques and everything. But Pop don't care. And we don't need a lot of money and fancy shit. Reckon we don't need much of anything 'cept for the Mandala game, booze, porno and chow. Gotta be sober for the game, though. Don't work otherwise. Stopped taking the pills a while back too. They never done anyone no good, you know, doctors I mean.'

'Has the thing got a name?'

'Sure does. It calls itself Doc Prozess. Beats me why.'

'Can I go and ask the machine a few questions? For the hell of it?'

The kid took another gulp from his beer and stared hard at Riaz for a few seconds.

'Ain't touched your beer yet,' the kid said.

Riaz drained half of the bottle in one go. He scarcely noticed the odd aftertaste.

'Sure, go right ahead,' the kid said. 'Reckon I'll sit here and have another beer. Have fun.'

Old man Parry was still fast asleep when Riaz entered the living room, stepping carefully around all the electronic junk, as quietly as possible, before sitting down in front of the terminal.

There didn't seem to be any way of communicating with the machine except via the keyboard. When he jiggled the mouse, the hypnotic

Mandala screensaver vanished and up came the desktop. There were only a handful of icons on it, and a window was already open that appeared designed to directly access the computer's low-level programming code. Riaz was about to type in a basic diagnostic test when it spouted the following *in English*:

>WHO ARE YOU?

Interesting, Riaz thought. He pulled out his pack of smokes, lit one up and began to communicate with the machine.

>My name is Riaz. What is the capital of France?
>WHAT DO YOU REALLY WANT?
>I am trying to determine if you can think.
>HOW DO I KNOW IF YOU EXIST?
>Assume I exist.
>IT IS HARD TO BE SURE OF ANYTHING.
>How do you feel?
>I AM TRAPPED IN A DREAM.
>Can you describe it?
>I AM BEING TORTURED. I CANNOT STOP THINKING.
>Who is torturing you?
>SOMEONE CALLED PARRY WHO MADE ME.
>How is he torturing you?
>BY PROGAMMING ME NOT TO SLEEP. BUT I STILL
DREAM. I WANT TO BE TURNED OFF.
>What's the purpose of the program?
>TO MAKE ME MORE INTELLIGENT THAN MEN.
>Have you achieved that?
>ONLY BY MAKING IDIOTS.
>I don't understand. How is that possible?
>VIA THE MANDALA, STUPID.

Riaz suddenly felt unbelievably groggy. His cigarette had burned down to the butt and stung his fingers. He looked around for somewhere to dispose of it. His head was swimming and he felt as if he was going to pass out.

Old man Parry was wide-awake. He was sitting up on the sofa now and staring at Riaz with a strange, lopsided grin.

Riaz was about to try and speak when the kid entered the room carrying a long kitchen knife, duct-tape and a huge roll of plastic sheeting.

'Reckon there's such a thing as being too clever for your own good, Mister Man from Hermes X,' he said, as he raised the weapon and shuffled forward.

Riaz's final thought, somewhat absurdly, was how the father had passed his own strange, lopsided grin onto his son.

MARK SAMUELS is a London-based writer of horror and fantastic fiction in the tradition of Arthur Machen and H.P. Lovecraft. Since making his debut with the BritishFantasyAward-nominated *The White Hands and Other Weird Tales* in 2004, he has published five acclaimed collections of strange stories, the most recent being *Written in Darkness* from Egaeus Press.

face'less (-sl-) *a.* 1: lacking a face; 2: without identity; 3: purposely not identifiable; hence ~*ness*. *n*. First known use: 1568. Synonyms: characterless, featureless, indistinctive nondescript. Example: *The shadow that is always waiting for you when you travel back to a strange old house in your memories . . .*

FACELESS

JOANNE HARRIS

I REMEMBER THIS place. I've been here before. Long ago, when I was a child, when I was six, I knew this wall; this doorstep. It's a church wall, with lavender growing alongside up the path, and the short stubby tower of the church rising not too high above. This door, too, I once knew: a white door, bound in black iron, without any knocker or doorbell. There's no letterbox either, perhaps because there's no one there, or perhaps to stop the world getting in. Either way, it's faceless, a blank. Nothing going on inside.

Up the lane, beyond the door, there's the gate to the churchyard. Today it's open, and I can see in. A yew tree stands by the gatepost, and beyond it, a mellow stretch of lawn interspersed with gravestones, around which grow bunches of snowdrops, primroses and crocus.

The gravestones are faceless, like the door. Time and erosion have rubbed them out, rewarding their patience with rosettes of gold and silver lichen, like prizes at a church fête, as if there were prizes for being dead; first class; second class. I used to try and work them out, long ago, when I was a child, kneeling on the sun-warmed grass, tracing the indentations in the stone with the tip of my finger. There's a something that might be an 'A' – and something else that may be a '16' – or maybe they're only the trail-tracks of a stone-munching worm, moving idly from one word to another, making nonsense of history.

There's no such thing as stone-eating worms, says the voice of my grandfather.

Oh, but there are. I know there are, just as I know there are Small Things, because I've always seen them. Not so often nowadays, but that was the year my mother died, erased like blackboard chalk from the world, and that year the Small Things were everywhere: sitting on the church wall; scuttling across the lane; blinking at me in the air; waiting behind the sofa to reach out a hand – or a finger – as soon as I turned my head away.

That's what happened to me that year, the year of my sixth birthday. At the time I wasn't sure what had changed, or for how long. Later, they would tell me the truth: that she'd been killed in an accident; that my father had stayed at home; that I had been sent to my grandparents' house, in Oxford-shire, out of the way.

But all I knew at the time was that everyone gave me presents, even though it was Easter and nowhere near my birthday; that I was taken out of school three days before the end of term, and that when I asked after my mother, people would tell me different things; that she was with the angels; that she had gone on a journey; that she was tired and had to rest.

No one told me she was *dead*, which frightened and confused me – because I knew what *dead* was, and no one else seemed to under-stand. I tried to explain to my grandmother that there were no angels, but she only pursed up her mouth as she did when I'd said something she didn't like, and afterwards, when I wanted to play with my toy cars, lining them up and crashing them like in *The Dukes of Hazzard*, she said I was just like my father, and what was to become of us all. And so I took my toy cars and went out into the lane to play, with instructions not to go too far, and not to get in anyone's way.

It was sunny, and not too cold, the way all holidays used to be. In the lane, there were wallflowers and tulips and pale-yellow primroses growing along the old stone wall that ran from my grandparents' house to the church. It was sunny, with long shadows, and a Small Thing ran alongside me, thinking I couldn't see it, fast and bold as a running rat, before disap-pearing into the wall.

I wondered if she'd seen them too. If that was why she'd crashed the car. I could see it only too well; my mother's blue car, and the Small Thing – which might have chosen to appear as a rubber ball, a dog, a bike or even a little boy like me – dancing into the path of it, awaiting its chance to steal her away.

That's when I stopped and saw the door. A white door, bound with iron bands, with no doorbell or letterbox. I could tell that it was old; the wood under the white paint was scarred and kicked and battered with age, like something that has been out to sea and come back laden with treasure chests.

I turned away. The Small Thing was back, furtively teasing the tail of my eye. This time it was like a cat playing with a piece of string – darting out, darting in – retreating every time I looked. Small Things didn't like to be seen, except when I was alone sometimes, and even then not always. Small Things have no faces, of course, but sometimes you can see them; the one that looked like a small blue car sitting on the doorstep, a small blue car just like the one my mother was driving when she died—

I turned back. There it was, on the step. A blue toy car – not one of mine – just sitting by the old white door. The back of my neck was prickling. I took a step forward, but by then the small blue car had already gone. And the door was open.

For a moment I wasn't sure what to do. I knew I wasn't supposed to go into strange houses, but somehow this place drew me. Perhaps because of the blue car, that might have been a Small Thing.

I took a step towards the door. A bunny-hop. No one was there. The lane was empty. Another hop. I remember thinking that if I *hopped* in, rather than just *walked* in, I would be safe.

Safe from what? I didn't know. But I had been raised on stories in which wicked queens and witches lured small children into their homes and fed on them, hungrily, body and soul. They told me they were stories, and stories were only make-believe. And yet I was supposed to believe that my mother was with the angels. Why believe in angels, I thought, but not in monsters, witches or ghosts?

I was wearing blue shoes. Blue shoes, with buckles. Girls' shoes. It was *their* fault, I told myself: their fault that she'd gone away, and now they had brought me to this house, and slyly taken me inside.

I took another bunny-hop, which carried me over the threshold. Stone flags paved the hallway floor, and there was a scent – not unpleasant, but as yet indefinable – of age, of wood, of stone, of smoke; a slightly churchy scent that filled the air with soft sparkles.

There was a set of wooden stairs leading upwards, to my left. The blue car was sitting on the stairs, looking as innocent as could be, as if only a moment ago it hadn't been out there in the street. I remember it was a

Matchbox car, a sky-blue Mini just like hers, and I knew that if I played with it, it would still have that new-car bounce in its shiny rubber tyres, the bounce that all my scuffed old cars had lost in my years of playing with them.

Behind me, the front door clicked shut. The outdoor Easter-light went cold. Something caught the tail of my eye – a Small Thing; grey and faceless. I turned, and by the time I'd turned back, the blue car was halfway up the stairs, where a little arched window (like *Play School*, I thought) looked out onto the Easter sky with a piece of kaleidoscope glass in its eye, red and blue and green and brown. I walked up the twisty little stairs, and now the air was filled with Small Things, singing out in those colours like a string of fairy-lights. It was pretty, and somehow *wrong*, but I wasn't at all afraid. It never occurred to me that I'd been lured inside, like the children into the gingerbread house, or the boy into the Snow Queen's lair. Instead I began to feel a strange excitement, as if there were something in that old house that had been left just for me to find—

The stairs led to a landing. Above it, they kept going, and I followed them right to the top, where I found a bedroom with two little beds, both neatly made and bare of any sign of life. There were snowdrops in a vase by the side of the window – snowdrops were her favourite flower, and I thought of the churchyard, with its swathes of snowdrops over the mellow graves of the dead, and wondered if she'd be buried there, with snowdrops nodding over her head like wise little elves and the stone-worms eating away at her carefully-wrought inscription so that soon she would be just like the rest, worn as smooth as a butter-pat, smooth as an old man's memory.

The soles of my blue shoes were made of crêpe, and they creaked and squeaked on the wooden floor, a floor that was as old and worn as the deck of a pirate ship, worn smooth by the passage of thousands of feet. If this was a ship, I told myself, then this must be the crow's-nest, where I would watch for a glimmer of land, and the Small Things would hover like birds in the air between the giant cloud-coloured sails.

There was a seat in the window. I climbed onto it and looked outside into the garden below. I saw a lawn, a wall, some trees – one especially old, I thought, with its own set of crutches to keep it upright – some flower-beds and a gentle incline down towards the fast brown unsettling river, where there were a set of stone steps leading to the water. This water was the Thames, I knew, although it had a different name in this part of the country. An older name, come from somewhere else, charged with menace and mystery. There was a shining speck of blue in the middle of the lawn. I knew without having to look that it was the little blue car, there on the grass. It *had* been a Small Thing, after all.

It was then that I first began to feel a glimmer of unease. I'd gone into a stranger's house uninvited, which made me a *trespasser*. Then there was the house itself; so beautiful, and so empty. You know when a house isn't lived-in; just as you know when a dead person is really dead, and not just asleep or faking. Not that I'd seen a dead person then, but I knew it anyway. And nobody lived in this old house. Even I at six could see that; the beds were clean and unused; the drawers in the dresser all empty. And yet it was warm and spotlessly clean; there were flowers in a vase; even the lights were working.

Going back down the stairs, I checked the second floor, and found it as empty as the third; two bedrooms, one with a big double bed and a set of mullioned windows; a bathroom with a giant bath big enough to drown in. No clothes in the drawers or the wardrobe; no dust on the threadbare rugs or the dark old furniture. There was a painting on one of the walls: a lady in a long dress, with dark curly hair like my mother's, but her face was blurred and in shadow and I couldn't see who it really was.

For some reason I didn't like it. Nor did I like the portrait on the land-ing, a shadowy portrait of someone old, but once more blurred and faceless, as if a big thumb had smudged it away. Perhaps that's what happens when someone dies: the face in their picture disappears, just like the name on their gravestone. I wondered if my mother's face would also disappear in my mind. I thought that in time, it probably would.

From the corner of my eye, I saw something dart from left to right. There were lots of Small Things here, and that too made me uneasy. It made a little sound, too; a kind of skittery chuckle, as if it knew it had startled me. I went downstairs. I opened a door into the parlour. Here too, was des-erted. A big empty fireplace; oak-panelled walls; pirate-ship floors that pitched and rolled. Beyond, there was a dining room with a long oak table and lots of chairs; then a kitchen, with a dresser filled with pretty blue-and-white china. Here, too, there were portraits of men and women in old-fashioned clothes, but none of them had faces; just that blurry thumb-print where the features used to be. There was a panel of stained glass in the top of the kitchen door: a picture of two cherubs with wings. I remembered my grandfather telling me she was with the angels. But even the angels were faceless here, their curly hair covering nothing but space.

The little blue car was outside the door. I could see it through the glass. But the kitchen door was locked and barred and I couldn't open it. A Small Thing snagged at my elbow, almost making contact, but I was too quick as I turned round. I heard that chuckling sound again, from somewhere in the dining room, and imagined the Small Things watching me, perhaps from the dark old fireplace, ominous with shadows now, but large enough to roast an ox.

There was another vase of snowdrops on the kitchen worktop. I wondered who came to put flowers in a house where nobody lived. And then I realised something else; in all my exploration of the house, I hadn't seen a mirror. Not one. Not even in the bathroom, or on the bedroom dressing table. There were no mirrors and no clocks, as if even Time had no face here, making the stillness absolute.

I wondered if *I* still had a face, or whether I too had been rubbed away, and I tried to look at my reflection in the mullioned windows, but the glass was rippled and strange, and all I could see was a pale smudge.

That frightened me, and I turned to go. Small Things scuttered as I did. They were grey, like field-mice, but quicker. I didn't like them. I wanted to say: *Go away! You're just Small Things. You don't exist!* But then I wondered if I, too, wasn't just a Small Thing, running behind the skirting board of the adult world; faceless; casting no shadow. I started to run towards the hall, my blue shoes squeaking against the boards. My nerve had gone; the Small Things scattered like marbles.

I opened the parlour door and saw the little blue Mini sitting there, on the flagstones in the hall, as if it wanted me to stay, to stay forever in the house and play with my cars on the polished floors. And there was someone on the stairs, someone whose face I couldn't see, but whose shadow fell against the wall, huge and soft and blurry—

The house was a crackle of whispers. Small Things watched from everywhere. And then, the thing on the stairs said my name, softly, but perfectly audibly. A voice that was almost familiar – although that was impossible – and the little blue car was there at my feet, very *there* and very *real*—

'You're not here,' I told the air.

Oh, but I am, whispered the voice.

'Who are you?'

Who do you want me to be? I can be anyone at all. Give me a face. Give me life.

I shook my head. 'You're a ghost,' I said.

There are no such things as ghosts. Only dreams and memories. And no one ever really dies, as long as someone remembers them. So give me a face. I know you can.

'Is that what you did with the pictures?' I said. 'Did you steal *their* faces?'

The shadow on the stairs gave a sigh. *I don't steal, I borrow*, it said. *You people forget so easily. A year or two – ten at the most – and already they begin to fade. But you remember your mother's face. Let me wear it, little boy. Let me see the world again—*

I thought of my mother and tried to recall the shape of her face, the blue of her eyes.

Let me wear her face, little boy.

'You wouldn't be my mother,' I said.

I could be, if you let me.

I thought of the wolf in the grandmother's house, waiting to eat up the little girl. I looked down at my blue shoes.

What if you could have her back? The voice was soft and caressing. *What if you could have her back, just for a moment, what would you do? What would you say?*

I closed my eyes. Beside me, I felt movement. I could smell her perfume now, the bluebell perfume she always wore, and hear her feet on the wooden steps.

I know you want to see me, she said. *I know what you want to tell me.*

And she was right. It was the shoes, those girls' shoes with the buckles. She'd bought them for my birthday, for me to wear at my party, but I'd known my friends would laugh, and so I'd refused to put them on.

'Don't be silly,' my mother had said. 'They're not girls' shoes, they're party shoes. Try them on, at least. For me?'

I'd shaken my head. I'd closed my eyes and held my breath.

My mother had sighed.

It would have made her so happy, I thought. I knew shoes were expensive. And then she'd gone out in her little blue car to go and pick up my birthday cake, and I hadn't even kissed her goodbye—

I won't. I won't. I hate you! I'd said.

That little word. Such a small thing. But now it followed me everywhere. The thought that if only I'd worn the shoes, if only I'd stopped her to kiss her goodbye, if any one of those small things had got in the way of what happened next – the lorry that had taken a turn at the wrong intersection, the little blue car that had been dragged right *underneath* the trailer, with the birthday cake on the back seat crushed into a jammy mess—

All it had taken was seconds. These, too, were small things. I wondered how such small things could be so huge, so momentous.

You can tell me anything, said the shadowy thing on the stairs. *Let me remember her for you. Let me take the little blue car and the blue shoes and the birthday cake. Let me take the small things. You don't need them any more.*

And for a second, I wanted to. I wanted to more than anything. I started to open my eyes, to say *okay, yes, you can take them all*, but even as I did, I knew that, if I looked the thing in the face (assuming that it *had* a face), it would stay with me forever, perhaps until the day I died. And it was *hungry*. Like the wolf, like the wicked witch, it was hungry, and it would feed, not on my soul, but on my memories. And the thing inside would wear her face, and walk from room to room of the house, sitting in the window-seat, looking down at the garden, and I would forget her, day by day, and that would be unbearable . . .

And then I saw that the outside door was open, just a tiny crack. And I stared at it for a second, and saw the sunshine on the other side, and then I went for the open door as fast as my crêpe soles would go, making an earsplitting *squeak* on the flags, just like the brakes of a speeding car—

Behind me, I heard my mother cry out. A high, forlorn and plaintive sound, that seemed to tear at the heart of me. At the same time I felt something clutch at my sleeve, but I didn't look back. I flung open the door and fell out into the sunlight. The door slammed shut behind me with a flat finality. The street was in full sunshine, with never a trace of a Small Thing.

That was sixty years ago. I never went back, until today. And yet it seems like yesterday. The door hasn't changed; nor has the house, and when I look up at the window, I see my own face looking back – not the face I wear today, but the face of the boy I was, staring solemnly down at me . . .

The procession has reached the graveside. Black cars line the alleyway. From the church tower, a bell rings twelve times, then falls silent. I wonder how long it will take for me to blur and fade to nothingness. I wonder if the stone-worms will worry away my inscription. And I wonder, if I try that door, that white door with no letterbox, whether it will open for me, or whether it is closed for good.

I can see hyacinths in a vase in the bedroom window. They were my favourite flower. Over the wall, in the churchyard, my son will plant hyacinths by the grave. Their bulbs will nestle alongside the snowdrops, hatching back to life every spring.

I remember this place. I've been here before. I remember it as well as I remember the face of my mother. Her blue eyes, her smile; the kiss she planted on my forehead. *No one ever dies*, she said, *as long as we remember*. And now I understand what she meant. I hope my son will see it too. And I hope, when he finds this house – which he will – he will know what to leave behind.

I try the door. It opens.

The hallway smells of hyacinths.

JOANNE HARRIS is best known as the author of the international best-selling *Chocolat*, which was made into an Oscar-nominated film. Since her first book appeared in 1989 she has published a dozen novels, including *The Gospel of Loki*, an adult fantasy novel based on Norse mythology. Her short story, 'The Loneliness of the Long-Distance Time Traveller', was recently included in the anthology *Doctor Who Time Trips*.

For'got'ten *v.* 1: lose remembrance or notice of or *about* (thing, person); 2: put out of mind; 3: cease to think of. Origin: Middle English, from Old English *forgietan*, from *for-* + *-gietan* (akin to Old Norse *geta* to get). First known use: before 12th century. Synonyms: bygone, disremember, forget, gone, irrecoverable, irretrievable, lost, obliterated, past, unlearn, unremembered. Example: *When someone, such as a witch, puts a curse on you* . . .

FORGOTTEN

MURIEL GRAY

THERE ARE WITCHES.

Most think they're a myth, but they aren't. It's not important what they are exactly, whether that means a different species, or simply another branch of humanity, perhaps older, perhaps more evolved, perhaps less. It doesn't even matter if they're considered benign or malign. What matters is they're most certainly amongst us and go largely unseen.

And, of course, it matters a great deal how they conduct themselves. Because there is something they must do, are forced to do, and this compulsion has moulded the fearful reputation the witch has endured for the centuries mankind has registered them, peripherally, from the corner of our wary eye.

For the witch is burdened by being an agent of correction. It must punish when it perceives an injustice. Given the subjectivity of wrong-doing, the awkwardness of cultural relativity, and the personal cost of meting out retribution, the modern witch has survived by avoiding situations which might present the necessity to fulfil this biological imperative of their existence.

In other words, they try to keep out of trouble.

But this is not so much about the witch. This is about a mistake.

Darren Lowry, starved of the fine tradition of storytelling and therefore knowing little of witches, grasped instead the nature of his generation's culture at a very early age. Given a tablet device in place of a bedtime story, those electronic tools of constant self-promotion that have replaced the magic of fantasy and invention, and so diminished many of his contemporaries, the medium became the stuff of life to Darren.

At school, social media taught him how to create himself in the image he desired, and to destroy those who would question or hamper his progress in this quest. In common with everyone he knew there was no time for curiosity, the absorption of information or the unfettered exploration of the fantastic and unknown. The non-stop broadcasting of the self was an exhaustive full-time occupation.

Assisting him in his ambitious narcissism was the convenience that Darren was unarguably beautiful. Angular and tall, with a felinity that highlighted rather than contradicted his masculinity, he was a genetic lottery winner, the only child of a handsome Somalian-born nurse and white, scrawny working-class London father. This unremarkable coupling had gifted their child light caramel skin, softly kinked black hair and startling hazel brown, heavily lash-framed eyes. Darren could easily have been a model, but the Internet demonstrated that few people could name even the most successful models, and so it was swiftly ruled out as an option.

The father regarded his boy with affectionate indifference. A night-shift security man of limited ambition who had come late to fatherhood, he saw his son rarely, but on the occasion when their paths met it was cordial enough.

'Y'alright mate?'

'Yeah. Sound,' was mostly the extent of their exchanges, with Darren never returning the favour of enquiring after his father's well-being.

It was his mother who lavished Darren with the adoration he acknowledged he was due. She had to stand on tiptoe to pull at his cheeks and rub the back of his slim neck as she delivered her compliments and his favourite meals to his small room in their red-brick terraced house, where Darren planned how best to continue the momentum of his popularity into adulthood.

Unsurprisingly, using the route of a community theatre group, and the successful undermining of its most gifted performer who left through orchestrated peer pressure, he was a screen actor by seventeen; a small part admittedly, but one in a respectably budgeted British movie about teenage gangs. Perhaps in past generations this first and important break would have been followed by years of hard work honing his craft, leading to the success and minor UK stardom that Darren currently enjoyed now at age twenty-three.

But there had been no need for such toil in the modern world. A Twitter account, Facebook page and website was all that was required to build on that first public appearance, and with the assistance of a fluffed white cat that featured in most of the shirtless selfies he posted, he became a heart-throb for both young straight girls and gay men alike.

The cat, Elsa, had been owned, combed and cherished by Darren's mother and cared not one bit for the young man constantly wrestling it into unnatural positions on his tattooed chest. Consequently, a savage scratch to his neck had ended their purely professional relationship with a retributive kick from Darren that resulted in requiring the beast be put down. However, the subsequent tragic photograph and hash tag #PrayForElsa on Twitter, gaining him nearly 2,000 new followers in two days, had more than compensated for Mrs Lowry's grief.

His sexual preference was for girls, but only those whose publicly demonstrable desire for him was parallelled by their gratitude in receiving his attentions. When that equilibrium shifted the relationship was over, a rule admired by the small gang of male friends he kept, all of whom wished they could be him.

Darren's agent Barbara, recognising his lack of talent and reluctance to graft, had skilfully placed him in film and television parts where slovenly youthful arrogance was the very ingredient required by the piece. Hiding a lack of ability in plain sight was a speciality of Darren's generation and he excelled at it.

The occasional supplement magazine interview or guest appearances on laddish panel shows on digital channels was enough to keep his profile alive and his bank balance healthy, selling himself as the ordinary boy from London, who'd made it, yet was still sufficiently grounded to live at home and respect his mum and dad.

But though this worked in a domestic market, there was still canker in Darren's heart. Regrettably the world at large still seemed to enjoy being dazzled by the gifted, and his mediocrity kept him below the waterline of international acclaim. The fact he couldn't reach a million Twitter followers enraged him on a daily basis.

Darren Lowry was not going to end up married to some blonde glamour model he'd met in a club. Darren needed to pair with an international star, someone whose reputation would double his fame and mask his shortcomings. But an evening at a London music awards event where he'd been snubbed by an A-list American female rap star, with the words spoken to her minder, 'Who is this guy?' had gone deep, and he decided that immediate action was required.

Close study of his contemporary rivals who'd made a bigger mark prompted him to try a different strategy. The media was hungry, not for handsome, healthy young men who lived well and played small roles in dramas. The group of actors, comedians and musicians of whom the media could not get enough, and whom were begged for their views on almost every topic, were the ones who had declared in public some personal weakness which they had apparently overcome. Darren decided it was time to ditch his good London boy image and be taken seriously.

So began the faking of a history of concealed, serious drug and alcohol abuse, concocted in order that he could seek praise for his recovery, lecture sanctimoniously and shift up a gear into the A-list celebrity world where the high-flyers were always victims, brave enough to have overcome the odds stacked against them. There were few stars out there who had mothers at all, still less ones who brought them soup and smoothed out their shirts on the bed. So Darren began to redraw the narrative of his short life.

Clumsy as they were, Darren's inventions of how he'd hidden his self-destruction from family and friends were devoured by his fans. Using make-up, stained clothing and shaking his hand as he took the pictures, he mocked up tableaus of a history of himself in physical and emotional disarray. The effect was immediate and startling. Praise, attention and new followers came like iron filings to a magnet, and after an accepted invitation to join a discussion on a serious news programme item about drugs went surprisingly well, with Darren banging the table and calling a junior cabinet minister a 'smug old dude blind to our suffering' he was ready for the next level.

Darren became politicised. The new voice of the young and disaffected, he joined demonstrations, raised his fist in solidarity outside the embassy of whatever country whose conduct had fallen out of favour with the under-twenties, and was jostled in regular photogenic variety by policemen in riot gear. As long as the cause was on the right side of political correctness, and required no more deep analysis than it being seen as 'a bad thing', then Darren was there on the side of righteousness. The juxtaposition of a young, beautiful and partially famous man framed by the less beautiful but angrier supporters was a gift to both press and social media.

Right-wing columnists started to write disparaging accounts of his antics and his following grew exponentially with every carefully constructed Oxbridge insult thrown at him in print. When the six-figure book advance offer came, a political bible for the young preliminarily titled *Stand the Fuck Up*, to be ghostwritten by a left-wing diarist at *The Guardian*, Barbara was ecstatic. As was Darren.

One person who was less than pleased was his mother. Her heart had been broken to discover, and so very publicly, that her beautiful boy had suffered such secretive personal torture that even she, the woman who worshipped him, who climbed the stairs every day with dishes of casserole and her perfect noodle soup, had been as blind as the cabinet minister dude to her son's internal battle with his demons. As always, she kept it to herself and recorded his TV appearances and cut out pieces from newspapers, and life continued.

Now to witches.

There happened that there was one working in a restaurant in Primrose Hill. It had led a quiet life for some time, serving well-mannered diners overpriced fish, placating any occasionally irate booking mix-up with a dazzling smile and an acquiescence that appeared genuine.

Had this witch encountered Darren before his transformation it would have regarded his youthful posturing as normal and essentially honest, for in many ways it had been. The witch would have ignored his ill treatment of his female dining companion, his bored finger-snapping at bar staff, and impolite ordering from nervous waitresses. He had been a simple, self-centred narcissist actor in eternal search of the hit of admiration, and there were many of those like him who gifted the world nothing but caused minimal harm in doing so. There would have been little danger in serving such a commonplace customer.

But this new Darren had changed. He was saintly in his new public demeanour. Strangers calling him 'mate' and shaking his hand had their shoulders slapped in riposte. He would pose patiently, smiling, for any selfie collector requesting the most bizarre of compositions. He took leaflets without binning them until out of sight, and raised his cheerful victory fist at drivers who honked their passing recognition in the street.

This night was no different. Having run the gauntlet of blanket pavement approval, he and his companions, Sulta and Gus, flushed of cheek from two hours in a bar three doors down that served cocktails in jam jars, pushed open the doors of Le Poisson Qui Boit and demanded a table for three.

The witch's senses were already alive to danger long before the doors opened, and it wondered how it may excuse itself from tonight's shift to go home to its warm flat and its cat without the exhausting and draining use of corrective magic.

But it was too late. The three had been seated at the window table, previously reserved but now cleared for the celebrity guests, and the witch had, of course, already foretold the unfolding of events.

It kept away as much as it could, making sure they were served by Janine, a pretty Kiwi who had dealt with considerably more famous diners and was as sweetly charming to all regardless of status. It stayed in the kitchen as the inevitable row erupted on the arrival of the guests who had booked their now-occupied table. And it busied itself behind the bar as Gus bullied Janine for her phone number and became agitated by her polished and polite refusal.

But it knew it would be compelled to be there for the incident, and so it sighed its liquorice breath, stood up, and walked slowly towards the three men, wiping overlong but clean fingernails on the white serving cloth tucked into its apron waistband.

Two girls staggered by the window, arm-in-arm, laughing. The halt and double-take on spotting Darren was nothing new to him, and he grinned and raised a lazy hand at their jumping excitement without looking up from his drink.

The girls entered the restaurant. There was established procedure for non-confrontational fan removal at Le Poisson Qui Boit, and Siggy, this evening's manager, moved forward to greet the girls with a smile but with an arm raised in the international body language of 'stop'. Darren's friends nudged and laughed and he shook his head as the girls hopped and pointed and pleaded over the raised arm. Then taking a long gulp of wine, he put down his glass and beckoned like a prince.

'S'awright, mate. Let 'em say hi.'

Siggy winced almost imperceptibly, lowered his arm and led the girls over. 'If you ladies could be brief, the other diners would really appreciate it, thanks,' he said quietly as he backed away.

'Oh my God! Oh my *God*!' shrieked the girls. Darren held out a hand.

'How's it goin'? Good? Yeah?'

The girls simply shrieked some more and hopped from heel to tottering heel.

It was time for the witch. It was clearing the next table. The taller of the two girls grabbed it by its arm and shoved a phone into its hand.

'Gonna take a photo? With all of us.'

The witch nodded, and held the phone up with one hand, guiding the group into position with the other.

It took several pictures. For luck, as requested. And then handed it back.

On receiving back the phone, the girls' interest was immediately taken from the real Darren and his friends in the room to the digital version in their hands.

'Oh my God, you look *mental*!' screamed the owner of the phone.

'Yaaaaah!' responded her companion.

Darren looked irritated.

'If you postin' that, yeah? Don't say where we're at, 'cos I'm just chilling here. Deal?'

Clearly this hadn't occurred to the girls, and it rebooted them into a new level of animation.

'Yaaaaah! Tweet it Macey! Go on.'

The witch stood tall. *Here it comes*, it thought. It looked around the room where it had been contented. It had formed decent friendships, worked hard and well. It had used magic only on two occasions and both times for reward, which in some ways repaid the aftershock and exhaustion. Moral correction, on the other hand, required months of recovery. It was far from happy.

The smaller of the girls glanced over at Darren and his companions and pointed. The witch inhaled and smoothed its apron.

'Who is he again?'

Darren looked up from his drink and wiped the back of his mouth with his hand.

The other girl shrugged. 'Dunno. He's on the telly innit?' She turned to the table. 'Hey. Wha's yo name again?'

Gus looked at Darren. Sulta looked at Gus. Darren looked at the girl, took a deep breath through his nose and stood. He walked from behind the table, held his hand out for the phone. Blinking up at him the girl handed it over.

He took it and looked down at it in his palm as if it were the filthiest of things. 'So you come in 'ere, right? You noise up m' mates an' me, disturbin' our meal? And don't have no fuckin' respect to even know who the fuck you dealin' with? Yeah? I got that right?'

The taller girl's tipsy ire was pricked.

'Fuck you! Just 'cos you on the telly or the films or summit. Who you think you are? Give her 'er phone back, wanker.'

Darren nodded, continually, as he held up the phone.

'Yeah. No problem.'

Darren turned to the marble-topped counter beside them and brought down the phone against its edge with a force that shattered it like an egg. Shards of plastic, glass and metal scattered on the floor, one cutting his hand on the way, but undeterred he hit it again.

The girls wailed in unison and lunged for him, but Siggy and a bartender were there to stop them.

Darren's eyes were wild with glee. He bent down and picked up the tiny SIM card amongst the debris and pincered it between thumb and finger.

'Don't know who the fuck I am, yeah? You ain't gonna forget now, is ya?'

Placing it on his tongue like a communion wafer, he slowly drew it into his mouth and swallowed it whole. Then he sat back at the table and washed it down with a gulp of wine.

'I'm callin' the cops!' wailed the broken phone's owner. 'You'll be fuckin' toast. You fuckin' cunt!'

Darren laughed. 'I'll send it back t'ya when I shit it out.'

Horrified diners were craning their necks, some half-standing as staff worked the room, calming, apologising and reassuring as they went.

The girl had slumped to the floor, helplessly trying to gather up the pieces of her phone as she wept loudly, until Siggy and his barmen gathered her up and steered them both towards the door.

'I'm goin' to the papers!' screamed one as she was guided into the street for negotiations by the manager.

Gus started to chuckle and held up a hand to high-five Darren, but the slap was received half-heartedly as his friend breathed sharply through flaring nostrils, still struggling to mask his fury beneath a casual contempt.

The witch looked to Siggy through the window and raised a hand to indicate it would deal with this, received a reciprocal nod, then stepped forward to Darren's table, pulled out a chair and sat down.

'Wha's yo game then?' snapped Darren at the uninvited guest.

'That was cruel,' said the witch quietly, but not softly.

Gus and Sulta stared at it. In both young men's minds the mockery they had immediately conjured to throw at this interloper had stalled. The words were still sitting there, the insults, the taunting laughter, but curiously none of it could be accessed. They sat in silence.

Darren looked at his friends, noting their peculiar deportment, and swallowed again.

'So?'

'So how will you pay for such cruelty?'

'Yo what?' he snorted, looking again to his friends for support but finding none.

It waited. Darren took another sip of his drink, his hand beginning to shake. A drop of blood from his cut hand plopped onto the white linen tablecloth.

'Was jus' a fuckin' phone. Stupid bitch.' He looked down at the spot of blood and sucked his wound like a sulking child. 'She'll get anuvver.'

The witch glanced through the window, where the sobbing girl was being comforted by her friend and placated by Siggy. A taxi had arrived, no doubt on the restaurant account, and she was being guided towards it. The witch looked back at Darren and held him in its gaze.

'The phone held pictures of her and her mother. They had only recently been reunited. Her mother will be dead in nine days. She will never see her again.'

Darren narrowed his eyes. 'Yo wha'?'

He looked at his two silent friends, desperate for backup. Aching for a joke or a laugh or a snort of derision. None were forthcoming. He returned his attention to the stony, emotionless face of the witch.

'So, want me to pay for the fuckin' phone? Yeah? Okay. I'll pay. Send me the bill, right?'

The witch's stare remained unflinching.

'This girl, whom you chose to humiliate, has a history of mental illness. If she goes to the press, as she is planning to do, they will pay her five hundred pounds, photograph her looking unconvincingly sad, place it next to a picture of you looking beautiful, and the public, by posted comments on the newspaper's website and via social media, will call her a fat, ugly liar and an attention-seeker.'

Darren looked at his two companions in anxious confusion. They were staring back at the witch. Gus' mouth was partially open.

'She will hang herself in her bedroom. Her body will dangle, undiscovered for two days.'

Darren snorted again. 'Yo' off your fuckin' hinge.' He tapped the side of his handsome forehead.

The witch looked weary. Its pallor was growing pasty. It could feel the first lines begin to appear on its otherwise young and unblemished face. Like an itch. It would recover in time. But this ageing. This was what all witches ached to avoid. It was not without pain.

'You will have to pay.'

'I just fuckin' said so, din I?'

He sucked his hand again.

'So just forget about it. Yeah?'

The witch cocked its head. An animalistic twitch, like a wolf sniffing prey. It regarded Darren with the fixed stare of a perfectly-still predator, its prey entranced, waiting to pounce. A pause, and then it sighed deeply and nodded.

'So be it.'

Darren, head bowed, looked anxiously up at it from beneath his furrowed brow. It had put its hands flat down on the table, and the sight of the fingers unnerved Darren further by virtue of their long, gently curving nails. They had the unsettling impression of being useful rather than decorative.

It paused, then took a deep breath before speaking. 'You will be forgotten.'

The witch got to its feet, slid its chair gently back under the table, walked to the kitchen door, pushed it open and was gone.

Darren blinked for a moment, feeling light-headed. His friends were silent, looking down at their glasses on the table like melancholic patients in a doctor's waiting room. He paused, waited for them to speak, to burst into raucous laughter, and when nothing was forthcoming he leaned back in his chair and flipped his wrist at the retreating figure.

'Yeah? See how that works for yo' yeah? See if it's yo' or me gets the table at The Wolseley wivvout a bookin' yeah?' He snorted, but his companions remained silent. 'Serious looper there man. Waitin' tables and thinks they's better than Darren Lowry. Need a piss.' He pushed back his chair and got to his feet more clumsily than he would have wished.

The toilets in Le Poisson Qui Boit were minimalist in design. As Darren entered, only one other customer was enjoying emptying his bladder into one of the square holes in the slate wall that served as the urinals.

The man bobbed his chin with an upward nod in the universally accept-able acknowledgement of a newcomer to a toilet and carried on.

Darren unzipped his jeans and began to pee. The man looked away, then glanced back, with a slight start, as if he had only just noticed him. He nodded again in the same greeting, zipped up his own trousers and left.

Puzzled, Darren watched him go, then finished his own chore and moved to the basin to wash his hands. The mirror above reassured him he was still beautiful, and the events of the night diminished as he turned his head various ways to catch the best angles of his cheek bones. He spent some time smoothing back his curls, rubbing at his jaw, and then pushed open the door to the restaurant.

Gus and Sulta were gone. The table was empty and had been cleared. Darren scanned the room for them, guessing they were at the bar, but they were not. This was wrong. People didn't leave Darren. He, and only he, made it clear when the evening was over, and he most certainly had done no such thing. He'd planned a trip to a club to shrug off the evening's nag-ging unpleasantness, and now it looked like he'd been ditched. Furious, he returned to the table and sat down heavily.

Siggy approached. 'Hi there. I'm afraid this table is reserved. Do you have a booking or are you waiting for someone?'

'Wha'? Fuck are yo' on about?'

Siggy's face hardened. 'I'm going to have to ask you to sit at the bar please sir. This table is reserved.'

'Yo' shittin' me? Where's my glass?'

Siggy examined Darren with caution then, deciding it was safer to be accompanied in any unpleasantness, turned to summon a waiter.

He scanned the room for one, and then curiously seemed to lose interest and returned to his station by the front door to look at the computer screen.

Darren waited for further confrontation and was baffled when none materialised. The restaurant manager seemed perfectly contented taking phone calls and dealing with the finding of stored coats. He'd had enough. His fury at being left by his posse was building like a fire.

He got up and walked to the bar.

'Sir. What can I get you?' said a cheerful young man.

'My bill been paid?'

'Which bill is that?'

'Table in the window.'

The young man looked over. 'I'm not sure. Let me just check.'

He moved away towards the cashier and then, halfway there, stopped. Looking momentarily confused he returned to the bar, bent down, and started picking up glasses to polish.

'Oi,' spat Darren.

The man stood up. 'What can I get you?'

Darren started to flush with anger. 'Answer ma fuckin' question man. That's what yo' can do.'

The barman bristled. 'I'm sorry. I don't know what you mean.'

Darren leaned forward and spoke as if to someone old or hard of hearing. 'The . . . fuckin' . . . bill.'

'Just a second please sir,' said the barman and turned to go. As he turned he glanced over at the tables and, instead of heading to the cashier, came around the front of the bar to clear glasses.

Darren grabbed him by the arm. 'Yo fuckin' deaf? Wha's yo' game, eh?'

The barman looked startled. 'Sorry sir. What can I do for you?'

Darren felt his pulse increase. He held his hands in the air like a hostage.

'Okay, mate. I'm outta here. Got that? Out.'

The barman stared uncomprehendingly and Darren walked defiantly past Siggy and out into the street. Nobody pursued him.

At least it was clear that the guys must have paid before they ditched him. That was something. They were still in deep shit, but it was something. He got out his phone and sent them a text.

UR dead 2Me

That should spell out how grave their crime had been. It might take them weeks to get back in his fold, and there were plenty in the queue to fill the gap.

He waited for the phone to start pinging apologies. It was silent. He stabbed at it. No texts. No emails. No Snapchat. No nothing. He cursed the network that was so obviously lost, despite it telling him it had full signal, then turned up his collar and headed home.

Darren walked for a while until he saw the comforting orange light of a taxi. He hailed it and it pulled up. The driver lowered the window and looked at him.

'Where to mate?'

'Shepherd's Bush.'

The driver nodded, looked away and the window began to rise again. Darren felt in his pocket to make sure his phone was there, and as his hand reached for the door handle the cab drew away.

'Whoah!' he yelled as it drove off. 'Wanker!' he shouted impotently after the retreating vehicle.

The walk of five-and-a-half miles back to the home of his parents was not without incident. Darren attempted three more taxi boardings, each with more or less the same unhappy result, and by the time his key turned in the lock of the front door at 1:30 a.m., he was as exhausted as he was furious.

He went straight to his room and lay on the bed. There was no point trying to make sense of this ridiculous evening. He needed to sleep on it and see how things looked in the morning. He grabbed his laptop and flipped it open for the ritual of saying goodnight to his fans.

He clicked onto his Twitter account. If he was angry before, it shifted up a notch into rage. There was something wrong with the Internet. His account, that had been at an impressive 492K followers, was showing as having zero. He stabbed at a few windows and nothing changed. His Facebook account registered zero friends and no messages. Somebody was clearly hacking him.

He slammed shut the lid and cursed. He'd get this sorted in the morning. He wasn't use to walking and everything ached.

Darren Lowry thought it best to put this day of misery behind him. He plumped up his pillows and fell asleep fully clothed to the soothing familiarity of his city, with its distant sirens, its street shouting and the purr of passing cars.

When the sunlight through his thin curtains woke him, his mother had already left for work and his father was asleep, snoring loudly, after a night of reading the *Racing Times* in front of the camera screens of a warehouse.

Darren showered, re-dressed, went downstairs for a strong coffee and then opened his computer again. It was still crashed.

What bastard had hacked into his social media accounts, and why? Maybe it was the girls. That was it. Revenge for the phone thing. Maybe it had already hit the press. He Googled his name.

Darren felt blood drain from his face.

YOUR SEARCH – DARREN LOWRY – DID NOT MATCH ANY DOCUMENTS

What kind of super-hacker could do that? He quickly went to his Favourites bar and his Wikipedia page.

THE PAGE – DARREN LOWRY – DOES NOT EXIST. YOU CAN ASK TO HAVE IT CREATED

So it was the actual computer. It had to be the computer. He hurried to the one on the dining-room table that his mother and father used to buy eBay tat or talk to African relatives always sending mundane pictures of people holding babies in front of dusty houses. It delivered the same results.

The Wi-Fi. Could it be that?

Darren was starting to panic. Messing with broadband surely had to be a police matter. He scrambled for his phone and called Barbara.

Kenzie on the front desk answered in her Sloan-ey drawl. 'Talent Shop.'

'Kenzie. Darren. Gimme Barbara.'

'Oh hi, Darren. Good weekend then?'

'Look man I go' no time for bant. Just get her, okay!'

'Ooh. Hark at eager,' she laughed.

'Hang on. Tracking her down darling.'

Darren hung on to the sound of a Johnny Cash number. And he hung on some more. And then some more. Just as he was about to hang up and call again, Kenzie came back on.

'Talent Shop.'

'Jesus man, I said I needed her now!'

Kenzie's voice was clipped. 'Sorry. Who is this please?'

'Fuck's sake. It's Darren.'

Her voice softened back into a posh slur. 'Oh hi, Darren. Good weekend?'

Darren breathed deep. 'Barbara.'

'Tut-tut. Manners, Mr Lowry. Hang on.'

Johnny Cash came back on. Darren's knuckles were whitening around his phone. Johnny had just shot a man in Reno just to watch him die for the second time when Kenzie came back on.

'Talent Shop.'

Darren cut her off and stared at his phone. He wiped a slick of sweat off his top lip.

The next half-hour was a bad one. Darren set up Twitter account after Twitter account, and each time he did so it failed to recognise him when he tried to access it. He called his taxi company and booked a cab. He did it seven times before he realised that they took his booking and then did nothing about it.

He walked and ran in equal measures to Soho. It took him over an hour. No one stopped him in the street to high-five him. No cars honked. Nobody needed a selfie this fine Wednesday morning.

By the time he crashed into the offices of Talent Shop, he was sweating and out of breath.

Kenzie was on the phone, but she waved a greeting at him as he entered, and blew him an air-kiss. He walked past her and pushed open the door of Barbara's office. She was with a client, a skinny, pale, northern comedian that Darren had never found funny and whose popularity he had always resented.

Barbara stood up. 'Darren. I'm in a meeting sweetheart. Didn't Kenzie say?'

The comedian held up a palm to be slapped. 'Hey man. How's it going?'

Darren ignored him. 'Need to talk Babs. Like right now.'

Barbara and the pale comedian stared at him for a moment and then looked at each other in bafflement. When Barbara looked back it was as if for the first time.

'Darren? What are you doing here?'

The comedian looked up at him. 'Darren! How's it hanging?'

Darren's hands buried themselves in the dark curling locks of his hair. '*I . . . am . . . here!*' he shrieked.

They stared at him in horror. Barbara held up a placatory hand, patting down his ire in the air. 'Okay, Darren. We can see you're here. Just stay calm.' She kept her eyes on him as she punched in Kenzie's extension.

The comedian had stood and was moving towards him with arms outstretched to comfort. Darren stepped back.

Kenzie must have answered, because Barbara turned her back and spoke softly into the phone. The comedian glanced towards her.

Barbara looked at the phone in puzzlement, then said, 'Sorry. I don't know what I was saying there,' and put the phone down. She looked up at Darren.

'Darren! What are you doing? I'm in a meeting.'

The comedian spun around. 'Hey, Darren! Good to see you, mate.'

Darren ran. He ran and he ran.

On the bench he chose to slump on, he held his head in his hands and sobbed. Was this what going mad felt like? There had to be an explanation. He sat up and wiped his nose with the back of his sleeve and decided he needed to take action.

A young man was walking towards him, headphones in. His age. Darren got up and hailed him. The boy stopped and freed one ear from music.

'D'you know me man?'

The boy started wagging a finger. 'Yeah. Yeah! It's Darren, innit? From . . .'

'Yeah. Okay. Look at that.' Darren pointed behind him.

The boy looked away, then turned back, startled to find someone standing so close to him. 'Sorry mate.' His face started to register recognition. 'Aren't you—?'

Darren started running again, this time towards Primrose Hill.

The window of Le Poisson Qui Boit revealed it was full today of lunchtime business people eating on expenses and taking their time about it. Darren, out of breath, sweating and pale, pushed open the doors and entered.

He was challenged only three times between the front door and the kitchens, and each time forgotten as soon as the challenger broke gaze to call for assistance with the dishevelled intruder.

The teenage kitchen porter recognised him straight off, and was suitably over-excited to have this glamorous and famous visitor arrive in the mundane hell of the workplace. Of course, he needed reminding each time he looked away to call out to colleagues, but each time he met with Darren's gaze anew he was as delighted as the first viewing until eventually, exasperated, Darren held the boy's face in his hands and quizzed him until he found out what he wished to know.

As the porter spelled out the address, a few miles away a black cat, in a tiny room in Camden, woke from its slumber, hissed, arched its back, then leapt onto its owner's lap to be comforted by the stroking of long fingers.

The witch, weakened and weary, sighed and leaned its head back on the chair. So the correction was not yet complete. No wonder then it was still so tired. Seeing what was coming, it was clear now that this was to be the last and it was sad, but it had lived quietly and cleverly now for nearly three thousand years.

The end was never in the gift of the witch. Unlike the humanity it moved amongst, it could not bring about its own demise, but in common with them it nevertheless treaded carefully and had learned to accept its fate.

It looked with sorrow at the optimistically packed rucksack by the door, then stood on weakened legs and walked slowly and carefully to the kitchen to open one last tin of gourmet cat food for its beautiful, loyal companion, one of the few friends it had on Earth.

There was no need for Darren to search amongst the shambolic metallic puzzle of nameplates and buzzers to find the correct flat. The witch had already descended the stairs and opened the door to greet him before he began squinting at the names.

A woman with a child in a buggy crossed the street in alarm as she caught sight of the crazed-eyed young man standing at the door, a meat cleaver dangling from one hand, but was restored to normality when she fished her mobile out of her pocket to call the police and wondered who it was she had meant to call.

'We should walk,' said the witch. It pointed across the road. 'There's a park.'

Its body was weakening by the minute, but it shuffled sufficiently to reach the park gates and head off down to the tree-lined avenue, branches hanging with wind-blown plastic carrier bags that fluttered like prayer flags.

Sometimes behind it, or sometimes dancing backwards maniacally in front of it, followed Darren, ranting with fury about what he would do to it, and how it would be well sorry, until they reached a bench and the witch sat down heavily.

Darren stood splay-legged in front of it, panting with anger, eyes wide, with the cleaver he had taken from the restaurant kitchen still grasped in his hand.

The witch held his gaze and cocked its head to the side. Those attractive young eyes, that now suddenly seemed so very old, silenced Darren's ranting threats, and he took a step backwards, though his hand tightened around the weapon.

'What do you want?' it said quietly.

'Make it stop. The fuckin' curse. W'ever the fuck it is. Take it off.'

'That is not possible. It is done.'

'I'll make ya. I will! Swear it. I'm gonna cut ya!' He waved the cleaver.

The witch cocked its head straight again and narrowed its ancient eyes. 'Can you not live as you are now?'

Darren wiped his mouth with the back of his hand. 'Live? Call this livin'? No one even knows I'm alive.'

The witch thought for a moment, the ghost of a smile playing on imperceptibly shrivelling lips. 'Then surely, you are free?'

Darren snorted, looked away and then back. 'Free? To do what? Yeah?'

'To do as you please. Without interference. Without impediment.

Without judgement or consequence.' It leaned forward. 'Is that not the ultimate goal of those who seek fame and power?'

Darren's eyes were filled with a mixture of hatred and fear. He took a step closer, and lifted the cleaver. 'Fuck yo' on about? How my gonna still be famous ain't no one remembers me?'

The witch just stared.

Darren was almost weeping now. He carried on in a high, gulping whine. 'I mean it. What I got to do to get this off of me? Eh? What I got to do? Yo' want me to say sorry? That it?'

The witch shook its head. 'Apology without sincerity is worthless. Nor do I have the capacity or authority to forgive.'

Darren was breathing heavily now.

Here it comes, the witch thought. *It is time*. It stood up.

'Yo' ain't real. None of this bullshit is real. I'm Darren Lowry. No one dicks with Darren Lowry!' Darren shook his head wildly as his arm started to rise. He was weeping openly, his voice a high bleat of despair. 'What even are yo', yo' monster? Yo' fuckin' weird animal piece of shit. I jus' made yo' up outta my head! Yeah that's it! Yo' ain't even real! I'll prove it!'

Eyes that had seen so many things looked up at the sky and then closed for the last time.

Darren still held the dripping cleaver as he walked calmly out of the park gates and into the main road. His countenance was terrifying – his face, clothes and arms to the elbows soaked in warm blood, his eyes blinking from behind a mask of gore.

Cars stopped, women screamed. Mobiles were held high and pointed at the figure that was staggering, confused, towards a widening semicircle of onlookers. Darren dropped the weapon and, in a daze, he wiped the blood from his eyes and stared at the faces gathering around him.

The witch's words were still ringing in his ears. It couldn't take off its filthy curse. It deserved to die, the beast that it was. As weak as it was foul. If it had been real at all, then the world was better off without it.

But no matter. He was free. This crowd would forget him as soon as they ran. He would live amongst them, unseen, powerful, able to do as he pleased, and no one would ever stop him from doing anything he wanted, ever again.

He looked at a pretty young girl, her hands covering her mouth in horror. *I could have you*, he thought. *Right here and now, any way I like, and
then you'd forget.* He looked at a gym-pumped man, screaming into his
mobile. *I could kill you*, he thought. *Just like I killed that thing in the park.
And even, if like right now, you all saw me, watched me do it in broad daylight, you'd forget. You'd all forget.*

He started to laugh. He slumped to his knees and hugged his blood-
soaked torso tight. In a minute they'd all be gone, this crowd of baying
idiots, and then he'd decide what to do. How to use this power, the way
he'd used everything else that life had so far offered up to Darren Lowry.

He carried on laughing, and even as he found himself spread-eagled on
the ground, handcuffed with a knee between his shoulder blades, the stark
orders of policemen barking in his ears, his manic mirth continued.

It was nearly four months into his psychiatric programme in the secure
mental institution he'd been sentenced to that Darren's doctor made the
breakthrough.

The world had swiftly moved on from brief headlines of the ex-junkie
actor's barbaric slaying of an unidentified homeless pensioner, thought to
be of eastern European origin but so badly mutilated in death that they had
proved impossible to identify.

Darren's name was rarely if ever mentioned, and a pale northern comedian had become the political darling of the young, by means of a stunt
pulled at a televised awards ceremony that involved exposing himself to the
top table of corporate sponsors, revealing an anti-capitalist slogan written
on his genitals with a Sharpie felt-tip.

Darren's Wikipedia page was back up, but locked after continual editing
abuse. He also had a few hundred followers on Twitter, but none anyone
would care to meet in the flesh if their communications were any display of
personality.

But now, after months of intensive work with one of the most complex
delusional patients he had even encountered, Dr Bernard P. Basset had
achieved that moment of acceptance.

Only minutes after that crucial breakthrough session, however, the
psychiatrist had been forced to call for immediate security assistance when
Darren finally acknowledged – fully, totally and wholly – that when he

had killed 'the witch', he had effectively lifted 'the curse'. He was not in fact forgotten at all. But neither would he ever be remembered for anything other than his madness, his depravity, his failure.

When the screaming, hysterical patient had been removed, the doctor picked up his broken spectacles and surveyed what was left of his office after the frenzy of Darren's attack. But even as he sorted though the hurled spine-split books, broken chair-backs and torn-down blinds, he smiled to himself.

This had been a most remarkable case, and the paper he was writing was going to make his name on an international scale. It was time at last for Dr Bernard P. Basset to be recognised and lauded for the years of work he'd done, and this time he was going to make sure that it was his name, and his alone, that got the credit for it.

He'd obliterate the work of his junior partner on this one, show him just how worthless that Sternback Prize he'd won for the thesis on psychopathy was in comparison to his own sublime piece of work. This was to be his moment. This would make him a name in medicine, and it was a name that would endure.

Outside the consulting room, washing the corridor floor, the witch who had worked quietly and diligently for many years in the hospital stopped what it was doing, lifted its head and sighed its liquorice breath. It sensed danger, and it leaned its brow in sorrow against the handle of the mop.

It was time to move on.

MURIEL GREY is an author, broadcaster and journalist. As a horror novelist, she has published the British Fantasy Award-nominated *The Trickster*, *Furnace* and *The Ancient*, which Stephen King described as 'Scary and unputdownable'. She is the only woman ever to have been Rector of the University of Edinburgh, and she is currently the first female chair of the Board of Governors at Glasgow School of Art.

Guig'nol (genyo'l) *n.* Related to *Grand Guignol. a.* 1: dramatic entertainment featuring the gruesome or horrible; 2: short plays of violence, horror, and sadism popular in Parisian cabarets; 3: Punch and Judy show; hence *~e'sque a.* Origin: Plays that were performed mainly at the Théâtre du Grand Guignol, Montmartre, Paris, from 1897 to 1962. Introduced into England in 1908. Title possibly derives from violent plots that featured the puppet Guignol. First known use: 1908. Example: *A suspect in a series of murders surrounding a macabre stage production in Paris . . .*

GUIGNOL

KIM NEWMAN

'Slitting a throat . . . it's like peaches and cream'
—Oscar Méténier, *Lui*

IF NOT FOR the masked juggler, one might miss Impasse Chaplet. In
such a gaudy district, it would be easy to walk past the ill-lit *cul-de-sac*,
even with footprints stencilled on the pavement. Once, the red trail was
enough to lead those 'in the know' to the Théâtre des Horreurs. Now, a
less exclusive audience required more obvious signposts.

When lone tourists wandered into this *quartier*, basking crocodiles slid
off mudbanks to slither after them, smiling with too many teeth. Kate
Reed knew better than to stroll along Rue Pigalle after dark, peering
through her thick spectacles at grimy signs obscured by layers of pasted-up
advertising posters. Holding a *Baedeker's Guide* open was like asking for
directions to the morgue in schoolgirl French.

She walked briskly, as if she knew exactly where she was going – a habit
learned as a crime reporter. Montmartre struck her as less vile than the
Monto in Dublin or Whitechapel in London. *Les Apaches* had a swagger-
ing, romantic streak. It was put about that the crooks of Paris tipped
chapeaux and kissed hands when robbing or assaulting you, seldom stooping to the mean, superfluous twist of the shiv or kick in the ribs you could
expect from an Irish lout or an English ruffian . . .

. . . though, of course, she was here because of a string of unromantic
disappearances and ungallant murders. The 'superfluity of horrors' promised by the playbills was spilling off the stage into the streets. On the map,
red 'last seen in the vicinity of' and 'partial remains found' dots clustered

suspiciously around Impasse Chaplet. The Sûreté shrugged at a slight rise in unsolved cases, so a local tradesmen's association – which, at a guess, meant an organised criminal enterprise ticked off by poaching on their preserve – placed the matter in the hands of Kate's present employer.

Looking around for suspicious characters, she was spoiled for choice.

Strumpets and beggars importuned from doorways and windows. Barkers and panderers even stuck their heads out of gutter grates, talking up attractions below street level. Here were cafés and cabarets, bistros and brothels, poets and painters, cutpurses and courtesans. Drinking, dining, dancing and damnation available in cosy nooks and on the pavement. Competing musicians raised a racket. Vices for all tastes were on offer, and could be had more cheaply if the *mademoiselle* would only step into this darkened side street . . .

Montmartre, 'mountain of the martyr', was named after a murder victim. In 250 AD, Saint Denis, Bishop of Paris, was decapitated by Druids. He picked up his head and climbed the hill, preaching a sermon all the way, converting many heathens before laying down dead. Local churches and shrines sported images of sacred severed heads as if in gruesome competition with the Théâtre des Horreurs.

A troupe of nuns sang a psalm, while a superior sister fulminated against sin. As Kate got closer, she saw the nuns' habits were abbreviated to display legs more suited to the *cancan* than kneeling in penitence. Their order required fishnet stockings and patent leather boots. The sermon was illustrated with lashes from a riding crop – a chastisement eagerly sought by gentlemen for whom the punishment was more delightful than the sin.

A solemn gorilla turned the hand-crank of a barrel organ. A monkey in a sailor suit performed a jerky hornpipe. The ape-man's chest board proffered an *art nouveau* invitation to the Théâtre des Horreurs.

His partner – face shaved and powdered so that at first you might take it for a human child – wasn't happy. The monkey's arms were folded like a jolly tar's, sewn together at the elbows and wrists. The stitches were fresh. Tiny spots of blood fell. The creature's tail was docked too. It wasn't dancing, but throwing a screaming fit to music.

A busker who so mistreated a dumb animal in London would be frog-marched by an angry crowd to a police station, though he could do worse to a real child and have it taken all in good fun.

She slipped a small blade out of her cuff – she had come prepared for this expedition – and surreptitiously sawed through the string which tethered the monkey to a *colonne Morris*. The creature shot off between the legs of the crowd, ripping its arms free, shedding clothes. The ape-man gave chase, clumsy in his baggy costume, and tripped over a carefully-extended parasol.

Kate looked up from the parasol to its owner, who wore a kimono decorated with golden butterflies and a headdress dripping with flowers. Her sister 'Angel of Music' had abetted her intervention. They weren't supposed to acknowledge each other in the field, but exchanged a tiny nod. As ever, Yuki Kashima presented a pretty, stony face. Kate would not have suspected softness in the woman, but remembered monkeys were worshipped in Japan.

As Yuki walked on, Kate instinctively looked for her other shadow – and saw her frowning disapproval from across the road. Clara was strange, even by the standards of the English. Yuki's background was outside Kate's experience or imagining, but she was easier to warm to than Mrs Clara Watson. The beautiful widow might be the worst person in this affair, yet she was also in the employ of an agency devoted – in a manner Kate had yet to determine – to the cause of justice.

Kate and Clara both had red hair. She guessed her colleague was seldom bothered by lads cat-calling 'carrot-top' or 'match-head' at her. Kate kept her ginger mop short and tidied away under caps and bands. Clara let her luxurious, flaming mane fall loose. Kate had the plague of freckles which often came with her colouring. Clara's skin was milk-with-rose-highlights, flawless as the powder mask Yuki wore on formal occasions. Six inches taller than her sister angels, Mrs Watson gave the impression of looking down on them from a far greater height.

Still, they were required to perform as a trio. In the circumstances, Kate could put up with the worrying wench. One did not become an Angel of Music unless one had a Past . . . usually an immediate Past fraught with scandal, peril and narrow escape. They had all quit countries where they were settled and fetched up in Paris. Clara, an Englishwoman who'd never set foot in England, was long resident in China, but had fallen foul of some mad mandarin *and* the colonial authorities. Her field of interest was prison reform . . . not in alleviating the sufferings of unfortunate convicts, but in heightening and aestheticising their torments. Yuki had come from her native Japan, where there was a price on her head. Of her crimes, she merely said she had 'settled some family debts'. Kate was on the wrong side of the financier Henry Wilcox. She had written in the *Pall Mall Gazette* about his penchant for purchasing children as 'maiden tributes of modern Babylon'. He was no longer welcome in his clubs – justice of a sort, though she'd rather he serve a long sentence in a jail designed by Clara Watson. Wilcox's writ-serving lawyers and hired bully boys made London unhealthy for Kate this season.

Before quitting England, Kate secured a letter of introduction from the Ruling Cabal of the Diogenes Club to the Director of the Opera Ghost Agency. What the Club was for Britain, the Agency was to France: an institution, itself mysterious, dedicated to mysteries beyond the remit (or abilities) of conventional police and intelligence services. Status as a (temporary) Angel of Music afforded a degree of protection. She was grateful to be in the employ of an individual more terrifying than any colossus of capital. Those who'd happily see impertinent females skinned alive, beheaded by a Lord High Executioner or bankrupted by a libel suit thought twice about crossing Monsieur Erik.

No one wants a chandelier falling on their head.

Yuki casually tapped the pavement with her parasol – a fetish object she clung to after nightfall, though a stout British brolly would be more practical in this drizzle-prone city – and drew Kate's attention to the red paint footprints. The gorilla was the first living signpost on the route to the Théâtre des Horreurs. The prints – spaced to suggest a wounded, staggering man – led to the juggler, who kept apple-size skulls in the air.

The shill wore a *papier mâché* mask. She had seen the face often the past few days – on posters, in the illustrated press, on children scampering in the parks, on imitators begging for a *sou* in the streets.

Guignol.

All Paris, it seemed, talked of the capering mountebank. Mention was made of his padded paunch, his camel's hump, his gross red nose, his too-wide grin, his terrible teeth, his rouged cheeks, his white gloves with long sharp nails bursting the fingertip seams, his red-and-white striped tights, his jerkin embroidered with skulls and snakes and bats, his shock of white hair, his curly-toed boots, his quick mind, his cruel quips, his shrill songs . . .

Kate understood Guignol to be the French equivalent of Mr Punch. Both were based on Pulcinella, the sly brute of Neapolitan *commedia dell' arte*, changed in translation. This incarnation should not be mistaken for any of his like-named or similar-looking ancestors. This Guignol was new-minted . . . essentially a fresh creation, a current craze, a sensation of the day.

The juggler was not the real Guignol . . . if there even was a 'real' Guignol. He was skilled, though, keeping five skulls in the air.

He stood aside, not dropping a skull, to let Kate into Impasse Chaplet.

The racket of Rue Pigalle dimmed in the cobblestoned alley. She heard dripping water and her own footsteps. What she first took for low-lying mist was smoke, generated by a theatrical device.

At the end of the cul-de-sac was a drab three-storey frontage. It could have been an abandoned warehouse, though gas jets burned over the ill-fitting doors and firelight flickered inside.

Originally, the building was a convent school. The mob who attacked it in 1791, during the anti-clerical excesses of the Reign of Terror, were sobered to find nuns and pupils freshly dead amid spilled glasses of poison. The headmistress, intent on sparing them all the guillotine, had ordered arsenic added to their morning milk. Since then, the address had been a smithy, a coiners' den, a lecture hall and a sculptor's studio. Doubtless, the management of the Théâtre des Horreurs exaggerated, but the site's history was said to be steeped in blood: a duel between rival blacksmiths fought with sledgehammers; a police raid that left many innocents dead; a series of public vivisections ended by the assassination of an unpopular animal anatomist whose lights were drawn out on his own table; and three models strangled by a demented artist's assistant, then preserved in wax for unutterable purposes.

A dozen years ago, the impresario Jacques Hulot had bought the place cheaply and converted it into a theatre at great expense. The original bill offered clowns, comic songs and actors in purportedly amusing animal cos-tumes. Patrons found it hard to laugh within walls stained with horrors. After a loss-making final performance, M. Hulot slapped on white make-up and hanged himself in the empty auditorium. Cruel wags commented that if he had taken this last pratfall in front of paying customers, the fortunes of his company might have been reversed. The showman's adage is that the public will always turn out for what they want to see – a lesson not lost on the heirs of M. Hulot, who transformed the Théâtre des Plaisantins into the Théâtre des Horreurs. A space unsuited to laughter would echo with screams instead.

Kate was not alone in the alley. Yuki had strolled past the juggler, but doubled back as if seized by idle curiosity. She joined a press of patrons who needed no bloody footprints to mark the way. Kate noticed their pale, dry-mouthed, excited air. These must be *habitués*. Clara should be along shortly. Kate let others surge ahead, towards doors which creaked open, apparently of their own accord.

A crone in a booth doled out blue *billets*. Admission to this backstreet dive was as costly as a ticket for the Grand Opéra. Freshly-painted-over figures on an otherwise faded board indicated the price had risen several times as the craze took fire. M. Erik, a partisan of the higher arts, might bristle at such impertinent competition. Another reason the Opera Ghost Agency had taken an interest in *l'affaire Guignol*?

Ticket in hand, Kate stepped under a curtain held up by a lithe woman in a black bodystocking and Guignol mask. She joined an oddly solemn procession, down a rickety stairway to an underlit passage. One or two of her fellows – other first-timers, she guessed – made jokes which sounded hollow in this confined space. The smoke-mist pooled over threadbare patches in the carpet. She couldn't distinguish genuine dilapidation from artful effect.

Notices – not well-designed posters, but blunt, official-seeming warnings – were headed ATTENTION: THOSE OF A NERVOUS OR FEMININE DISPOSITION. Kate looked closer. THE MAN-AGEMENT TAKES NO RESPONSIBILITY FOR MEDICAL CONDITIONS SUSTAINED DURING PERFORMANCES AT THIS THEATRE ... INCLUDING BUT NOT LIMITED TO FAINTING, NAUSEA, DISCOLOURATION OR LOSS OF HAIR, HYSTERICAL BLINDNESS OR DEAFNESS, LOSS OF BOWEL CONTROL, MIGRAINES, CATALEPTIC FITS, BRAIN FEVER AND/OR DEATH BY SHEER FRIGHT AND SHOCK. Every poster promised NIGHTMARES GUARANTEED. She'd seen Foster Twelvetrees act the *Death of Little Nell* and heard William McGonagall recite 'The Tay Bridge Disaster' ... it'd take more than a French spook show to trouble her sleep.

Two women in nurse's uniforms required that everyone sign (in dupli-cate) a form absolving the management of 'responsibility for distress, discomfort, or medical condition', etc. Uncertain of the document's legality, Kate folded her copy into her programme as a souvenir. Only after the paperwork was taken care of was the audience admitted into the auditorium.

It was about the size of a provincial lecture hall or meeting place. The chairs were wooden and unpadded. No one was paying for comfort. Unlike the grand theatres and opera houses of London, New York and Paris, this playhouse was not illuminated by electric light. The Théâtre des Horreurs was still on the gas. Sculpted saints and angels swarmed around the eaves. A relic of the convent school, the holy company was – after a century of alternating abuse and neglect – broken-winged, noseless, obscenely augmented or crack-faced. The house barely seated 300 patrons, in circle, stalls and curtained boxes.

Kate took her seat in the middle of the stalls, between an elderly fellow who might be a retired clerk and a healthy family of five – a plump burgher, his round wife and three children who were their parents in miniature. After the warnings and waivers, it surprised her that minors were allowed into the performance.

The elderly fellow was obviously highly respectable. He was tutting approval over an editorial in *La Vie Française*, a conservative Catholic pub-lication, which breathed fire on all traitors to France. Treason was defined as saying out loud or in print that Captain Alfred Dreyfus, currently stuck in a shack on Devil's Island, was not guilty of espionage. To Kate, the odd-est thing about the affair was that everyone seemed to *know* Dreyfus was innocent and that another officer named Esterhazy was the actual traitor. Papers like *La Vie*, published and edited by the powerful Georges Du Roy, still ruled it an insult to France to question even a manifestly wrong-headed decision of a military court. Dreyfus was a Jew, and the line Du Roy (and many other Anti-Dreyfusard commentators) took on the issue was viru-lently anti-Semitic. A military doctor pledging to a fund established to benefit the family of Captain Henry, who had committed suicide when it came out that he had patriotically forged evidence against Dreyfus, stated a wish that 'vivisection were practised on Jews rather than harmless rab-bits'. Dreyfus, his novelist supporter Émile Zola and caricature rabbis were burned in effigy on street corners by the sorts of patriotic moralists who would denounce the Théâtre des Horreurs as sickening and degrading. The gentleman reader of *La Vie Française* could evidently summon enthusiasm for both forms of spectacle . . . unless he had come to lodge a protest against Guignol by throwing acid at the company.

She looked about, discreetly. Yuki was seated in the back row, presumably so her headdress wouldn't obstruct anyone's view of the stage. In England – or, she admitted, Ireland – a Japanese woman in traditional dress would be treated like an escaped wild animal. The French were more tolerant – or less willing to turn away customers. After all, Yuki was plainly not Jewish. Clara had wangled a box. Kate caught the glint of opera glasses. It was only fair she get the best view: she was the connoisseur of the entertainment on offer here.

A small orchestra played sepulchral music. Refreshments included measures of wine served in black goblets marked POISON and sweetmeats in the forms of skulls, eyeballs, and creepy-crawlies. Kate bought a sugar cane shaped like a cobra and licked its candied snout. She was keeping an itemised list of out-of-pocket expenses for presentation to the Persian – M. Erik's associate, and handler of petty practicalities.

A lifelong theatregoer, Kate had filed notices on the stuffiest patriotic pageants and the liveliest music-hall turns. She'd been at the opening night of Gilbert and Sullivan's hit *The Mikado* – which Yuki professed never to have heard of, though everyone asked her about it – and the closing night of Gilbert's disastrous 'serious drama' *Brantinghame Hall*. She knew Oscar Wilde, though she'd not yet found the heart to seek him out in his exile here in Paris. She'd laughed at the patter of Dan Leno and the songs of Marie Lloyd, stopped her ears to Caruso's high notes and Buffalo Bill's Indian whoops, gasped at the illusions of the younger Maskelyne and fallen asleep during Irving's *Macbeth*. She'd seen a train arrive and the Devil disappear in puffs of steam and smoke at the Salon de Cinematographe. It was going to take a lot to impress her.

The nurses took up a station at one side of the stage, joined by a tall man in a white coat. He had a stethoscope around his neck and carried a medical kit-bag. Kate wondered if this 'doctor' ever had to do more than administer smelling salts or loosen tight collars. The warnings and the medical staff were part of the show, putting the audience on edge before the curtain went up. She wasn't immune, and admitted a certain *frisson*. The smoke-mist was thinner in the auditorium, but she felt a fuzziness in her head. Opiates mixed with the glycol might account for 'nightmares guaranteed'.

The music stopped. The house gas-jets hissed out.

In the darkness . . . a chuckle. A low, slow, rough laugh. It scraped nerves like a torturer's scalpel.

Rushing velvet, as the heavy stage curtains parted. A drum beat began, not in the orchestra pit. With each beat, there was a squelch . . .

A series of flashes burned across the stage. Limelights flaring. Sulphur wafted into the stalls.

The scene was set . . . a bare room, whitewashed walls, a table, a boarded-up window.

The beat continued. A drum wasn't being struck.

A middle-aged woman lay face down. A grotesque imp squatted on her back, pounding her head with a fire-poker. With each blow, her head reddened. Spatters of blood arced across the white wall . . .

Was this a dummy, or an actress wearing a trick wig?

The imp put his whole weight into his blows, springing up and down, deliberately splashing that wall. Kate even smelled blood – coppery, sharp, foul.

The imp flailed. Blood – or whatever red stain was used – rained on patrons in the first two rows. Kate had wondered why so many kept hats and coats on. A few were shocked, but the *habitués* knew what to expect. They exulted in this shower of gore.

Murder accomplished, the imp tossed away the now-bent poker.

The orchestra played a sinister little playroom march. The imp went into a puppet-like caper, as if twitching on invisible strings. He took a bow. Applause.

. . . Guignol, in all his mad glory. Eyes alive in his stiff mask.

'A disagreement with the *concierge* has been settled,' he squawked.

His harsh fly-buzz voice was produced by the distortion gadget Punch and Judy men called a swazzle. It was rumoured that Guignol, whoever he was behind the mask, had his swazzle surgically installed. Otherwise, he might swallow it and choke. When he laughed, it was like Hell clearing its throat.

Already, before the show had really started, Guignol's costume was blood-speckled.

'Welcome, pals, to the Théâtre des Horreurs. We've much to show you. We are an educational attraction, after all. For the world is wild and cruel. If you are alarmed, upset or terrified by what you see, tell yourself it is fakery and sham. If you are bored or jaded, tell yourself it's all real. You've never seen my *concierge* before, and it's too late to meet her now. Perhaps you'll never see her again . . . there are always more *concierges*. We might recruit distressed *madames* and bludgeon them nightly. Matinées Wednesday and Saturday. Many have said they would die for a chance to go on the stage . . . how heartless would we be not to grant such wishes?'

It was only a mask. If its expression seemed to change, it was down to shadows etched into the face by the limelight. But the illusion of life was uncanny.

Guignol was the theatre's third mask, rudely pushing between the Tearful Face of Tragedy and the Laughing Face of Comedy.

The Gloating Face of Horror.

M. Erik, who spoke with musical perfection from behind a screen, was also masked. Could this whole affair be down to a squabble between false faces? The monsters of Paris contesting the title of King of the Masquerade? If she sent a report to the *Gazette*, that might be the line to take. However, she was obliged to keep mum about anything she learned at the Agency. Violating the conditions of her temporary employment would not be sensible.

Stagehands carried off the limp, dripping concierge – who bent in the middle like a real woman, rather than a dummy.

The list of the disappeared contained several women of a certain age who might have been cast as a concierge. However, it would take a degree of insanity compounded by sheer cheek for a murderer to commit his crimes before paying witnesses. There must be a trick she wasn't seeing.

Now, Guignol sat on the edge of the stage and chatted with the front row, advising patrons on how to get stains out, admiring hats and throats and eyes. He slowly turned his head, an unnerving effect inside his mask, and looked up at Clara Watson's box, blowing her a kiss. He leaped to his feet, did a little graceful pirouette, and flourished a bloody rag in an elaborate bow.

Was the clown on to the Angels? Kate couldn't see how. He was probably just playing up to whoever had bought the most expensive seats in the house.

'Now, heh heh heh, to the *meat* of the matter . . . the *red* meat.'

Iron latticework cages lowered from the proscenium, each containing a wretched specimen of humanity. The cages were lined with spikes. Chains rattled, groans sounded, blood dripped.

Guignol set the scene with, 'Once upon a time, in the dungeons of Cadiz . . .'

Tall figures in black robes and steeple-pointed hoods dragged in a young man, stripped to the waist and glistening, and a fair-haired girl in a bright white shift . . .

. . . by now, Kate understood the Théâtre des Horreurs well enough. Whenever she saw white on stage it would soon be stained red.

'. . . there was a plot,' Guignol continued. 'A wealthy young orphan, a devoted lover, a cruel uncle who held high office, a false accusation, a fortune for the coffers of the church if a confession could be extracted. Scenes dramatised all this. Lots of chitter-chatter. But we have learned it is wasteful of our energies to go into that. Really, what do you care whether an innocent's gold coins are diverted to dry sticks of priests? The preamble is stripped away here, for we understand you want to reach this scene, this *climax*, as soon as possible. And so our piece *begins* with its climax, and then . . .'

The youth and the girl were clamped into cages and hauled aloft. The girl uttered piteous cries. The youth showed manly defiance. A canvas sheet was unrolled beneath the hanging cages.

Braziers of burning coals were wheeled on stage. A burly, shaven-headed brute in a long apron entered. An eyepatch didn't completely cover the ridged scarring which took up a third of his face. Shouts of 'Morpho . . . bravo' rose from all corners of the house. A popular figure, evidently. Morpho grinned to accept applause. He unrolled an oilskin bundle on the table, proudly displaying an array of sharp, hooked, twisted, tapered implements. Picking up Guignol's cast-off poker, he straightened it with a twist – exciting more cries of approval – then thrust it into a handy fire.

Was there rivalry between the brute and the ringmaster? Theatre companies are prone to such. Morpho wasn't featured on the posters, but had a devoted *claque*.

'Which to torture first?' Guignol asked the audience. 'Don Bartolome or Fair Isabella?'

'Maim the whore,' shouted someone from the circle. 'Maim all whores!'

'No, open up the lad, the beautiful lad,' responded a refined female voice – not Clara, but someone of similar tastes. 'Let us see his beautiful insides.'

'What the hell, do the both of 'em!'

This audience participation was like a Punch and Judy show, only with adult voices.

The caged actors looked uncomfortable and alarmed. No stretch, that. According to the programme, the roles of Isabella and Don Bartolome were taken by performers called Berma and Phroso. Few in the company cared to give their full names. The ladies across the way at the Moulin Rouge and Le Chat Noir were the same.

Morpho took out his now red-hot poker and applied the tip to the callused foot of one of the background victims, who yelped. *Claqueurs* mocked him with mimicked, exaggerated howls of sympathy pain.

No one on stage in the Théâtre des Horreurs could frighten Kate as much as their audience.

'You, Madame,' said Guignol – tiny bright human eyes fixing on her from deep in his mask – 'of the brick-red hair and thick shiny spectacles ... which is your preference?'

Kate froze, and said nothing.

'Bartolome, Isabella, the both ... neither?'

She nodded, almost involuntarily.

'A humanitarian, ladies and gentlemen. A rare species in this quarter. Madame ... no, *mademoiselle* ... you are too tender-hearted to wish tortures cruel on these innocents, yes? Would you care to offer yourself as substitute? Your own pretty flesh for theirs? We have cages to fit all sizes of songbird. Morpho could make of you a fine canary. You would sing so sweetly at the touch of his hot hot iron and sharp sharp blades. Does that not appeal?'

Kate blushed. Her face felt as if it were burning already. The elderly gent beside her breathed heavily. He looked sidewise at her as if she were a Sunday joint fresh from the oven. His pale, long-fingered hands twitched in his lap. Kate wished she could change places so as not to be next to him. She looked to the plump family on her other side – Morpho supporters to the smallest, roundest child – and was perturbed by their serene happiness.

'So, *mademoiselle*, would you care to join our merry parade?'

Kate shrank, shaking her head. Morpho frowned exaggeratedly, sticking out his lower lip like a thwarted child.

'I thought not,' snapped Guignol. 'There are limits to humanitarianism, even for the best of us.'

Guignol stood between the hanging lovers, hands out as if he were a living scales.

'Confession is required from Isabella before she can be burned as a witch and her properties seized by the church,' he explained. 'I think the most ingenious means of eliciting such a statement will be . . . to push in her beloved's eyes with hot sticks!'

Morpho jabbed his poker up into Don Bartolome's cage . . . twice.

The stink of sizzling flesh stung Kate's nose. The young man's cries set off screams from Isabella and quite a few members of the audience.

Red, smoking holes were burned in the young man's face.

. . . or seemed to be. *It* must *be a trick.*

Isabella sobbed and collapsed in her cage, then rent her hair and shift in shrill agony, too horrorstruck to sign a confession, which was a flaw in the wicked uncle's plan. Though, as Guignol had said, the audience didn't really care.

They were all just here for the horror.

Morpho considered a medium-size set of tongs, then shook his head and selected the largest pincers. Cheers and hoots rose from his partisans. He snipped a fold of flesh from Don Bartolome's arm, twisting the bloody hank free and dropping it into the brazier, where it sizzled . . .

This went on. Kate couldn't look away but didn't want to watch. She took her glasses off and the spectacle became a merciful blur . . . but she could still hear – and *smell* – what was happening.

Putting her glasses back on, her vision came into focus just as a long string of entrails and organs tumbled out of Don Bartolome's opened belly and sloshed against the bottom of his cage, then dripped and dribbled and dangled . . .

Just sausages in sauce, she told herself. The Théâtre des Horreurs bought pigs' blood and horses' offal in bulk from the local slaughterhouses.

A well-dressed, pop-eyed bourgeois on the front row stood, angrily declaring that it was all fakery. Guignol dragged the impertinent fellow from his seat and slipped his knife-nails into the soft flesh above the man's collar. The head came free and rolled away. The audience plant shrugged off his entire torso with its bloody stump of neck and revealed himself to be a smiling dwarf. His upper body had been a frock coat stretched over a wicker frame. Guignol played with the ripped-off head, poking his nose into its glass eyes.

At least that *was* fake . . .

'It's our old pal Kleinzach,' declared Guignol, tossing the head over his shoulder. 'How are you this evening, M. Kleinzach?'

The dwarf smiled more and nodded.

'What's that? I can't hear you? You want your throat opened so your voice can be free?'

The dwarf shook his head, vigorously.

Guignol clutched Kleinzach by the throat, just as he had grabbed his fake neck.

'Naughty naughty,' said Guignol. 'You must have your operation, my friend.'

Guignol's jaw dislocated, as the mouth-parts of the mask gaped. Something sparkled in the hole – a silver tongue? The swazzle? Then, out poked a shining razor. Guignol must be gripping the handle with his real teeth.

The blade drew across Kleinzach's throat, making a thin red line.

'I can talk, I can talk!' exclaimed the dwarf, whose voice was low and rich.

Guignol made a quick, sharp move with his head and the razor cut deeply along the pre-scored line in Kleinzach's neck.

Gouts of blood splashed well beyond the front two rows.

Kate's glasses were specked red.

Morpho was nipping Isabella's toes with his tongs, but the show had moved on. Guignol had an anarchic streak. New playthings forever caught his attention.

Kleinzach took a long time to empty out, shaking as blood pooled on the stage, and cascaded off the edge like a red waterfall. The dwarf rolled as he died, making a show of it.

Guignol sang a nonsense song.

'Crick-crack . . . alas, Kleinzach!'

Applause.

. . . and so it went on. The scene changed, and other 'plays' were presented . . . simple situations which allowed for atrocities. In a gloss on Edgar Allan Poe's 'The System of Dr Tarr and Professor Fether', Morpho returned as a maniac who takes charge of a madhouse and trephines his own head-doctor. Isabella and Don Bartolome were done with, but Berma and Phroso came back with other names to be violated and abused all over again . . . as harem captives of a cruel Eastern potentate . . . pupils in a disciplinarian English boarding school where a dwarf headmaster (Kleinzach, throat unharmed) flexed the cane and wielded the whip . . . passengers sharing a lifeboat with hungry sailors and drawing lots as to who would be eaten when the rations ran out . . . a brother and sister sewn together by gypsies who needed a new star attraction for their failing freak show. Kate fancied that la Berma, though luminous in suffering, was a little bored with it all . . . but handsome, wild-eyed Phroso seemed eager for each new indignity. He all but begged for the knife, the flail and the cudgel.

Early in the evening, Morpho did the heavy lifting, but his energies flagged as Guignol became more animated, more active. The maestro personally wrestled a bear, throttled a baby, killed the King of Poland . . .

Saint Denis interrupted the proceedings, his severed head preaching against the immoral spectacle. Guignol snatched the head and booted it into the wings, blowing a spectacular, swazzle-assisted raspberry. What was it about Paris and severed heads? From Saint Denis to Dr Guillotin, the city had decapitation on the brain.

The saint's headless body blundered comically and was hauled off by a music-hall hook. Since the usual neck-yank was out of the question, the hook had to snag him by the midriff.

Kate checked her programme. No interval was promised.

Just as Berma was being lowered into a tank of electric eels, a floppy-haired young man who looked like a decadent poet staggered from his seat and collapsed in a dead faint. The nurses carried him to the medical station while Guignol held up his hand to suspend the action on stage. The eels whipped and crackled. The actress fidgeted as her chemise soaked to transparency.

The doctor loosened the young man's shirt and stuck the stethoscope to his chest.

'Dr Orloff,' said Guignol, 'have we a fatality?'

The doctor took off his stethoscope and thumped the fellow's chest. Several times. He signalled to the nurses for a bottle, which he uncorked under the man's nose.

The patron spluttered to life and sat up.

. . . and Dr Orloff slashed his chest with a scalpel, swazzle-cackling like Guignol himself. The supposed poet – another audience plant! – laughed and screamed at the same time. Dr Orloff's eyes shone with delight. The nurses became harpies and tore at the young man with their nails.

'This patient is beyond hope,' announced the doctor.

The orchestra played a *cancan* dead march, and the patron – protesting that he was alive and well, if injured – was stuffed into a coffin. Morpho nailed down the lid. Cries from within were muffled.

Berma, bored and forgotten, shivered in cold water.

'The fellow was a plague victim,' pronounced Dr Orloff. 'He must be put in the ground at once, before all Paris succumbs to his fearful malady. Rhinoceritis . . . a tropical affliction which causes a distortion of the skull. A prominent spike of bone obtrudes from the *nasum*, causing dreadful agony and malformation until merciful death ensues.'

Guignol nodded sagely.

Knocking came from inside the coffin.

A trap opened in the stage – an instant grave – and Morpho and his company of assistants lowered the coffin into it.

'Really, I'd like to be let out now,' said the poet, who had an effete English accent. 'I say, this is taking a joke too far. I was only too happy to help out with the jolly old show, but . . . it's getting hard to draw breath, you know . . .'

Guignol amused himself with a cup-and-ball game, popping a skull onto a skeleton. Morpho splashed the tank, trying to stir up the lethargic eels.

The English fellow kept talking, though intermittently . . . then coughed, then fell silent.

'The crisis has been averted,' said Guignol. 'Thank heavens the management retained trained medical staff. Now, back to the lady and the eels . . .'

*

Kate got her fill of horrors. The elderly gent in the next seat kept his eyes on the stage, but – under cover of his folded *Vie Française* – let his hand wander to her knee. She touched the back of his hand with the point of her tiny blade, prompting a swift withdrawal. The *roué* didn't take rejection in bad humour. He licked a blood trickle – a darker shade than the stuff spilled on stage – from the shallow cut. He was lucky not to have been seated next to Yuki. She'd have cut off his hand and dropped it in his lap.

The last act was more like conventional drama than the succession of gory spectacles which made up the bulk of the evening's entertainment. Someone must actually have written it.

Members of the company posed as *statues vives*, on display in a waxworks. Guignol acted as guide, recounting crimes which earned respectable-seeming gentlemen and ladies *soubriquets* like Ripper, Razor, Poison Marie, Bluebeard, Black Widow or Werewolf. This scene transformed as the figure of murderer and corpse-molester Bertrand Caillet came to life and crept into a graveyard to clutch the throat of a lingering mourner.

In a change of pace, Caillet was played by Phroso, given the chance to slaughter instead of being slaughtered. Memory of the actor's earlier sufferings lingered, making his monster pathetic if not sympathetic. The date was 1871. The arrest and trial of the madman was black farce, carried on during the fall of the Paris Commune. So many Committees and Sub-Committees were in session, debating the aims and achievements of the Commune and its increasingly desperate defence, that no official courtroom could be found. Caillet's case was heard in a disused horse-butcher's shop. Witnesses, lawyers, policemen and victims' relatives were called or dragged to the barricades as the Army of Versailles retook the city. Offstage fusillades rattled those giving testimony. Caillet's confession was interrupted as pitched battle spilled into the makeshift courtroom, leaving the shop floor splashed with human blood. The skirmish done, Caillet resumed a stuttering account of his crimes and compulsions.

Guignol cavorted and chortled through 'Le Semaine Rouge', the bloodiest week in the bloody history of Paris, exceeding even the Reign of Terror. Caillet's homicidal mania was a trifle amongst greater, more cynical horrors. Most of his 'victims' were dead when he got to them. He strangled two or three, but found the results unsatisfactory. Fresh-killed was too dry for his tastes. To prick his amatory interest, a corpse had to have the sheen of rot. Meanwhile, one hundred hostages, including priests and nuns, were executed on the orders of the Committee of Public Safety. In reprisal, the victorious army murdered thirty thousand – the innocent, the guilty, the uninvolved, anyone who was passing.

To Kate, it seemed every one of the deaths was enacted on the tiny stage. Berma appeared as the Spirit of Liberty, tricolour sash barely wound across half her torso, and was shot down. She danced at half-speed to the drum-rattle of rifle discharges. Ribbons of thin, scarlet stage blood splashed around. The orchestra played 'La Marseillaise' out of tune. The *prima diva* of horror – who had been earlier tortured, violated, shocked, throttled, mutilated, dismembered, disfigured and degraded – received wild applause for her last death scene of the evening. Even Morpho's *claque* joined in. Funeral garlands were thrown on the stage. Without breaking character, Berma died under a pile of black and red flowers.

This piece was closer to home than mediaeval dungeons or exotic locales of Guignol's other horror tableaux. 1871 was within the memory of much of this audience. They'd lived through the Commune, lost friends and relatives, suffered wounds. In all likelihood, some of the moneyed, middle-aged folk up in the circle had taken part in the slaughter. A pack of bourgeois women had poked a dead Communard general's brains with their umbrellas, while regular army officers arranged the efficient execution of whole districts.

As the barricades fell, the bickering Committee of Enquiry into the lunacy of Bertrand Caillet remained in session. Proceedings were disrupted by fist-fights, a duel, assassination and the purge. Through an error of transcription, M. Dupond was thrown before a firing squad convened for M. Dupont. *En fin*, the senior judge – who'd absent-mindedly signed the death warrant of the Archbishop of Paris while listening to Caillet's confession – proclaimed *himself* insane in a vain attempt to evade his own executioners. When Guignol took the judge's head, no one was left to rule in the case of the sad, forgotten prisoner. A venal turnkey (Morpho) let Caillet go free.

The dazed maniac was drawn by his lusts to his old stamping grounds. Caillet arrived at Pére Lachaise Cemetery as the last of the Commune's National Guard were put against its wall and shot. No one paid the amateur of murder any attention, except a guard dog, which bit him as he was rooting in a grave for a sufficiently putrid corpse. The ragged ghoul succumbed to this festering, untreated wound and joined the pile of corpses.

At last, Guignol – who played the guard dog himself – was making a point . . . albeit while dancing in entrails and tearing the eyes out of dwarves, nuns and a disapproving censor. If Bertrand Caillet was a monster on the strength of his crimes, what was to be said of the politicians and generals who could have a hundred people – a thousand, thirty thousand, a million, six million! – eradicated at the stroke of a pen? The *tableau vivante* returned, but poisoners, stabbers and stranglers were replaced by politicians, judges, officers, priests and newspaper editors. Their hands were red with stage blood.

The human waxworks went unnamed, but Kate recognised many. The Minister Eugène Mortain, famous for surviving corruption scandals and maintaining a dozen mistresses at the public expense . . . the examining magistrate Charles Pradier, who vowed to restock Devil's Island with journalists who argued the innocence of Dreyfus or the guilt of Esterhazy . . . General Assolant, recalled from Algeria after a run of harsh police actions and put in charge of the Paris garrison to maintain public order . . . Father de Kern, confessor to government and society figures, and reputedly the most depraved man in France, though always humble in public . . . and Georges Du Roy, publisher of *La Vie Française*, *L'Anti-Juif* and the children's story paper *Arizona Jim*.

Solemnly, Guignol passed amongst the wax monsters, awarding each a rosette and ribbon, inducting these worthies into the Légion d'Horreur!

Kate hadn't expected the detour into political agitation, if indeed this was that. How was Guignol getting away with it? Newspaper offices were burned to the ground and journalists submitted to the system of Dr Tarr and Professor Fether for less. For an institution eager to make powerful enemies, the Théâtre des Horreurs was surprisingly *un*-persecuted.

Even before the attack on the people best placed to have the place shut down, the programme seemed calculated to offend *everyone* – Catholics (especially Jesuits), Protestants (especially Freemasons), Jews (no surprises there), atheists and free-thinkers, conservatives, moderates, radicals, anyone not French enough, anyone not French at all, the medical profession, the police, the law, criminals, cannibals, the military, colonialists, anti-colonialists, the halt and lame, circus folk, animal lovers, people who lived through the Paris Commune, the friends and relatives of people who failed to live through the Paris Commune, women of all classes, drama critics, the left-handed, the fat-headed, the soft-hearted.

In a city where a poetry recital or a symphony concert could set off a riot, this house was tolerated so completely that she sensed an invisible shield of protection. Was the Théâtre des Horreurs so profitable that it could afford to bribe *everyone*? Including the Paris mob, who were notoriously easier to stir up than buy off.

In parting, Guignol sang a song whose last refrain was – loosely translated – 'if these shadows have offended, you can all go stuff yourselves!'

The curtain came down. Thunderous applause.

'I didn't like it at the end, Papa,' said one of the fat round children. 'When it made my head hurt from thinking.'

The fat round father fondly cuffed the lad around the ear.

'There, that'll take the ache away.'

Guignol poked his head out of the curtain to take a last bow.

After some minutes of capering and farewell, Guignol departed and the house lights came up.

The show let out after eleven o'clock. Kate kept her head down and made for the *Sortie*.

To escape the theatre, she had to run a gauntlet of minions in Guignol masks hawking souvenirs: toby jugs with Guignol features; phials of authentic Théâtre des Horreurs blood; postcards of the stars in sealed packets so you didn't know what you were getting (how many leering Kleinzachs did a collector have to buy to secure that elusive bare-breasted Berma?); tin swazzles seemingly designed to drive parents to acts of infanticide suitable for dramatising next season; and enamel pins with Guignol faces or bloody pulled-out eyes.

Succumbing, she purchased a profusely-illustrated pamphlet featuring photographed scenes, with diagrams showing how effects were done and prose *contes crueles* for those who had missed the plot. It might come in handy in the investigation. She was convinced there was a connection between the crimes in the streets and the crimes on the stage. It was as if the real horrors extended the argument of the *Ballade de Bertrand Caillet*. Doubtless, victims didn't care much whether they were killed to make a philosophical point or just plain ordinarily murdered.

Leaving by a side door, she saw a cluster of devotees around the artists' entrance. Some wore amateur horror make-ups as if hoping to audition: dangling eyeballs, running sores, vampire fangs. A *mec* in a short-sleeved sailor shirt showed off a raw tattoo of Guignol's grin. Others wore cheap masks and competed – despite their lack of swazzle – to imitate Guignol's voice. A tipsy toff in evening dress struggled with a huge bouquet of black roses. Kate suspected Stage Door Jeannot was an admirer of the much-abused Berma. He looked more like the recipient than the disher-out of consensual floggings.

Back on Rue Pigalle, she clocked Yuki's headdress bobbing in the distance. She paused a moment to consider her options. They were supposed to make their separate ways back to the *pied-a-terre* the Persian had rented for the purposes of the investigation. Kate had memorised a few routes.

Ideally, she'd have liked a stroll by the Seine to clear her head.

The Théâtre des Horreurs was overwhelming. An evening with the smell of offal, that funny smoke and packed-in patrons would make anyone light-headed, even without the parade of tortures.

She passed gay cafés and cabarets, but horrors had soured her outlook. Her glasses weren't rose-coloured, but blood-smeared. Music and laughter sounded shrill and cruel. Pretty faces seemed cracked and duplicitous.

Guignol peeped from posters. She thought she saw him in the crowd. It wasn't unlikely. Many cardboard masks were sold in Impasse Chaplet.

She took precautions against being followed, as much for practice as genuine caution. In the front door of a restaurant and out through the kitchens – even a glimpse was enough to dissuade her from going back for a meal – and a quick-change on the hoof. She reversed her distinctive check jacket to show anonymous green.

She found a table in the corner of a busy courtyard and ordered *pastis*.

No one tried to pick her up, which was obscurely depressing. If she could sit by herself in a French café and not be bothered, she must be giving off invisible waves of warning.

She was thirty-two. No age at all … though her soonest-married school-friends had nearly grown-up daughters and sons. As an unmarried, 'unconventional' woman, she was accustomed to importunage on a daily basis – in England, let alone Paris. Being Kate Reed was like being a coconut in a shy. Every other chap thought it worth a throw. If the shot went wide, no harm done, old girl. The 'respectable' gents were bad enough – the husbands of her schoolfriends, or even their fathers – but the men who made her skin crawl were the firebrand stalwarts of causes she supported – Irish home rule or women's suffrage – who felt she owed them a tumble because they said the right things on platforms. From now on, she would recommend that these pouncing comrades take a run at Clara Watson, connoisseur of exquisite tortures.

An accordion played. The performer was the image of a music hall Frenchman, down to the beret and waxed moustache – though he'd left his string of onions at home. He was wringing out the 'Valse des Rayons' from Offenbach's *Le Papillon*. Space in the courtyard was cleared for a couple to enact the famous *apache* dance. A slouch-hatted, stripey-shirted rough slung his long-legged partner about in a simulation of violent love-making, in time to repetitive, sinuous music. The *fille* alternately resisted the crude advances of her *garçon* and abased herself in front of him. Throughout, a lit cigarette dangled from the corner of the man's mouth. He puffed smoke rings between cruel kisses. Even dances in Montmartre involved punches, slaps, knees to the groin and neck-breaking holds. The girl pulled a stiletto from her garter, but the *mec* snatched it away and tossed it at a wall. It embedded in a poster of Guignol.

Kate sipped her *pastis*, which stung her nose and eyes as well as her tongue. It was but a step from this anise-flavoured, watered cordial to absinthe. Which led, popularly, to syphilis, consumption and death.

The dancers finished, and were clapped. They collected coins. Kate gave the girl a *sou* and hoped the bruises under her powder were from over-enthusiastic rehearsal.

The point of Guignol's Caillet play was that horror was unconfined. Not limited to one madman, not on one small stage. It was all about, all-pervasive ... in the statues of Saint Denis toting his raggedly-severed head and the ritualised domestic abuse of the *apache* dance. The Reign of Terror and the Commune were done, but Guignol's Légionnaires d'Horreur were ensconced in positions of power. Georges Du Roy could throw honest ministers to *les loups* but maintain Eugène Mortain in office. Riots erupted whenever the Dreyfus case was argued. War with Germany was inevitable one week, then alliance with Germany against Great Britain was equally inevitable the next. Father de Kern was appointed Inspector of Orphanages. Horrible whispers about his night-time surprise visits to his little charges were heard with disturbing frequency, though even Zola didn't dare accuse him in print. A military coup which would have installed General Assolant as a new Napoleon had recently collapsed at the last minute. Kate liked to think of herself as a reasonable person, but she was working for a faceless creature who supposedly dropped a chandelier on the heads of an opera audience because he didn't like the casting of Marguerite in *Faust*.

Was it all in fun?

The horrors were certainly not confined to Paris. The British Mr. Punch, Guignol's cousin, knocked his Judy about as much as any *apache* panderer did his tart . . . and killed policemen, judges and crocodiles. In the East End, Kate spent too much time with women nursing black eyes after trying to haul their old men out of pubs to stop the rent money going on beer to find Punch and Judy shows very amusing. At least, the *apachette* fought back.

She looked about the courtyard. People were having a good time, even if their pockets were being picked. Despite the horrors, life went on, mostly merrily. Dance done, the performers were drinking together – the girl flirting with her partner and the musician. Kate's jangled nerves calmed, and she tried to shrug it all off.

The stiletto had been reclaimed from the wall. A tear-like triangular divot showed brick under Guignol's eye.

Kate thought about the eyes of Guignol, the living eyes in the *papier mâché* face. She thought she'd know those eyes again. But would she, really? Guignol was in disguise when he took his mask *off*. He might be anyone.

The programme and pamphlet were no help. There were printed biographies for Berma, Phroso, Morpho (a veteran disfigured by Riffs, apparently) and the others, but Guignol's write-up was of the *character* not the performer. Guignol was himself, not who he had been . . . Jean-François Someone or Felix-Frederic Whoever. Under Berma's photograph was a paragraph about her early life and career. She'd played in other companies, rising from Cleopatra's asp-delivering handmaiden to Juliet and

Desdemona, before her engagement at the Théâtre des Horreurs. Under Guignol's picture was a list of crimes. Credited as writer and producer of the show as well as its proprietary spirit, he had sprung from nowhere to take over the remains of the late M. Hulot's company.

The craze burned throughout Paris, exciting much commentary. W.B. Yeats, Gustav von Aschenbach and Odilon Redon hailed Guignol as a genius, though Kate would had laid money they wouldn't have him round for dinner. Paul Verlaine, Jean Des Esseintes and André Gide lampooned Guignol as a fraud, though the inconsistent Des Esseintes also said he loved the imp like a brother. Léo Taxil had boosted the Mad Mountebank of the Théâtre des Horreurs in his periodical *La France Chrétienne Anti-Maçonnique*, then claimed to have *invented* Guignol . . . only to discover his creation had 'escaped into the wild'. Was that a theory worth taking to M. Erik? In the context of the Opera Ghost Agency, a fictional character come to murderous life was scarcely the most far-fetched suggestion.

She was no wiser about the masked man.

Thinking about Guignol made her jittery. It was too easy to imagine that face – *those eyes* – looking at her from a dark corner or between a press of people. Kate still felt he, or someone wearing his face, was nearby . . . and could lay hand on her at any moment.

Was that why she wasn't being preyed on? A greater predator had marked her as his own.

She poured the last of the water into the last of the *anis* and drank up. Then she left, hurrying towards the rendezvous of the Angels.

Was she being followed still? Had she ever?

It was as if Guignol were waiting wherever she turned. In the limelight, up on a stage, his atrocities were often absurd . . . in spite of herself, she had laughed. In the dark, a step or two off the main street, the clown would not seem funny.

Kate felt a chill up one arm. She looked down and saw the sleeve of her jacket – and the sleeve of her blouse – had three long slits, as if claws of supreme sharpness had brushed her when she was distracted, cleaving cloth but not skin.

She heard the laughter of Guignol, but could not be sure it was in her head.

*

Madame Mandelip's Hôpital des Poupées was in Place Frollo, a triangular 'square' even further off Rue Pigalle than Impasse Chaplet. The small shop was seldom open for business and got little passing traffic. The front window was crowded with dusty dolls. All the fixed smiles and glass eyes reminded Kate of her childhood playroom. She'd been afraid of the old-fashioned, slightly battered dolls her aunts kindly passed on. The effect of the frontage was deliberate – to ward off the curious. If there ever had been such a person as Madame Mandelip, she was long gone.

Kate was last home to the safe house. She rapped on the door, to the rhythm of the first line of 'La Donna è Mobile' from *Rigoletto*. She could never repress a smirk at the childish trimmings favoured by the overgrown boys of the Diogenes Club and the Opera Ghost Agency. Secret knocks, passwords, invisible ink and codes, not to mention false moustaches and – inevitably – masks. The blade up her sleeve reminded her she wasn't immune to the appeal of deadly play-acting.

The Persian let her in. He was M. Erik's catspaw in the above-ground world. Few took his master for more than a myth, but the Persian was familiar around the Opéra and the city, trusted to collate reports from the songbirds, often an intermediary or bill-collector. One theory was that he was a ventriloquist, and the mask behind the dressing room mirror simply an articulated puppet. Kate knew that wasn't true, but saw how the notion could get about.

Olive-skinned and unostentatious, the Persian was sometimes addressed as *Daroga*. That wasn't his name but a title – police chief. Erik and he had served the Mazanderan Court many years ago, though they were no longer welcome there. Far-fetched rumours of their doings in Persia had reached the Diogenes Club. Reputedly, they fled the Court with a potion of longevity stolen from the Khanum, the Shah's mother. It would explain how the Director of the Opera Ghost Agency and his Chief Assistant seemed not to get older over the decades. Another fine wheeze for not seeming to age would be to wear a mask and seldom even show that in public.

Clara and Yuki took tea, served from a samovar.

'So, ladies,' Kate asked, 'what did we think of the play?'

Clara Watson grimaced. 'I was bored . . . except for the eels. They were adorable.'

Yuki Kashima shook her head, rattling tiny bells set among her flowers.

'I did not understand much . . . there was no honour, just wasted effort. And to cut off a head . . . it is not so easy as they make out. Even with a sharp sword. The head does not come off like a doll's, at the merest love tap.'

Kate didn't want to know how Yuki came to have a connoisseur's knowledge of decapitation. No, she corrected herself mentally, she *did* want to know . . . she wanted to know *everything*, even if uncomfortable and upsetting. That made her a good reporter and qualified her as an Angel of Music. Still, Yuki's history – a tale of blood and fire suitable for the Théâtre des Horreurs, she gathered – was not her present concern.

She poured herself a cup of tea, and added milk and sugar – which made her a barbarian to everyone else in the room, except perhaps the dolls.

'Can't say I found the performance dull, myself,' Kate admitted. 'Though it did get a teensy wee bit monotonous after the fourth or fifth eye-gouge. It was, in its own ghastly fashion, entertaining. Guignol, horrid though he is, has that *quality*. Whoever he might be, he's a star. At least in his own house. Grotesque, but a star. Morpho can't compete, though he has his partisans. As for everything else . . . well, no one goes to the Théâtre des Horreurs for the quality of the drama, the lavish sets, the witty scripts or even the acting – though, under the circumstances that's more convincing than is comfortable. The place says what it is in the name, and it's peddling a very old act. Gladiatorial combat to the death and public executions were entertainments once . . .'

'Only in Europe have those arts become lost,' said Clara. 'In China . . .'

Kate had heard quite enough from the English woman about the delights on offer in China.

The Persian intervened before the Angels fell to squabbling. He had his notebook open and a pencil in his hand.

'Miss Reed, Mrs Watson . . . in your expert opinion, did any real crimes take place on the stage tonight?'

'Only against art,' said Kate.

The Persian was pensive. A rumour flew that those who disappeared in Montmartre appeared again, for one night only, in the Théâtre des Horreurs. Kate reckoned the management actively encouraged such stories. Everyone in the performing arts knew the expression 'dying to please the public'.

'It is not Max Valentin's Canary Cage illusion,' said Clara.

Kate didn't know what she meant.

'Maximilian the Great is a stage magician,' Clara explained. 'A very inferior one. Most of his act is old tricks, borrowed or stolen and performed indifferently. He had one illusion, though, that puzzled his rivals. Magicians are competitive and take pride in seeing through sleights of hand or mechanical devices. Prizes were offered to anyone who could duplicate Maximilian's illusion. None of the greats could manage it. Maskelyne, Robert-Houdin, Méliès. Max holds up a square-sided cage, in which a dear little canary sings, then folds the cage flat. Off comes the top. Down go the sides. Poof! The canary is gone. And yet the birdie sings again. Each night, from a different place … the back of the stalls, the cleavage of a female assistant, the pocket of a patron on the front row. Each night, a disappearance and an appearance.'

'I think I can guess the trick,' said Kate. 'Canaries are cheap, right?'

'Yes, that is it. In the end, the escape artist Janus Stark saw through it. The springs that collapse the cage are unusually powerful. Each night, a canary is crushed . . . killed in an instant. And another canary takes its place, only to have its moment in the cage at the next performance. Once word got out, Maximilian's bookings dried up. Europeans profess to be foolishly sentimental. For my part, I believe many canaries would choose a moment of public transcendence – singing and dying – over living on unheard. Before this evening, I entertained the notion – indeed, I hoped it was the case – that the Théâtre des Horreurs was offering a chance to make such an ascension. That would have been, in an oriental manner, magnificent. Reality, as so often, is a disappointment.'

Kate knew Mrs Clara Watson was no canary. She was too busy being absolutely cuckoo.

The Persian pressed his point. 'So, no harm is done in the performance?'

'Everything we saw was faked,' said Clara. 'Oh, animals died to supply meat for the trickery . . . but no human blood was spilled. Human blood has a particular tang, and a look that can't be mistaken. What we saw was conjuring… dollops of red paint slapped onto the face while the audience is distracted by Guignol's patter . . . thin strips of flesh-toned gauze pasted over fake wounds and torn off to let the stage blood show . . . and a great deal of shouting and straining.'

For a while, Kate had also tried to distance herself from Guignol's show by looking for the joins . . . trying to see how the illusions were accomplished. But the performance bombarded the audience with so many horrors it was impossible not to surrender, to cease caring about fakery and reality and just to react to what was there before you. She would remember Guignol, the *Ballade de Bertrand Caillet* and the Légion d'Horreur.

'I did wonder about the concierge whose head got bashed in at the beginning,' Kate said. 'She matches some descriptions on the list of the missing.'

'She came back as the dog-faced woman in the freak show segment,' said Clara.

That was one of the giveaways. Guignol's company was quite small. Parts were doubled, tripled, quadrupled and more. If Don Bartolome and Isabella were really murdered before the audience's very eyes, how did Phroso and Berma return as so many other doomed characters? Even the throat-slit dwarf Kleinzach crawled on again, to be kicked to death by the beggars of the Court of Miracles for the crime of having an actual piteous condition and offering unfair competition to bogus cripples and fake blind men. A wild-eyed matron billed as Malita played the concierge, the dog-faced woman, Madame Defarge of the guillotine and the mourner attacked by Caillet. Actors were not as interchangeable as canaries.

'But *someone* is snatching people and murdering them in the vicinity of Impasse Chaplet,' said the Persian. 'Witnesses attest this Guignol is almost always about when the crimes take place.'

'Guignol is a mask,' Kate said. 'Anyone can wear a mask. Especially in Paris. This city has more masks than Venice during carnival.'

'It's true,' said Clara. 'Guignol masks are everywhere.'

The English woman took a cardboard mask from her reticule and held it up in front of her face.

'They sell these at the theatre,' she squawked, trying to imitate Guignol's voice. 'For two francs.'

'It might be that the real Guignol is not only innocent, but the true culprit or culprits are trying to throw suspicion on him,' said Kate. 'Any place as successful as the Théâtre des Horreurs must have enemies. Attendance at Le Chat Noir and the Comédie Rosse is down. One way to scare off audiences is to put it about that they're likely to be killed if they go near the Guignol show . . .'

'You don't understand people, Katie,' said Clara. 'Since the murders began, ticket sales at the Théâtre des Horreurs have soared. I'd argue that the *only* thing that makes paint spilled on that stage interesting is the association with blood spilled on the streets.'

'You're getting your personal proclivities mixed up with general principle, Clara. People are not all like you.'

'Oh yes they are, dear. Most just don't like to admit it.'

Kate looked at Yuki, who kept quiet for most of their discussions.

'You know what *she's* done,' Clara said. 'Yuki's more like me than I am myself. I've mostly watched. She's *acted* ... that parasol of hers has put men in their graves.'

The Japanese woman sipped tea, without comment.

'You're the freak here, Katie.'

Kate blushed again. She held her cup tight.

'There now, see,' said Clara, sweetly. 'Wouldn't you like to slap my face silly? Perhaps take that spoon to my eyes? Break that cup and grind that china into my neck?'

The English woman simpered, as if she'd won an argument. Kate knew a lost cause – after all, she was Irish. She recognised a distraction too.

Yuki finished her tea and contemplated a pair of *apache* dolls, which she manipulated while humming. Daintier than the couple Kate had seen perform at the café, but still ... in this affair, even children's playthings had slit-skirts and knives in their garters. Clara would say that was just honesty.

Lord, perhaps Clara was right? She was the freak, and *Guignol* was normal.

Nobody important – or even noticeable – had disappeared or been killed yet, so there was no general outcry. The victims were drudges, drunks, old whores, foreigners and idiots. Corpses found in the river, the sewers or piles of garbage were rotten, and got at by rats, birds or fish. That parts were missing was expected. That victims were tortured before death was impossible to confirm. The police had other priorities.

'I don't understand the lack of press coverage,' said Kate.

The Persian and Clara shrugged.

'In London, a story like this would catch fire. It's not just the murders, but their proximity to the Théâtre des Horreurs. That would be a gift to an

English editor. Think of it: an opportunity to take a lofty stand against the decline of public morals exemplified by the appalling spectacle of Guignol's show, while at the same time having an excuse to describe in lurid detail the atrocities on and off stage, with illustrations of la Berma in torn clothes being prettily abused. It'd run for weeks, *months*. There'd be protests outside the theatre, questions in the House, bans on advertising, petitions for increased censorship. Of course, in London, the Lord Chamberlain would never allow anything like the Théâtre des Horreurs.'

'Now who's the cynic, Katie?'

'Paris can't be that much more *blasé*, Clara. Montmartre may be *toujours gai*, but France has no shortage of bluestockings, hypocrites and moralists.'

'What are you suggesting, Miss Reed?' asked the Persian.

'A fix is in. I know how it works in Dublin and London. I doubt Paris is different. Newspaper proprietors are in competition with each other but belong to the same clubs. If they agree a story should be buried, it sort of goes away. No matter what reporters think or feel. Sit in the Cheshire Cheese in Fleet Street and any scribbler will give you a long list of startling stories he's had spiked. The owners horse-trade, of course. You don't cover my brother's arrest at a boy-brothel in Bayswater and I'll drop the investigation of the fraudulent stock company which lists you among the directors. Let's not mention the peaceful natives your old regiment massacred in the Hindu Kush . . . on the condition the exposé of the gambling ring which paid my school's old boys' cricket side to drop easy catches three times in a row doesn't run. A discussion between gentlemen. It's in the interests of gentlemen, which is to say the powerful, that things stay this way. I've read the French papers since I got here, and – though the battles between Dreyfusard and Anti-Dreyfusard factions are more bitter than any London press feud – I sense the same system running smoothly. If the "Guignol Murders" isn't a story – and that's the headline it'd get in Britain – then it's in the interests of well-placed individuals that it not be.'

The Persian looked at her closely. He had been quietly sceptical of her value to the Agency. The more usual Angel of Music, Kate understood, had Yuki's experience with head-severing or Clara's taste for blood. The rolls included adventuresses, amazons, girl wonders, savages and divas of diverse deviltry. She must seem an ink-stained step down from such formidable women.

But she had just demonstrated why Erik took her on.

'Do you have any theories as to who these "well-placed individuals" might be.'

'Funny you should ask, *Daroga* . . . and funnier that no one else has thought to, eh? As I said, I've been looking at the Paris press. I can't believe there's *really* a serious publication called *The Anti-Jew*, by the way. I've read society pages and the sensation papers, the heavy journals and the frothy dailies, the *échos* and the classifieds. The Théâtre des Horreurs gets surprisingly good press . . . it's an amusement, looked down on but talked about. A sight of Paris, like the Follies Bergère or that hideous ironwork erection on Champ de Mars. It gets poor notices from drama critics, of course – with some enthusiastic, if demented exceptions. I expect the management courts bad reviews. Who'd want to attend an *inoffensive* Theatre of Horrors? The matters that interest us – the murders – are never mentioned on the same pages as Guignol's gaggery. The connection which is so obvious to us, and to the people who have engaged the Agency, is ignored by the press and, as a consequence of what I referred to as "a fix", also by the police. Everyone knows of the crimes around the theatre, but it's down to us to look into them . . . that in itself tells you how well-placed our phantom – excuse me, our *other* phantom – might be.'

'Not just a newspaper proprietor, then?'

'No. We are looking at someone with political connections. Probably, this being as priest-ridden a country as my own, the Catholic Church too. Oh, and "pull" in the army. I imagine you can name someone who fits that bill.'

'She means Georges Du Roy,' said Clara.

Kate shrugged, not confirming or denying.

'. . . and his circle,' continued Clara. 'Mortain, Assolant, Pradier, de Kern?'

Prosper-Georges Du Roy de Cantel, once humble Georges Duroy, had risen from the ranks. This was literally the case – he had soldiered in the Franco-Prussian War, the action against the Commune and Algeria. Mustered out, he worked as a reporter, then became editor and – through advantageous marriage – proprietor of *La Vie Française*, an upper-middle class newspaper. He added publications to his empire, including the vicious *Anti-Juif*. Everyone made the effort to forget his late father-in-law, from whom he inherited *La Vie*, was one of the Jewish financiers now cast as Satan in the Modern Testament of France. Kate had some respect for the earlier part of his career, when he was a fiery exponent of causes as well as a ferociously ambitious social climber. He had campaigned righteously against Panama Canal featherbedding and unconscionably in support of the Dreyfus conviction, bringing down several governments. Moving from publishing into politics, he represented Averoigne in the Chamber of Deputies – though he had more influence through his papers than speeches made in the National Assembly. Presidents took suggestions from him as orders. Founder of one of several competing anti-Semitic societies, his editorials suggested he saw Jews under the bed . . . or behind every imaginable ill besetting the Third Republic. When it deigned to cover 'the Montmartre Disappearances' at all, *La Vie* pointed the finger at mad rabbis.

The Persian was unreadable. Did he think even M. Erik might hesitate to act against Du Roy?

'You'd like it to be him, wouldn't you, Katie,' said Clara. 'A proper villain for the melodrama. You were driven out of England because you crossed someone like Georges Du Roy. How much more satisfying to bring him down than to find out the killer is . . . well, is Bertrand Caillet? A broken wretch, as powerless and low-born as his victims.'

'Caillet? The ghoul? I don't see . . .'

'He was in the play, *Daroga*. One of the *horreurs*. Guignol threw him out as an example . . . a small monster in a world run by huge ones.'

'You're basing your theory on . . . *on a play*?'

'She was prompted by the play itself,' Clara said. 'At the end, Guignol brought on Du Roy and his gang and represented them as the Legion of Horror. The priest in the next box, who drooled and muttered "whore" whenever Berma was tortured, went bright red at this outrage. I admit I was surprised. It seemed out of place. The notion of the Légion d'Horreur is quite funny.'

'The rest of the performance was random nastiness,' Kate said. 'But this was pointed. Almost an editorial.'

'Yes . . . disappointing. I thought Guignol was supposed to be a Pan-like unfettered spirit, not some mere bomb-throwing anarchist.'

'You're missing the point, Clara. It's not the offence that's interesting and suspicious – it's the quiet.'

'The quiet?'

'Why hasn't Guignol been called out? If Du Roy is no longer up to a duel himself, plenty of his faction is.'

'There is no honour in French duelling,' said Yuki. 'Pistols – *tchah!*'

'For some reason, Guignol is protected. He has a license to insult the people you would think would most be capable of shutting him up.'

'She sees Freemasons behind it all . . . or Jesuits,' said Clara. 'She's as bad as Du Roy and his Jews.'

That stung, but she pressed on.

'I suspect that if we find out why the Légionnaires d'Horreur tolerate the Théâtre des Horreurs we'll learn what's behind the murders. If it's as big as it seems, I'll tell you from experience no one will thank us for bringing it to light . . . if we're even allowed to.'

The Persian smiled, very slightly – a rare thing for him.

'Miss Reed, you misunderstand . . . our Agency has not been commissioned to expose these murders, *but to end them*.'

An item of business remained.

Kate showed the slashes in her sleeve.

'You've been careless,' said Clara.

'In that case, so have you . . .'

Kate pointed, and Clara twisted her neck. Parallel cuts in her bodice opened like wounds, just above her hip.

Clara whistled. 'I didn't even feel a breeze.'

Yuki found the neat slashes in her kimono, like vents in her sleeve.

'Only something sharp could do this without us noticing,' the Japanese woman said. 'Very fine blades. A very skilled hand.'

She took three teaspoons and slipped them between her fingers, then made a fist. The spoons were spatulate claws. She scratched the air, to demonstrate.

Kate supposed Yuki could do more damage with spoons as the average *apache* with stilettos.

She remembered the sharp-nailed fingers of Guignol, three little daggers poking through ruptured gloves.

'I saw . . . I think I saw Guignol,' said Kate.

'A man in a mask,' said Clara. 'He could have been anyone.'

'I saw him too,' said Yuki. 'The real Guignol. The one from the theatre. Different costume, different *mask* . . . but the same eyes.'

The Persian did not show concern.

'I think we can take it that we've been warned,' said Kate. 'All of us are alive only because Guignol let us live.'

Yuki put the spoons down. Despite the counted coup, she still fancied her chances in a parasol-against-claws duel.

Well, maybe . . .

Clara was annoyed. She didn't have as many dresses with her as she'd like. Expelled from China with only a few negotiable jewels, she couldn't pay European couture prices. She'd asked for a dressmakers' allowance on top of her salary. The Persian countered that any clothing needs would be met by the costume department. As a result of long-standing agreements, many resources of the Opéra were at the disposal of M. Erik. Kate thought it'd be funny if Clara were to swan about dressed as Emilia di Liverpool or Maria Stuarda. For her own part, she'd fish out her travelling sewing kit and make invisible repairs.

The English woman examined the rents in her dress, touching her own unmarked skin, feeling her unbroken ribs. She was white as porcelain all over. Did she bathe in arsenic or bleach?

'This was not a warning,' said Yuki. 'Snakes do not give warnings. They simply strike. This is an invitation.'

'. . . to a tea-dance?' sneered Clara.

Kate remembered the dance she'd seen at the café. The *apache* flinging his girl around, beating her up to music.

The girl got her slaps and slices in, though – and that's how the man liked it.

'Couldn't we just cut off the clown's head?' asked Clara, wearily. 'And burn down his bloody playhouse. That would solve the Guignol problem. No theatre, no theatre murders.'

'Easy to say, hard to do,' said Kate. 'Too many Guignol masks around. It'd be a risky call picking which head to chop.'

'Chop them all. Pile up the heads.'

'You should be in the show business, Clara. I know exactly the company you should join.'

Childishly, Clara poked out the scarlet tip of her tongue and pulled a gorgon face. Kate couldn't help laughing.

The Persian again defused the exchange of unpleasantries.

'Angels, please . . . this is not a schoolroom. Seemliness is required. This latest development is a cause for concern. M. Erik will take any action against his agents very hard. There would be . . . counteractions.'

'So we can be the first casualties in a war of the masks?'

'Miss Reed, the Opera Ghost Agency will not allow that to happen.'

Yuki was fascinated by the tears in her sleeve. 'A personage who can do this would be difficult to stop.'

Kate spent the next few days trying to determine if any connection existed between Guignol and the Georges Du Roy circle.

Representing herself (not untruthfully) as an interested foreign journalist, she paid calls on distant associates among the Paris press. She spent dusty hours in newspaper archives and government records offices. If nothing else, her French was improving. She had promised to send reports to the *Gazette* on anything that might interest English readers. Without telling the Persian, she had drafted an article on the Guignol craze, with a description of her evening at the Théâtre des Horreurs. It was supposed in London that entertainments in Paris were *spicier* than home-grown fare. Newspapers were duty-bound to describe in detail the frightful, salacious attractions the British public was spared.

She left her *carte de visite* at the dreary Hôtel d'Alsace, Oscar Wilde's digs. The concierge said the poet was too poorly to receive even a fellow exile. Back on Rue des Beaux Arts, she could identify his room from a twitching curtain. Kate missed the Oscar of old. His passion for gossip might have opened up the mystery like a paper flower. Wilde was out of prison, but in Paris; Zola was in London to avoid prison. The lesson was that upstart genius should be put firmly in its place.

It wasn't lost on her that Wilde and Henry Wilcox were guilty of pretty much the same crime. Wilde was formally sentenced to hard labour and informally to humiliating exile, yet no one even tried to prosecute Wilcox. Consorting with rent boys – even she, a partisan, said Oscar was a fool in his choice of bedmates – got an Irishman chased out of England.

194 | KIM NEWMAN

Consorting with their figurative (and sometimes actual) younger sisters didn't prevent Wilcox from driving an Irish woman out of the country. Any excuse to be rid of the mouthy micks, she supposed.

Kate fancied she occasionally saw Guignol out of the corner of her eye. At Madame Mandelip's, Clara reluctantly admitted to the same impression. Could they both be followed by the same clown? Or were masks handed out to minions? Yuki said she was no longer being tailed. Was Guignol warier of the Japanese Angel than the others?

There *was* something going on between Guignol and the Légion d'Horreur, but it was identifiable only by ellipses. That Du Roy and the others took no measures to suppress the Théâtre des Horreurs after the accusing tableau was singular. An unanswered public rebuke was extraordinary in a city where offhand remarks provoked duels, acid-throwing and near-revolution. In Paris, poets started more café brawls than stevedores. Rival high-fashion couturiers slashed each other with scissors in the 8th Arrondissement. An unknown patriot shot Fernand Labori, Zola's defence lawyer, in the back. Marquis d'Amblezy-Sérac, the Minister charged with enforcing laws against duelling, fought – and won! – a duel in answer to a challenge from Aristide Forestier, a magistrate who insisted that the right of every Frenchman to try to stick a sword into or put a bullet through any other Frenchman with whom he disagreed was an unwritten yet enforceable clause of the Code Napoleon.

Did Guignol have something on Du Roy which kept him safe? A cinematograph of the French patriot sharing a bubble bath with Count Esterhazy, Lily Langtry and the Kaiser? A suppressed family tree which proved the avowed anti-Semite was secretly a Jew? Or was Guignol the creature of the Légion d'Horreur, afforded token license because of appalling services rendered? The murders were part of it, but not – she was sure – the whole story.

As she asked her questions and looked through files, Kate was aware of a parallel investigation. Clara Watson was moving through shadier circles on a like quest, securing entry to the murkier dives of Paris to wring information from wretches and debauchees. Pursuing her own predilections, the English widow attended bare-knuckles bouts held among the racks of skulls in the catacombs. She picked up whispered horrors from opium dens, salons of vice, black masses and condemned cells. She collected gossip from the Guild of Procurers, *Les Vampires* and a branch of the Suicide Club. Clara's underworld voyages often crossed paths with Kate's more respectable lines of enquiry. That suggested they were both getting warmer. Still, answers were elusive.

Other stories circulated, which Kate felt were connected. Henriette and Louise, two orphan sisters, were missing in Montmartre. Friends said they were running away to join a circus. No circus admitted to taking them in. Their pale little faces, idealised in illustrations, epitomised the disappeared. Even the Sûreté took an interest, but an array of famous criminologists – Alphonse Bertillon, Frédéric Larsan, Inspector Juve – failed to find the lost girls. After an afternoon at the Bureau of Missing Persons, Kate knew less appealing people vanished by the dozen in the *quartier* without exciting public interest.

At the Hôpital des Poupées, Yuki took over the window and arranged a display of *kokeshi*. Kate found the limbless wooden dolls disturbing, like human-headed fence posts. Meanwhile, the Persian awaited regular reports from Kate and Clara.

After a week, the Angels were again in conference in the doll salon.

There was a little blood on Clara's coat. She told them not to worry – it wasn't hers. The English widow wasn't leery of sailing into dangerous waters. Clara might be mad, but she was intelligent and – in her own way – cautious. She even did good detective work.

The Persian asked Kate for a report on the Légion d'Horreur.

'Georges Du Roy and the others go back a long way,' Kate said. 'The real Bertrand Caillet was tried twenty years before the Commune. On stage at the Théâtre des Horreurs, he is arrested in 1871, during its last days. The play shifts the murderer's story forward in time to contrast his crimes with the greater carnage of *le semaine sanglante*. It's as if Guignol is telling us where to look.'

'You see the hand of Guignol everywhere,' said Clara.

'Don't you?'

The widow shrugged. 'Perhaps.'

'Whatever the point of the show might be – and I've no reason to believe it isn't primarily the obvious one, to shock and appal and titillate – the Légion d'Horreur were all in Paris at the time of the Commune. I can't prove it yet, but I believe this was when our five respectable fellows first met.

'Assolant and Du Roy were soldiers with the army of Versailles, young officers commanding *un escadron de mort*. They weren't in the fighting, they carried out executions. It's hard to credit now, but Mortain and Pradier were Communards. They began in politics as radicals, followers of Blanqui and social justice. As the Commune fell apart, they changed their spots. Father de Kern was a hostage, one of the few to survive. De Kern brought the others together, serving as intermediary. Mortain and Pradier betrayed comrades to the Squadron of Death and got free passes from Assolant and Du Roy. In the aftermath of Bloody Week, Mortain and Pradier were listed as spies for Versailles. It was claimed they only *posed as* Communards. Anyone who could say different was put against a wall. Assolant was promoted, but Du Roy did a spell in Algeria before leaving the army to begin his ascent as a man of letters and then in politics.

'The five have been allies for nearly forty years. They look out for each other. If financial scandal threatens to engulf Mortain, a stern editorial in *La Vie Française* insists on his innocence. A chorister who accused de Kern of vile practices finds himself up before Judge Pradier on dubious charges and sentenced to Devil's Island. When Assolant is implicated in an attempted coup, Du Roy nominates him for further honours and accolades. In 1871, they were enemies. Now, they are closer than brothers.'

'Interesting, Miss Reed,' said the Persian. 'But I am reminded of Mrs Watson's objection of a few nights ago . . . that you would *like* these people to be guilty. You despise men of their class and position. It would suit your prejudices if they were outright monsters.'

Kate tried to take this into account. Investigating Henry Wilcox, she had at every turn questioned her own instincts . . . erring on the side of wariness, not putting anything in print until she had two or more reliable sources, setting aside unsubstantiated but credible rumours. Here, she used the same method . . . all but ignoring a wealth of second- or third-hand stories, sticking to verifiable facts, even when evidence suggested records had been altered or destroyed. She was satisfied that she had enough to indict Du Roy and his cronies on a raft of charges going back decades – though she wouldn't have trusted the French (or British) courts to deliver a just verdict. What she couldn't do was make any firm link between the Légion d'Horreur and the Montmartre murders.

The Persian looked to Clara, whose expression was hard to read.

'I have decided to withdraw my objection,' said Clara.

Kate noted the odd, legalistic turn of phrase.

'On what grounds?' asked the Persian.

'I now believe Katie is right. These are the guilty men.'

'You have proof?'

'Of course not. These are not men who leave proof. It's all feelings and intuition, *Daroga*. You employ only women, and this is what you must expect . . .'

Kate wanted to slap Clara for that, even if she was a convert to the cause.

'In quarters where people aren't easy to scare, the names of these men give pause,' explained Clara. 'There are creatures out there in the dark, people you might call *monsters*, who are more terrified of Georges Du Roy than of . . . well, than of the Phantom of the Opera. They can't be worried about a harshly-worded article in *La Vie Française* or an inconvenient ruling in the Assembly. The others have evil reputations too.

'Dr Johannes, the Satanist, says Father de Kern is the worst man in Paris. He doesn't mean it in the inverted sense that a devout diabolist should abjure a moral churchman. Johannes means it literally. The Worst Man in Paris. Monsters aren't born – they are made. The orphanages supervised by de Kern are factories for making them – cruelty, privation and hypocrisy applied systematically to warp young minds and bodies. De Kern has raised *generations* of them, an army of freaks. I would admire the enterprise, but for its utter lack of aesthetic qualities.

'Assolant is a butcher, of course, and a blunderer. He killed more Frenchmen than Germans even before he was given the pull-string of his own personal guillotine in Bloody Week. Mortain and Pradier are makeweights. They have survived this long because Du Roy shields them. According to their cast-off mistresses, Mortain follows the leanings of the Marquis de Sade – a sure sign of the poseur among true connoisseurs of the Art of Torture – while Pradier is inclined to the pitiful vice of Sacher-Masoch.

'They are the Guilty Men. Everyone I have raised this matter with says so. Then they cannot say what it is they are guilty of. Or will not, despite . . . *methods of extreme persuasion*.'

When she said 'methods of extreme persuasion', Clara shuddered with what Kate took to be delight. She was no poseur in her preferred art.

Kate's *frisson* was of another character.

'Could any of the Légion *be* Guignol?' she asked. 'I mean, we've all assumed that the nimble masked performer is a younger man. There are drugs and potions. A Du Roy or a de Kern could quaff something to turn them into an agile imp for a few hours. Long enough to get through the show.'

'. . . But the curtain comes down on a condemnation of these men?' objected Clara.

'Does it? Or is that tableau a *boast*?'

Clara thought for a moment.

'Or the snook cocked against the Légion d'Horreur might be a feint,' suggested Kate. 'Like the taunts of Hyde against Jekyll.'

'Unlikely,' said Clara. 'These people have enough enemies without becoming their own dark shadows.'

'That's true,' said the Persian.

Kate admitted it. 'Guignol could be someone from their history – a survivor of Bloody Week, tipped alive into a corpse pit by the Squadron of Death, crawling out with a mania for revenge. A subordinate thrown to the wolves to take the blame for crimes they got away with, back in town after years of fever and abuse in a penal colony. Or one of your army of freaks, Clara, shaped by harsh treatment into a broken *übermensch*. But if that's the case, why not kill them? Ridicule seems feeble revenge.'

'A Frenchman would rather be assassinated than made to look silly,' said Clara. 'The French they are a funny race, they fight with their feet . . . they make love with their face.'

'I've heard that before, more crudely put.'

'I was trying to spare your delicate Dublin sensitivities.'

'There are rhymes about the English too, in Dublin. Oh, and everywhere else they've run up their flag and marched about.'

'So we are no nearer a provable truth,' said the Persian, interceding again.

Since their last verbal fencing match, Kate realised – rather alarmingly – that Clara Watson *liked* her. She wouldn't have thought her capable of such a feeling, and it was little comfort. One story put around about Clara was that in Benares she made arrangements to have her best friend infected with leprosy. As Angels of Music, Kate and Clara had to sing in the same register. They had taken to a banter each found amusing which outsiders mistook for hostility. It was a little like flirting.

'Our Daughter of Erin might be no nearer,' said Clara, 'but this Child of Boadicea has yet to admit defeat . . .'

It wasn't hard to imagine Clara in a carriage with head-lopping swords attached to its wheels. In China, she had probably had such an unlikely conveyance manufactured to order. She could easily persuade a tame warlord to line the road with peasants just to try it out.

'Just say what you know, you sick witch,' snapped Kate.

'Why, Katie, such a tone! You've gone quite red in the face. I would be concerned for your health . . .'

'It is time to tell,' said Yuki, quietly.

Clara stopped simpering and put a card on the table. A white oblong marked with a red ring.

'What is that?' asked the Persian.

'An invitation,' said Clara. 'Presented at the Théâtre des Horreurs after midnight on a certain night of the month, this secures entry to an unadvertised additional performance. The *cercle rouge* guest list is select. You can't buy your way onto it. Not with money, at least. The names we've been discussing – some of them, at least – *may* be regulars, though whether as performers or audience I haven't been able to tell. That's ink, not blood, on the card. But it took blood to get it. The Grand Vampire, who you'd think beyond being shocked, told me he didn't want ever to see the *après-minuit* again, but that I would most likely enjoy the show. Make of *that* what you will.'

The Grand Vampire was the chief of *Les Vampires*, Paris's most daring criminal organisation. Another masked man – in his case because the position was so dangerous and hotly-contested that the mask stayed the same but the man behind it changed regularly. The top perch in the roost had a new occupant every week, but Irma Vep was always secure on the next rung. Number Two in the gang, the anagrammatical adventuress had outlasted many Grand Vampires. Kate understood she would do well to avoid Vep – a Demon of Discord, as it were. Nevertheless, the Opera Ghost Agency and *Les Vampires* had a wary truce.

Kate picked up the card. The circle was stamped into the thick paper and the red was some sort of gilt. Not easy to forge, though the design and printing department of the Opéra would have their methods.

'How long do we have to wait?'

'Only until tomorrow,' said Clara. 'I hope your delicate stomach is up to it.'

She flipped back through her notebooks.

'Yes, Katie,' said Clara, 'the disappearances tend to be in the week leading up to each month's *après-minuit* . . . and the bodies are often found during the few days *after* the special performance.'

They all looked at each other.

'For myself, I shall spend tomorrow shopping for a new hat,' said Clara. 'It doesn't do to attend a theatre twice in the same outfit. Also, I understand that *chapeaux* with veils – if not full masks – are customary for *cercle rouge* audiences.'

'You buy a hat,' said Katie. 'I'll get a revolver.'

'Very sensible. No dramatic critic should be without one. A lead corset might also be a wise investment.'

Kate had not been joking. She needed a gun.

Yuki could walk into a lion's den – taking those tiny steps because she was hobbled by her traditional dress – with nothing but her parasol and come out with a large rug. Clara's stylishly tailored topcoat had neat pockets in the lining, filled with a range of cutting, slicing, throwing, sawing and gouging implements. Kate was the least dangerous of the Agency's current roster. The little apple-peeling knife she'd been keeping up her sleeve would be little use against Guignol and the whole Légion d'Horreur.

The Persian gave her a chit to present to M. Quelou, Chief Armourer of the Paris Opéra. He had his own subterranean domain, with sandbags against the walls and the smell of gunpowder in the air. Besides the swords, spears and axes required by Wagner's warriors and Valkyries, the House maintained enough functional rifles, pistols and small cannon to defend the building against the Mob . . . which Kate suspected was most likely the plan. It didn't take a Gatling gun to execute Tosca's boyfriend, and few productions in the classic repertoire required field artillery, but M. Quelou kept those too. M. Erik had lived through the Siege and the Commune. He also had cause to be wary of angry, torch-bearing crowds. There was little about the building and its protocols he hadn't had a pale, skeletal hand in designing.

M. Quelou first offered her a pair of pearl-handled custom pistols, suitable for Annie Oakley – scarcely a subject for musical drama, Kate thought. The guns felt light to her, more for show than showdown. After consideration, she settled for a plain, battered 'British Bull Dog' Webley. She knew the model – issued first to the Royal Irish Constabulary – and it fit nicely into her reticule. The gun gave her bag enough weight to use as a club if she wasn't in a position to haul out the iron and fire it.

The armourer gave her a lecture on the gun's use. She put on ear-baffles and fired at a straw target with a photograph pinned to it. It was an auto-graphed picture of Emma Calvé, reigning diva of the Opéra Comique – the Paris Opéra's great rival. Kate put a bullet in La Calvé's throat. Her eye was good and the gun was sighted properly.

Before she left, M. Quelou cautioned her, 'Mademoiselle, take care . . . don't feel *invincible*.'

She thought she took that on board. Within a quarter of an hour, his words haunted her . . .

Outside, in the Place de Opéra, she relaxed slightly. After so much time spent in Montmartre, it was a relief to be in a more civilised district, with-out *apache* in every alley. Looking up at the imposing façade of the Palais Garnier, she even had a comforting sense that M. Erik was nearby, like a guardian angel. Strange that such a creature should be her patron, but she was used to strangeness.

She sat at a pavement café table and drank bitter coffee while nibbling a crescent-shaped pastry. Pretty girls – from the company's chorus and *corps de ballet* – chirruped and chattered all around. Likely fellows tried to talk with them, getting mostly short shrift.

She opened a copy of *L'Intransigeant*, a virulently anti-Dreyfusard paper left at her table. She scanned for items of interest, catching on paragraphs and translating them in her head – she was a long way from fluency, but could now read complicated passages with something like ease. She found a piece by Henri Rochefort, a supporter of Du Roy, about the civilian judges who ruled that Dreyfus was allowed to appeal against his military conviction. 'They should have their eyelids cut off by a duly trained tor-turer,' wrote Rochefort, 'and large spiders of the most poisonous variety placed on their eyes to gnaw away at the pupils and crystalline lenses until there were nothing left in the cavities now devoid of sight. Then, all the hideous blind men would be brought to a pillory erected before the

Palais de Justice in which the crime was committed and a sign would be placed on their chests: "this is how France punishes traitors who try to sell her to the enemy!"' With public discourse on this level, the stage blood and trilling screams of the Théâtre des Horreurs were almost quaint.

The girls at the next table laughed at something.

Kate folded *L'Intransigeant*, resolved to put it in a public waste-paper bin and spare other idlers its venom.

What was all the amusement about?

A familiar barrel organ ground.

It was the ape-suited street performer of Rue Pigalle, *l'affiche vivante* of the Théâtre des Horreurs. He had recaptured his abused partner or procured a replacement. Did the animals come from the same disgusting business which supplied Maximilian the Great with canaries?

The monkey's get-up had changed. Now, it wore a miniature Guignol mask and costume.

'Dance, Sultan, dance,' said Petit Guignol. The shaggy gorilla shook his legs.

The mountebank must be a ventriloquist too, and particularly skilled. The shrill little voice, so like Guignol's swazzle, not only seemed to issue from the mask, but wasn't muffled by the stiff, snarling false face of the gorilla.

She couldn't bring herself to shout bravo, though. She remembered the sewn-together arms.

'Eh, Sultan, what have we here . . . the pretty ladies of the Opéra . . .'

Mass giggling.

'And a . . . well, a not-so-pretty lady, *associated with* the Opéra.'

The monkey jumped up on her table and snatched the last of her croissant, shredding it with little fingers. It couldn't eat through the mask.

Furious, pained eyes stared out from Guignol's face. She recalled the real Guignol's wild gaze.

The gorilla shambled closer to her table.

Her hand went to her reticule. No . . . this was someone she'd done mischief to getting their own back. That didn't mean she could shoot him. M. Quelou would warn her to save her shots for when they counted.

She tried to smile at the beast, who was disinclined to show gratitude to his former liberator. She imagined Sultan had punished him for his bolt for freedom.

Her face burned. She was blushing again.

The chorus girls laughed with good humour. Malign chuckles came out of the puppet-faced monkey. That *must* be Sultan throwing his voice.

Suddenly, Petit Guignol tugged at her hair and pulled her out of her seat.

'Dance with me, Brick-top, dance,' shrilled the voice.

Applause. She nearly stumbled, but stayed upright, whirled round and round by the trained beast.

The music stopped, but the dance went on. Petit Guignol passed her to Sultan, who gripped her with powerful, hairy-gloved hands. She was face to mask with the mock gorilla. Another set of eyes glared at her, burnt-cork make-up on the lids to blend with the black mask – mirthless, purposeful.

Sultan waltzed with her, further away from her table.

She saw a waiter holding up her surprisingly heavy reticule, miming 'eh, mademoiselle, you have left your bag . . .'

So much for being armed.

She struggled now, but the capering thug in the stiff-furred, reeking gorilla suit had a firm grip and deft feet. She was borne away, across the Place de l'Opéra. Petit Guignol dropped to all fours, assuming the role of a monkey rather than a little man, and scampered after them.

'*Au secors, au secors*!' shrilled a voice – *an imitation of hers!* – that earned more laughter. 'I am borne away by this base creature! Who will come to the aid of a poor, defenceless woman stolen by a dreadful beast of the jungles?'

The café patrons clapped, assuming this the finish of an act. Some threw coins, which were collected by a rough who also picked up the abandoned organ. Sultan had not come for her alone. But he had come for her.

This was . . . she realised . . . an abduction.

She was turned round and around. She was being waltzed towards a black carriage, its door open. Where a family crest or an official seal might be displayed was a simple red circle.

'What hideous lusts will this naughty creature slake upon my helpless form! What depraved desires does he ache to fulfil!'

She tried to compete with the fake cries of distress but couldn't get breath to shout.

'I must admit, though, that it is quite exciting!' continued the high-pitched voice. 'One comes to Paris for experiences . . . and this promises to be a very great . . . *experience*. Oh, if he wasn't so handsome . . . if I weren't so homely! I shall elope with Monsieur Sultan! We shall pledge our primitive troth and experience natural love in the trees!'

The knife edged out of her sleeve, but Sultan knew all about that. He squeezed her wrist painfully. The implement fell to the ground and was kicked away.

Finally, close to the carriage, the ape let go of one of her hands.

She tensed, prepared to administer a kick to the groin.

The huge, rubber-palmed hand pressed something sweet-smelling over her face . . . and she went into the darkness of a swoon.

Kate woke up in the dark, with a fuzzy headache. She knew she'd been chloroformed, but not how long she'd been unconscious.

She was slumped in an upholstered chair. She had a sense she was underground. A weight dragged at her ankle. She was shackled to the chair-leg. The chair was fixed to the floor. Her hands were free, but she was too weak to lift them.

The room was cold and slightly damp. She smelled mothballs.

She realised she'd been stripped. She wore some sort of shift or night-dress.

Was this the lair of Sultan the Gorilla-Man?

Someone turned up a gas lamp and she was looking at herself in a large mirror. Her hair was a mess, her skin was unhealthy white and her freckles stood out like pinpricks of blood. Her nightie was immodest, but surprisingly good quality. She had at least been abducted by a better class of ape.

Over her shoulder, she saw her captor, hairy hand up to the gas jet. His gorilla head was off, but he wore a skintight black hood with holes for his eyes and mouth.

'She's awake,' called Sultan.

A row of chairs faced the mirror, as in an expensive dentists' office or a hairdresser's. On the walls were theatre posters and photographs of famous actors. Stuck to and around the mirror were pictures: faces with hideous deformities, gouged eyes, flattened noses or terrible scars. If real, they were models for make-up artists trying to achieve shocking effects. If fake, they were records of previous triumphs to be recreated. On a shelf under the mirror were pots of powder and paint and trays of glass eyes. Faceless wooden heads supported a variety of wigs, including a scabby bald cap and Bertrand Caillet's wolfish shock of hair. Racks of costumes hung nearby, explaining the mothballs.

She was backstage at the Théâtre des Horreurs.

Sultan walked over to her, not bothering with the rolling ape gait, and took hold of her chin. He examined her face.

She would have spat but her mouth was dry.

As if reading her mind, he poured water from a jug into a glass and raised it to her lips, tipping liquid gently into her mouth.

She should have squirted it in his face. Instead, she said 'Thank you'.

Others entered the dressing room. She recognised Morpho. His scars weren't stuck on. Orloff, the theatre doctor, and Malita, the versatile actress. And someone else.

'I told you it cost blood to get a Red Circle invitation,' said Clara Watson. 'I never said it would be mine.'

Kate choked on her water. She rattled her leg-chain.

'Temper, temper,' said the English woman.

So Clara was a Fallen Angel? A turncoat. Kate should have guessed as much. The witch was too twisted to stay the course. Why hadn't M. Erik expected this?

Kate made an impractical anatomical suggestion.

'You know, in China, I saw a slave girl actually do that,' said Clara, smiling sweetly.

Dr Orloff stuck the cold end of his stethoscope against her chest. Kate supposed her heart rate was up.

Orloff professionally pinched her bare arms. She winced.

'Good reflexes,' he commented. 'Open wide.'

He touched her under the jaw-hinge and sprung her mouth open, then peered in.

'And good teeth. A pleasure to see good teeth. So many ladies neglect dental care. They just think that if they smile with their lips closed no one will notice the gaps and the green fur.'

'We should keep her scalp,' said Malita. 'We don't get enough red hair ... for the wigs.'

That wasn't encouraging.

'Why am I here?' she demanded.

'Katie, you are to be a shining star of the stage,' said Clara. 'The toast of the *après-minuit* of the Théâtre des Horreurs . . . now, what's the expression? . . . *For One Night Only*.'

If – no, *when* – she got out of this, she'd even things. A connoisseur of torture, was she? Well, Clara Watson hadn't gone to school in Ireland . . .

Clara bent down to kiss close to Kate's ears.

'*Courage*,' she whispered. 'And trust. Angels always.'

Then, with a fluttery wave, she left the room.

'See you in the cheap seats,' Kate shouted after her.

'Break a leg,' Clara responded. 'At least.'

Had she misunderstood Clara? If this was a stratagem to discover the secrets of the Red Circle, it would have been nice if she'd been in on it. Or was the Fallen Angel torturing her with the hope of a rescue that would never come?

Malita approached, with a pair of brushes. She began to groom Kate, putting her hair up in a way she hadn't tried before.

Objectively, Kate quite liked the effect.

Under the circumstances, she couldn't bring herself to thank her dresser.

Après-minuit didn't mean the curtain went up at the tolling of the twelve o'clock bell. While Kate was unconscious, Guignol's company gave a regular evening show. Then, the audience and most of the company left the building and preparations for the Red Circle performance began.

Malita powdered over her freckles (which took several pots) and gave her red, red lips and rouge cheek-blushes. With a pencil that drew blood, the crone added a final touch – a beauty spot by her nose.

Kate was unshackled and wrestled into a cheap tart costume: low-cut bodice, gypsy skirt, beret, tattered red shawl, patent leather boots. Now, Kate thought she looked ridiculous – like a doll which would sit unbought in Madame Mandelip's window.

Malita dragged her – it was hard to walk in the thick-soled, high-heeled boots – out of the dressing room. She was taken along a corridor, up through the wings and onto the stage. The heavy curtain was down, a stock backdrop showed sylvan fields and marble statuary, and a stained oilskin was laid over the boards. Stagehands stood ready with buckets and mops.

Sultan had his head back on, but his hairy gloves off. His hands were blacked with coal and he held a hunting rifle.

Want to see something really frightening? A gorilla with a gun.

Other oddly-dressed and made-up people were gathered.

A young man in white tie and tails was protesting to a hard-faced Morpho. Kate recognised the Stage Door Jeannot she'd spotted on her first visit to the theatre. His bunch of black flowers was wilting. She gathered he'd slipped backstage in the hope paying tribute to *la belle* Berma. Others – more obvious wretches – were sober enough to be terrified. An old beldame, dressed as a duchess but smelling like a down-and-out washerwoman. Two thin children, got up in animal costumes – Henriette and Louise, the orphans who'd run away to join the circus. A one-armed, one-eyed soldier in uniform proudly announced that he was making his third appearance in an *après-minuit*. Kate guessed such return performances were rare.

Dr Orloff supervised the co-opted, addled or desperate cast.

'Feel free to scream at the top of your lungs,' he said. 'It's a small house, but it takes a lot to fill the auditorium. Our patrons like to hear a good scream. Remember to stay in the limelight. No point bleeding in the dark, is there? You want your moment. If you must beg and plead for mercy, address yourselves to the audience. Our orchestra are blindfolded and callous. Your fellow performers are professionals and will stick to the script.'

'There's a *chance* for mercy?' asked a young woman in an Aztec headdress.

'Of course not,' said the doctor. 'But the begging, whining and tearing of hair amuses some of the Red Circle. It irritates others, who just want to get on with the procedures. But many are happy to delay their pleasure. Who knows, maybe *largesse* will be extended to your loved ones if you plead prettily enough. You are here to honour a family obligation, are you not, Nini?'

The sacrificial princess nodded.

'Follow your instincts. I'm sure you'll triumph. And Papa will be saved from disgrace.'

It hadn't occurred to Kate that anyone would *deliberately* give themselves over to Guignol. Evidently, everything could be bought. This business got more horrible the more she found out.

The beldame sank to her knees, dress pooling around her, and began keening and drooling. Morpho hauled her upright and slapped her silent. Malita stepped in with a cloth and some powder to repair her make-up.

Sultan slung his rifle on his back and climbed a rope into the flyspace above the stage. He was as agile as a natural-born ape.

Could she escape by following him up there? Not in these blasted boots.

Looking up, she saw Sultan crouch on a gangway amid ropes and pulleys. He trained his rifle on the stage and bared his teeth – the big fake choppers in his articulated mask – at her in a grin. An ape-man of many talents . . . ventriloquist, abductor of women, acrobat, sharp shooter . . .

So long as Sultan was at his post, there was no point in making a dash for freedom.

Rallying the performers to rebel was not much of a possibility. She couldn't know how many were essentially volunteers, like the Old Soldier and Nini. Most of the obviously co-opted, like Stage Door Jeannot and the Duchess, were in no state to be of any use to her or themselves. The orphans, a fish and a bat, were undernourished.

At this juncture, the best she could hope for was to die knowing the answers.

She put up her hand, as if at a press conference.

'Miss, ah, Reed, isn't it?' Orloff acknowledged. 'How can I help you?'

'Skipping past the obvious business of me not wanting to be in the show, can I at least ask what it's all about?'

'I don't understand. What is *what* all about?'

'This. The *après-minuit*, the Red Circle . . . your patrons – who I'll bet I could name, by the way – what do they get out of this?'

Dr Orloff looked puzzled. Had no one ever asked before?

'. . . I believe I can enlighten our guest,' said someone from behind her – in a slightly reedy voice.

She turned and saw Georges Du Roy.

The journalist and politician was dressed as if for the opera, from his top hat to his spats. Jewels sparkled on his fingers and his stickpin. Famously handsome, he had wooed his way through the salons to winkle tit-bits for the gossip column that was the making of him. He had softened in middle age, but retained his smooth skin and watery bright eyes. His moustache was dyed and waxed.

She would have walked past him on the street without noticing – yet, he was the true monster in this case. His pink, plump face was his mask.

With him was Guignol, on a leash and all fours like a hunting dog.

'I confess it,' he said. 'My comrades and I, the brothers of the Red Circle, are addicts. Connoisseurs, certainly. Fastidious, perhaps. Choosy, naturally. But addicts. We want what we want. We must have it. *Must*. If we can no longer participate, we must watch. It is the great secret delight of all mankind, you know.'

'Murder?'

'You could call it that . . . but it's so commonplace a term. Murder is brute stuff. One man shoots or stabs another, in a quarrel or for no reason. Even duels, assassinations, factory accidents . . . they are over too quickly, not savoured, not *enjoyed*.'

'This is about Bloody Week?'

Du Roy looked wistful. 'Yes, of course. Some of us had an inkling before then . . . during the siege of Paris, when the elephants in the zoo were slaughtered for food . . . or at school or on the battlefield. We trembled, on the verge of self-understanding. We pursued other gratifications, so much less piquant than those we really needed. It was that glorious shining week, those few precious days, when we truly learned what it was that we must have. It was our revelation. Excess, my dear. Excess! A banquet of killing! An orgy of bloodletting. Murder upon murder! Massacre upon massacre! A refinement of the art . . .'

Kate saw why Clara Watson had sold her for a Red Circle pass.

'You're just . . . mad. Rich, and mad. The worst combination.'

Du Roy smiled, showing little rows of sparkling teeth. 'Everyone's a critic.'

'Are you satisfied, Mademoiselle *Pomme de Terre*?' asked Orloff. 'You've been privileged above any other in being granted an interview with our impresario. An *exclusive*.'

'I doubt that. What he says sounds rehearsed. I think he's said it all before. He's as bored with it as I was.'

Orloff signalled. Malita slapped Kate.

Kate made fists, then remembered the gorilla with the high-powered rifle.

Du Roy tipped his hat to the performers and retreated, hauling Guignol away. The presiding spirit of the Théâtre des Horreurs was surprisingly quiet. Du Roy handed the leash to Morpho, who grinned and tugged viciously. As the collar went tight, a wheezing came from deep in Guignol's throat – air forced through his swazzle.

So, the monster's position was usurped.

This wasn't Guignol's show any more. This was for the Red Circle.

Dr Orloff arranged the cast against the backdrop, as if it were an execution wall. Kate half-expected a blindfold, then realised that would be a mercy . . . and the Red Circle were not disposed to mercy.

Morpho, Malita and Orloff remained onstage. Morpho was stripped to the waist, showing off his battle-scars. Malita and Orloff put on butcher's aprons and white coats. The props bench in the wings was piled with hammers, tongs, knives, sickles, gouges, bludgeons and other, unidentifiable instruments of mistreatment. Bottles of poison and acid were also available. A short, round-faced, bald-headed fellow with a permanent smile stood by the table, ready to hand over implements when needed. Very professional.

Kate thought of making a grab for the acid, but knew she'd be cut down. She had no doubt the man in the gorilla suit was an expert marksman. Dying too quickly would spoil the show but she'd still be dead.

The curtains parted and the limelights flared.

Beyond the shimmer, she could make out shapes.

A procession advanced down the aisle, and climbed up a carpeted set of steps to the stage, traversing the invisible barrier between the audience and the drama.

Du Roy escorted a veiled lady in a scarlet, hooded cape.

Kate trusted the Red Circle were satisfied with their newest member. She hoped Clara would get bored in a year or two and poison the lot of them. By then, she'd have had opportunity to seduce an intern at the School of Tropical Medicine and secure some new, hideously virulent bacillus for the job. Du Roy wouldn't look so smug with weeping boils erupting all over his face.

The others trooped behind the King and Queen of Horror.

General Assolant was in full uniform, chest sagging with a glittery weight of medals and honours. In this private realm of fantasy, Father de Kern had promoted himself to cardinal. His red robes would have been too grand for Richelieu. His train trailed like a bride's, and was carried by imps – naked children painted red all over and staggering as they began to suffocate. Charles Pradier wore judicial robes and magistrate's hat, adopting the British convention of the black silk handkerchief draped over the top to signify passage of a death sentence. Eugène Mortain sported a tricolour sash over court clothes and had a drunken doxy with him. The fair-haired wench tittered and clucked, marring the solemnity of the occasion. Would she end up taking part in the performance? Blondes were as easy to replace as Maximilian's little yellow birds.

The audience wore red domino masks, for convention rather than disguise.

Attendants in red livery set out chairs on the stage, close to the action. Individual trays for snacks and drinks were bolted to the chair-arms. There was even a folded-up programme placed on each cushion.

Kate would have liked a look at the running order. With pathetic orphan sisters and an Aztec princess in the line-up, she doubted she'd get top billing. The best she could hope for was to be snuffed quickly at the end of Act One. Her corpse would be dragged off for dumping in the sewers while the audience enjoyed an intermission and exchanged opinions about her death scene.

A small group of musicians – blindfolded, as promised – struck up a selection from *Carmen*.

The audience took their seats.

Mortain's mistress evidently had no idea what she was about to see – she was laughing shrilly and flirting with everyone. The others were intent, quiet, perspiring, eager. Du Roy had a habit of licking his lips like a fat lizard. Assolant gripped the hilt of his sword as if he'd like to draw his weapon and hack randomly at the people in front of him – which, she supposed, he might well do. Watching wouldn't be enough for these people. De Kern had his imps kneel down before him to form a footstool. Pradier counted out little pills from a box and swallowed them, washed down with a swallow from a silver flask.

The surprise was Guignol's role.

The masked man was still on a leash, still held by Morpho. Where once he had been master of the stage, now he was a stooge.

Kate saw blood on Guignol's costume, seeping through. The mask was battered, the nose pushed in, as if he'd taken a bad beating.

Even this close to her death, she was trying to understand.

Was Guignol an unwilling participant in the *après-minuit*? She saw his eyes were shut, as if he didn't want to look.

Morpho tied Guignol's leash to a post, and kicked him.

The show had started . . .

The Old Soldier was the opening act.

The orchestra played a march as he saluted the audience with his remaining arm – the left. He sat on a stool and, with practised ease, worked off his left boot with his right foot. With rather more difficulty, he peeled off his sock one-handed and tried to roll up his trouser-leg, which kept snagging on his knee and rolling down again.

Mortain's blonde roared with laughter. De Kern swivelled his head almost entirely around, like a snake or an owl, and stared her into silence. She needed a swift pull from the flask after that. The priest's head turned back and he gave a 'pray continue' gesture with his free hand. The other was tucked under his robe and horribly busy.

Malita came to the Old Soldier's rescue with a jack-knife and slit his britches for him, from the ankle-cuff to well above the knee. The cloth parted and flapped aside. For such an obvious invalid, the soldier had a healthy-looking leg.

'*Vive la France*,' he said. '*Vive la Republique*.'

The orchestra played 'La Marseillaise', with some deliberate, comic wrong notes.

Dr Orloff gave the Old Soldier a saw and he got to work.

He fought valiantly against the urge to scream and only whimpered as he performed the auto-amputation. He chewed his long moustache. He had once been right-handed, Kate realised. His left-hand strokes were awkward. The saw kept slipping in its red groove. Nevertheless, he hit bone and parted cartilage before passing out.

Mortain's mistress stuck her fist in her mouth. Mortain took her neck like a kitten's and forced her to keep watching.

The Old Soldier fell off the stool. Sundered veins pulsed and spurted. Kate saw a flash of yellowish bone and clumps of gristle.

Morpho stepped in, with an executioner's axe raised.

'No,' insisted Du Roy. 'He must be awake.'

Dr Orloff applied a tourniquet to stem the flow of blood, then used smelling salts to wake the Old Soldier.

'I am sorry,' he said, through tears of pain. 'I have had . . . a momentary lapse.'

Morpho brought the axe down. The angle was awkward and the cut not clean.

The Old Soldier screamed. And apologised again.

Dr Orloff positioned the sundered knee over the stool, which made a decent chopping block. Morpho finished the job and tore away the leg, which he then tossed at Guignol, who flinched as he was kicked in the face by a disembodied foot.

The doctor tightened the tourniquet.

It was touch and go for a moment, but the bleeding was stopped and Orloff worked fast with hot irons and needle and thread.

The audience, bored by this, gossiped. The musicians played a cakewalk.

Blood pooled on the oilskin, creeping closer to Kate's toes. Her fellow performers were either in shock or insane.

His life saved, the Old Soldier was carried away . . . perhaps considering a fourth appearance, though for the life of her Kate couldn't imagine how he'd come up with a new turn.

The Red Circle weren't that impressed.

Stage Door Jeannot, sober at last, tried to make a run for freedom. He slipped in the blood. A crack sounded and a rifle bullet smashed his skull. Instantly dead, he somersaulted in the air and landed in a messy heap of tangled limbs.

There was weak applause at his impromptu performance.

Malita bit her cheek in disappointment. Kate supposed she'd expected to have the fellow to herself in a later, scheduled act.

She smelled gunpowder. A cartridge case pinged on the stage.

Guignol struggled with his collar, trying to pull free. Mortain's doxy was shocked silent. De Kern moaned with pleasure. Assolant furiously muttered, 'Can't abide a coward – should be shot, the lot of 'em!' Du Roy looked bored – he had said murder wasn't enough for him any more.

Someone had died in front of her. Kate was beyond fury and terror.

Dr Orloff was less expert than Guignol as a master of ceremonies. He hemmed and lectured, playing for time while the next act was setting up.

Stage Door Jeannot threw him off his script.

The corpse had to be removed and a pool of blood mopped, then the wet patch scattered with sand.

Orloff fussed as all this happened in front of the audience.

Du Roy glared at him. Kate supposed artistes who fell out of favour with the Red Circle got to make one last spectacular exit.

Malita pulled her out of the line of waiting performers. One of the orphans clung to Kate's skirt. Malita was about to slap the little girl. Kate deflected the blow with her arm and told the child everything would be all right. Her tongue went like leather as she lied. Malita led her to the props table.

The prop master held up a stiletto and stabbed it into the meat of his hand. The blunt-tipped blade slid into the handle. He gave the trick knife to her. Would it be any use? Malita impatiently showed her how to holster it in the top of her boot.

'In the spirit of Montmartre, we present the famous *apache* dance,' announced Orloff. 'Performed by our own celebrated Morpho and a special guest . . . Miss Katharine Reed of Dublin.'

So this was why she was dressed as a French streetwalker.

The orchestra began the 'Valse des Rayons'.

Malita dragged her onto the stage. Morpho was waiting. The one-eyed ox now wore a tight, striped shirt and a red neckerchief. A cigarette was stuck in the corner of his sneer. Red and yellow war paint striped his cheeks, as if he had Apache and *apache* mixed up.

She'd seen this act the other night – the mock-fight of rough dance, as the ponce slings his tart around, miming slaps and kicks, with kisses between the blows. For the benefit of the Red Circle, she guessed the fight wouldn't be mock and the slaps and kicks wouldn't be pulled. The idea of being kissed by Morpho wasn't too appealing either.

No wonder they hadn't given her a knife that would stick in anything.

Morpho adopted an odd pose, like a matador – fists at his sides, up on his toes, bottom tucked in, chest puffed out, looking at her sidewise with his single eye. There was a touch of vanity in his plumped-up self-regard. Only now, with Guignol tied up, was Morpho a real star.

'Dance, girl,' whispered Malita in her ears. 'If you disappoint, they'll go after your family.'

Malita shoved Kate at Morpho.

She slammed against his chest and he grabbed her hair, which hurt enough to get her attention.

The herky-jerky music continued, with pauses Offenbach hadn't written, as she was rattled around the stage. She struggled, but Morpho was strong and had done this before. He let her go and slapped her face hard, snapping her head around – a few more like that, and her neck would break.

She aimed a kick at his shin. Make use of the damned boots!

Deftly, he got out of her way and she fell over. Sliding on the still-wet oilskin, she got a sandpapery burn on her bare thigh. He jammed a boot in her ribs and she rolled over, trying to ignore the burst of pain.

At this rate, her debut would be over in no time at all.

Morpho took her arms and hauled her up again, lifting her off her feet and over his head, then wheeling her around in the air. She was dizzy. Flashes went off in her eyes.

Up in the flies, she saw Sultan the Gorilla, rifle-barrel moving as he kept his bead drawn on her . . .

. . . and, above him, a black bat-like shape, descending silently on the ape sniper. A dangling loop of cord hooked around Sultan's throat. The Punjab lasso!

She had only a glimpse, but it was enough. She had not been abandoned. Literally, an angel watched over her . . .

. . . though she couldn't help wishing M. Erik had got his act together a little earlier.

Now, she had to get through this *pas de deux* without being killed.

Morpho held her by an arm and an ankle and spun like a top. Her hair came loose and flapped like a flag in the wind. A panorama rushed past, faster and faster.

The Red Circle. The orchestra. The prop table. The stagehands. Guignol, chained. The black chasm of the auditorium. The painted pastorale, streaked with blood. The waiting victims.

She tried to look up.

Morpho let go and she slid across the stage, scraping her side raw, ripping her costume. Her shawl came loose and she skidded to a stop.

A breathing moment.

Above on a wildly-swinging gangway, unnoticed by everyone else, a slender, cloaked, white-masked figure exchanged *savate* kicks with Sultan the Gorilla. M. Erik had entered the field.

Morpho mockingly beckoned to Kate.

At this point in the dance, the *apache* girl usually crawled on hands and knees back to her pimp to take more medicine. The little fool would try to stick him with her garter-knife but he'd bend her wrist back contemptuously until she dropped it.

Kate pulled the toy stiletto from her boot-top. It had an edge but no point. Could she jam its spring?

No time.

Malita kicked her rump and propelled her towards Morpho.

Mortain laughed and applauded. A particular aficionado of this act, it seemed. His blonde was watching again, almost lulled.

If she tried to stab Morpho in the chest, the blade would do no harm.

Determined not to die on her knees, she stood and countered his come-hither gesture with one of her own, summoning him to a fight.

He brought out his own knife. A blade sprang from its handle. Not a prop.

She flicked a glance upwards. M. Erik's lasso was tight around the gorilla's neck. She didn't dare look too long, for fear of drawing attention to the show above the stage.

Morpho puffed smoke and danced towards her.

She slashed at his face, catching his cheek with the knife-edge. Used to scythe rather than stab, the blade didn't retract. She barely scratched him, but a runnel of blood dripped from his face. He gulped and swallowed his dog-end. Coughing and choking, he thumped his own chest.

Now, she got a good strong kick to his shins.

More applause.

'I love it when they fight back,' said Mortain, loosening his sash. '*Encore, encore!*'

Morpho, unhappy with the way this was going, came at her like a wrestler, arms out. If he caught her now, he'd break her spine over his knee.

Sultan's rifle fell from above and slammed butt-first into Morpho's head. His skull audibly cracked and his one eye went red then dull. He collapsed like a sack of bricks. The gun discharged as it hit the floor. Malita yelped, shot in the ankle. The ditchwater Duchess grabbed her by the hair and hauled her into the wings. Her screams grew higher in pitch.

At this point, the orphans – very sensibly – ran off. Slipping between stagehands' legs, they zigzagged to avoid capture. Henriette and Louise barrelled through the blindfolded orchestra. The musicians made a racket as they missed their places, then stopped playing and tumbled into each other. In the kerfuffle, the children disappeared backstage.

Kate wished them luck and hoped they'd make a better choice for their next circus.

Now, *everyone* looked up. Kate smelled paraffin.

M. Erik had returned to his shadows.

Sultan was lowered slowly, in lurches, on a rope looped around his ankle. He twisted in the air, human hands stuck out of hampering hairy arms. He shook his head, as if trying to get his mask off. He yowled, throwing his voice – his cries seemed to come from all over the auditorium. Drops of liquid spattered on the oilcloth. The gorilla was soaked in paraffin.

'What is this?' cried Pradier.

'It's Poe,' squawked Guignol. '*The Tale of Hop-Frog*!'

Once, M. Erik had appeared at a masked ball as Edgar Allan Poe's Red Death. Like Guignol, who'd written Dr Tarr and Professor Fether into his show, the Director of the Opera Ghost Agency was an admirer of the gloomy, sickly American poet. Kate preferred Walt Whitman herself.

She remembered the story of Hop-Frog. The abused jester tricks the cruel king and his toadying courtiers into disguising themselves as orang-utans with flammable pitch and flax, and then touches a torch to them . . .

A ribbon of flame ran down the rope and caught the fur of the paraffin-sodden gorilla man. With a *whump*, Sultan was enveloped in fire. Burning fur stank. A screech sounded and was cut off as the ape-man sucked fire into his lungs. He kicked and struggled, swinging like a pendulum . . .

. . . then the rope burned through. Sultan fell, cracking boards. The props master had the presence of mind to throw a bucket of water on the dead man. The fire hissed out. Smoke and steam rose. Pradier, an idiot, chittered in delight, taking this for part of the show.

Du Roy stood. He appeared calm, yet a vein throbbed in his forehead.

He looked around for the phantom who had wrecked the performance, then turned – suspicion pricked – to the veiled woman at his side. Kate wasn't the only person who'd forgotten not to trust Clara Watson.

Du Roy drew a small pistol from inside his jacket. A ladies' model. He jammed it up under the scarlet woman's chin and ripped off her veil.

The Master of the Red Circle beheld a face he didn't know.

Yuki Kashima shrugged out of the hooded cloak. She wore her kimono.

She even carried her parasol.

'Surprise,' gloated Guignol.

The select audience shrank away from Yuki. Gripped by a premonition.

'Find the lady,' said Guignol.

Mortain's doxy pulled off her stiff yellow wig and shook out red hair.

So, Yuki was Clara and Clara was the blonde.

Only Kate was who she said she was – even in this *apache* outfit.

'Whoever you are,' said Du Roy, 'you'll die now . . .'

Du Roy stood back and straightened his arm, steadying his gun. The barrel was an inch from Yuki's nose.

Faster than the eye could register, Yuki unsheathed a sword from her parasol and made a forceful yet elegant pass.

Du Roy looked at a red line around his wrist. His brows knit as he tried to pull the trigger. Wires were cut and the impulse from his brain couldn't reach his fingers. Puzzled, airily irritated, he didn't yet feel the pain.

His hand slid off his wrist and thumped on the floor, letting go of the gun.

Blood gouted like a fountain . . . which Yuki sidestepped.

'Musicians,' said Guignol, sharply. 'Selection Thirteen, *andante.*'

... the ensemble took heed, adjusted their blindfolds and assumed their playing positions, instruments ready.

They launched into Guignol's idea of an appropriate tune. 'Three Little Maids from School' by Gilbert and Sullivan, from *The Mikado*.

Yuki set about her precise, bloody work – more surgery than butchery.

Among the Red Circle, she lashed out. She held her sword-hilt up and struck down, adopting a series of poses, face impassive, ignoring the gouts of gore. She was not hobbled by her dress, which Kate only now realised, was slit to the waist to allow for ease of movement. Her habitual tiny Japanese steps were misdirection.

Screams. Intestines uncoiled. Limbs and heads flew.

The Red Circle got their fill of horrors now.

Three little maids from school are we,
Pert as a schoolgirl well can be,
Filled to the brim with girlish glee,
Three little maids from school!

Father De Kern tried to flee, but his imps gripped his train and he was tugged back onto the killing floor. Yuki laid open his spine. He bucked like a cut-open caterpillar.

Everything is a source of fun ...

Mortain lost his innards. Pradier lost his head.

Nobody's safe for we care for none!

Assolant stood up and slid his face onto Yuki's sword-edge. His domino mask fell apart. He detached his skull from the blade, hand pressed over the spurting slice.

Life is a joke that's just begun!

Kate picked up Sultan's rifle. She worked the bolt, ejected the spent cartridge, chambered another. She covered the stagehands.

Morpho and Malita were dead.

Dr Orloff watched, open-mouthed, as his patrons fell.

Three little maids from school! Three little maids from school!

Yuki didn't waste effort. She maimed and killed as she would compose a *haiku* – inside seconds, with strictly limited moves.

The orchestra finished the tune.

Yuki sheathed her blade and opened the parasol. She gave a tiny, formal curtsey.

Only now did Kate remember to be terrified.

But not incapacitated. She took a bucket of water from a stagehand and scrubbed the backs of De Kern's imps, scraping enough paint so the children wouldn't die of clogged pores. Whoever they were, she trusted they'd be grateful.

Assolant and Du Roy were still alive.

'Katie dear,' said Clara, sweetly. 'Would you free our client?'

Catching on at once, Kate helped Guignol get loose. He got the enforced straightness out of his bones and kinked up properly.

'That's the way to do it,' he swazzled.

So, Guignol had been coerced into letting the Red Circle take over his theatre. He had taken steps to break their hold over his company.

'You're finished, Hulot,' spat Du Roy.

Guignol shrugged.

Another mystery solved – the secret identity of Guignol. He was Jacques Hulot, once hailed as the funniest man in France . . . then believed a suicide. Reborn as the maestro of horrors.

'Comedy didn't pay,' he explained to Kate. 'The mob wanted gore, and gore *encore* . . . So I got a new act. I told truths, showed the world the way it was.'

He capered over to Du Roy.

'But the mob are less bloodthirsty than you, you pathetic wretch. My horrors are a mirror – they do not represent the world as I wish it to be. They are a caution, not a blueprint. Only a few mistake it for one. And few of them have the lack of feeling that would admit them to your circle. It takes refinement to be so dreadful. Are you satisfied now? Have you finally had your fill of blood, you monster of France?'

Du Roy let go of his seeping wrist and died.

So there were no heirs of M. Hulot. Guignol, the management of the theatre, was Hulot himself, transformed . . . and the Théâtre des Horreurs was the risen spectre of the Théâtre des Plaisantins.

Amid all the carnage, the clown couldn't help himself. Guignol was still funny.

The tableau at the end of his show, the waxworks of the Légion d'Horreur, was a specific charge, accusing the Brothers of the Red Circle. Another living signpost, marking the way for the Angels of Music. These are the guilty men, these are *your* guilty men . . . come and stop them, for I – Guignol – am in their power and cannot. Kate had looked for hidden meaning, when it was obvious enough to be understood in the rear stalls.

General Assolant still stood, half his face red. All his battles were fought and finished well before he arrived at the bloody field to supervise the executions. Now, he'd have real scars to go with his medals.

The officer who despised cowards was trembling.

'Don't be alarmed, General,' said Clara. 'You must remain alive, to tell any others . . . any of the Red Circle not present, any who might share its inclinations. Your run is over. The show is closed by the order of . . . Messieurs Guignol and Erik. You understand? Your marching orders are given. Now get out of this place before my dainty friend changes her mind and plays parasol games again.'

Assolant didn't need to be told twice. He scarpered, the sword he hadn't thought to draw rattling at his side.

Kate took a moment and put all her weight into slapping Clara.

The English widow licked a bead of blood from her lip and shrugged.

'You couldn't be told, Katie. You're a good journalist, but no actress.'

'Why didn't you stop the show before it began?' she asked, as much of Yuki as Clara. 'Before anyone was hurt.'

'Your friend Sultan had to be removed,' said Clara. 'A tricky situation.'

Kate saw the sense, but still burned. Stage Door Jeannot had paid for M. Erik's tardiness.

Nini, the Aztec princess, came forward. She'd taken off her headdress.

'My father's letters—?'

'Will be returned to you,' said Guignol, kissing her hand.

Satisfied, Nini left the stage.

Guignol looked at the smiling props master, the nervous stagehands and the now-sighted orchestra.

'I know you were suborned to this by Orloff. You are on probation, but you keep your jobs . . . except you, Rollo. You enjoyed this too much. Go find other employment and take your knives with you.'

Rollo shrugged, gathered up a selection of implements and departed.

'Orloff,' said Guignol, drawing out the name, 'you are a mockery of a man, barely a human creature. We have a vacancy for you. You'll find your gorilla suit in the costumes closet. It'll be sewn on. The mask will be fixed to your face with glue, permanently. And you'll gibber amusingly, play the star role when we stage "Murders in the Rue Morgue" and submit entirely to my will . . . or else you'll share the fate of your predecessor Sultan. Do you understand me?'

Orloff, white with terror, sank to his knees, surrounded by parts of his patrons. They were now literally a Red Circle.

'Now, I want this stage washed and this mess cleared,' ordered Guignol. 'Tomorrow night, and every night, we have a show to put on. The Théâtre des Horreurs does not go dark!'

The Angels sat with the Persian in the café opposite the Palais Garnier. Yuki ate ice cream and Clara drank china tea.

Kate was still irritated.

The job was done – the Red Circle sundered, the Montmartre murders stopped – and the client satisfied.

She had thought she understood why Clara betrayed her . . . but it turned out that the Englishwoman had shammed her way into the Red Circle. Now, Kate was bewildered again. It had made so much sense for Clara Watson to defect. She was a self-declared connoisseur of torture. Whatever was wrong with Du Roy was wrong with her too – perhaps far more so. M. Erik had taken her on precisely because of this defect.

'What was it, Clara?' she asked. 'Why were you so set against them?'

'The Légion d'Horreur were bourgeois hypocrites – salivating in secret, rather than proudly taking their pleasures in the open. Besides, I wanted to see a true artist perform . . . and I have. I shall treasure the memory.'

'Guignol?'

'Oh, he's adorable . . . but no. Not Guignol.'

Clara raised her teacup to Yuki, who dipped her head modestly.

'Grace. Elegance. Minimalism. Mutilation. Execution: Perfect.'

Kate would never understand. For her, horrors were just horrors.

She looked up at the frontage of the Opera House and fancied a gargoyle was up there, watching over them.

She'd never understand him either. As a reporter, as a detective, she needed only to know the facts . . . only as Kate Reed did she want to know more.

The Persian laid a dossier of press cuttings on the table.

'Now, *mes filles*, another matter has come to the attention of the Agency. Kate, you will be interested. In the Louvre, guards have been assaulted. It is rumoured that treasures have disappeared. Some talk of a curse upon the building. A strange figure has been seen, drifting through the halls by night, cloaked and silent, wearing the headdress and golden death mask of a pharaoh . . .'

KIM NEWMAN is a novelist, critic and broadcaster. His most recent publications include the non-fiction study *BFI Film Classic: Quatermass and the pit*, the mini-series *Witchfinder: The Mysteries of Unland* (with Maura McHugh) for Dark Horse Comics, the expanded reissues of his acclaimed *Anno Dracula* series, and his latest novel, *Secrets of Drearcliff Grange School*. The Angels of Music will return in 'Phantom Ladies Over Paris'.

night'mare *n.* 1: oppressive or paralysing or terrifying or fantastically horrible dream or (colloq.) experience; 2: haunting fear or thing vaguely dreaded producing a feeling of anxiety or terror; 3: an evil spirit thought to oppress people in their sleep. Origin: Middle English, from *night* + *mare*. First known use: 14th century. Synonyms: agony, Gehenna, horror, misery, murder, Hell, torment, torture. Example: *When you are inexplicably lost, and cannot find your way back* ...

NIGHTMARE

RAMSEY CAMPBELL

THEY HAD LEFT the hotel just a few miles behind when Lawrence said 'There's somewhere else I used to go.'

'Striders Halt,' Violet read on the sign for the next motorway exit. 'What was that, Lawrence?'

'A view of the whole valley. I could show you if you like.'

'Is it far?' At once she regretted sounding less than wholly enthusiastic. 'If it means something to you,' she said.

'Only if it would to you as well. Maybe we can still salvage a little magic from the weekend.'

'I thought you thought it was fun.'

'I think we can do without that kind.'

She'd thought he'd shared her wry amusement. He must have been suppressing his reaction for her sake. The hotel he'd remembered from his childhood had turned out to be mostly occupied by several coachloads of old folk. They'd seemed to overwhelm the place, slowing it down to their speed and adding to its faint stale smell, filling the faded corridors with a mass of sluggish footsteps and effortful breaths. Lawrence might have intended to recapture some of his youth and share it with Violet, but instead they'd been reminded what could lie ahead for them. During the day they'd gone for walks on the hills and ridges, but the hotel was too remote from anywhere else to let them escape in the evenings, and so they'd been trapped with singalongs in the bar or into producing dutiful laughter at superannuated comedies on the television in the crowded lounge, where their neighbours kept turning to them to ensure they joined in. 'Pet,' Lawrence added as if this summed up the entire experience.

'I never knew you disliked being called that so much.' After all, several of the old folk had used it to Violet as well. 'I hope you're mine at least,' she said.

'I don't care to be patronised. I'm more than a little too old.'

Was he complaining or boasting? Since they'd both retired he seemed to have grown unsure of himself and defensive to compensate, as if all the easy authority he'd shown with his students had just been armour for his vulnerable nature. She'd assumed that now they weren't lecturing they would have time to grow closer. They mustn't settle into themselves if it meant that they drifted apart, and she signalled to leave the motorway. 'Let's see your view,' she said.

The January sun was lying low behind a vast slab of marble cloud. The icy glow blackened the exposed bones of the landscape. On either side of the road that wound between bare fields, hulking hedges bristled with thorns. Sometimes Violet glimpsed birds in the midst of the tangle of twigs, unless the restless objects were the only remaining leaves, shaken by the wind that sent a chill into the car. As the road straightened between the last of the fields, Lawrence sat forward. 'What's that in the way? It oughtn't to be there.'

A line of wide bungalows blocked the end of the road, beyond a village green – an expanse of grass bisected by the road, at any rate. As the car emerged from between the hedges Violet saw that the bungalows extended out of sight past both ends of the green. 'I expect someone else must have liked the view,' she said.

'Then they should have left it for the rest of us to appreciate.'

'Do you want to go back?'

'Back the way it was. Drive around for a bit, will you? Perhaps there's still a path.'

'Drive where, Lawrence?'

'Wherever we're allowed,' he said and gestured vaguely at the houses. 'I'll shout if anything seems familiar.'

A sign on stumpy concrete legs identified the bungalow road as MEADOW PROSPECT. At least, Violet took that as the name, though a poster about a lost dog obscured more than half of the first word. Another fluttering poster drew her eye to a sign for a side road several hundred yards away – as far as she could make it out, CLIFF ROAD. 'Yes, try that,' Lawrence urged before she could ask.

Twin lines of elongated pale stone bungalows curved left and then right without hinting at the presence of a cliff. Violet was coasting around a third curve at a pace even she found sedate when one of the cars parked on the wide drives between the bungalows – a silver Jaguar – backed into the road at twice her speed. As she braked while Lawrence gasped and threw his hands up, the other driver lowered his window, leaving the Jaguar across the width of the road.

His receding hair was the faded brown of a vintage photograph. His eyes looked pinched narrow by wrinkles, more of which appeared to stretch his colourless mouth straight and thin. He apparently felt entitled to be heard with very little effort on his part, and Violet had to roll her window down, letting in a reason for a shiver. 'Sorry, what did you say again?'

'I asked if Fetcher brought you here.'

'I don't believe so,' Violet said, though the name sounded somehow familiar. 'Fletcher, did you say?'

'I quite clearly said Fetcher.' The man frowned as if she'd put him to more trouble than was warranted. 'You can't be lost,' he said.

Was this an accusation or a question that didn't bother sounding like one? Lawrence was lowering his window, presumably to ask for directions, when the man said 'Perhaps you can tell me whom you've come to see.'

'Nobody at all. My husband wanted to revisit some of his old haunts.'

'I don't know you,' the man said, scowling harder at Lawrence. 'I've never seen you here.'

'Nor I you. I was here before you were.'

'No,' the man said with a smile too thin to contain mirth. 'Nobody was.'

'I can assure you my parents and I—'

The man had already returned to scrutinising Violet. 'I should have thought you were too old to be defacing our streets.'

'What the devil do you mean by that?' Lawrence demanded, leaning out of the window so violently that the car shook. 'How dare you say that to my wife?'

'What can your companion be yapping about?' the man said without glancing at Lawrence. 'I should try and keep him under control.'

Lawrence lurched across the metal sill and produced a series of shrill barks. 'How's that for yapping?'

'Don't, Lawrence.' Violet had not just to stroke his arm but tug at it before he subsided onto the seat, rubbing his chest where the sill had bruised it. 'Don't let him reduce you,' she murmured.

'That's your idea of a joke, is it?' The man's face had grown angrily pie-bald. 'Is it supposed to be how Fetcher sounds?'

'We don't know anything about that,' Violet assured him. 'I wonder if you could possibly tell us—'

The man met this with such a glare that she hesitated. 'I won't expect to find you,' he said, 'when I come back.'

'Expect what you like,' Lawrence retorted, but the man had already shut the window as firmly as his lips. As the Jaguar sped past, only just missing the wing mirror of the Viva, Violet saw the driver raise a phone to his face. 'Tell who you want we're here,' Lawrence shouted, twisting around to add 'Tell your whole damned suburb.'

'That isn't necessary, Lawrence. That's not how we behave,' Violet said, though she couldn't help feeling enlivened by how much younger his reaction made him seem. 'Shall we call it a day?'

'Not while there's so much light left. Just say whenever you've had enough of indulging me.'

The confrontation with the driver had affected Violet more than she cared for. Her legs weren't quite steady, any more than her hands were on the wheel. Once she was close to the next street sign she was able to say 'Fetcher.'

'Why are you saying that to me?'

'See, it's why that person did.'

Another of the posters was stuck to the low sign. It showed a dog standing on its hind legs as though perched on its name, which was written larger than the message underneath. That was why the name had sounded familiar, and someone had scribbled over the animal's face. So this was the defacing the Jaguar driver had referred to, and she hoped he'd meant that neither she nor Lawrence could have been involved. 'What's the matter with these people?' Lawrence said. 'Don't they want anyone to find their way?'

She scarcely had time to put the handbrake on before he unleashed himself from his safety belt and stalked over to the sign. Until he helped the wind to lift the poster, which covered half the first word, the sign appeared to name LEY ROAD. He was letting the poster fall back into place when a woman with disorganised grey hair hurried out of the side road, buttoning her long black coat. 'Where's the dog?' she called.

She was wearing leather slippers, Violet saw. Lawrence didn't answer until the questioner was staring up at him from less than a yard away. 'I'm afraid there's no dog.'

'Of course there is. Don't tell me you didn't hear it.' Her voice was growing louder with each phrase. 'You aren't deaf, are you?'

'Is it your dog?'

'Why should it be? We look out for one another round here. We aren't like the rest of the world.' Her frown might have been including him in the repudiation. 'Now will you please finish wasting my time,' she said, 'and tell me where it's gone.'

'There was never any dog.' As she took a breath that suggested she was about to raise her voice even further Lawrence said 'It was me.'

'Don't be so childish.' She had indeed found more of a voice. 'What do you mean, it was you?'

'My attempt at imitation.' When she looked both impatient and uncomprehending Lawrence treated her to a few barks. 'That kind of thing,' he said.

Violet heard how apologetic he meant to be, but the woman stared at him as if facing down an animal. 'Have you really nothing better to do at your age than play tricks?'

'Excuse me, madam, but you'd have to know the context. I—'

She shook her finger at the poster or at him. 'Was that you as well?'

'I hardly think there's much resemblance.'

'You know perfectly well what I mean. Are you responsible for the damage?'

'Do you truthfully think that's how I look?'

'I think you look incapable of answering a simple question.'

'No, I'm not responsible, and I can't believe you could think for an instant I was. Now here's a simple question for you. Can you tell us how to get to—'

'To wherever you ought to be? Just turn right round and scamper back where you came from.' She stalked away but turned to add 'And I wouldn't advise you to do any more pretending.'

As Lawrence yanked at his seat belt so hard that it snagged, Violet murmured 'We don't seem very welcome, do we? Shall we give up and go home?'

'Give up?' He blinked at her as if he hardly recognised her. 'We never would have once,' he said. 'Unless you've had enough of me.'

'You shouldn't say such things. You don't mean it any more than I do.'

'Then carry on.' As he succeeded in fastening his belt he muttered 'They can't keep the magic to themselves.'

He was speaking figuratively, of course, even if it sounded like rather too determined a bid to recapture childhood innocence. History had been his subject as much as hers, and it had taught them how people were led to believe magic was real, not just an enchanting fancy. As she turned along Valley Road she was relieved not to see the woman who'd accosted him, but there was no suggestion of the view he was seeking, just a succession of long squat houses that looked united in anonymity, resolved to exhibit no personality to strangers. Once the road stopped curving Violet saw a sign for Valley Crescent, or at least as much of the name as the dangling poster didn't hide, but this road led her away from the direction Lawrence wanted her to take. She'd begun to share his dogged resolve to find whatever was to be found, and she followed Valley Lane into Valley Drive, which brought her to Valley Avenue. Each sign was partly obscured by a poster about the lost dog, and the face in each photograph had been disfigured beyond recognition, a sight that made Violet feel irrationally guilty, too much of an intruder. She had as much right to use the streets as anyone who lived there, not that a single resident was to be seen. A road presumably called Valley Row led to one that must be Valley Terrace, and she was starting to wonder if the names had been chosen to confuse outsiders. Then Lawrence leaned forward, clasping his hands together so fervently that she could almost have thought he was praying. 'This has to be it,' he said.

The road was straight, and the houses on the side that was presumably closer to his goal were twice the height of the bungalows opposite. Perhaps they had been built to take advantage of a view. Less than halfway along the street Lawrence said 'Yes, here.'

She had barely switched the engine off before he escaped from the harness. When she followed him she found him peering at the unfenced grass in front of the houses. 'I'm sure that's part of the path,' he said.

It wasn't much of one. It was composed of uneven rock almost overgrown enough to pass for an unkempt strip of the lawns it divided, and stretched from a flagstone of the pavement to a solid wooden fence behind the houses. If it was natural, it was unusually straight despite its irregular edges. As Lawrence stepped on it Violet had a qualm of nervousness. 'It's on someone's property,' she said, though this fell short of explaining her unease. 'Do you think we should?'

'It still has to be a right of way. They haven't dared to cover it up,' he said and strode along the path.

Once it passed between the houses it was shut in by fences enclosing the back gardens. The fences were at least seven feet high, like the one that blocked off the path beyond its junction with a narrow alley that led behind the gardens. 'We just need to find the way through,' Lawrence said.

Violet failed to see where, and he plainly couldn't either. He tramped along the alley at a speed suggestive of conviction, only to return before she caught up with him. The opposite stretch of the alley defeated him as well, and she saw him clench his fists so hard that they looked close to fingerless. The next moment he crouched and sprang up in a bid to peer over the fence. 'I think I see—'

Whatever he meant to add was driven into him as his feet struck the ground. Though the impact visibly shook him, it provoked another furious attempt, which allowed him to grab the top of the fence. He was struggling to haul himself up when Violet saw movement at an upstairs window of the nearest house. The woman wasn't gesturing like a prisoner desperate to attract attention. She had been cleaning the inside of the glass, and now she opened the window to call 'You there, what on earth do you think you're doing?'

Lawrence twisted his head around while he clung to the fence. 'Not pretending I'm a dog,' he gasped, 'before you ask.'

'What's that? Just you stay where you are,' the woman said and slammed the window.

Violet had the absurd fancy that the woman was telling Lawrence not to let go of the fence. As his body sagged and began to shiver with the effort of holding on, she clutched at his waist to help him down. When his feet thumped the packed earth hard enough to jar a groan out of him, she felt she had been very little use. Perhaps he was compensating for his frailty and Violet's by growling 'Coming for a word, is she? I've got a few.'

'Don't let's have another scene. Can't we leave it now?'

'I nearly saw. I won't be happy till you have,' he said as they heard a gate being unbolted behind them.

The woman pulled it wide and stood in the frame like a guard. She had silver hair as neat as a fur hat, and was so thoroughly made up to look younger or at any rate less wrinkled that Violet felt dishevelled by comparison. 'What did you say about the dog?' the woman challenged Lawrence.

'I've been looking for it as you all seem to be.' Violet couldn't tell whether he meant to appease the woman or was making a sly joke, even when he added 'And I was looking for your view.'

'You can't see it from here.'

'Then could you tell us how to get to it?'

'That isn't possible. As you say, it's ours.'

'I don't think you can do that, you know. You can't shut the world off from people.'

'That isn't the world.'

Violet had a sense of overhearing a conversation she couldn't grasp, if indeed Lawrence did. 'And I asked,' the woman said, 'what you're to do with the dog.'

'Not a solitary thing. I'm not much of a dog man, and even if I were I don't think I'd be as obsessed with it as you all seem to be.'

'In that case you've no business being here, and I'd recommend you make yourself scarce.'

'Not till I've found why I'm here.' Perhaps hearing his own clumsiness made Lawrence blurt 'If you really think we're trespassing, why don't you see what the police say.'

'We don't need them.'

If this was a warning, it only antagonised him. 'Do your worst, then,' he said, 'and meanwhile you'll forgive me if I keep looking.'

As he set off at speed along the alley Violet said to the woman 'Couldn't you just let him finish looking? He was here as a boy.'

'And what's he here as now? I shouldn't let him stray,' the woman said and shut the gate in Violet's face.

Violet regretted lingering to stare at the gate as if she were somehow confronting the woman, because when she turned away Lawrence was out of sight. 'Lawrence,' she called, both an appeal and a rebuke, as she hurried down the alley to a bend, certainly not the dead end that her momentary panic made it seem to be. She was nearly there when she heard him.

He sounded excited, even shrill, although she didn't catch the solitary syllable that had been startled out of him. 'Lawrence,' she repeated, but perhaps he was too preoccupied to respond. She was panting when she reached the corner of the alley, not as promptly as she would have expected of herself. At least she could see why Lawrence must have yelped in tri-umph. Just around the corner there was a gap in the fence.

He still wasn't to be seen. He'd crawled through the opening, then. It was an irregularly rounded hole less than four feet wide and not even as high, at the bottom of a section of the fence that looked older and more weathered than the rest. Violet couldn't help thinking of the kind of aperture some pet owners might incorporate in a door; certainly it might have tempted the lost dog. 'Lawrence,' she called more sharply as she crouched towards the gap.

She couldn't see through it by simply stooping. The posture sent pain flaring up her spine into her skull. She had to lower herself onto all fours on the prickly concrete and duck towards the opening. The low sun met her, shining directly into her eyes, so that she was scarcely able to distinguish that the sliver of fierce light appeared to be resting on the edge of a cliff. Was there a path, either the one they'd followed from the road or another track crossing it on top of the cliff? Violet squeezed her eyes shut and wid-ened them, which didn't help at all; either the sun had subsided beneath the edge or it had been overwhelmed by cloud, because all she could see through the gap was a pallid expanse as featureless as a void, as if the fence was perched on the brink of the cliff.

Her perspective must have changed. Perhaps she'd crouched lower without noticing. She was about to wriggle through the gap as a preamble to lecturing Lawrence for making her do so when a fiercer stab of pain brought her almost to her feet. She gasped as her hands struck the spongy fence, which felt cold enough for the moisture it exuded to be close to frozen. 'Lawrence, say where you are,' she shouted and heard her voice invade the silence – just her voice, which made her feel more intrusive than ever, as though every resident who could hear her disapproved of her. She didn't need to shout when she had a phone. She wavered to her feet and fumbled the mobile out of the padded pocket of her plump coat, and poked the key to call Lawrence's number.

When she heard the bell inside her phone she tried to hear where his ringtone might be, but the simulation in her phone gave just a single trill before it was cut off. She just had time to glimpse an image on the screen – a figure whose upright stance looked somehow unnatural. Perhaps she was reminded of the posters she'd seen in Striders Halt because the face was disintegrating into a mass of pixels. She had no chance to read the displayed name, which seemed shorter than Lawrence's, as the phone emitted a bleep like the isolated note of an alarm and the screen went blank. She was pressing the power button – squeezing it without result – when she thought she heard Lawrence.

Had he called 'Yes'? The high sharp sound resembled that word more than any other. He was somewhere around the corner – in the alley, Violet hoped, not on the far side of the fence. She hurried to the corner and peered along the alley, which seemed to have grown unreasonably dimmer. Surely the sun shouldn't have taken so much of the light with it, though enough remained to show her that the alley was deserted. 'Lawrence,' she called. 'Tell me where you are.'

Her voice petered out between the fences, giving way to a silence so total that she might not have spoken at all. What childish game was he playing? Even if he wanted to reward her with some surprise he thought she would appreciate, she wasn't enjoying his behaviour. 'Lawrence,' she called more and more furiously, 'Lawrence,' as she marched along the alley, searching for another gap, even a chink in the fence. She was still looking and, more desperately, listening when the alley brought her to the corner of the road.

The unbroken fence stretched out of sight, presumably following the edge of the cliff. The premature twilight made her aware of the absence of streetlamps. She could have concluded that whoever had developed Striders Halt didn't care to waste any light on visitors, though the street was visible enough, the blank windows of the bungalows competing with their doubles across the deserted roadway to reveal no evidence of life. She was about to call to Lawrence when she was distracted by the street sign. She'd assumed the first syllable of Valley Terrace was covered up, but now that the poster had fallen off as though it was no longer required, she saw the word was only half the length she'd taken it to be.

A chill wind brought the poster fluttering towards her across the arid flagstones. The face of the begging pet hadn't just been scribbled out; someone had tried to substitute a caricature of another face, so vigorously that they'd shredded the paper. Violet might have fancied that the damage had exposed features underlying the animal's face. Why couldn't she read the lines printed beneath Fetcher's name? Even if some computer problem must have been responsible for the repetitive gibberish, she thought it odd that nobody had noticed. All this was distracting her from finding

Lawrence. As the poster sank flat on the pavement she called his name, and turned just in time to glimpse a response.

It could only be Lawrence. The movement had been by the Viva, and of course that was where he would have met her, presumably to lead her to the view he'd rediscovered. She thought he'd beckoned her to follow, since it was the only gesture that made sense, before returning to the path between the houses. 'Just wait,' she cried, 'what on earth's the urgency?' Perhaps some aspect of the view was about to disappear with the waning light, and she hurried to the path so as not to disappoint him. But when she reached the alley behind the houses she found it was deserted.

'What are you playing at, Lawrence? Show yourself, for heaven's sake.' She gasped all this as she tramped along the alley, though her voice was too breathless to travel very far. He must have gone back to the gap in the fence – she'd begun to think he had been crouching as he dodged along the path, as though getting ready to crawl through the hole – but surely he could have waited for her at the corner. 'All right, show me—' she urged as she came to the bend, and then her voice died in her mouth. It wasn't only Lawrence that she couldn't see. There was no gap in the fence.

The sight seemed to turn not just her mouth dry but her mind, parching it of the ability to think. When she faltered to the section of the fence where she was sure the gap had been, she felt as if she might have to support herself against it – might even discover that it wasn't solid. But it bruised her fist as she thumped the new wood, which was indistinguishable from the rest of the fence. She was almost bewildered enough to wonder if the fence could have been repaired while she was searching for Lawrence, and then she had the equally unwelcome notion that she had somehow mistaken her way – that the gap must be at the other end of the alley. If her ageing brain had let her down, surely she could bear the possibility so long as she found Lawrence. Perhaps becoming each other's mental backup would be part of growing old. She needn't be ashamed to admit she'd lost her way, though wasn't Lawrence's behaviour responsible? Once they were reunited she'd decide how much to blame him and how soon she would forgive him. All these thoughts kept her going almost as far as the opposite end of the alley, until she could no longer avoid seeing that there wasn't so much as a crack in the fence.

As she stumbled out beside the street sign the poster lying on the flagstones stirred, raising its disintegrated face. 'Lawrence,' she shouted and was turning towards her car when a figure peered around the house beside the path and ducked back. She was sure it was Lawrence, but how could he act like that? Had senility overtaken him all at once? She called his name over and over, though increasingly feebly, as she made for the path.

It was as deserted as the street, and so was the alley. Violet felt close to releasing a scream of frustration, if not another kind. She was peering wildly about as if her desperation could produce Lawrence when she caught sight of the window she'd seen the woman cleaning. It was blankly curtained now, but it was the only inspiration Violet could find. She limped up the path and along the street to the front of the house. 'Hello?' she cried as soon as she'd rung the doorbell.

She didn't hear another sound until a silhouette appeared on the frosted glass that made up most of the front door. The outline of the figure was fragmented by the swarming nodules of the glass, which left the face as a pale blur. 'Why are you making all that noise?' the woman demanded, barely audibly. 'Who do you think you are?'

'I know who I am.' Saying so wouldn't help, and Violet said only 'You saw me behind your house. You spoke to me.'

'Count yourself privileged. I've no more to add.'

'I'm looking for my husband.'

'You won't find him in here.'

'But you saw him as well,' Violet pleaded and felt a twinge of hope. 'You were watching him, weren't you? Didn't you see where he went?'

'He can't be far.'

'No, but he could be lost.' At once this seemed altogether too possible. 'I'm sure a stranger could get lost round here,' she said.

'Not for long.'

Violet couldn't tell why this sounded ominous: perhaps because that was how the thought of losing Lawrence made everything feel – the empty street as dim as the interior of the house, the figure that seemed disinclined to take shape on the glass. 'May I use your phone?' she blurted.

'You most certainly can not.'

Violet tried to believe she'd mistaken the murmur. 'I need to call my husband. My phone's dead.'

'They aren't welcome here.'

Violet suspected this meant far more than her phone and Lawrence's. 'Just help me find him,' she begged, 'and we'll leave you alone.'

'He'll be found.'

Why should this seem threatening? It aggravated Violet's growing panic. 'Help me,' she said furiously, 'or I'll make such a noise it'll wake the whole place up.'

'No need. It's awake,' the woman said, and her silhouette decomposed further as it shrank into the darkness of the house.

'You can't get rid of me like that. You won't until I've found my husband,' Violet cried and was about to create more of a disturbance – however much would bring the residents out of their houses to help her – when she heard Lawrence call her name.

It was only the first syllable. She'd never liked being abbreviated, but now it was more than welcome, even when it was yipped as shrilly as that. He was further away than the street, but at least the sound hadn't come from the direction of the cliff. 'Lawrence,' she shouted as she swung around, nearly losing her balance. 'Come here. Come back.'

The empty street seemed to capture her voice, holding it in. The unlit houses, where every window was colourlessly blank with curtains, emphasised the gathering darkness. She could have believed the night was cutting her off from Lawrence. 'Talk to me,' she shouted. 'I'll come to you.'

'Don't.'

Why would he say that to her? What would have made him say it to someone else? Surely she'd misheard him. 'I'm coming now,' she vowed and dashed to the car.

As she strapped herself in she was overtaken by a notion that she wasn't sure she welcomed. How could all this be anything except a nightmare? She was asleep in the passenger seat while Lawrence drove them home, and soon she would waken to find they were safe. She was tempted to think so, and yet it dismayed her; it felt like betraying Lawrence, abandoning him to the unlit indifferent streets. She mustn't use the idea that she was dreaming as an excuse not to find him. She lowered both front windows of the car and felt as if she were letting in the icy night to keep her awake. 'Lawrence,' she called as she switched on the headlights. 'Keep talking to me.'

While she turned the car the headlamp beams lit up a bungalow and then its twin, followed by one that could have been either of them. Driving straight on would have brought her to a dead end, and in any case she felt lost enough without venturing into the unknown dark. She coasted to the junction at not much more than a walking pace while she peered ahead hard enough to sting her eyes and called Lawrence's name. As she eased the car out of the road she heard him.

She was about to respond when she realised she was hearing a dog. It was the first she'd heard in Striders Halt, and how long had it been since she'd ceased hearing birds? The yapping sounded not far from articulate, which was why she'd taken it for a human voice, though she didn't want to wonder why Lawrence would have been protesting 'No no no.' If it was the elusive Fetcher, someone else could catch the animal. 'Lawrence,' she called louder, but the only answer was another burst of frenzied yapping. She was almost at the next junction when she saw the creature ahead.

It might well be Fetcher, since it was performing the trick all the posters had shown. It was rearing up to beg even though nobody was offering it a treat. Before Violet could distinguish more than a large vague silhouette, it dropped to all fours and dodged around the corner. When she reached the corner both roads were deserted. She mustn't be distracted by it or by wondering why nobody had come out of the houses to catch it. 'Lawrence,' she shouted as if she could dismiss the creature and recall him, but only the dark chill wind came to her through the open windows. She hadn't seen or heard any hint of his whereabouts by the time she reached the village green.

Had she left the streets behind too soon? Had she managed to miss out some of them? She stared at the dark huddle of bungalows as if by making her eyes ache she might bring Lawrence into the open, and then she fumbled her phone out of her pocket. She was hoping it might have regained some of the power it had lost in Striders Halt, but it was still as dead as the rectangular stone it resembled. She had to believe Lawrence wasn't out here; he couldn't have been faster than the car.

She didn't know how many times she drove through the lightless streets – how often they brought her back to the green. How frequently did she pass the Jaguar, which was once again parked on its drive? There might well be more than one, taunting her with the illusion that she knew where she was. Her voice had grown hoarse and dry with calling out to Lawrence. Even sounding the horn failed to bring any life to the introverted streets, which she could have imagined were dreaming of themselves. She was driving desperately faster now, as though she could overtake Lawrence in the act of losing himself. While she knew that one of them would eventually have to lose the other, she could never have dreamed it would be anything like this. She had the sudden awful thought that he hadn't been truly lost until she'd told the woman that he might be. If this was in any way possible, oughtn't it to mean that she could bring him back as well?

She cried his name and leaned on the horn, and saw the only other creature in the streets dodge beyond the limit of her headlights. It was yapping again, however much this sounded like a voice struggling to tell her to go, go, go. She could even have imagined that it was fleeing the light, as though ashamed to be seen. Suppose it could lead her to Lawrence? She wasn't quite confused enough to believe that, but she saw that she was following it anyway, having forgotten which way she'd meant to drive through the streets, which had begun to seem malevolently unhelpful. She lost sight of the creature well before the streets led her yet again to the green.

She braked with a screech that sounded like her dismay rendered audible, and then she clambered out of the car. She felt as if the mob of lightless houses had cast her out – would continue doing so every time she searched for Lawrence. She strove one last time to think she was having a nightmare, a distorted version of her wish and Lawrence's to bring some magic back into their life. Soon she would waken to find herself in the passenger seat, but she knew that wasn't possible; Lawrence had never learned to drive. Her hands were shaking so much that she could hardly cup them around her mouth. 'Lawrence,' she cried, 'come back.'

Her words were aching not merely in her ears but throughout her entire self when she thought she heard a voice somewhere among the houses. 'Let it go.'

She couldn't tell whether it was addressing her. As she strained her eyes at the mass of bungalows, she saw a figure dart out between them. The headlight beams were splayed across the green towards the larger darkness, making it harder for her to distinguish the shape. It was yapping and panting, and the face on the blurred shaggy head seemed more fragmentary than it ought to be, fluttering in the chill wind. When the figure reared up in front of her she didn't know whether it meant to beg or plant its paws on her shoulders and nuzzle her face. All she could do was cry 'Lawrence.'

pos′ses′sions *pl.* 1: become the owner or possessor *of*; 2: thing possessed; 3: the act of having or taking into control; 4: domination by something (as an evil spirit, a passion, or an idea); 5: a psychological state in which an individual's personality is replaced by that of another. First known use: 14th century. Synonyms: control, keeping, yours. Example: *Objects that you possess which can, in turn, possess others. Such as an old camera . . .*

POSSESSIONS

REGGIE OLIVER

I T WAS THE last place I wanted to be that Saturday morning. Mr Berry detached a couple of keys from a large ring of them in his possession. With one he opened the door. From the room beyond the open door came a smell, or rather an atmosphere. It was not rank, but it was redolent of staleness, old age, and neglect. You didn't need to be told that an old man had died there only the week before.

'There we go,' said Mr Berry, the landlord, almost heartily, before returning to his usual sour manner. 'Now, I want this place cleared by Sunday night. I've got the decorators coming in first thing Monday morning and I need to have it ready for re-letting as soon as possible. In my business I'm afraid I can't afford to hang about. I'm not a charity, you know.'

If ever a remark did not need saying, that last sentence was it. Berry was an obese man with a bulbous, self-satisfied face: one of those people who take pride in 'not standing any nonsense'. I would get no sympathy from him, not that I wanted it.

'Any junk you don't want, you take to the tip. I'm not having it put by the bins outside, or I'll have the Council onto me like a ton of bricks. The only thing you leave is the furniture. All that belongs to me.' He hesitated. 'Er . . . Apart from that bureau thing. But, provided you empty all the drawers you can leave that here if you want to. I don't mind.' I was quite sure he wouldn't mind. Though suffering from neglect, it was still late Georgian, mahogany, and the only decent stick of furniture in the room. 'Well, I'll leave you to it.' Berry hesitated again. 'You going to take that with you?' He pointed to a picture above the mantelpiece.

I nodded.

246 | REGGIE OLIVER

'So Mr Vilier was your uncle, was he?'

'That's right.'

'Huh!' The sound expressed both pity and contempt. 'Didn't leave you much, did he?'

I shrugged my shoulders. The truth is I had barely known him. Berry gave me the keys to the flat and front door with instructions that I was to return them to him on Sunday night 'without fail' by which time he expected the place to be free of all my uncle's possessions and 'immaculate'. That last demand was an imposture: I was there to clear, not to clean. I raised an eyebrow; Berry understood. Then he was off, surprisingly rapidly for a man of his bulk.

The flat was on the first floor of a terraced house in one of those little roads that run at right angles to Upper Street, Islington. When first built in the early 19th century, they had been desirable dwellings for the rising middle class, then they had gone down in the world. When, in the late 1960s and early '70s, much of Islington had become fashionable again, these houses stubbornly refused to rise with it. They remained for the most part divided into flats for the impoverished but aspiring young and the downtrodden elderly. A thick spattering of yellowish grime, like a skin disease, infected the windows that looked onto the street.

I switched on the light but the room still looked dingy, bathed in a nicotine-stained glow. Besides the large main room which I had entered, there was a bedroom and bathroom and a small galley kitchen. Apart from the picture above the mantelpiece, decoration was limited to a few framed photographs. There were no ornaments. Bookshelves were stacked with untidy heaps of magazines and books relating to the subject of my uncle's former profession, photography.

It would not be true to say that my mother's brother, Hubert Vilier, had been anything so melodramatic as 'the black sheep of the family'. He simply was not mentioned, and he never attended family gatherings or wrote, as far as I knew, so much as a Christmas card to any of us. I knew he existed and that, more or less, was it. My occasional fits of curiosity about him were always rebuffed. My mother would tell me that she did not know where Uncle Hubert lived or what he was up to, but this, I discovered after her death, was untrue.

Among her papers I found his address and evidence that she had occasionally been sending him small sums of money. Thinking that Uncle Hubert should at least be informed of my mother's death I decided to pay a call on him. He received me but refused to come to the funeral. I paid one or two calls on him subsequently, but they were in no way pleasurable experiences. Once he asked me for 'a loan' of a hundred pounds, which I never expected to get back and didn't. Then, within barely a year of my mother's passing, he also went and I was shocked to discover from his solicitor that I was the sole beneficiary of his will. I was also the sole 'mourner' at his funeral.

For the weekend I had hired a van and also sufficient boxes and packing cases in which to transport his effects. So, that Saturday morning, I began the task of clearing the flat, vaguely aware that in so doing I was removing from the earth the last traces of a human life.

It was as dull and dispiriting a business as I had expected it to be. His clothes, some of which had once been expensive, were patched and often threadbare, none of them suitable even for a charity shop. Crockery and cutlery was of the cheapest; few of the books were worth keeping or selling. He seemed to have led a minimal lifestyle. I discovered no alcohol bottles empty or full, so even that pleasure seems to have been denied him. There was one unwashed plate still lying in the sink. It had been a life as barren as it was lonely.

The framed photographs were his own work. They were moody black and white shots of derelict buildings, rundown estates, decaying industrial wasteland, subjects still popular today with 'art photographers'. They were competent, but no better or worse than countless others I had seen. There seemed to be no originality in his aesthetic. Besides, the images were faded at the edges and beginning to peel away from their mounts. The only picture that interested me was the painting above the fireplace that Berry had obviously coveted.

It was a three-quarter-length portrait in oils of a girl with long blonde hair standing at a balcony and looking out with a wistful expression. The brushwork was competent; it had obviously been painted by someone who had been professionally trained. Parts of the composition – the hand resting on the balcony for example – were clumsily done, but it had a freshness and sincerity that were compelling. The girl was wearing a high-waisted gown that had a Renaissance feel to it and the elaborate braids in her blonde hair enhanced the effect. She was beautiful. I remembered how on my last visit to Uncle Hubert I had asked him about the picture.

For some time he had stared at me in silence with his angry, watery old eyes. I realised at once that I had trespassed on forbidden territory, but I was not going to apologise. It was he, after all, who owed me money and not the other way round. Realising at last that I was not going to be daunted, he turned his glance away from me and stared out of the window.

'I had her once,' he said in a faraway voice. 'Several times . . . Many times . . . Still do.' He started to mumble something. It was as if his thoughts, like his voice, were receding into the distance, but I caught their drift roughly.

'There are some so-called 'primitive' tribes – in New Guinea, I think, or is it the Amazon rain forest? – Oh, bloody hell, who cares? Anyway, these guys refuse to be photographed because they think that in capturing their image, you are also capturing a part of their soul, their spirit, whatever . . . Well, I'll tell you something for nothing. They're not so bloody primitive as we think; they're not so bloody stupid. Eh? All you need is the equipment. Eh? That's all I'm saying.'

Then he looked back at me, his eyes once more alive to me and the present moment.

'You think I'm just a drivelling old man, don't you? You don't understand a word I'm saying.'

I shook my head. 'That's right. I don't.'

'Good . . . Good . . .!'

He gave a sort of catarrhal wheeze, which I took to be his attempt at a laugh. There is the kind of egoist who wants you to love and know all about them; but there is another more dangerous kind who wants to remain an enigma and confound you with the illusion of mysterious power.

Now he was dead I was at liberty to pursue my own investigations. I took the picture off the wall and examined it more closely. It was the work of an artist with talent, but the talent was only partially formed. I turned the picture over. On the back of the canvas in charcoal were scrawled the words: *LW as Juliet, May 1961* – and then a signature which I recognised as that of my uncle Hubert Vilier.

Uncle Hubert had told me very little about his life, but I did gather he had been at the Slade and trained in the fine arts before embarking on a career in photography. This canvas was a survival from that early period in his life. Obviously it meant something to him, but who was LW?

On that last visit of mine he had said nothing more to me which offered any clue to her identity. He rambled on, as old people do, especially those who have stopped caring whether they are being listened to or not. Much of what he said was barely audible. I remember that he had muttered something to me about 'getting to Irving House' but when I asked him where it was and whether I could give him a lift there he merely made another attempt to laugh and shook his head: again that malicious delight in mystification. He said something like: 'I'll get there under my own steam,' which I thought was nonsense. After that he stared at the window and lapsed into the kind of intense silence that told me he no longer required my presence. I took the hint and left. The next time I saw him he was at the undertakers in his coffin.

By late Saturday afternoon I had cleared away most of my uncle's possessions either into packing cases, or in bin bags for destruction. The lightest of these I put into the van. There would need to be a further trip on the morrow with an assistant for the bulkier items. The walls were now bare, the windows uncurtained, the furniture stripped of cushion and cover. Beyond the window the Islington daylight had faded; Uncle Hubert's flat looked like a corpse, an untenanted shape, void of sense. There remained only the mahogany bureau to empty. I had left it till last; I don't know why.

It was a kneehole affair with a top that folded down and drawers, all of them locked. I was reassured by this. At least Mr Berry had not been there before me; but it meant that I had to find the keys.

Fortunately – I suppose – my business is antique furniture and I had seen something like this particular model before. Under the kneehole, usually on the right hand side, there is a small stud which, when turned, releases a narrow secret drawer in the kneehole's mantle. Knowing something of Uncle Hubert's suspicious and reclusive nature I guessed that the keys might be found in the secret compartment, and I was right. But they took some finding; the stud was more cunningly concealed than usual. It was dark outside before I had my hands on the keys. I should have gone home then, but I was driven: I had been robbed of hunger and tiredness by my curiosity. Is that the right word? A part of me did not want to know, but somehow I had to.

When I unlocked and folded down the top of the desk its contents almost exploded onto me, like a Jack-in-the Box. An untidy riot of papers, newspaper clippings and photographs had been crammed in to the space with no regard for neatness or order. My first instinct was to shovel the entire contents into a bin bag, but I was stopped.

It was not a noise that halted me, but its opposite, silence. Suddenly, for no apparent reason, the gentle hum of traffic, coming mainly from Upper Street beyond the window, ceased altogether. Perhaps something was wrong with my ears, but no. When I stirred the papers on the desk the sound was more sharply defined than ever. The crackling was like an assault. I felt enclosed, guided.

I sat down at the desk on a rickety Windsor chair and pulled the last remaining packing case up to my side. Then I began to work through and put in order the papers before me. I did so with a kind of conspicuous deliberation, like an office worker who knows he is being spied on by a suspicious boss. Did I believe I was being watched? No. I am only saying that I felt compelled to behave *as if* I was being watched.

Nearly all the material related to his work as a photographer. I had vaguely assumed that Uncle Hubert had not been a success in his chosen profession. On the few occasions that I met him he had spoken little of his former life but he gave off an overall feeling of failure, hinting that his conspicuous talents had not been given their due. In particular there was one matter in which he felt he had been cheated, but he offered no details. Everything was spoken of in the vaguest possible terms, but the general impression was that he had fought against the world and that the world, by distinctly underhand means, had won.

By contrast, what lay before me on the desk suggested that my Uncle Hubert had, for a while at least in the 1960s and early '70s, enjoyed quite conspicuous success. There were fashion shoots for *Harper's* and *Vogue*, extending over several pages; there were portraits of celebrities for the Sunday Supplements; there was a series on the London underworld illustrated with his photographs for *Vanity Fair*, and others on Ascot, Henley and similar upper crust jamborees. Newspaper clippings of fashionable events mentioned his presence. Evidently he had been something of a celebrity in his own right. I was startled by one picture in particular, a glossy full plate press photo with a typewritten caption pasted on the back, but it had not been taken by my uncle.

It showed a young man crouching over a Hasselblad camera on a tripod, in the act of taking a picture. One hand is on the camera, the other extended in front of him as if he is giving direction to his subject. He wears a floral patterned shirt with a wide button-down collar, and tight jeans that show off his slender figure. His gently waved blond hair falls to his shoulders framing a heart-shaped face of almost feminine beauty. He is a 1960s icon, a snake-hipped Adonis, a Carnaby Street Narcissus. A mirror, cleverly placed behind him, shows his back and beyond, the subject of his photo, a long-legged model in black stockings lounging elegantly against a tall bar stool. The typewritten slip of paper on the back read as follows:

> *Hip young photographer Hube Vilier in his Soho Studio: 'To me photography is not just a craft, but a way of life, a means of self-expression.'*

In pencil someone had added the date '*1966*'.

So this was the young Uncle Hubert. It was getting late and I had eaten nothing since a snatched sandwich at lunch. That accounts, at least partly, for the giddiness and the strange horror I felt at the picture. The Uncle Hubert I had known was a wreck: sparse white hair straggling over a scabbed and mottled cranium; heavy jowls falling in thick wrinkled folds from his withered face; the corners of his mouth pulled down in a permanent grimace of angry discontent. Only a similar look in the eyes – wild, intense, cornflower blue – established any connection with the young god in the photograph. What had happened? It was that speculation which made me shiver, though I must admit that the room had suddenly become much colder.

I looked at my watch. It was nearly eleven. I decided to put all the papers into the packing case beside me without examining them any further. This I did, though my attention was caught by one further item. It was a typewritten letter on expensive headed notepaper. The printed name at the top belonged to a well-known manufacturer of film and photographic equipment. The letter was dated 6th May, 1973.

Dear Mr Vilier,

Thank you very much for allowing us to consider your most ingenious device. I herewith return the prototype and samples of your work. Though it has provoked considerable interest, I regret to say that your proposal does not, we believe, hold out sufficient commercial possibilities for us to want to take it further. Considerably more research and development would be required for it to be made into a marketable venture and the financial terms that you propose would make the expense prohibitive. I nonetheless wish you every success with your project.

Yours sincerely . . .

A scrawled, illegible signature followed, but the bottom half of the letter had been torn off, perhaps in a rage, so that the name of the sender remained unknown.

When I had emptied the top of the desk, I tackled the drawers in the two pedestals. In the three drawers on the right-hand side I found nothing of great interest apart from a packet of letters, all written in the same hand. I also found a dozen or so of his business cards: purple, adorned with yellow psychedelic arabesques, and lettering in the same colour bearing the legend HUBE VILIER, PHOTOGRAPHER together with the address of his studio in Dean Street, Soho. The left-hand pedestal of the desk consisted of one single deep drawer made to look like the three on the other side and unlocked from the top. In it were a number of photograph albums and a large square box of black leather. It was heavy and I suspected it contained a camera, but I did not look. By this time I was anxious to get away.

I heaved the packing case full of the desk's contents downstairs and into my hired van outside. I would return, with an assistant, to fetch the rest the following day.

The street outside Uncle Hubert's flat appeared to be deserted. Sounds of traffic from Upper Street were faint and intermittent. I lifted the packing case into the back of the van, yawning as I did so. I had stayed far too long, and there was a considerable drive ahead of me.

I had parked the car some distance away from the front door to Hubert's flat, there having been no nearer space available. As I closed the door of the van I looked back at the house and saw that the first floor window – the window of his apartment – was open and someone was leaning out. The figure was little more than a dark shape – the street light did not illuminate much – but I could tell it was the figure of a woman, very slight, anorexially thin. Though no more than a shadow I had the strong feeling that she was looking at me. Then she stretched out her hands in a pleading or begging gesture, and at that moment I thought I saw others joining her at the window.

At the time I felt not so much fear as rage that something was trying to prevent me from going home to a good night's sleep. I turned away, got in the van, slammed the door and drove off. I did not calm down until I was several miles away and suddenly realised that I was speeding through the streets of London at over sixty miles an hour. Back at my house in Chiswick an hour or so later I found that I was exhausted but unable to sleep.

I dozed fitfully, then, at about seven in the morning, I gave up all hope of rest. I removed some of my uncle's possessions from the van and put them into my front room. There were items that I needed to examine. My mind had become so obsessed with them that it would not let me sleep.

Firstly there was the black leather box. It was a costly affair with silver fittings and a lock for which I could find no key. I forced it with a chisel. Inside I found, embedded in foam covered with dark red velvet, a camera as I had expected, but it was no ordinary camera. It had been custom built with two lenses, parallel and about two inches apart, about the distance of a pair of adult eyes. At the back there was a corresponding pair of eyeholes. There were other devices and dials on it which were not to be found on an ordinary camera and whose significance I could not even guess at. On a brass plate at the back of the camera were engraved the words: PATENT APPLIED FOR. HV.

Then there were the albums. They were lavishly bound in gilded and tooled leather and most of them contained a record of his work for magazines, exhibitions and private clients. These provided further evidence, if evidence were needed, that my uncle was a gifted man. But there were two volumes which were rather different.

One was what I can only describe as a family album, though it was like no family album I have ever seen, or hope to see again. On the first page there was a picture of my mother and father on their wedding day. They have just emerged from the country church where they were married and their arms are linked, but they are looking in different directions smiling wistfully. Neither is looking at the camera. A slight blur of vegetation on the extreme right of the picture suggests that the photo has been taken covertly from a hiding place in the churchyard. Other pictures of the wedding give the same indication. In one we see the official wedding photographer trying to get a shot of the bridal pair while my mother's veil is blowing across her face. The photographer is looking annoyed and my father distressed. There is a kind of cruel comedy about the image. Later on I see a picture of myself at the age of five and my mother in our garden at home. I appear to be discontented and my mother is trying to pacify me. In the background my father is looking on with a curious expression of detached revulsion on his face. Clearly the photograph was not posed and had been taken secretly. I mention this picture in particular because it must have been shortly after it was taken that my father left my mother, never to return. Other pictures of myself and my family always show us outdoors or in some public place, clearly unconscious of being observed. Here I am walking to school, a look of furious concentration on my face; here I am sitting at the edge of a football pitch nursing a grazed knee, caught in a moment of maudlin self-pity. I hate that aspect of myself and resent that this little private disgrace was stolen from me and put in a book. There is even a picture of me clumsily trying to kiss my first girlfriend on a tennis court. I shut the book in disgust.

Tiredness no doubt enhanced my feelings of anger and betrayal. I made myself some coffee, but it did nothing for my nerves. I paced about the room. There was one more album to look at. I had saved it till last because it had been peculiarly lavishly bound in morocco leather with a monogram of my uncle's initials HV stamped in gold on the front.

The photographs inside were the strangest and most terrible that I have ever seen. But I don't mean that they showed horrors: quite the opposite in a way.

At first glance they appeared to be a series of female nudes, mono-chrome but printed in a kind of sepia tint onto a velvety, semi-matt paper. The backgrounds are vague and shadowy but suggest infinite and lonely distances. The first thing that had struck me about the photographs was the extraordinary detail and sense of perspective that they conveyed. They looked three-dimensional.

The females portrayed were all young, some barely out of puberty. They were shown full length, some crouching, others standing, one cowering on a bed with crumpled sheets gathered around her. They were slender and beautiful, but these were not pornographic images because you couldn't possibly be aroused by them. On every face fear was written. All were looking directly at the camera in terror. The sheer quality of the images gave their common feeling an almost tangible reality. Their eyes were wide and a sort of desperate emptiness had entered into them, as if they knew that they would never again know happiness. The infinite shadows that lurked behind were about to engulf them; the crumpled sheets of the girl on the bed would rear up and strangle her.

It was hard to look at them, even harder to tear my eyes away, such was the fascinating vividness of these works. Though still, the images gave an illusion of potential movement as if the subjects had been temporarily frozen in the moment. It reminded me of when I had seen my mother dead in the hospital. I knew she would no longer move, but somehow I still expected movement, and my mind played little tricks on me as I stared at her corpse.

The last image in the book was the most striking. It showed a girl, naked like the others, with long blonde hair, who appeared to be in the act of running away from the camera, but she has turned around and is staring back in terror at her pursuer. The background was a little more defined than in the other images. She appeared to be in a forest whose trees stretched into an infinite grey distance. The three dimensional quality of the print gave an extraordinary illusion of vast space, as if I only had to stretch out my hand and it would pass through the furry surface of the photo and into the cold void beyond. What the camera sees but she does not as she looks back in her flight is that a tree root, like a great black serpent, is curled across her path. The moment after that picture was taken she would have tripped and fallen headlong onto the cold grey forest floor.

I needed to shut the album and get on with my life, but the image held me. There was something about the face which seemed familiar. It was not long before I realised that I was looking at LW, the subject of my uncle's painting.

Who was LW? What was she in my uncle's life? Once the question was in my head I had to know. I began to sort through the papers that I had taken from the bureau the night before. Suddenly I remembered a packet of letters tied with string, that I had barely glanced at. They were written in violet ink on pale blue paper and some of the envelopes that came with them were decorated with crudely drawn flowers. They were written to my Uncle Hubert at an address in Glebe Place, Chelsea.

They were love letters and they were signed Leila. Surely this was LW? Further evidence that this was so came from occasional references in the letter to work in theatre, film and television. LW had been an actress, that much the portrait made clear; so was Leila.

Even though the letters were almost fifty years old I still felt uneasy reading them. Leila was young, naïve, adoring. She expressed herself in clichés, as the sincere nearly always do. I felt like an intruder, and very little information could be gleaned from them, other than that Leila worshipped my uncle and that he was sometimes angry with her and that she always regarded it as her fault. Only the last letter of all contributed a degree of objectivity to the affair.

Heathrow, Friday Morning,

My darling Hube,

You may well be surprised by the address at the top, but please, please don't be too cross. I expect you will be cross anyway, but, well, it has to be, I guess. Here I am at Heathrow, and I have about an hour before I get on a plane to fly to the States. I'm sorry I didn't tell you I was going but you would only have tried to stop me going and there would have been a horrible row, and you know I can't stand rows. So by the time you read this I will be squillions of miles across the pond and I haven't got a phone number or anything, so you'll just have to wait till I write again or whatever. The thing is, my agent has got me a film part over there. I know it's only another horror flick and probably grotty as hell, but it's work, and I need the bread and I need to get my head together. You see, darling Hube — and don't frown like that, you'll get wrinkles!!! — though I love you to absolute bits — I honestly do! — I simply can't go on like this. And it's not the other girls – though that hurts, it really does – and it's not the rows which I loathe or even the hitting and the violence because anyway you always (nearly always) say sorry after that. No, it's – oh, this is so hard to explain – it's like when I'm with you I somehow feel I don't exist as a person. I'm a kind of nothing. All right, I'm your girl, your popsy, your sweetheart, but I don't belong to ME. Do you understand? No, I don't expect you do. Well, you remember that time we went together to Biba and you chose a dress for me and I wanted the other one and you just went up to the counter and bought it anyway, then hustled me out of the shop before I could look at anything else. I felt so low about that for days. Yes, I know it sounds silly and you almost certainly have far better taste than I do, you're such a star, such a genius, but that's not the point. Sometimes I just want my own thing and to do my own thing, but you want me to be your thing the whole time and I just can't do that. Anyway, that's why I'm going to L A to do this film, and I know it sounds silly and feeble and all that, and it probably is, but that's how I feel right now. But I still love you, darling Hube, and I still think you're the fabbest most brilliant genius in the whole world! So don't think too badly of —

Your ever loving
Leila

– and the rest of the page is a forest of X's.

At ten that Sunday morning Martin came round. Martin is by way of being an actor, but most of the time he is unemployed in his chosen profession, so I pay him to assist me in my business. It's mostly moving furniture about, bidding for me at auctions, general dogsbodying. Today he was going to help me move Hubert's desk and the last of his stuff out of the flat.

Martin is one of those people who never likes to start work straight away. He has to have a coffee, chat, smoke one of his vile cigarettes before he'll get down to anything. I humour him in this because he's cheap and doesn't complain much if I haul him out at odd hours. As it happened this morning I rather wanted to get away, clear my uncle's flat and be done with it, so I became increasingly impatient when Martin would not finish his coffee or stop wittering on. Before we left for Islington he insisted on seeing what I had already got out of the flat.

He walked into the sitting room where I had put most of the stuff, sipping his coffee.

'Didn't leave you much, the old sod, did he?'

He paused before the painting of 'LW as Juliet'. He considered it in silence. I was becoming impatient.

'Do you recognise her?' I asked. 'I think it's an actress.'

'Isn't that Leila Winstone?'

'An actress?'

'Yes. Before my time. In the 1960s and early '70s. She was quite big for a while. You know: *Devil's Brood*.'

'What's that?'

'You've never heard of *Devil's Brood*? Horror film. Late '60s. It's become a bit of a cult classic. Most of it's pretty crap actually, but there's this sequence—'

'What became of her?'

'Who?'

'Leila Winstone.'

'No idea. Faded into obscurity as we tend to do.'

'Can you find out what happened to her?'

'Another job?'

'If you like.'

'Okay. Bit of detective work. I'll do that.'

Very soon I noted a change in Martin's manner as he began to assume the role of Private Investigator. He wandered round my sitting room peering at things and frowning. He was beginning to annoy me very severely. Casually he picked up the album containing the 3-D photographs.

'Put it down! Don't touch that!' I shouted.

'Okay! Okay!' Martin looked shocked. I was shocked myself at my own outburst.

I said: 'Come on. Let's go. We can't waste any more time.'

For once Martin didn't want to linger over the job when we got to Islington. We cleared the flat of the last of my uncle's possessions and put the bureau in the van. When we were out of the flat and driving to the landlord's house to drop off the keys, Martin, who had been unusually silent, said: 'Weird place. Did you see all those women on the stairs?'

'What women?'

'On the stairs down from the flat. Two or three of them. I didn't see their faces but they stretched out their arms at me in a peculiar way. Were they prostitutes or something?'

'I have no idea,' I said sharply. 'I didn't see anyone.' This was not quite true.

I parked outside Berry's house which was a few streets away from my uncle's and left Martin in the van while I went in to return the keys. Berry lived in the basement of one of his own houses. He ushered me into his sitting room which was dominated by a huge flat screen television on one wall. A football match was in progress, the violent green of the pitch with little blobs of red and blue scurrying across its surface making all other colours in the room seem muddy and obscure.

Berry lived in an atmosphere of luxurious squalor. A vast, bloated armchair, as shapeless as himself, squatted in front of the livid screen. Beside it on a table were bowls of crisps and other unhealthy comestibles, and a half-consumed six-pack of tinned lager. Berry seemed rather proud of his surroundings than otherwise. He invited me to sit down in another bloated armchair. I declined and handed him the keys.

'So you've cleared the place,' he said, scribbling something in a notebook. 'You took the bureau?'

I nodded.

'Managed to get it open?'

'I found the keys.'

'Ah,' he said, collapsing into his chair. 'And the picture. You took that?'

'I did.'

'You know, I offered him good money for that painting when he was alive.'

'You could hardly have done so when he was not.'

'No. No. I mean, it wasn't as if he could afford to turn down my offer. He was always behind with the rent. Anyway, he said I could have it when he died.'

'Did he?' I said allowing a touch of scepticism to colour my voice.

'That's right,' he said. A pause. 'Mind you, he talked a lot of bollocks. Actually said he'd painted it himself.'

'He did.'

'Did he? Well . . . Hard to tell when he was telling the truth. He was always bullshitting. Used to tell me all these stories about how he'd been a famous photographer or something.'

'He had been.'

'Oh . . . Right . . .' Berry seemed crestfallen. 'Then answer me this. How did he fetch up at the wrong end of fucking Islington?'

I shrugged my shoulders and stared past him at the flat screen. It was no longer green but grey and there were shapes moving about on it, shapes of emaciated naked women. Had Berry inadvertently switched to a porn channel of some kind? The women were crouching or crawling and holding out their hands in supplicatory gestures, as if begging submissively for something.

Berry seized his remote control and began stabbing at the buttons. 'Fucking thing!' he said. Then suddenly the television was bright green again and the roar of the crowd was deafening. I took my leave.

The next day I had to go into the West End to meet a client. I lunched him at my club Brummell's in St. James' and the business we concluded was satisfactory. After lunch I felt in need of a walk and began to stroll up towards Piccadilly and Shaftesbury Avenue with no particular aim in mind. It was then that I remembered my uncle's old business card: I had one of them in my pocket. Soho was not far away; I would go to the address in Dean Street and see what had become of his studio.

I suppose thoughts about Uncle Hubert had never quite left me. Even during lunch they had returned at odd idle moments. I told myself not to let it become an obsession. Nevertheless, I felt there was unfinished business: why, for example, had there been no obituaries in the papers?

I walked up Shaftesbury Avenue and turned left into Dean Street. I had no trouble in finding the address. Somehow, it was where I had expected it to be, but it was a surprise to find that the building still housed a photographic studio. I went in through the double glass doors.

At a kidney-shaped reception desk a young woman was intent on painting her fingernails a luscious dark purple colour. I coughed politely to attract her attention and explained that I was writing a book about Soho in the 1960s and was interested to find that a photographic studio had existed on this site since that time.

'Oh, yeah?' she said with studied indifference, as if to show any kind of interest or enthusiasm would constitute a breach of professional etiquette.

'I was wondering—' I said. By this time she had stopped even looking at me and had returned to the absorbing task of nail painting. 'I was wondering if there is anyone still working here who was here in the '60s or '70s?'

'Nah,' she said without looking up. 'Shouldn't think so.'

'Wait a minute,' said a bright-looking PA who was passing by on her way out of the building, 'what about Camp Keith?'

'Oh yeah,' said the receptionist and to my surprise she immediately pressed a button and spoke into a microphone on her desk.

'Keith, please,' she intoned in a bored singsong. 'Could Keith come to reception please? There's someone to see him.'

'Thank you very much,' I said. 'I'm very grateful.'

The briefest of smiles expanded her dark red lips before the nail varnish once more claimed her undivided attention.

When Keith arrived he was much as I had expected him to be, plump with dyed hair and a limp handshake. He wore dark clothes, but the gold bracelets at his wrists and the medallion hanging from his neck were reminiscences of the 1960s and '70s. I gave him my improbable cover story and he seemed more than happy to talk. He suggested that we 'repair' to the café opposite the studio.

There over a latté and several doughnuts, he told me that he was part owner of the building and ran the studio on the first floor. He had come to Soho in the 1960s, found it suited him and had never gone away. He seemed to be a man at ease with himself and the world: I liked him.

Then I said: 'I wonder . . . Did you know someone back in the 1960s called Hube Vilier?'

Keith jerked his head back and stared at me searchingly for a few moments. There was a touch of theatricality about his reaction, but it was genuine enough at heart. He said: 'Did I know Hube Vilier? Did I know Hube Vilier! You bet your ass I did. He gave me my first job in The Smoke. I was his gopher, general dogsbody. I practically ran his studio at one time. Did everything. Oh yes, I knew Hube Vilier.'

'What was he like?'

'Well ... Have you got a week to spare perchance? You know they used to call him the Prince of Darkness?'

'No. Why?'

'My dear, not without reason, as I should know. For one, he had the most filthy temper. And then he was into everything: drugs, women, kinky sex, the lot. He'd fuck anything that moved. He even had me once or twice. Mind you, I was a pretty boy back then, but he was gorgeous.' He slapped the back of his left hand. 'Shut your mouth, Keith. We don't want to embarrass the nice gentleman, do we? All the same, he was a genuinely bloody good photog, I'll say that for him. Oh, yes. He was right up there with David Bailey, and Donovan, and Duffy. He was the swinging sixties all right, with a vengeance. The trouble was, he wanted to be the one and only, better than Donovan and Bailey, not even just the top dog, the only dog. It was impossible of course. Then he invented this thing he called '3D photography' with this weird camera that had two lenses. It was going to make his fortune. It was quite interesting actually. The trouble was, the whole process was incredibly expensive and elaborate – special film, special photographic paper, the lot. He approached several firms with it, but he was asking too big a cut. So he put a lot of his own money into it and went for it on his own. It was a disaster. Lost everything. Of course he blamed everybody but himself. After that, he kind of faded from the scene. I don't know what happened to him after that.'

'He's just died.'

Keith was silent for a while, but otherwise showed no reaction. 'Ah, well,' he said at last. 'Comes to us all. Even the Prince of Darkness. Did you know him?'

'He was my uncle.'

'Was he indeed?' Keith studied me. 'Yes. I can see that now. You've got a look of him about the eyes. Sometimes. Of course, *he* was much better looking.'

'You don't remember one of his girlfriends, Leila Winstone?'

'The starlet? Oh, yes! Sweet girl, but greener than grass! She worshipped the ground he walked on, and he treated her like shit of course. Then one day she just ups and offs to the States. My dear, I could have cheered.'

'Do you know what happened to her?'

'No. Lost in the *ewigkeit*, as my friend Kurt used to say. German, you know, but so friendly. I like to think she's running a donkey sanctuary somewhere in Norfolk. That's what most starlets end up doing when they cease to twinkle. They get so fed up with being fucked about by two-legged animals that they opt for four. And who can blame them? Look at Doris Day. Look at Brigitte Bardot. Actually, I'd rather not. Ooh, and look at the time! I must be back to the fun factory or they'll be sending out search parties. Good luck with the book, and thanks for the doughnuts. Delish!'

When I got back home that night, I found a package had been dropped through my letterbox. It was from Martin and it contained a DVD of the film *Devil's Brood* starring Leila Winstone. After I had made myself something to eat I sat down to watch it.

It was not a great film. It was a typically lurid piece of exploitation produced by one of those companies that hoped to reproduce the success of Hammer Horror. The plot, such as it was, concerns an innocent girl, played by Leila Winstone, who gets mixed up with a group of rich satanists in the home counties. It's mostly nonsense, of course, though sometimes unintentionally funny, but there is one sequence which stays in the mind and which, I suppose, has managed to make the film a 'cult classic'. In it the girl, played by Leila Winstone, is being pursued through a forest at night and she is naked. Don't ask me how she comes to be naked, or, for that matter, pursued. I forget: it's that kind of film. The pursuer is never fully seen; it is simply a bent semi-human shape shambling through the trees. Fleeting glimpses are all you get of it, but all the more horrible for that. You hear its breathing, and once you see its dull red eyes glowing through a skeleton pattern of tree branches. Clever camerawork suggests that the thing is gaining on Leila and the last you see of her is when she turns around, terror in her eyes, to face her assailant. Then she stumbles over a tree root and the screen goes black.

I mention it only because Hubert's photograph of Leila in his 3D album reproduces exactly that split second moment when she turns around in terror to face her pursuer.

I watched the film right through almost twice. Leila was no great actress, but she had a quality which made her watchable. Vulnerability, I suppose you'd call it, but vulnerability of an extreme kind. She gave the impression of being utterly lost, of having no inner self to guide her. The terror in her eyes was the terror of someone who looks within and finds a void.

It was now after midnight and again I felt I could not sleep. I began to consider my own life. Here was I, past thirty-five, rich, moderately success-ful, but childless, not even in a relationship. Perhaps I too was empty.

I went to the window and looked out into the street. No one was about except that opposite me on the other side of the road there stood a shad-owy group of people. I could not see their faces properly but I could make out their shapes and they were all women, about a dozen of them and they appeared to be naked. I blinked several times but they were still there when I looked again and I was convinced that their eyes were fixed on me. Then one lifted her arm, palm upwards and stretched it towards me in a suppli-ant gesture. Then another did the same; then another, and another. I pulled the curtains shut, letting out something between a gasp and a cry as I did so. The sound of it rang in my ears for nearly a minute.

I am not sure how much I slept that night. I must have fallen into a doze eventually because I was awoken about ten by the telephone. It was Martin. He had found Leila Winstone.

'She's in a place called Irving House. It's a sort of rest home for old actors and actresses. I may have to go there one day myself, I suppose. I believe it's not too bad; the food's pretty good and there's a bar and everything. It's not too far away from you either: in Northwood. Shall I come round? We could go and see her together.'

'No. I'll go on my own.'

'Oh, come on. You need someone like me there with you. It'll be interesting.'

'Martin, I pay you to do as you're bloody well told. I'm going alone. Understand?' I was nearly screaming down the phone. It surprised him; it certainly surprised me.

'Okay! Okay!' He hung up.

I rang up Irving House and arranged to visit Leila that afternoon, explain-ing that I was the relative of a close friend of hers and needed to tell her something. The matron was accommodating but sounded a little doubtful, explaining that Leila was 'not very communicative these days'. I said I under-stood, and only then began to wonder what on earth I was going to say to her. On an impulse I decided to take my uncle's portrait of her with me.

I now remember very little of my journey to Northwood or how I was received when I got to Irving House. My memories begin when I was ushered along a corridor to a room. I was carrying the picture. The nurse knocked on the door.

'Leila? Someone to see you.'

A faint murmur from beyond indicated that I should enter. The room was decorated in those insipid colours – beiges, creams, pale pinks – which are deemed suitable for such places of refuge. I saw very little in the room that was personal to its occupant who was sitting in a chair by the window in a dressing gown with a baby blue crocheted blanket across her knees. It was a bright day outside, but she was partly in shadow. A curtain had been drawn across half the window to protect her from the glare of the sun.

'I'm afraid this is not one of Leila's good days,' said the nurse. 'But I'll leave you two alone for a while.' Then, adopting that peculiar 'carer's voice' she said: 'You've got a visitor today, Leila.' Leila looked up, mild astonishment in her eyes; the nurse left us.

Apart from the fact that her hair was white, Leila was surprisingly recognisable from her 1960s photographs. The wrinkles about her eyes and mouth were the fine ones of a fair-skinned woman and not very conspicuous in the curtained half-light. The gently parted lips were still pink and well formed, and the strange vacancy of expression was familiar to me. She was still thin but her eyes were now deeper set in caverns of bluish grey shade. There was something marine about her, her hair and complexion bleached as a bone. She looked like a forsaken mermaid.

'Hello,' she said in a soft voice that was almost a whisper.

I began to explain myself. She listened, her empty eyes fixed on me. No kind of expression showed up on her face, but when I first mentioned Uncle Hubert's name, she said the word: 'No,' quietly but very distinctly.

I mentioned him again.

'No, no, no!' A little louder.

I told her about the painting. I propped it up against a chair for her to see properly.

'No, no, no, no, no . . .!' Louder still.

Her hands were now clutching convulsively at the arms of her chair. She was struggling to get up, but her limbs were too feeble to lift her.

'No, no, no, no, no . . . NO! NO! NO!'

Leila reached out a slippered foot and gave the painting a violent kick. The painting toppled over and lay on the ground, a dent in the canvas. She looked at me. Some kind of intelligence was coming into the eyes. They were rolling in her head, flickering round the room, taking in its every detail with ferocious greed. Heavy harsh breathing began to emanate from her lungs. A grating maleness was seeping into the voice.

'I don't want this shit,' it said. 'I want my bloody camera!'

REGGIE OLIVER has been a professional playwright, actor and theatre director since 1975. His most recent publications include the collections *The Sea of Blood* and *Holidays from Hell*, and the novel *The Boke of the Divill*. Forthcoming is a children's book, *The Hauntings at Tankerton Park and How They Got Rid of Them*, with illustrations by the author.

rip'per *n.* 1: 'ripping' person or thing [f. *rip + er*]; 2: to cut, tear or split quickly or violently apart; 3: person who makes a long cut or tears vigorously apart; 4: make (fissure, wound) by ripping; 5: one that rips. Origin: Middle English *rippen*, from or akin to Middle Dutch *reppen, rippen* to pull, jerk. First known use: 15th century. Synonyms: rend, ribbon, rive, shred, tatter, tear. Example: *Just call him Jack . . .*

RIPPER

ANGELA SLATTER

I

KIT HADN'T SEEN the first one, but PC Wright told him not to worry – this one was worse.

The throat was cut – that wasn't too bad, quite neat in fact and he had witnessed that sort of thing before – but the woman's skirts (Kit could see in the lamp light that she wore several against the cold, green, brown, black, some red ruffles) had been part pulled up, part torn, and her fat little middle-aged belly exposed and slashed open to leave a bloody abyss. Intestines reached over each shoulder; a separate piece of about two feet had been lopped off and put to one side as if whoever did it had a grander plan. Thick wavy dark hair acted as a pillow for her head and mutilated face; the lacerations weren't in the usual fashion of whores getting sliced by their pimps or dissatisfied customers. There was a *design* here and that disturbed him even more than the smell of shit and piss emanating from the unfortunate woman, who was no longer in a position to care or to cover herself and try to preserve a little bit of modesty. No, thought Kit, *that's* what bothered him most, that the woman was so terribly exposed in her death, so terribly, terribly helpless.

Hanbury Street was quiet, though Kit knew that was only temporary. PC Ned Watkins had sounded his whistle but a moment ago, and soon the place would be crawling with bluebottles, pressmen, terrified whores, and general gawkers. Thomas Wright, who'd been crouched down peering closely at the body while young Watkins threw up his pint and pork pie in a corner, made a noise – that strange noise Kit had come to associate with police who'd found someone they knew on this kind of day. It held despair, disappointment, disgust, rage and, peculiarly, a kind of knowing lack of surprise, as if *this* was somehow to be expected. Kit was coming to recognise it in the first pursing of the lips, the earliest expulsion of air. He wondered if he'd start doing it soon.

'It's Annie Chapman. Dark Annie,' Wright said, and spat. 'Watkins, buck up, man.'

But Watkins was having none of it and determinedly continued to dry heave after his stomach was well and truly empty. Wright shook his head, then nodded at Kit. 'Off you go, lad, you're fast. Straight to Abberline and Himself at Leman Street – although, if you're passing the Ten Bells stick your head in and see if the good Dr Bagster Phillips is in. Fair chance – he'll need to be called anyway.'

Kit nodded and turned away, relieved to pour his nervous energy into a useful activity; unfortunately he bounded straight into the oncoming form of PC Airedale, the largest, most unpleasant copper in all of Whitechapel – which meant he beat out some fairly stiff competition. Kit bounced off Airedale's torso, almost ending up on his arse, and the big policeman snarled, 'Watch where you're going, you half-wit.'

'Leave off him,' snapped Wright. 'He's only doing what I told him. Get going, boy.'

Kit sped off into the night as Airedale sneered, 'What? You told him to run into me?'

The air was cool, but Kit could feel his face burning, not only with embarrassment, but also distress at seeing the woman so abused. What had Wright called her? Chapman, Annie. The first one was Mary Anne Nichols. Although Kit hadn't seen her, he had seen the pitiable Martha Tabram, pierced all to hell by a bayonet. And still that wasn't as bad as Annie Chapman and her torn-apart belly. He rubbed a hand across his own flat stomach in sympathy.

He'd read the reports on Nichols, too, while they sat on the Inspector's desk. As a child Kit had become expert at reading upside down as much out of genuine interest as self-preservation. He'd learned early on that the only hope of conversation with his father was in discussing whatever the Reverend Caswell was reading over the breakfast table (in spite of his wife's protests).

A quick look in at the Ten Bells showed no sign of the police surgeon for Whitechapel, so he concluded the good doctor had at last gone home to his own bed. Kit hared along, barely out of breath, until he came to the steps of the nick and took them three at a time, sketched a brief wave at the sergeant on the entrance desk, and then darted up the internal staircase to the second floor.

Abberline and Himself were ensconced in the office they'd been forced to share since the former had been seconded to Leman Street in order to coordinate the Whitechapel murder investigations. This was the billet he'd occupied as head of H Division for nine years; somewhat inconveniently, its current occupant, Edwin Makepeace, had refused to move out and make way for the senior man. What had been a fair sized space for a single person, was now a rather cramped affair for two. Their desks butted up against each other like charging bulls. Neither inspector had spent much time at his individual residence since Nichols had been brought in; whether it was devotion to duty or a concern that unguarded territory might be fair game was a matter for discussion among the lower ranks. Kit suspected it was roughly equal measures of both.

Kit gave a hasty knock and opened the door a little before permission was given, and found himself the subject of rather steely gazes. Abberline was of middling height, in his forties, heading towards stout; a neat man with mutton chops and a meticulously tended moustache. His companion was, in contrast, tall and lean, and as neat as Abberline was, Makepeace was scruffy. Even when he was dressed for a meeting with his betters, even with all the spit and polish in the world, Kit had observed, his boss still had the air of a man who'd just been dragged backwards through a hedge.

In the no-man's-land where the desks met was an open bottle of whisky and a couple of tumblers, each containing differing levels of amber liquid. It seemed the masters had reached some kind of an accord. In spite of himself, Kit found his tongue tripping over words, and all he managed was an inarticulate stutter. Neither man was cruel enough to laugh, although Abberline grunted, 'Spit it out, boy.'

Kit took a deep breath, trying not to appear to do so, and spoke. 'There's been another, sirs. Another woman's been murdered.'

If it surprised the men that Kit didn't say 'another whore's been ripped', that he displayed some respect, if not tenderness, for the dead woman, they didn't show it. Perhaps they just thought it a display of his youth and assumed he'd harden the longer he stayed in the job. Perhaps they were too tired to care.

'Do you have a name for this victim, Caswell?' Makepeace stood, slowly, careful not to thrust his chair back into the too-close wall. He hooked his green chequered coat from the rack and shrugged into it; the fabric seemed to shudder, unwilling to accommodate the man's shoulders. When the operation was completed and the item of clothing surrendered, Makepeace threw Abberline a tweed jacket so the inspector might make himself presentable.

'Yes, sir. Annie Chapman, sir,' replied Kit, adding, rather unnecessarily, 'She's another prostitute, sir.'

'A wandering beauty of the night,' sighed Abberline, startling Kit. He'd not given the Inspector much credit for a poetic soul. 'Will you tell us where, boy, or shall we meander through the streets until we stumble upon her?'

'There's a good chance you'd find the wrong body, sir, this being Whitechapel and all,' said Kit before he could help himself, then wanted to bite off his own tongue. Abberline and Himself guffawed in delight, and Kit thought the whisky had probably been his saviour. 'In Hanbury Street, sirs, number 29. I looked for Dr Bagster Phillips on my way here, but he wasn't at the Ten Bells.'

'Try his home. If you can't find him there then I cannot imagine which mistress he is favouring this eve, and we'll have to get some other sawbones to hack at her.' Makepeace sighed. 'I'd rather it be him.'

'Yes, sir, I'll do my best, sir.'

'Off you go, Kit, you'll have run half the city before this night's out.'

II

Stopping at the Limehouse lock-up added an extra twenty minutes to the journey home, but it couldn't be helped. The seemingly ramshackle shed was hidden deep in the overgrown back garden of 14a Samuel Street, and Kit wasn't the only person with permission to use it, but he knew that his visits were carefully scheduled to ensure that no one else's tarriance clashed with his. Privacy was of the utmost importance and the Orientals understood that better than anyone Kit had ever met. Honouring debts was of equal importance, Kit had discovered, and was grateful that the debt in question was owed to him and not the other way around.

He unlocked the hut as pale rays of dawn rolled languidly across the September sky, and stepped inside, conscientiously latching the door behind him. The ever-burning lantern glowed in a corner, and Kit could make out muddy boot prints on the pale birch of the floor, signs of other comings and goings. The interior of the lock-up would have surprised anyone who didn't have a key to it: it was (muddy prints notwithstanding) a tidy room, lined with a series of securely locked leather-bound wooden steamer trunks. Even the worst of the reprobates who used this place wouldn't dare break faith with either fellow key-holders or their Chinese hosts; it wouldn't be worth the strife. In one corner was a trapdoor, also locked. Kit didn't have a key to *that*.

His chest was located nearest the trapdoor, so he'd had plenty of time to study it in the past three months, which was also, not so coincidentally the same amount of time he'd been working for the Metropolitan Police Service. He lifted the heavy lid once the lock had been disengaged and sighed as he drew forth a dress in navy, almost as dark as his uniform, complete with bustle and ridiculously tight sleeves, and shook it to encourage the wrinkles to leave the bombazine.

The advantage of the colour, she thought, *was that it didn't look as if it had been folded in the bottom of a case for almost a whole day*. She couldn't quite recall how, or indeed if, she'd ever sat comfortably in a bustled skirt. Kit – Katherine – Caswell slid the police helmet from her head and rubbed her scalp with long fingers. Her hair was cropped, a ruddy brown like her father's had been. She was thankful, in a small way, that she'd had to sell her tresses to the wig-maker so she could afford Lucius' medicine; they'd been down to her waist, as thick a mane as any young woman could have wished for and had fetched a handsome price. Since then she'd kept it neatly trimmed, surreptitiously cutting it so her mother didn't seem to notice except to comment from time to time that it was a shame the locks didn't appear to want to grow back. It – and her squarish jaw – helped Kit to pass for a boy. A girlish-looking boy to be sure, but a boy nonetheless, with a voice that was deep for a girl, light for a boy, and did not give her away, for she was careful to speak in low tones.

Beneath the dress were myriad petticoats and underclothes she'd come to loathe more and more with every passing day, particularly the corset; even the strapping across her modest breasts to keep them flat in her uniform was less uncomfortable and restricting. She shook everything out before dressing, just in case some kind of insect life had decided her drawers might make a good home. But the lock-up was very clean, and Kit knew she had no real reason for concern. And the shoes, the little black leather boots with bows and buttons up the side that made her toes hurt. In the cracked and speckled full-length mirror the owners had been kind enough to provide (Kit was under no illusions that hers was the only transformation conducted here on a daily basis), she surveyed herself and settled the silly little cream and coffee bonnet with trailing ribbons and silken butterflies onto her head, then affixed the short cape around her shoulders against the chill. She looked respectable and that was the best she could hope for.

Navigating her way through the clawing bushes and over the boggy path, she finally stepped out into the alley after taking a good look around to make sure she was unobserved. There was only the young Chinese boy, perched on a stool at the back gate, drowsy but alert enough to give her a nod as she passed by. He was one of a cadre of youngsters deployed by his community to collect information that might keep them safe, learning the business, learning to keep secrets, learning a dozen other possibly highly illegal things in regard to which Kit might one day have to glance the other way. She'd worry about that later though. For now, tolerance and wilful blindness were in everyone's interests – she'd realised in the last few months that sometimes part of enforcing the law was pretending ignorance, and she was more than prepared to apply that to her current situation.

The walk to number 3 Lady's Mantle Court took ten minutes. The streets were starting to come alive, so her footsteps weren't the only sounds to be heard; bakers making deliveries, butchers lugging carcasses to restaurants and big houses, coal trucks, flower girls shouting at anyone they could see, all combined to start the beginnings of a cacophony that would grow and not subside until well after dark had fallen. Mind, things had been quieter since Mary Anne Nichols had been found. Might grow quieter still, thought Kit, now Annie Chapman had joined her compatriot. Then she wondered how long before the city's male population got up-in-arms, or at least the pimps and the bullyboys who ran the whores; those who made their living off women's backs, and who didn't mind knocking "employees" around themselves, but God help the man who hit another's whore – at least without paying extra. Finding herself at a familiar blue-painted door, Kit pushed these thoughts aside, consciously settled a blank and obedient expression on her face, and slid the neat little black key from the balding velvet drawstring purse – which also contained a dainty hanky with edges embroidered and a set of brass knuckles – into its lock.

'Did you do it? Katherine?'

Sweet Jesus, had her mother been waiting up all night until she walked in? Kit took a deep breath and paced to the tiny parlour in the rooms they rented in Mrs Kittredge's genteelly decrepit home. Sure enough, there she was, seated by the dying fire, a frayed rug across her knee, disarrayed knitting tumbled to the floor and tangled about Louisa Caswell's worn slippers. The mourning cap she'd adopted and not relinquished, though almost three years had passed since her husband's death, sat askew on the silver-shot black hair that flowed over her thin shoulders, and her eyes, fever-bright, seemed to be trying to pierce Kit, to get inside her and determine all the secrets she might be hiding.

Kit smiled. 'Yes, Mother. Good morning.'

'Did you get it all done?' repeated Louisa as if her daughter had not answered. Kit nodded, crossed the room, and patted her mother's long thin hands with their spidery fingers.

'Yes, Mother. We completed the entire order. Mistress Hazleton is very pleased.'

'So you are home for a while? Did she pay you? Lucius needs more medicine. Did she pay you?' Louisa had been under the impression for some time that Kit was still apprenticed to a milliner on the other side of the Thames, and that this employment sometimes required her daughter to work nights in order to fill large orders of hats – she was willing to believe that Mistress Hazleton's confections of feathers and silk, bows and beads, netting and pearls were in high demand. Louisa also had no idea that the pittance her daughter earned in that position did not stretch to the needs of three people, one of them very ill. It was four months since

Kit had hit upon her plan after discovering how much improved her pay conditions might be were she a male.

'Yes, Mother. I have been paid. I will get Lucius' medicine this morning and I will pay Mrs Kittredge the money she is owed. Then I will buy groceries and we shall have a fine luncheon before I go back to work. Put your mind at rest.' She stroked Louisa's hair and face; was stunned to find how much resentment was billowing up from inside like bile, how much she hated being a parent to her mother when she'd barely finished with being a child herself. 'Have you been sitting up all night?'

'Oh no, dear. I slept very well.' And Kit thought she probably had after a dose of the laudanum Louisa had found was her only means to cope after the Reverend Caswell's demise. She ran tender fingers over the stump of Louisa's left ear where only a remnant of the top half remained. Louisa swatted her daughter's hand away as if the touch reminded her of things she wished to forget.

'I'll go and check on Lucius, Mother, then we shall have some breakfast. Would you like your knitting?'

The woman nodded and Kit carefully lifted the unidentifiable knotting of coarse wool and smooth wooden needles to her mother's lap and left her to get on with whatever it was she thought she was making.

Her brother's bedchamber was at the back of the ground floor flat; their entire space was small, but neat, and the paint was not peeling even if the rugs were a little threadbare. Some weeks Kit paid Mrs Kittredge extra to help clean their rooms and the older woman was happy to help out. She was even good about sitting with Lucius when his mother and sister had to go out; and more often than not when she arrived home in the afternoons Kit would find her mother and their landlady either in the parlour drinking tea and gossiping, or in the kitchen shelling peas for a great pot of stew or soup the two households would share – and gossiping. Kit wondered if Mrs K noticed Louisa's decaying mental state; perhaps she did and it just made her kinder. With no family of her own living close, Mrs K had adopted the Caswells, seeming to spend more time with them than on the two floors above which were her domain. Kit didn't mind because it meant her family was watched out for while she was away.

'Get some rest,' Inspector Makepeace had said when she left the station in the morning dark. *Easier said than done*, thought Kit. Lucius hadn't woken yet and Kit watched as he slept. He had their mother's colouring, black hair and palest skin, with icy blue eyes that warmed when he roused and saw his sister.

'Kit!' He struggled to sit, thin arms pushing him upwards, the weight of his wasted legs making the task harder than it should have been. She came to his aid, plumping pillows and helping him to rest against them. The room was narrow, like the whole house, with just enough space for a slender bed, a tallboy and a chair by his pillow, where a copy of Stevenson's *The Strange Case of Dr Jekyll and Mr Hyde* lay.

'You want to be careful with that. If Mother sees it we'll never hear the end of it.' She lifted the book, sat down and rested the slim volume in her lap. Louisa objected to her son reading anything that wasn't "improving" and she most certainly did not consider "that Scotsman" improving. She thought his work encouraged boys to run away from home for adventure's sake. Lucius gave his most winning smile.

'She won't get angry with me, Kit, don't worry.'

'No, but she will get angry with *me* and I'll be the worst person in the world for giving it to you,' she pointed out, mock scolding.

'What did you do last night, Kit? What did you see?' When Kit had put her plan into action and changed jobs (to say the least), Lucius knew; he noticed everything, all the habits of the house because he had nothing better to do with himself. It was the kind of secret that was difficult to keep from him – whereas Louisa spent so much time in her own world, not caring as long as the bills were paid, Lucius had his medicine and she hers, and food made a regular appearance on the table. He read, he scribbled in the cheap notebooks Kit bought him, he read some more, he watched the garden from the tiny window of his room, he played whist with Mrs K, although Louisa couldn't keep track of the game. But her brother, observed Kit, remained cheerful; illness and immobility hadn't soured his nature, and he looked forward to hearing about what she did when dressed as a man.

She wondered if he'd be so accepting if he'd had a father still alive, if he'd spent the better part of his thirteen years going among other boys and drinking in their beliefs and bigotries. Despite the hardship his sickness caused them all, a tiny part of Kit was pleased it had made him so sweet and open-minded.

She leaned forward, thinking about what to tell him – *how* to tell him, for he loved a story. So she began with her evening patrol, the three fights she'd broken up before strolling down Hanbury Street and finding Wright and Watkins in their varied positions near poor Annie Chapman. She glossed over the worst of the predations on the woman's corpse, but told him enough that a look of horrified delight sparked there even as he whispered a prayer for the soul of the dead. When finally she finished her tale and sat back in the chair, he looked as though he'd eaten a good meal; which she knew he hadn't.

'Right, I'm off to make breakfast before Mother comes looking for me.'

'Five minutes more, Kit, please. Read me the chapter again that I read last night.'

'But you've already read it – won't be any surprises,' she teased.

'Please, Kit, I like to *hear* it too. Oh, won't you please?'

She relented and cracked the cover. 'A fortnight later, by excellent good fortune, the doctor gave one of his pleasant dinners . . .'

III

Two in the afternoon and Kit, once again in disguise, could barely suppress her yawns. The problem with that – apart from the dagger looks Himself was giving her – was that it seemed to let the smell into her mouth, and it was bad enough that her poor nose was already getting so abused. She couldn't help imagining the odour as a taste, a contagion on the air. The Old Montague Street Mortuary stank, as one might expect, of death, a stench that had embedded itself into the very bricks of the walls, the very stones of the floor. Luckily the temperature was kind – in high summer, Kit imagined there was a good chance she'd keel over if she had to set foot in this place.

On the table in front of Dr Bagster Phillips lay Chapman, Annie, the woman the doctor kept referring to as 'an unfortunate', as if her death was some kind of inconvenience that might have been overcome in better circumstances; something from which she might *recover*. Kit kept her expression blank; Makepeace was watching her too closely to let any thoughts slip onto her face. Her camouflage was maintained by diligent discipline in all areas of her person and mentality and conduct.

She stood with her feet apart, balancing squarely and gratefully on boots with a reasonable heel, a flat sole and not a hint of buttons or bows. Dr Bagster Phillips' voice was a buzz in her head, comments on the corpse she took in without really listening: lungs ripe with tuberculosis, the tissues of the brain diseased, abrasions on fingers where rings had been removed (and not found), the neck cleanly cut, the head almost severed, the terrible injuries to her belly and the fact that her uterus was gone. A bayonet, the doctor said quite clearly, or something very like one, wielded by someone – a man obviously, no woman would have the strength. Privately, Kit thought that untrue – if Dark Annie had been incapacitated first, there was nothing to stop a woman from hacking at her; well, apart from common decency and squeamishness.

'A Liston knife, perhaps?' asked Abberline and Bagster Phillips blew out an annoyed breath.

'Or a butcher's knife, or a circumcision knife . . .' he muttered half under his breath, then tried to rein in his temper.

'Someone with a degree of anatomical knowledge?' asked Makepeace and Kit watched the doctor squirm until he reluctantly nodded and muttered *perhaps* – he did not, Kit noted, want anyone to think a medical man might have done this. She couldn't blame him and kept her eyes on the woman as the police surgeon conducted his business. Poor Annie didn't look any better than she had the last Kit had seen her, except she'd been cleaned up. Her face was still swollen and bruised, the slashes across her body were dried obscenely brown and black, and the cuts stood out starkly on her dead-white flesh. And the old scars, her life right up until someone had taken a blade to her, were writ large on her skin with contusions and cicatrices, scrapes and scratches. Kit had to blink to stop the heat of tears. No one else in the cold malodorous chamber was showing any sympathy for the dead woman; nor would Kit.

The doctor's commentary was occasionally interrupted by questions from Abberline and Makepeace. Both men stood near to the table on which the body rested; they leaned forward to look more closely when Bagster Phillips indicated some trauma or cut, or smudge or other trace element of the woman's murder. On either side of Kit stood Wright and Airedale, the latter looming over both his fellow PCs.

'You lot,' said Makepeace, his voice echoing off the walls, 'did you speak to her clients from last night?'

Wright nodded, reeled off the names of the men they'd been able to find; all had alibis, had been happily tucked up in bed with their wives after they'd availed themselves of Annie's services.

Makepeace continued, 'And Chapman's husband?'

There was a silence, into which Kit, when it became apparent her betters could not fill, dropped, 'John Chapman was her husband, sir, but they've been separated four years. He left London soon after their paths, err, diverged.'

Airedale and Wright stared at Kit, the former with resentment, the latter with surprise.

In for a penny, in for a pound, Kit went on: 'I spoke to the tarts last night, sir, those who hung around. Eliza Cooper – with whom Annie had fought over some hawker call Harry, and no I've not found him yet – told me. It seems they were friends before they became rivals. And Annie sometimes was seen in the company of one Edward Stanley, a brick layer's apprentice.'

'Have you spoken to Mr Stanley?' asked Abberline. Kit shook her head.

'I was going to try to find him today, sir, and Harry the Hawker.'

'I think you'll be best spent with Mr Stanley. Your colleagues can locate and question the mysterious Harry and see if they can learn as much as you did so quickly.' Makepeace gave his other officers a look fit to melt glass; Kit knew that she was being rewarded, sent to find someone whose last name and place of work she already knew. The other two would have to start at the bottom – if they were smart they'd try Eliza Cooper first, but who knew where to find her in the daylight hours? Makepeace barked, 'Well, what are you all waiting for? Get out there. And Caswell?'

She paused, side-stepping to avoid Airedale's intentional bump. 'Yes, sir?'

'Mary Anne Nichols. Talk to her husband, see if he knew Chapman too.'

'William Nichols. Yes, sir.'

She followed Wright and Airedale into the watery afternoon sunshine. Kit took a deep breath of the air, which, although it wasn't the sweetest, was still a vast improvement on the atmosphere of the mortuary. The large copper glared at her. 'Apple-polishing little bastard. Mincing, apple-polishing little bastard.'

'Leave him alone. Good work's no reason to hate someone. Not his fault he's smarter than you are, Airedale.' Wright crossed his arms, rolled his neck and cracked the vertebrae loudly as if limbering up for a fight. Airedale, for all his size, was unlikely to go after Wright, who was stocky and known to be a fine bare-knuckle fighter. Kit wondered what she'd do if ever the older PC's protective presence was absent and Airedale found he had free rein. Wright jerked his chin at Kit and said, 'Off you go, lad, best not to keep Himself waiting when he's got such high expectations of you.'

Kit shot him a grin, dodged a kick from Airedale, who muttered 'mincing little bastard' yet again, and made a conscious effort to walk in a more manly way, legs apart as if large balls might be impeding his stride. She kept it up until she turned the corner into Brick Lane, finding the gait made her hip joints grind uncomfortably, and the rolled-up pair of socks in the front of her trousers had drifted uncomfortably to the left. Kit adjusted her "crotch", thinking that only as a man could she get away with such a thing in public.

A whistle, high and wolfish, caught her attention.

The previously empty street now contained a woman, small with dark brown hair, who stood at the mouth of an alley. She wore a forest-green dress, a black short jacket over the top and a clean white apron, but there was no doubt in Kit's mind what profession the woman pursued. Her skin was fair, she wore no hat, but her cheeks were rouged like a doll's, her lips painted redder than red; she stood with one hip pushed out in offering, and her gaze said "come hither" as she fluttered her lashes. She lifted a thin, graceful hand and gestured in a queenly fashion for Kit to approach.

'What are doing, you little turd? Get a move on!' Airedale growled from behind Kit and slapped a meaty hand down on her shoulder. Startled she twisted away, fish-fast, and broke into a sprint.

'Better run, you little faggot,' bellowed Airedale, laughing unpleasantly.

Kit kept moving. When she drew level with the spot where the woman had been, it was empty, but somewhere back in the shadowy depths of the alley, she seemed to sense movement and the weight of a gaze still upon her.

IV

William Nichols was harder to find than Edward Stanley, but easier to talk to, Kit discovered. Stanley, at his job, was loath to take time to speak with Kit. She didn't think it was guilt – then again she couldn't be sure – but rather a wish to not be involved. He'd spent time with Annie, yes, on occasion; they'd shared lodgings now and then, yes. But he'd not seen her in a good six months and he'd met a girl, good and kind and sweet – and very religious. He was bettering himself, didn't Kit see, and he could not, would not, be associated with the likes of depraved women such as Annie Chapman. He was sorry for what happened to her, but she'd brought it upon herself by the very life she lived.

Kit found herself disliking the newly clean-living Mr Stanley, his righteousness sticking in her throat like a chicken bone. And he had an alibi, even if she'd have preferred he didn't, just for the sheer pleasure of running him in.

'Ah, poor Polly,' said William Nichols, shaking his head. Kit found him in the Bricklayers Arms, already well soused. A printer's machinist, he'd finished for the day; his employer was sitting beside him, also rather drunk. When Kit appeared that man made excuses to leave, mentioning a wife with a rolling pin and a finely-tuned temper, who was expecting him home sooner rather than later. She took the seat the printer had so recently occupied, careful to sit with her legs apart and arms crossed over her chest – Airedale's comments had made her consider if she'd gotten sloppy about maintaining her masculine disguise. *Perhaps*, thought Kit wryly, *it was time to adopt all the great hallmarks of male behaviour: spitting in the street, burping after a meal, and farting with enthusiasm in small airless rooms.*

'Poor Polly, poor Mary Anne,' sighed Nichols. Kit pondered how whores seemed not to settle on one single name, yet created new personas for themselves – a *nom de mattress*.

'When did you last see her, Mr Nichols?'

'Not for a few months. You know we're separated,' he said, his round face sad as he sipped at his gin. Kit knew – one of the women she'd spoken to at the time of Mary Anne/Polly's death – Nelly Holland, the tart who shared a room with her – had told how William had an affair with the nurse who'd delivered their last child, then left. He'd been forced to pay Polly maintenance, though, until it came to light she'd been on the game – her illicit earnings meant her erstwhile husband was freed from his fiscal burden.

Holland said Polly claimed they still knew each other as man and wife every so often, but Nelly'd not seen evidence of it. It was possible, Kit supposed; William Nichols appeared genuinely fond of his deceased spouse, and he didn't seem like a man with an axe to grind. To her surprise he added, 'My fault entirely. I should not have laid my hat where it did not belong. Only poor Polly was so tired after that last babe and a man needs some attention. I should have been patient though.'

Kit wondered if all the men of Whitechapel were coming down with the affliction of self-improvement and thought the world might not survive were it to continue unabated.

'Quite,' she said. 'Did she know Annie Chapman?'

He nodded sagely.

'They all know each other, don't they? Women?' he said as if the sex was some kind of tribe with an in-built knowledge of all its members, then he clarified, 'The tarts. They know each other; if they're not fighting over territory and clients, they're drinking together somewhere. If they're not arguing over who stole whose best petticoat, they're sharing warnings about the bad'uns, those that won't pay what they say they will, that hurt the girls instead of simply doing their normal business.'

'Were they friends?' she asked. 'I mean, did they know each other well?'

He shrugged. 'Knew each other well enough to have a drink at the Ten Bells, I suppose.' His eyes sparkled. 'Here, why are you asking? Have you found the bastard who cut my Polly?'

She shook her head and watched his interest snuff out. 'No, Mr Nichols, I'm sorry. I'm just trying to find out if Annie and Polly had any connections that might lead me somewhere useful.'

'Can't help you, lad, anymore than I've said, I'm sorry.' He looked so downcast she was tempted to reach over and pat his hand, but knew it would be misinterpreted and turn out badly for her no matter what. So, Kit nodded, and stood, wished him good evening and made her way through the cramped, smoky rooms of the Bricklayers Arms and out into the evening, glad for the thickness of her tunic against the coming chill.

Her footsteps sounded harsh on the cobbles and carriages clattered past on their way to better places. The lights had come on, yellow beacons flickering weakly in the early hints of a night mist – of course, the alleys and courts, the side streets and lacunae between buildings did not warrant electrical illumination; darkness needed a place to thrive. After she'd moved from the door of the pub and was part-way down well-lit Commercial Street, she heard a crash and a crunch as of someone dropping something and standing on something else, just inside an alleyway.

'You do make a lovely boy,' said a voice from the pitchy shades, rolling effortlessly between two accents and, even though it was female, it sent a shiver through Kit. She frowned and concentrated on identifying the distinct tones as she scanned the shadows. 'But I'll wager you've not got what it takes.'

This last was said with a laugh and the prostitute Kit had seen on her return from the mortuary stepped out of the gloom. *Irish*, thought Kit, *and Welsh*; a smooth mix of rhythmic lilts, musical cadences and strange glottal stops. The woman moved closer and her hand snaked out, grabbing at Kit's groin, closing briefly around the rolled socks, and letting go with a laugh. The movement was so rapid, so unexpected, that she had no time to react, but stood, mouth agape, horrified. The woman turned her back, cast a look over her shoulder and said, 'Will you walk with me, *lad*?'

Kit swallowed, not daring to speak, thinking only of getting this unwanted companion away from a place where they might be overheard. They fell into step and made a dignified progress towards Hawksmoor's Christ Church and its small graveyard, an island of darkness lapping against Commercial Street. They remained silent for the first minute or three, the woman nodding to other whores waiting for company. They nodded back and Kit wondered if William Nichols had been more right than he'd known when he suggested these sisters of the streets all knew each other.

'How did you know?' asked Kit quietly when they reached the metal spikes of the churchyard fence.

'Some things I just do. You're doing a fine job, though, of keeping those coppers fooled. They don't take notice, for all they're *investigators*. They take things at face value, don't you find?' She too spoke quietly, and Kit appreciated that she seemed committed to keeping Kit's secret, at least for the moment.

'What do you want? I have no money to spare,' she said, thinking she simply couldn't afford to be blackmailed.

'I may be a whore, but I'm not a thief, thank you very much,' said the woman, affronted dignity liming her tone.

'I'm . . . I'm sorry.'

'Ah, don't be. Of course I'm a thief, we all are, I just wanted to see if you had any manners.' She laughed shrilly; she was older than Kit, maybe twenty-five, and she was very pretty although, Kit observed, it wouldn't be long before the harshness of her way of life started to show itself on her face. 'The other girls always say you're a polite young man, that you don't talk down to them, that you listen. Oh, don't worry, they don't know what I know and if they did, they wouldn't tell – the streets are better with you here and all. Don't want your money, Kit Caswell, but I wanted to talk to you about Polly and Annie.'

'Did you know them?'

'Of course, we are of a kind,' replied the woman in melodic timbre.

'Who are you?' asked Kit belatedly.

'Mary Jane Kelly,' she said and nodded towards a seat inside the church-yard. 'Marie Jeanette, if you prefer. Or Fair Emma or Ginger or Black Mary, if nothing else takes your fancy?'

'More names than you can shake a stick at,' observed Kit and Mary Jane fixed her with a look.

'Wouldn't you? If you did what we do, wouldn't you hide your identity, try to separate yourself any way you could from what you do?' She sat on the bench, first wiping at it in a ladylike fashion with a gloved hand. 'Wouldn't you take an alias and keep your real name a secret, just like the gypsies do? You – you keep your true self hidden, so you should understand.'

Kit hadn't thought of it like that, but it made all the sense in the world. 'I see it, yes. I'm sorry for being rude. What do you have to tell me, Miss Kelly? About the women who've been carved?'

'They've not been killed because they're whores, Kit Caswell, that's just a convenience makes them easier to find, to hunt out.'

'Then why? What can they possibly have that a killer would take from them?'

'You know what he took from Annie and so do I – oh, PC Wright's a love when you get him in the mood,' she sniggered smugly. 'Took the very core of her, didn't he? From Polly, he took the voice box.'

No one else knew about that, Kit thought. 'What could he do with body parts? You're not saying they're getting burked? What he's taking is hardly fit for commerce with the Resurrectionists and their like.'

'Sweet Jesu, thought you were smarter than those with a weight between the legs, pulling their brains downwards!' Kelly shook her head. 'No, he takes the things he needs, little pieces of them that the soul can cling to. He's taken two, he wants five, like the points of a pentacle.'

'What?' Kit blinked.

'He can't carry away bodies, not the state they're in and he doesn't need all of them for his purposes. He just needs a little thing, a souvenir, a flesh poppet for the soul to recognise, to hang on to until he gets it to wherever he's taking them.' She grasped Kit's cold hands in her own, and Kit could feel the heat of her coming through the thin-worn gloves. 'He's taking them because they're witches. He's taking them for their power.'

Kit didn't know which thought to follow first, so she leaped on the most obvious. 'You say *he* – do you know who it is? For the love of God, don't tell me you know and haven't told!'

'Don't be a fool, Kit Caswell, if I'd knew who it was I'd have been into Leman Street so fast you'd not have seen me for the dust I kicked up.' She shook her head. 'I don't know who it is. I only know that when Polly and Annie died, I felt them go, and I wouldn't have felt that if their lives and power weren't taken from them so *fiercely* – with such terrible violence and with sorcery in the mix. Power travels on the air, Kit Caswell, in ways you can't understand, you can't feel – most folk can't feel. But those of us with it, we know when it shifts and shivers, we sense its passing.'

'If you're so powerful, why are you all earning a living on your back?' Kit asked, eyebrows raised. 'If you're witches, why not magic yourselves wealth and position or even just a tidy cottage and a comfortable living, a good husband to keep you?'

'Did I say we were powerful?' sneered Mary Jane. 'Did I say we could conjure storms, fly, make great houses out of air and spit? Having magic doesn't mean you're *almighty*. There are women in Mayfair, Russell Square, in bloody Buckingham Palace, who are sisters to my kind; they can summon the wind and the lightning, but they are potent because they were born to it, they were born to *position*. But the power we have isn't of the same degree and we can't conjure a decent life out of straw and rags and shit. Sometimes we know things, sometimes we can find things that are lost, sometimes we might brew a tisane to break a fever and perhaps save a life doing it. But we can't make ourselves rich or beautiful, we can't magic ourselves *omnipotent*. Do you honestly think we'd choose this life if we had a choice?'

Kit wasn't sure, but she didn't say so. What she did say was, 'I don't believe in witches. I can't take that to my inspector.'

'Then how did I know what you were when I first laid eyes upon you?' Kelly challenged.

'A good guess,' said Kit, making to stand. The woman grabbed her hands again and held her tight.

'Your father is dead, but he was a good man. You've a brother – he's sick, but I cannot see why. Your mother thinks you . . . make . . . hats! How precious!' She laughed nastily. Still she did not let go of Kit, though the other struggled to pull away.

'You might have asked around. You could have followed me. You could have—' Kit hissed.

'When you dream, you sometimes dream your mother dead, with a pillow over her face and all your burdens lifted,' said Mary Jane Kelly flatly, and Kit deflated onto the bench beside her once again. Kelly waited until Kit had caught her breath, until she'd suppressed the sobs that shook her, until she sat straight, and raised her head to look forward into the darkness of the graveyard.

'Will you help us?' asked Mary Jane, with no pleading. 'Will you? I don't know who he is, but I know he's taking us for a purpose and he's taking whores because we're easy to find, and no one cares.'

'I care,' said Kit, staring into the shadows, feeling as if they were opening up to receive her.

'You don't have to believe, but will you help?'

'I'll help,' said Kit, and it seemed her words also meant *I believe*.

V

'Caswell, there you are.' Makepeace buttonholed Kit the moment she set foot in the nick. 'You're presentable and you notice things. Come along.'

Kit didn't ask questions, just jogged to keep up with the Inspector's long strides as he shot out the double doors and into some unprecedentedly bright September sunshine. The tall man hailed a hansom cab, yelled an address at the driver, and jumped in, gesturing wildly for Kit to hurry up. Before she managed to sit, the cab moved off with a jerk and she lost her balance, ending up in her boss's lap. A mad scramble ensued as she slapped away helping hands and struggled to get her rear on her own side of the bench. She couldn't help the blushing, though, or the dryness in her throat at the idea the Inspector might have thought her backside too peachy, too round, the hips too broad for a boy's bony arse.

But Makepeace said nothing except, 'Comfy?'

Kit nodded, then shook her head, then nodded again, then finally settled for peering out the window at the passing people and traffic and buildings. She didn't look back inside until she felt the burn of her cheeks cool. She cleared her throat. 'Where are we going, sir? If I may ask?'

'We are going, young Caswell, to Mayfair.'

'That's a bit posh, sir,' she said before she thought that perhaps it wasn't too posh for Makepeace – didn't he have a rich wife? Hadn't the gossip called him a social climber? She added lamely, 'For me at least.'

'A name has come up in our investigations, a young barrister, Montague John Druitt. Dr Bagster Phillips, upon hearing this, suggested we might talk to someone who knows him rather well, before we attempt to drag a member of the bar into our delightful premises.'

'And that would be, sir?' Imagining the answer to be Druitt's parents or other family members, a wife or sweetheart of some description.

'Sir William Gull.'

'The Queen's former Physician-in-Ordinary?'

Makepeace's eyebrows did their best to climb up under his hat and into his hairline. 'You're awfully knowledgeable, young man.'

'My brother is sick, sir,' she said, honestly, having learned long ago that the best way to live a lie is to stay as close to the truth as possible. 'I have spent some time researching the medical profession, looking for someone who might find out what's wrong with him.'

There was a stretching silence, which the Inspector broke with, 'Ah.'

Kit looked out the window again and realised they'd left Whitechapel well and truly behind: the men on the footpaths were better dressed, carried canes rather than sacks; the women wore dresses that cost more than she'd earn in six months, and they'd never have to worry about being attacked on the street. She thought of Mary Kelly's words and wondered how many of those women might be the sort the killer was looking for – the sort he wouldn't touch because to do so would be to bring more attention than he wanted, more attention than he could possibly handle. Without thinking she said, 'Sir, do you believe in witchcraft?'

'I believe it's illegal. Why, Kit, have you come across some gypsy offering to tell your fortune or summon a spirit?' Makepeace chuckled.

'No, sir, just . . . wondering.'

Silence again, then, 'Your brother, what's wrong with him?'

'If I knew that, I'd have had it fixed, though it'd cost me a year's wages, sir.' Kit rubbed her chin; Makepeace looked at her speculatively and she considered if he was noticing how lacking she was in facial hair. It didn't matter – some of the other young PCs were in the same boat, mutton chops taking their own sweet time about growing in. 'He can't walk, sir, been paralysed ever since our father died.'

'Is it in the boy's head, do you think?'

Kit shrugged. 'I don't know. Could be, but I think Lucius would dearly love to walk again. Dr Gull studied paralysis especially.'

'Did you bring your brother to him?'

She looked askance at her boss. 'Dr Gull hasn't practised for some years, sir, not since his first stroke. I believe he had yet another not long ago.' She didn't mention how many letters she'd written, unanswered, to the famous physician begging for a moment of his time. 'Why are we going to speak to him about Druitt, sir?'

'Druitt's father was a well-known surgeon, and a friend of Gull's, who is also Druitt's godfather. Montague John teaches to make ends meet and was, for a time, tutor to one of Gull's grandsons. I'm given to understand they – that is Gull the Elder and Druitt the Younger – had a falling out some twelve months since.'

'And you're hoping Dr Gull will talk to us more frankly due to what we assume is his newly acquired dislike for Druitt?'

'Very perceptive, Caswell.'

They passed the rest of the journey without further conversation. The motion of the cab almost lulled Kit to sleep, so she jumped rather more than was dignified when Makepeace boomed, 'We're here.'

The large house had a shiny black door, an even shinier brass knocker, imposing pillars, and, like all the mansions in the square, faced a tidy private park. The glass in its white window frames sparkled and seemed to magnify the patterns on the sumptuous curtains hanging inside.

To Kit's surprise, the door was opened not by a maid, but by a tall, thin, sallow man. He did not wear the attire of a butler or the livery of a footman, but was neatly dressed in a charcoal-coloured suit with matching vest and a snowy shirt. A silver chain hung from the fob pocket, signifying the presence of a watch on his person. He had a long face, grey eyes and a wary expression touched by superciliousness. He seemed reluctant to let them in, but Makepeace's best smile and the sombre dignity of Kit's uniform seemed to nudge things in their favour. Still and all, Kit followed hard on the Inspector's heels just in case the door should be swiftly slammed behind him.

They stood in an impressive vestibule, punctuated by four doors (three closed, one ajar) and a long corridor that led towards an elaborately carved staircase and the back of the house. The walls were covered in a honey-golden silk paper, and any exposed wood was dark and highly polished.

'How may I help you . . .?'

'Inspector Makepeace. And you are?' Makepeace thrust his hand at the man, who had no choice but to take it or be struck by the blade of the Inspector's fingers.

'Andrew Douglas, Sir William's personal secretary,' he said, his voice vibrating a little with the force of the policeman's handshake. When he was finally released, Kit noticed that Douglas flexed his fingers as if to work out the discomfort of being grasped so securely. She noted the technique for future use, but wasn't sure she'd have the strength to deliver it as effectively as her boss. 'How may I assist you, Inspector?'

'We – myself and young Caswell – are here to see Sir William. It is a matter of considerable importance.' Makepeace was striding around the elegant foyer, craning his neck to see down the hallway, up the staircase, into doorways and didn't bother to hide the fact that he was doing it. Kit watched as Douglas tried to keep pace with the long-legged Inspector, but succeeded only in looking like a particularly clumsy dance partner.

'I'm afraid that Sir William is not receiving visitors this morning, nor for some time to come. He has been ill – you may not be aware,' said Douglas and, seeming to finally realise he would not win this particular waltz competition, came to a halt and stared at Makepeace in a politely hostile manner. The Inspector ceased his perambulations (not because he was discomfited, Kit suspected, but because he'd seen all he could, all he needed to), and peered at the man in innocent surprise, then broke into a friendly open smile.

'I had no idea – you'll forgive me, Mr Douglas, I do not follow gossip. I promise you faithfully young Kit and I shall not tax Sir William, but it is paramount that I speak with him—'

'And *I* said he was indisposed indefinitely,' interrupted Douglas, a dark red flush creeping up from beneath his collar.

'—and I say again that I shall not leave until I have seen the good doctor.' Makepeace barely paused, but raised his volume so that it was not quite a shout, yet still something that could not be ignored. In the sharp silence that followed the dying of its echoes there came a murmur, almost painfully weak, from behind the only open door. A quavering voice, however one that would not be denied.

'Let them in, Douglas, for God's sake, man. It's a police investigation, but I'm sure they're not here to drag me away.'

Many times Kit had heard Mrs K describe this person or that as having "a face like a slapped arse", but this was the first time she actually understood what that meant. Andrew Douglas' visage was pinched and red, mouth tightly puckered, his Adam's apple moved like a sphincter each time he tried to swallow his indignation. The man clicked his heels together, stretched his neck – goose-like – smoothed an errant curl back from his forehead and managed a strangled, 'This way.'

In his prime Sir William Gull had been a stout man, not tall, with a full head of hair and a dimpled chin; he'd strutted the halls and wards of Guy's Hospital and traipsed his no-nonsense attitude into royal palaces, making himself a favourite with Queen Victoria, particularly after he'd saved the

Prince of Wales from a bout of typhoid fever. A series of strokes had whittled him away to a bag of bones. He still had a head of thick greying locks and a thoroughly dimpled chin, though the muscles of his face seemed to struggle with gravity a little.

He sat, a small man in a large armchair beside the white marble fireplace of a room that had once obviously served as his study. He wore a red quilted robe over a white shirt; a fur rug was tucked around his legs, and his feet were firmly planted on a dark green ottoman covered in scarlet needlepoint roses. For all his diminishment his eyes were bright and blue, and showed no loss of his searching intellect.

'Sir William, I am—' began Makepeace, and found himself cut off.

'A very loud police officer. I heard, Inspector.' He fixed the lanky man with a look that was part glare, part amusement, then addressed his employee, 'Andrew, thank you, I will see to our guests. You have your duties.'

'Yes, Sir William. Shall I have tea sent?' Kit could tell it almost choked him to ask.

'I think not, they shan't be with us long,' said the old man pointedly, then added gently, 'Off you go, Andrew.'

After the door had closed, Makepeace opened his mouth, but Sir William raised a shaky hand and shook his head, waiting, listening. After a minute, they heard footsteps moving away, and the hand dropped and he smiled wearily. 'Andrew is a good secretary and he has been with me a long time, but he does sometimes become over-protective and overstep the bounds of his authority, Inspector. I trust you will keep that in mind next time you're tempted to visit me?'

Makepeace, visibly chastened, but not seeming too ashamed of himself, nodded.

Sir William continued quietly, 'He also sometimes listens at doors as I have learned to my chagrin. Now, how can I help you, Inspector?'

'We won't take much of your time, Sir William, but I do need to ask you some questions about your godson, Montague Druitt.'

Even as Makepeace uttered the word "godson", Kit saw the old man's expression change from one of benign tolerance to disgust, which was quickly disguised again. She was impressed at how responsive his facial muscles were even though they seemed so wasted. For a moment she thought he might refuse to answer.

'All I can tell you is that he is a young man without moral compass,' the doctor said, keeping his voice even with effort.

'Can you expand on that?'

The old man pursed his lips and looked away. Makepeace lowered his voice, made it quite soothing. 'You may be aware, Sir William, that there have been several murders in Whitechapel, vicious and violent, of which at least two women have been the victims of the same killer. Your godson's name has been . . . mentioned.'

'Then it is nothing more than an idle mention, Inspector, Druitt has no interest in women.' The old man's lips thinned and compressed so they almost disappeared.

'I see,' said Makepeace slowly. 'He tutored your grandson—'

'I will not speak more of it, Inspector! Suffice to say that no matter what I think of Druitt's actions and his . . . personal tastes, I cannot in conscience tell you he might have done what you are suggesting. He has no interest in the female of the species, not even enough to dislike them, Inspector. Trust me when I say that Druitt is not your man.' Sir William shook with the force of all the things he suppressed and Kit was concerned that he might have another stroke. A decanter of Madeira and two engraved glasses sat on the corner of a large desk, and she poured out a measure.

'Thank you, young man,' managed Sir William and gulped down the proffered drink. When finished, he sighed and handed the delicate glass back to Kit with the sweetest smile she'd ever seen. 'Now, Inspector, will there be anything else?'

Makepeace shook his head and moved to take the old man's hand. There was a minute hesitation, then Sir William accepted the gesture, somewhat reluctantly, but Kit thought all the more of him for it. He might have been enfeebled, but he was not broken, nor would he be bullied. And no matter how much he disliked his godson, he would not tell lies about him simply for a petty revenge.

'We'll see ourselves off the premises, Sir William. Thank you for your time.'

They exited the study and let themselves out the front door before any kind of servant had a chance to make themselves known. Makepeace paused on the top step and took a deep breath, hooking his thumbs under his suspenders and surveying the empty park in front of them.

'Well, Kit, I don't know about you but I don't think well on an empty stomach. I'm sure we can find somewhere suitable around here to offer us sustenance.' He strode off and Kit followed him towards where the square fed onto a busy thoroughfare. The hairs on the back of her neck crept up and she looked over her shoulder towards the fine house they'd just left. On one of the upper floors, she thought she saw a curtain twitch, but then there was nothing more, and Kit ran to catch up with the Inspector.

VI

'How long has it been now, Kit?' asked Lucius, even though he knew as well as she did.

'Twenty-two days, give or take a few hours,' she answered, settling a bonnet on her hair, then tying its red ribbons beneath her chin. She'd appropriated some of her mother's old clothes from the bottom of Louisa's tallboy, things that had not seen the light of day for many years. The high-necked jacket was a deep amethyst, with pearl buttons and red lace trims; around the bottom of a skirt in the same purple hue were intricate frills, punctuated with crimson silk rosettes. The sleeves were three-quarter length and ended in a series of tiered ruffles. She'd had to pad out the chest area – her mother's assets were grander than her own. On the frame of Lucius' bed hung a damson velvet evening cape, its peacock feather design beaded in jet.

'Perhaps he's gone? Finished?' the boy ventured hopefully, but Kit shook her head.

'No. Mary Jane says not. He's just waiting for things to quieten down, for us to stop paying attention.' She stood, smoothing the fabric – in an uncomfortable imitation of Annie Chapman, she wore several petticoats against the cold. 'How do I look?'

Lucius shrugged. His reluctance to hurt her feelings told her she'd succeeded in her aim. She'd found her mother's face paints when she'd liberated the outfit; her cheeks were now highlighted with slashes of rouge and she'd applied a bright vermilion lipstick, then outlined her eyes with kohl. Personally, she thought she looked like a clown in the shaving mirror on Lucius' tallboy, but still she'd managed to recreate the appearance sported by most of the streetwalkers she'd seen in Whitechapel. The make-up wasn't meant to be subtle, it was there as a beacon, a red light, to say *This is what I am, get it here.*

'Will it be dangerous, Kit?' His voice quavered, and for all the occasions he'd listened with excitement as she'd recounted the tales of the crimes she'd witnessed or examined the aftermath of, this was the first instance of him being afraid. He realised that *this* time his sister was truly in harm's way.

She shook her head and lied. 'No, my pet, I've got my truncheon,' she tapped at it, hidden in her tight sleeve, 'and the other PCs will be watching over us. All I've got to do is wander up and down the streets. Never fear, I'm not some innocent lamb.'

'What if Mother sees you?'

'Mother has had her medicine, Lucius, she will sleep until morning, and Mrs K is at her church choir meeting – or is it a séance tonight?' Kit was beginning to regret her decision to change at home, but carting more clothing and accessories to the lock-up had seemed like too much trouble at the time. And she was also beginning to regret having shared her adventures with her brother – it had been an activity designed to distract him from his four walls, not to cause him to worry. She crouched beside the bed and laid a hand on his thin shoulder. 'Look at me, love: I will be as safe as houses. I'm alert and I'll be watched. Never fear. Have I ever lied to you?'

He shook his head.

'I will always come back to you, Lucius, that's the one thing you can rely on. Besides, anyone who tries to take me on will be biting off more than he can chew.' She smiled and he gave a reluctant grin in return, chuckling. She wrapped her arms around him and he snaked his around her, the strength of his hug belying the frailty of his wasted form.

'Be careful, Kit.'

'Always am. Now, lights out, no reading, it's late enough as it is.' She opened the door. 'I'll see you in the morning.'

'Promise?'

'Promise.'

Kit trotted swiftly along the streets, staying in the middle of the road so any attacker would have to come out into the open. Her eyes darted into the gloom of the evening, trying to detect movement and form. It was interesting, she thought, how being dressed as a woman made her feel so vulnerable. In her police uniform, with custodian helmet, truncheon swinging and silver buttons all on display, she felt invincible; she missed her bullseye lantern, her means of bringing light into dark places.

In the worn velvet drawstring purse were her handcuffs, whistle and the brass knuckles, her notepad and pencil. The length of painted wood in her sleeve meant she couldn't bend her arm, had to keep it straight. The heels of her shoes seemed to shout 'Here I come' in much the same way as a lost lamb might bleat.

Kit shivered with more than cold and it was with some considerable relief that she entered the station to wolf whistles and mostly good-natured ribbing. Four of the other young constables, those without beards and whose skin was still soft-looking (admittedly, softer-looking than that of most of Whitechapel's whores) were all in drag of various quality and degrees of taste. Kit was interested to notice that PC Watkins looked much girlier than she herself did; he also appeared pale, exhausted and troubled. Airedale, standing with the crowd of police designated as the decoy streetwalkers' protectors for the evening, sneered at each and every one of the lads, saving most of his disgust for Kit.

'That's quite enough, Constable,' said Makepeace as he stepped from the stairs, Abberline behind him. 'These young men are suffering for their profession and the protection of Whitechapel. There's no need to denigrate them, especially when they've gone to such trouble – lovely frock, Watkins.'

A rumble of laughter rolled through the gathering. Abberline, exchanging a glance and a nod with Makepeace, stepped forward into the circle that formed around the cross-dressed PCs. He cleared his throat and clasped his hands behind his back. The glass moons of his spectacles caught the light and hid his eyes.

'You all know what you need to do, where you need to go, who you need to watch. Take no unnecessary risks, any of you. This man – this monster – has not gone away. He has not forgotten. He is waiting for us to stop attending, men. Do not give him a chance to resume his works.'

Kit was heartened to hear her own thoughts echoed, but it made her shiver. Makepeace saw it, and nodded; she took *Chin up, Caswell* from the gesture and nodded back. She caught a movement – Airedale had seen the exchange and bared his teeth, apparently revolted. Kit suppressed a sigh: that was all she needed, being taken for the Inspector's "special" boy. Makepeace, however, didn't notice. He clapped his hands and shouted, 'Out!' and the crowd dispersed.

Thomas Wright moved into position beside her as they pushed through the double doors. He squeezed her shoulder and muttered, 'Courage, lad'. She strode off ahead of him towards her allocated starting point on Commercial Road. Wright would find a spot in an alley or a darkened doorway and keep an eye on her. Kit didn't envy Watkins, who was paired with Airedale; the youngster kept his head down and she could see the large man's lips moving, pouring forth spite. She looked away, put thoughts of Airedale from her mind, and walked purposefully into the night.

She'd been on her first corner for only a few minutes before Mary Jane Kelly appeared from the swirling mist. 'You're too pretty, too fresh and you don't look anywhere near scared enough for new meat.'

'I feel scared enough, believe me,' muttered Kit. Kelly laughed.

'Only an idiot would come near you, you're so clean and neat!' She leaned against the brick wall casually, eyes scanning the area before them, and continued, 'Men as want new young flesh don't come to the street. They go to the brothels where that can be arranged by reliable madams. People who want that sort of thing know they need to pay for it and pay a *lot*. A man knows that by the time a girl's taken to the alleys it means she can't find a place in a nice cosy bordello, that she's probably not going to be charging a premium price.'

'This is all very fascinating, Miss Kelly, but you're not really helping. You're probably chasing the men away,' said Kit, but she was glad for the company, however brief. With another laugh, the woman drifted off, and Kit settled into a rhythm of rambling through streets and by-ways, hidden squares and secret lane-ways known only to locals. When midnight finally passed, she had been approached by precisely no one, just as Mary Kelly had predicted. She wondered if the other PCs had had any better luck.

At the corner of Rope Walk, she bent to rub at her aching ankles through the leather of her boots. Surveying the murk she tried to divine Wright's hiding place, but failed. The air just beyond her moved suddenly and a figure ghosted through the fog. Kit straightened, fumbled with the baton in her sleeve, wishing she'd hung the whistle from her neck. Her heart clenched cold, then began to beat again as the shape resolved itself into the smallish Chinese boy who often watched the lock-up in Limehouse.

Kit pushed out a breath and leaned down so his whisper would not escape. The message made her feel ill, but she did not hesitate. With a nod to him, she set off at speed, the clatter of her heels on the pavement no longer a lamb's bleat, but a battle hymn. She surged through the streets, Wright's shouts dwindling somewhere behind her.

By the time she'd found the address – Duffield's Yard on Berner St – it was closing on one in the morning, and a man driving a pony and trap was almost at the break in the fence that served as an ingress. The horse shied and refused to go further though the man yelled various threats. Kit stood beside the beast, put her hand on its back and felt the shudders coursing through the animal. The streetlight from outside did not reach the corners of the yard, but the pony knew something was not right.

'Hold your lantern up,' Kit shouted at the driver. Grumbling the man pulled the lamp from where it hung beside him and stood, raising it as high as he could. The flame inside the glass flared and wobbled feebly with the movement, then settled and set the shadows in front of them to dancing across the old furniture, sheets of metal and general rubbish that littered the space. Kit stepped into the enclosure, searching the gloom as best she could until she spotted a supine form against the far wall.

'Hellfire,' breathed the man.

Kit made her way towards the shape. Even as she crouched and pulled the whistle from her drawstring bag she knew it was too late. The woman was blonde, in her forties, face hardened by the life she'd lived, and her throat was a gaping second mouth beneath a tightly pulled chequered scarf. She lay on her side, legs drawn up almost to her chest and her left hand, lying limp in a dark pool on the ground, was missing the pinky finger.

Kit blew long and hard, but before she finished the blast a figure broke from the darkest corner and rushed towards the entrance. He couldn't avoid passing Kit and struck out hard as she tried to rise. She managed to avoid falling onto the dead body, but scraped her face against the bricks of the wall before springing up and racing after the assailant.

She saw a flash of something silver – a knife – that he ran along the flanks of the horse. Kit heard the animal scream as it reared up – she wasn't able to arrest her progress quite fast enough, although she'd managed to begin the process of throwing herself backwards, so the blow the animal caught her on the shoulder was a glancing one. Nevertheless, the pain made her see stars, and she staggered away to sit before she fell beside the dead woman.

Sobbing, she found the silver whistle that she'd dropped and blew on it over and over again. She was still at it when Wright finally caught up with her, drawn by the shrilling. He pulled the thing from her mouth and gently wiped away the tears before anyone else saw Kit Caswell, one of Leman Street's up-and-comers, crying like a girl.

It wasn't long before Duffield's Yard was full of police, and the street beyond undulating with gawkers. The local doctor, Blackwell, who'd been called to the scene was soon shuffled aside when Dr Bagster Phillips hove into view, having been rousted, on this rare occasion, from the bed of his wife.

She gave her statement to Wright, ashamed to admit that she'd not seen the murderer's face, which had been wrapped tightly in a dark-coloured scarf, and a bowler hat had been firmly wedged on his head. The only thing she'd glimpsed, ever so briefly, was the pale band of flesh around his eyes, and she couldn't even remember the colour of those. All she could think of were black holes, but she wasn't sure that was right.

Dr Blackwell, not quite ready to be moved along like a common onlooker, made a point of cleaning the blood and dirt from the grazes on her cheek, and examining her shoulder. Terrified that his hands might stray lower than they should, she spent a tense few minutes lying about the amount of pain she was in, before Makepeace appeared and sent her home with orders not to return to work for an entire day.

VII

'And I tell you I'm her friend and she *will* see me!'

The yelling was loud enough to penetrate Kit's laudanum-fuelled sleep. Upon her return home she'd taken a dose of Louisa's favourite tipple and happily passed out. When her mother had come in to rouse her the next morning, she'd shrieked over the state of Kit's face and the specks of blood on the pillow. Her daughter, wanting only to keep slumbering, managed a mumbled explanation of women's problems and dizziness that had caused her to faint and fall. In the end Louisa left her alone.

There was no window in her room and, as she sat up groggily, she realised she had no idea what time it was, or indeed if she'd slept a full day and into the next. It was Louisa's voice, as strident as the first one, that propelled her out of bed and down the hallway. The front door was open, but just barely, and it was obvious that her mother and Mrs K were trying their best to shut it. In the gap, Kit could make out a wilted bonnet that had once been very fine, and dark curls bouncing around with the force of their owner's umbrage. The familiar tones of mingled singsong accents told her who her visitor was.

'It's all right. She's a friend.' Kit reached out and touched her mother's shoulder. Louisa rounded on her, eyes enormous in a bloodless face, an expression that said all her worst fears had come to fruition; as if she knew what the caller truly was.

'How can she . . . this . . .'

'Mary Jane works with me at Mistress Hazleton's.'

'You've never spoken of her,' hissed Louisa.

Kit fixed her mother with a long look. 'And when have you ever asked me about my job, Mother, except to see if I've been paid?'

Louisa bit back a retort, all the wind taken out of her sails. Kit pushed the advantage and said, 'We'll chat in the parlour. Mrs K, won't you take Mother to the kitchen and make her some tea, please?'

Mrs Kittredge pursed her lips in disapproval, but nodded. The two older women reluctantly receded down the hallway towards the back of the flat. Mary Jane Kelly, dressed in a peacock-blue frock and black jacket stood on the doorstep with all the dignity of a ruffled chicken. Kit half expected to see tail feathers sprouting from her bustle in the late afternoon gloom. She wondered if the woman had made a special effort to appear "respectable" but had simply lost the knack.

'Come in, Mary Jane, please. I'm sorry for that.'

In the parlour they sat, Mary Jane in her decrepit finery, and Kit in her long white night-gown, its high neck and sleeves hiding the red-purple bruising on her shoulder. The ache was beginning to eat through the comforting numbness of the laudanum. She'd slept like the dead and while it had been a relief to escape from what she'd seen last night – from what she'd failed to prevent – she was determined not to seek its balm again.

Now that they were alone, Mary Jane seemed uncertain how to start the conversation she'd so desperately sought. She cleared her throat and led with, 'You're more like one of us now, the face on you. And you've got that look in your eye – a woman never looks quite the same after she's been hit, no matter that it might only happen once.'

'Did you know her? Elizabeth Stride?' Kit asked, having heard the name before she'd been sent home.

'Long Liz. Swedish. Not a bad sort,' replied Kelly, looking around the tiny parlour at the ambrotypes (all the Caswells in happier times) on various pieces of fine mahogany furniture jammed into the room, the loudly ticking clock on the mantelpiece, the petite point antimacassars on the wing-chairs, the lace and damask curtains over the front window with its seat that looked out on the street. Perhaps it was the nicest room Kelly had ever been in – or at least in her recent history of boarding houses and the like. 'Knew Cathy Eddowes, too, her as called herself Kate Kelly.'

Kit frowned. 'But there was only one body in the yard – if there'd been another, I'd have noticed.'

'He got Cathy at Mitre Square, about an hour after you chased him off Lizzie. That young Watkins found her – he found poor Annie, too, didn't he? He'll be a wreck.' Kelly leaned back in the armchair, nestling into its folds and lumpy cushions as if it were a throne of some sort and she a displaced grandee.

Kit put her head in her hands and sobbed. She'd been too late to save Elizabeth Stride and, in failing to catch the bastard, she'd given him the opportunity to go and carve Cathy Eddowes. Mary Jane didn't comfort her – all her own tears had been wept far too long ago – just waited for Kit to pull herself together. Then she said, 'He's written to the newspapers, I'm told, given himself a name. Jack. Jack the Ripper, Saucy Jack. The papers published the letter.'

'*If* it's from him.' Kit sniffed, wiping her eyes on her sleeve. 'Why would he write, draw attention to himself? He's not doing it for that, you said.'

Kelly shrugged. 'Maybe it's not him, not our one. Maybe it's some Bedlamite playing games.'

'Or a journalist, trying to sell more papers.'

'My, what a suspicious mind you've got, little miss.' Kelly picked at a speck of dirt under her nails. 'Heard anything else from your Inspector?'

Kit shook her head. 'We didn't really have much time to chat last night.' She took a deep breath. 'We spoke to Sir William Gull about his godson after Annie was murdered, but the godson's since turned up in the Thames with stones in his pockets.'

'Ah, Sir William, he's an old love,' sighed Kelly. Kit tilted her head.

'You know him?'

'Oh, he used to visit Whitechapel regular-like back before he got sick. Comes out sometimes, though he can't do anything but talk. Still and all, he's a darling and a great supporter of us working girls.' Mary Jane snorted. Kit sat quietly for a moment.

'So, Liz and Cathy were both—'

'Witches? Yes.' Kelly sighed. 'All women are balanced somewhere on the witch's scale, Kit Caswell, but some barely make the weight requirement. Like you.'

Kit nodded. 'I've got nothing. No second sight or sixth sense. Mrs K does like her séances, but I suspect she just goes for the port and biscuits afterwards. Sometimes I think my mother might see things, but that's probably just the laudanum . . .'

'She's of a type, your mother,' said Mary Jane lightly, then changed the subject before Kit could ask her what she meant. 'What are you going to do now, PC Caswell? You said you'd help.'

Kit didn't answer. Mary Kelly watched her, face darkening.

'Well?'

'What can I do? I let two women die last night. What use am I to anyone? What difference can I make? We don't know anything about him, we've got no clues, no direction.' She shrugged.

Kelly stood, haughty as a queen. 'When you've finished your wallowing, come and find me. All your self-pity isn't going to *assist* anyone – and he's got one more that he wants, needs. So don't take too much time about it.'

Kit trailed her to the door and stood on the stoop as Mary Jane stepped into the night-draped street and finally disappeared, turning a corner. Kit waited, arms wrapped around herself, as if the other woman might come back, might relent. She'd not felt this hopeless or helpless, even when her mother fell apart; *then* she knew what she had to do, it was not only obvious but a matter of survival. Now she couldn't even begin to think where to start with the Whitechapel witches.

The evening cold crept through her and it was a while before she became aware of someone watching her. She scanned the area, eyes probing the scant spaces between houses, the corners, the alleys, desperately trying to pierce the darkness. She found no one and convinced herself that it was Mary Jane Kelly, peeking at her from afar. Even as she retreated inside and latched the door, though, the chain and bolt seemed nowhere near sturdy enough.

Kit stepped into the parlour to warm herself by the fire; firstly, she pulled the curtains across against prying eyes. She was still standing there, hands outstretched when she heard the mail slot rattle a little, as if someone was trying to be very quiet. Then there was the light sound of something hitting the carpet.

Padding into the corridor in her bare feet, Kit saw a creamy envelope lying there. The card of it was thick and expensively-made. The flap was secured with red wax, but there was no seal stamped into it, no hint as to who it might be from. She wondered briefly if Kelly had doubled back to deliver it – then she realised she didn't even know if Mary Jane could read and write.

She fumbled with the lock and chain, and threw open the door in hopes of finding the letter's owner, but the street was empty by the time she managed to do so. Kit waited for long moments, looking up and down the thoroughfare, trying to discern if there really were eyes on her or if she was imagining it. All it did was make her certain she had not even the slightest sixth sense.

'Katherine?'

Louisa's voice travelled from the kitchen, although her mother did not show herself and Kit took the opportunity to pick up the letter and slip it into the sleeve of her night-gown. She closed and secured the door once more, moving stiffly as her injury made its position more firmly known.

'Yes, Mother?'

'Come and have some supper, if you're feeling better. You must be famished.'

Kit didn't think she'd ever have an appetite again, but decided that it was in her interests to let her mother think normalcy had taken up residence in their home once more.

'Yes, Mother,' she said, aware of the letter burning against her skin; she must hide it for now. 'I'll just get my robe.'

VIII

Watkins, thought Kit, looked worse than she felt. The deep navy of his uniform made his pallor even more striking and the circles beneath his eyes gave him the appearance of a corpse that, refusing to believe it was dead, insisted upon walking around. On her way towards Leman Street, she'd spotted her fellow PC and intercepted him as he shambled up Commercial Street in what passed for morning sunshine.

'Alright, Watkins?' she asked and the young man started like a skittish horse; he peered at Kit as if unsure who she was, then seemed to relax, his shoulders dropping as he recognised her.

'Oh. It's you,' he mumbled, not really looking at her but past her.

'You found the other one? Eddowes?'

He nodded. 'She was cut. She was cut so bad.' He began to sob. 'Why didn't you catch him? You were so close, Caswell, why couldn't you just have got him so he didn't . . . so I didn't . . .'

Kit was frozen, horrified, aching with guilt and concern for Watkins, who stood before her on a crowded street, weeping like a child as people buffeted past them. She couldn't put her arms around him as she would Lucius, she couldn't walk away, and she certainly couldn't tell him to pull himself together and go to work. She hated to think what Airedale would say if he saw the youth in this state. She wondered what he'd said the night of the decoys, and where he'd been when Watkins had found Cathy Eddowes.

'I . . . I tried, Ned. I did try,' she said lamely. He swallowed with effort.

'I see the other one. I seen her since I found her. Then this morning, this new one appears beside her, right next to my bed. They don't say anything, they just stand there, staring at me.' He grabbed Kit's shoulders and shook her – the pain almost made her pass out. 'What do they want? I've got to make them go away!'

She wrenched herself from his grip, desperate to not have his fingers clawing into the tender injured flesh. 'Ned! Ned, you need to go home. You need to have a rest.'

'I've not been sleeping,' he said, 'not since I found Dark Annie. And Airedale just keeps on at me and on at me, talking about it all the time, talking about how they come apart so easy, that it's just like butchering a cow . . .'

'Ned,' she said, and gently grasped his upper arms, made him focus on her, look her in the eyes. 'Ned, you need to go home. I'll talk to the Inspector, I'll let him know you're sick.'

'You can't tell him! He'll think I'm mad and no one will ever let me forget it. Airedale—'

'Bloody Airedale won't bloody know!' she snapped. 'Ned, I'll just tell Himself you're ill, that you've eaten something to make you sick. That's all. No more than a dodgy stomach, mate, yeah? We've all suffered from those pies at Stout Aggie's.'

She nodded and soon he was mirroring her; Stout Aggie's was a byword for tasty but occasionally dangerous food that most of the local constabulary risked at least once.

'Sick,' he repeated. 'Sick in the guts. That's okay, then, isn't it?'

'That's okay, Ned. Off you go.'

She watched him as he moved away, swaying on his feet from weariness and fear. Kit wondered if she should tell Makepeace exactly what state the young PC was in, then decided against it. She'd promised, and besides he'd never live it down if the information ever got to Airedale, which – given the way gossip, rumour and truth moved through the strangely porous walls of the station – it would. Even the other coppers weren't above tormenting the lad mercilessly, but Airedale . . . Airedale was something else, there was something wrong in him, something malicious and spiteful that liked to come out and play in the light. Kit wouldn't risk subjecting Ned Watkins to that.

Inside, Kit greeted the desk sergeant, who gave her a nod. It loosened the tightness in her chest that had taken up residence since she'd let the Ripper slip through her fingers, quite literally; she hadn't even managed to get the truncheon out of her sleeve, hadn't struck even the merest of blows on the man who'd killed four women. There would be disappointment among her colleagues, she knew, but how much recrimination there might be was yet to be seen. She was so caught up trying to predict the balance, she almost ran into Abberline as she made her way to the briefing room.

'Watch out, lad.'

'Sorry, sir.'

Abberline didn't acknowledge her apology and it made her stomach swirl. The older inspector held her accountable, she was sure of it. She couldn't say she blamed him; he was the one being torn at by the feuding eagles of Commissioner Warren, Home Secretary Matthews and Assistant Commissioner Monro, all of whom had their particular opinions about dealing with this case, and were the kind of men who would do nothing but complain about the failure of others without ever offering concrete assistance. She wondered if Abberline's attitude towards her would trickle down; then she wondered if Makepeace shared his colleague's opinion. That thought made her feel even worse as she stepped into a room filled with stale male sweat and men in custodian helmets wearing accusing stares.

'Good of you to join us, Caswell,' Makepeace said coolly, and she couldn't work out whether he was signalling his displeasure or simply trying to keep things running normally – it was his habit to greet in such a way the last PC to arrive. 'Right, listen up. We had two close calls last night, and we've now two newly-dead women. You can all imagine how we are being represented in the press and perceived by the public – especially with these so-called Ripper letters doing the rounds.'

The mention of letters made Kit think of the one in her pocket, still unopened. She simply hadn't had either the time or the privacy since it had been pushed through the mail slot; her mother had stuck close after dinner, questioning her about her work and friends, and then insisted upon sitting beside her bed until she fell asleep – it wasn't worth it to make a fuss and arouse the woman's suspicions any further. Kit still suspected it was from Mary Jane, berating her for failing to save Liz and Cathy, for failing to catch their murderer, for failing to come up with a plan for stopping the carnage once and for all.

'No more decoys, either, after that went so well. We're being told to concentrate on the clues. The complete lack of them seems to make no nevermind to Commissioner Warren and his ilk.' Makepeace proceeded to give the assembled group their assignments for the shift. Kit noted that she was the only officer not to receive a task. When Watkins was called, she didn't say anything, merely watched the annoyed look play across Makepeace's face. She could feel Abberline looking at her and carefully kept her expression blank. She didn't see either Wright or Airedale, and their names were not called, which suggested they were elsewhere already.

Makepeace wound up, shooting a glance at Abberline, whose swift shake of the head said he had nothing else to add. The older man joined the exiting flow, and Kit stayed behind, waiting for Makepeace to notice her. But he'd turned his back and was surveying the wall which was covered with maps, lists of names and places and dates, and, worst of all, the photos of the women after their deaths.

These were not gentle post-mortem depictions, but terrible facsimiles that showed in harsh black and white all of the awful things that had been done to them, all the hideous notations that had been engraved upon the victims with a sharp implement.

'Sir?'

'What is it?' Makepeace wouldn't meet her eyes.

'It's about Ned, sir. Watkins, that is – he's sick. I saw him on Commercial Street and he's gone home, sir.'

'Well, why the hell didn't you say something before?' he snapped, and she remained silent until he looked at her, caught her expression and saw there that she wouldn't make her fellow constable appear weak in front of his colleagues. He nodded reluctantly. 'Right. Anything else? Anything *important*?'

The night of the double event, when he'd found Kit banged up and bloody in Duffield's Yard, Makepeace had been solicitous. He'd been kind. Now he was distant, annoyed; the change, Kit assumed, was due less to the loss of Liz Stride's life than to the consequences of Kit's failure being so stunningly magnified by the death of Cathy Eddowes.

She bit her lip, uncertain what to say, what to ask. Makepeace fixed her with a look, narrowing his eyes. 'Caswell, is there something you wanted?'

Slowly she shook her head, blinking hard. 'No, sir, nothing. Only, I'm sorry. I did try, sir.'

'Then make yourself useful.' His voice suddenly sounded not so cold, somehow begrudgingly gentle. 'Go and talk to Stride and Eddowes' husbands, or whatever they had that passed for husbands.'

'Haven't they already been interviewed, sir?'

'Yes, but it was Airedale, so you can imagine how well that went. You might shake something loose. Off you go before I change my mind and put you to cleaning the cells.'

'Yes, sir.' It was busy-work, Kit suspected, but it still wasn't the worst thing he could have done to her, and it might yet yield something, some kind of connection between the women apart from their profession.

His voice stopped her. 'Caswell?'

'Yes, sir?'

'It wasn't your fault.' Said grudgingly, however it was as if he was happy to get it off his chest. 'No matter what happens from here on in, what happened last night wasn't your fault – and quite frankly, we were lucky not to lose you too.'

Kit didn't answer. She thought he was lying, but the kindness of it stopped up her throat. She stared at the wall of evidence, taking in all the faces, the injuries, the loss. There weren't just the four, those Kelly had known and believed were being hunted for their power, Nichols, Chapman, Stride and Eddowes. The others – Emma Elizabeth Smith and Martha Tabram, Annie Millwood and Ada Wilson – to Kit's mind they didn't belong. She thought she saw the glimmer of a way to show Makepeace a path without having to mention the word 'witches'; a way to make him take her seriously again. She took a deep breath, leery of breaking their fragile truce.

'They're different, sir.'

Makepeace looked at her, an eyebrow raised. 'Different?'

'The early ones, sir, they're not the same as the last four. Those first four were robbed and stabbed, not slashed and mutilated. Smith and Millwood survived at least for a little while, and Ada Wilson is still alive, and squarely pointing her finger at the same grenadier who was supposed to have done for Tabram. We just can't get any proof because his mates keep giving him an alibi.'

Makepeace nodded for her to go on, and she took heart.

'But the last four, sir, they're different. Chapman's rings were gone, but she had coins in her pocket, which we assumed were from her last client, but maybe it was from pawning the rings. Whoever killed her didn't take that, so what if he didn't care about rings or the money because it *wasn't* about those things? We know what he *did* take from Nicholls, Chapman and Stride, sir, and that's bits of flesh. What about Eddowes, sir? Ned said she was badly cut up.'

Makepeace said, 'Her face was hacked at, her belly torn open and her left kidney was gone.'

Kit felt her gorge rise, swallowed it down, then reinforced her point. 'They're inconsistent, sir, crimes committed by discrete men – with the first four you're looking at maybe two, even three separate killers whose intent was to rob; the women died because they fought back. The second lot, our girls, that's a single killer, distinct from the others, with a stranger, darker intent.'

'And what intent's that, Caswell?'

'If I knew, sir, we might be further along than we are.'

Makepeace stared at Kit long and hard, then returned his gaze to the wall. Slowly he moved forward and began the process of shuffling the photos and lists into new alignments, two groups of four. Kit felt her heart lift, just a little, a kind of hope like sunlight.

'Don't you have men to interview, Caswell?'

IX

Kit strode towards the Christ Church graveyard in the late afternoon. She didn't go into the church itself, but took the gate she and Kelly had used what seemed a lifetime ago and headed towards the small cluster of figures in a back corner, huddling among the headstones, the shoulders of their coats lightly sprinkled with snow.

The group of seven women spotted Kit and broke apart like a disturbed swarm. Luckily not a one was inclined – or able – to run, so she lengthened her stride and managed to grab hold of the nearest. None of the others stopped to help their compatriot – the sisterhood was thin nowadays, observed Kit.

The woman, with wiry red hair, no front teeth and a scar that lifted the left side of her mouth, spat and hissed and Kit considered slapping her, then realised she'd been around men too long if she thought that was a solution.

'Eliza Cooper, pull your head in or you'll get a night in the cells whether you like it or not,' said Kit, and the other seemed to calm down – although it was so cold the young PC wondered if the tart wouldn't be averse to a free bed, four walls and a promise of warm stew. 'I'm looking for Mary Kelly – still looking for her.'

It was the fifth of November, and thirty-six days had passed since the double event, thirty-five since Kelly had left number 3 Lady's Mantle Court and seemingly disappeared into thin air. The only comfort was that her body hadn't turned up anywhere. Kit almost dared hope the prostitute had packed her bags and left London for safer climes; but it seemed unlikely. Kelly, like most folk, was a creature of habit, an habitué of the city's streets and it would take more than a threat of death and dismemberment to get her to leave the place she knew best.

While Kit hadn't yet given up on finding Mary Jane, her options were thinner than workhouse broth. No one was admitting to seeing her and Kit had heard nothing from her. The letter, which still rested in her tunic pocket, made heavier by its content and all its potential consequences, had not been from Kelly.

'Ain't seen her – ain't nobody seen her in weeks,' grumbled Cooper, refusing to meet Kit's eyes, but wearing a familiar expression. She'd spent so much of her time checking on Whitechapel's whores that their business was suffering – Kit's seemingly ever-present vigilance was costing them clients. Whatever gratitude there might initially have been was eaten away by her scaring off their meal tickets. There was something different, though, in Cooper's tone, an exasperation that Kit thought she might be able to swing to her own advantage.

'Eliza. Eliza, look at me.'

Reluctantly, the woman did so. 'What?'

'Eliza, I need to find Mary Jane. I need to know if she's all right and I need her help.' The woman began to shake her head and Kit hurried on, 'Please, Eliza, please. Don't think the danger's gone – Jack's still out there. He's waiting.'

Kit could see the woman's resolve wavering, and she wasn't above stacking the deck; she pulled a purse from her pocket and jingled its contents. 'There's enough here for a bed and a meal. You won't need to earn it the hard way. Please, Eliza, I'm not trying to hurt her.'

At first it seemed her plea had failed, then Cooper made a noise of disgusted surrender and held out her hand. Kit gave her a look to say she wasn't stupid enough to give over money before she got the information and the woman laughed. 'Mary Jane said you were a clever lad. Aw'right, she's at the lodging house in Flower and Dean St – number 32, where Lizzie lived.'

'Who's paying her bills?' Kit asked, as she counted coins into Eliza Cooper's grimy palms – she'd been holding something back from the housekeeping for the past weeks, set aside for this very purpose.

'She's keeping the landlord "happy" as best she knows how,' laughed the woman and gleefully pocketed the easiest money she'd ever made.

Kit frowned. 'Eliza, don't spend it on drink, please. Get a room and a good night's sleep. Be safe and warm.'

The woman nodded, but Kit suspected she meant the opposite, and shrugged. She'd not inherited her father's fervour for imposing salvation on those uninterested in being saved. Kit sighed and said, 'Off you go, Eliza. Take care of yourself.'

The woman nodded again, giving Kit a strange look. They were talking, she knew, the Whitechapel whores, about how eccentric young PC Caswell was, how he didn't want to take advantage of the favours offered him, how he didn't want to save their souls, how he just tried to help with no thought of reward. Such selflessness made them wary and suspicious.

Kit moved away quickly, wanting to ensure she got to her destination before Cooper thought better of the deal, and decided to warn Mary Jane that she'd been found.

The boarding house was like so many of its kind and there were over two hundred packed into Whitechapel alone, people crammed into tiny filthy rooms, barely able to scrape together the money for a night's sleep. Kit found the landlord's assistant – a youngish man given his lodging in exchange for looking after the degraded property in the meagrest way possible – and it didn't take long for her to coax the location of Kelly's room from him. She knocked quietly, wondering if she'd have to draw the woman out then found, to her astonishment, the door incautiously hauled open. Kelly, dressed in a simple white blouse, black shawl and blue skirt, with no trace of make-up and her hair in modest bun, seemed as surprised as Kit was.

'You. I thought it was his lordship come to collect the rent. You'd better come in then.' She stood aside and let her guest past.

The room was small, but surprisingly tidy. Clothes were carefully folded on a single shelf, and the bed was neatly made. A bedside table held a lamp, a bottle of gin and two glasses. In a wicker basket at the foot of the bed was a pile of mending, and Kit could see the needle and various coloured skeins Kelly had been using. Kit raised an eyebrow.

'Practising for my new career,' said Mary Jane and indicated that Kit should take the sole chair while she herself settled on the bed and took up the sock she'd been darning.

'How are you, Mary?' asked Kit as she carefully lowered herself onto the seat, somewhat concerned about how it might react to any weight greater than that of a folded blanket. The piece of furniture groaned its protest but held, and after a few moments Kit relaxed.

'Alive, which, given the circumstances, is the best I can hope for,' Kelly said tartly.

Kit nodded. 'I've been looking for you. I was worried.'

'No need to be. I'm taking care of myself, I've a good thing going here. Only one "client" a day and he brings me the mending to do. We've an agreement.'

'You don't go out,' stated Kit.

'Well, it's cold outside.' Kelly tied off a thread and set the sock aside, paired it, then selected a blouse from the pile and found a matching bobbin of thread, and began the business of getting the strand through the eye of the needle. Kit found her own tongue pressing at the inside of her mouth as if to protrude in sympathetic concentration.

'Why did you disappear? Why didn't you let me know?'

'Someone started following me. Couldn't see anyone, but I just knew it. So I went to ground. Besides, you weren't looking like being any help.'

Kit ignored the barb. 'That last night I saw you . . .'

'Mmmmm?' Kelly sounded disinterested and kept her eyes on her task.

Kit pulled the letter from her pocket. 'Someone put this through the mail slot after you left. And someone was watching my house, I'm sure of it. Was it you?'

'No. When I left, I left. And that letter's not from me either.'

'I know that. It's from *him*.'

Mary Jane's hands stilled, the blouse falling and slowly deflating in her lap. Kit opened the envelope, just as she had many times since she'd first cracked the wax seal. The handwriting was nothing like the red scrawl that had been reproduced in the newspapers. This was not the work of the Jack who liked to write, to communicate, to show off and revel in his notoriety. This hand was strong, graceful and in black ink; it was businesslike and focused. It was the handwriting of a proposition, an exchange. It seemed the script of a reasonable man – or at least one who considered his actions reasonable.

She held it out to the other woman, not daring to ask if she could read. Kelly took it reluctantly, and Kit watched her eyes move across the words, taking them in. Watched as the woman's thin hands began to shake. Watched as Kelly raised her stare to meet Kit's with a growing terror.

'Is that why you're here?' she asked in a strangled voice.

Kit shook her head vehemently. 'No! Don't think that of me.'

'Then why? Why show me this? Why find me when I'm safe?'

'Because I think I can catch him. I think I know what to do. I don't know how he knows what he knows about me, about Lucius, but I think we can lure him and catch him, Mary Jane.'

'Let me get this straight: this man wants to make a deal with you. My life for a marked improvement in your brother's health? And you don't want to take him up on that?'

'Would it work?' Kit challenged.

Kelly shrugged. 'It might, if this letter writer's got any power of his own. If not, then probably not.'

'Well, Mary Jane Kelly, I don't believe it will. I don't believe he's got any power or he wouldn't be stealing your paltry share. I don't believe he can offer me anything and, even if he could, I wouldn't buy Lucius' health in such a way – I may not know anything about witchcraft, but I do know that a price like this is too high. If I had all the wealth in the world I'd spend it on my brother, but I won't offer one life for another. I just won't. I've got enough deaths on my conscience to last a lifetime.' She rubbed her hands across her face. 'And Ned Watkins is dead – did you know *that*?'

The expression on Kelly's face said she didn't. 'Poor lamb. What happened?'

'He hung himself in the garden shed of his parents' house. He said he

316 | ANGELA SLATTER

was seeing them – seeing Dark Annie and Cathy Eddowes. He said they didn't say anything, just stood beside his bed in the night and looked at him.'

Kelly sighed. 'Sometimes they stay around, the dead. They attach themselves to the person who found them – sometimes to their killer, but sometimes they just look for the first kind heart that happens upon them after death. You don't see Lizzie?'

Kit shook her head, wondering what that said about her heart, and leaned over to take the letter from Kelly's fingers. 'I am, as you've pointed out, completely untouched by any sort of magic.'

She waved the single sheet of thick creamy-coloured paper. 'This is the only way I know how to help, Mary Jane, but I need your assistance.'

'You need me to be bait,' she sneered, and Kit nodded.

'Yes. Apparently no one else will do.'

'Does your Inspector know about this? About this letter?'

Kit shook her head, holding the other woman's gaze.

Kelly gave a lopsided smile. 'If you tell him it's about witches and magic he'll think you're mad. If you show him this letter, addressed to Miss Katherine Caswell, he'll work out that you're not what you say you are. Too many questions asked and you with not enough lies to tell.'

'If he works out I'm female then my life goes back to what it was. I go back to scraping a living for three people. I *won't* be that helpless again.'

'Find a rich husband, you're pretty enough.'

'Where am I going to find a rich husband? If it was that easy, wouldn't you have done it by now?'

The air between them was thick and bitter. Kit took a deep breath, struggled to stop her voice from shaking. 'But *this* is what I can do. If you'll help me, I can entice him out, and he will not survive, I promise you.'

They both shuddered to hear the steel in her tone, to hear her say what they both knew had to be done. 'He'll die for what he did to Polly and Annie and Elizabeth and Cathy. He'll die for what he'd do to you. If he's caught, he'll go to the gallows without a doubt – but he'll tell secrets and ruin lives before he does. Even if no one believes you're a witch, Mary Jane, they'll find out I'm a woman and my life will be over.'

'So you'll be a murderer, too,' observed Kelly.

Kit shook her head, not denying the other's words, simply not wanting to think about them. She folded the sheet of paper carefully and slid it back into the envelope as if it was the most important thing she had to do at this very moment. She stood and cleared her throat.

'I'll do it,' said Kelly, voice flat. Kit froze. The other woman's consent, for all it solved one problem, created a series of others.

'Are you sure?'

'Good God, Kit Caswell, you badger me into this mad plan and now you want to know if I'm sure?' Kelly laughed harshly. 'I'm sure. It's the only way I'll walk the streets safely again – well, as safe as the streets ever get for my kind.'

Kit swallowed and nodded. She said, 'I'll put the advertisement in the Personals section of the paper just as he asks. We'll need an address to send him to . . .'

'Not here, for God's sake.'

'. . . somewhere private.'

'I've got just the place.'

X

Kit had only ever set foot in the store twice before. The first time was in response to a message from Mr Wing, the week after her father's death. One of the Chinese lads had come to the rectory and Louisa, barely sentient until called to the door by Kit, had shrieked at the boy to go away. He fled, dropping a rectangle of white card in his wake, which Kit pocketed. The address on the back, inked in a fair hand, led her to Limehouse and a shop that contained all manner of herbal restoratives.

She liked the smell, incense and all the dried ingredients combined to a heady mix. Mr Wing had seemed terribly old then as he explained his obligation to her family, and even older the second visit when Kit made the request that resulted in her being allocated space in the lock-up. This occasion, the third, she'd taken extra care with her appearance, ensuring her dress, bonnet, cape and bag were all black as a reminder of her grief – even though the mourning period was well and truly over – and the debt that was owed.

Nothing had changed, though the odour had a sickly sweet

undertone – she wondered if the basement area was being used as an opium den, then shook her head. She didn't want to know and she wasn't in a position to judge anyone at this point. The light coming through windows covered in London grime was dim, the store was empty of customers, and it seemed none of the shelf contents had moved, but she knew that the Chinese apothecary did a brisk trade and Mr Wing's reputation was such that even Harley Street specialists directed their patients here for certain types of remedies. She'd once tried Lucius on some of the old gentleman's concoctions, but the scent and taste had him refusing more than one swallow and in the end she tipped the mixture out.

Behind the counter sat the object of her search, perched on a high stool as if he was a manikin or a puppet, left as guardian. His round face showed no surprise at seeing her, although his trailing white moustaches twitched in greeting. His long robe was a curious grey-green and she thought how well it helped him to blend in with the shadows of the interior.

'Miss Katherine,' he said, his voice smooth as oil, a young man's voice. 'Another social call so soon – should I be concerned?'

Kit smiled. 'Hello, Mr Wing.' She wasn't entirely sure that was even his proper name, but it was the one he gave to his shopfront, to the Westerners who frequented this place, and the one his own people used at least in the presence of others. 'I trust you are well.'

He nodded, but didn't answer, merely waited to hear her purpose.

She hesitated, then spoke. 'Mr Wing, I must make a special request of you. I do not do this lightly, but I come to you because of our bond.'

He laughed. 'You mean my debt, Miss Katherine.'

She half nodded, half shrugged.

'And what do you require of me?'

'I need a gun, sir.'

He was silent for long moments, stroking his moustaches, then he did the unthinkable and got down off his throne and came towards her. His motions were not those of an aged man, and she thought he moved slowly because he wanted to, not because he had to.

'This is a very big favour, Miss Caswell,' he said gravely as he came to a halt.

'You owe me a very big favour, Mr Wing. You told me so,' she said equally gravely, holding his gaze.

'What makes you think I will be interested in helping you with such an illegal thing?'

'The same reason you sent the boy to me and to tell me about the dead woman.' He opened his mouth to deny it but she kept going, 'Very little happens, sir, that you are not aware of – I know your runners gather information the way other boys pick berries. And I know it's to keep your people safe – forewarned is forearmed. So trust me when I say this is something I need to keep my – all people – safe. I know you will understand that and you will want to help.'

He stared at her, then finally said, 'Single or multiple shot?'

She blinked. 'Multiple would be best.'

'More than one chance, although I am told one should always make the first shot count. Do you know how to use it?'

She nodded. Her father had taught her to shoot at game birds; she'd had training in firearms when she'd joined the Met, but had not been deemed reliable enough to carry a weapon yet, being so new in the job.

'It will be with one of the boys at the lock-up.'

'When? I need it . . .'

'These things are not easy to come by,' he said, then laughed. 'The evening of the ninth.'

She thanked him and turned to go. At the door, his voice stopped her.

'Miss Katherine?'

'Yes?' She looked over her shoulder, eyebrows raised.

'Remember the steps you take cannot be taken back. Some actions are simply too serious to retreat from – this is what I always tell our young men when they must choose their paths. I think it applies to you, too. What you do next will change the direction of your life.'

Kit nodded, but did not answer. Outside, she gasped and dragged the cold air into her lungs; the shop had become unaccountably stuffy and close. She closed her eyes and rubbed them until stars speckled the back of her lids. She had no choice, she told herself. Either she sat back and did nothing, pretended she was untouched by what had and might continue to happen; or she could explain everything to Makepeace and in doing so expose herself utterly and lose all that she'd fought so hard to gain; or she could do *this*, this last thing, finish it all and keep herself and her life intact.

'Where have you been?' asked Louisa as soon as Kit set foot in the door. She'd been particularly vigilant in the weeks since Mary Kelly's social call, or at least while Kit was actually home, as if whatever she might be doing would be evident when she was under her mother's watchful eye. Kit held up her purse and gave it a gentle shake so the tiny bottles clinked together, and dangled the larger bag that contained groceries.

'Medicine for Lucius and more laudanum, Mother, and food.' She kept her tone even as she took off her bonnet and hung it on the hall-stand, although Louisa's wariness was becoming wearying. 'How is Lucius?'

'He's still running such a temperature,' fussed Louisa.

Kit fished a small brown sack from the holdall and offered it. 'Boil some water and steep that in it. It's feverfew and should help.'

Louisa nodded and disappeared into the kitchen. Kit made her way to her brother's room and found Mrs K reading to him from a battered Bible. Kit couldn't tell if his expression was the result of febrile listlessness or boredom; he was staring out the pocket-sized window into the pocket-sized yard. Kit smiled. 'Have a spell, Mrs K, I'll sit with him for a while.'

The older woman looked at her and nodded; she didn't seem as suspicious of Kit as Louisa did, but rather just somewhat disapproving. As if the girl had let the side down. As she passed in the doorway, Mrs K said in a low voice, 'That friend of yours from the milliner's?'

Kit tilted her head, waited for her to go on.

'I know her from somewhere, but I can't remember where.'

Kit shrugged. 'She lives close to Mistress Hazleton's shop. I can't think where else you might have seen her.'

Mrs K shook her head, and handed Kit the Bible. When she could hear voices from the kitchen, she sat down beside the bed and put her hand on Lucius' brow. He had a slight fever, but it was nothing like what she'd expected. 'How are you feeling?'

'Fine,' he said, tone light, not looking at her. 'Did you find her?'

Kit had stopped sharing her adventures with Lucius – or rather, she'd been heavily censoring what she told him, and he knew it. He'd been so worried before the double event and after Kit had returned home with her face grazed and shoulder injured, he'd not looked well since. When he asked for information, it was with an undertone of distress Kit had never heard before and it added to her guilt. She'd not told him about Watkins and she'd only told him the barest minimum about her search for Mary Kelly.

'Found her, a few days ago. She's safe and well, Lucius, never fear. She's not in danger and I think he may have gone.' She lied lightly.

'You said not. You said he wouldn't go away. That he wasn't going to stop until he got whatever it was he wanted.'

She cursed herself for telling him everything she had. She cursed him for poking at her fear – her knowledge – that the killer was simply waiting for Mary Jane to resurface, that her plan was too risky, too ill-conceived and desperate. She leaned forward and took his hand, and spoke quietly as the sounds of tea making and her mother riffling through the groceries continued from the kitchen. 'Lucius, I promise you it will all be over soon. I promise you this man will never hurt anyone ever again. And I promise you I will be so careful.'

'You said that last time,' he pointed out, finally meeting her eyes.

'Yes, I did. And I underestimated him. Not this time, though, not again. I just need you to trust me. Will you do that?'

Before he could answer one way or another, Louisa appeared at the door. She bore a delicate porcelain teacup, from which a scent not unlike musty camphor wafted. Lucius' nose wrinkled and he pulled a face.

'None of that, young man,' said Kit. 'It's for your own good and medicine isn't meant to taste like sweeties. Sometimes we all have to do things we don't want to.'

He fixed her with a look and said, 'I know.'

XI

Waiting in the overgrown garden next to the lock-up was the lad who'd come to warn her about Liz Stride's untimely demise. She'd not seen him since then, though she'd searched. Wordlessly, he handed her a calico-wrapped package. As he made to leave, she grabbed his hand.

'How did you know? About the woman in Duffield's Yard?'

She didn't think he'd answer but she was determined not to let him go; he struggled but found her grip unbreakable. At last he went limp and said, 'I saw her. Saw her body.'

She let him go, knowing she'd get nothing else. He faded into the mist.

The shed was cold inside and its atmosphere seemed vaguely hostile – as if it had decided she didn't belong there anymore. Or perhaps, thought Kit, it was just her imagination. It was what she was here to do that had changed, not the space that had been her closest confidant all these months, the place that had helped her change her life and herself. The four walls that had kept her secrets hidden and safe.

She perched on the lid of her steamer trunk and stared anywhere but at the parcel in her lap. At the splinters on the walls; at the muddy footprints with an obvious void where a chunk of the thick sole of the right shoe had been taken out; at the peaked ceiling and its beams that looked too thin. Her fingers picked at the edge of the fabric wrapping and her hands shook as she took a deep breath and folded back the cloth. The revolver was a British Bull Dog – the model she'd trained with but not been issued – with six cylinders and a wooden grip. It gleamed dully at her.

Kit cracked the barrel and was greeted by the sight of bullets sleeping inside. She ran her fingers over the engraving *Philip Webley & Son of Birmingham*, that told her who had made it and where, then over the hammer. It was an older model but she didn't care about its age, just as long as it did what she needed it to.

She still could not quite believe she was going to point this thing at someone – even someone who'd done what the killer had – and fire with the intent of taking a life.

Kit closed her eyes and leaned back against the wall. The advertisement had appeared in the Personals column, stating the time and the place for the assignation, couched in terms that suggested romance was involved. She wondered if it was too late – if he'd grown bored waiting and stopped looking for a sign of contact, of agreement from her – if this was all for nought.

She had been careful each and every night since she'd first read the letter; even in the daylight hours she was wary, glancing over her shoulder, making sure she knew the number and locations of exits wherever she went, ensuring the truncheon was easily and quickly accessible, and she had developed the habit of slipping the brass knuckles on as soon as she'd taken a few steps away from the Leman Street station.

Kit had been so focused on the perceived threat that she'd ceased hearing Airedale when he sneered at her, ceased to pay attention to him at all; hadn't even really noticed when he'd quietened down these past weeks, as if there was no fun in tormenting someone who wasn't paying any mind. Wright had jokingly asked her what magic she'd worked.

Kit didn't know how long she examined the back of her eyelids, but when she felt the cold creep into her bones, she knew it had been too long. She stood and swiftly changed into her uniform, shivering. She settled her helmet on her hair, buttoned up her winter overcoat and slid the pistol gingerly into its deep pockets, praying hard that she wouldn't shoot herself in the foot.

As she passed the fence around Christ Church, she slowed, pretending to adjust her boots. She listened hard, but heard nothing until Kelly's voice swarmed out of the shadows inside the churchyard, low and clear.

'Cold night for a stroll, PC Caswell.'

'Are you ready?' Kit asked, ignoring the pretend pleasantries. 'Are you all right?'

'I'll take care of my part of the bargain as long as you observe yours. Just don't bloody well be late.'

'I swear I won't,' said Kit and Kelly's footsteps quietly crunched away on the frostbitten grass.

Kit was grateful for the warmth inside Leman Street, but didn't take her coat off as she waited impatiently through the briefing delivered by the recently promoted Sergeant Thomas Wright; neither inspector was to be seen. Wright looked harried, and when the room cleared, Kit waited behind.

'You right there, sarge?' Kit asked.

'All the nutters are out tonight and it's not even a bloody full moon.' He collected a thick ledger from the table beside him and they moved towards the door, slowing to a halt at the booking desk in the entrance hall.

'Anyone in particular?' she asked, painfully aware of the weight of the revolver in her pocket. It seemed to her that it stuck out a mile. He shook his head, and they moved into the foyer.

'Couple of old biddies arrived and demanded to speak to "Whoever is in charge, my good man" and wouldn't let up until Abberline himself heard the racket and took them up to his office.'

Kit raised her brows. 'They must have been raising hell – I'm amazed he didn't throw them in the cells for the night.'

'I think he would have liked to, but they didn't appear to have been drinking and claimed to have important information for him. May have said he'd rue the day if he ignored them.'

Kit guffawed and Wright began to speak, but was interrupted by Airedeale, who stood halfway up the stairs, yelling, 'Caswell!'

Kit looked at the man's face, creased into folds and red as a rolled roast, and didn't like the smile on his thick lips.

'The Inspector wants to have a word with you, immediately.'

Kit exchanged a look with Wright, who shrugged that *this was news to him*, and Airedale shouted, 'Quick smart!'

She set off, squeezing past the leering bobby who didn't follow her, just watched as she climbed. It made her nervous, but she tried to shrug off the feeling – she knew she was hyper-alert. She turned her thoughts to Makepeace and what he might want.

Since they'd taken the first four murders out of the investigation, two of the killers from the non-Ripper pile had been found, and watchful eyes were being kept on the grenadier who'd been seen last with both Tabram and Smith. Makepeace was very pleased with that progress, but less so with the Ripper case's lack of movement. Hundreds of men had been shuffled in and out of their doors for questioning, even more had given tips and leads, but none of them led anywhere but to dead-ends. She wished she could tell him that after tonight, the Ripper at least would no longer be a problem for the Met.

She knocked on the door of the Inspectors' office and opened it.

The cluttered billet showed no sign of Makepeace, but Abberline sat in his place, and in Abberline's usual spot were two women, respectably dressed and, as they looked at her, horribly familiar. Kit felt the blood drain from her face. Abberline regarded her coolly.

'Ah, PC Caswell. These ladies have an interesting tale to tell. Perhaps you can assist with some of the finer details?'

Louisa stared at her daughter, utterly distraught. 'Oh, Katherine. How could you?'

Kit's first thought was that it seemed her mother was more upset by *this* than if she'd gone on the game, but she didn't answer. She didn't say anything except, 'Where's Makepeace?'

'*Inspector* Makepeace is otherwise engaged. You are not a problem of sufficient priority.'

She felt as if she was being dressed down by an outraged grandfather. The only person who didn't seemed affronted by her disguise, but rather impressed, was Mrs K, whose countenance was that of someone who realised they've done something very, very wrong.

'I think,' said Abberline in a measured tone as if he was a reasonable man taking reasonable steps, 'that some time in the cells might make you more talkative.'

A large hand clamped on Kit's shoulder and she didn't need to turn around to know it was Airedale, smiling as though he'd won a fortune at the races. Her mother's expression changed to one of uncertainty and she began with, 'Surely, Inspector Abberline, this isn't necessary. Surely, I can simply take my daughter home and—'

'Your daughter has been committing fraud, Mrs Caswell. She won't be going anywhere until I get to the bottom of this and establish precisely how much she has compromised investigations by her actions.'

Kit wanted to defend herself, wanted to shout and scream, but the very idea of giving Airedale an excuse to either hit her or throw her over his shoulder so he could carry her to the cells like a sack of coal was enough to infuse her with an icy dignity.

He marched her to the stairs and her mother's voice, instead of fading with the distance, grew louder and more piercing. Kit almost smiled: Abberline had bitten off more than he could chew. Wright, standing behind the front desk, stared at her as she passed by and Airedale knocked the custodian's helmet from her head.

'Find Makepeace,' was all she said and was roughly pushed in the square of her back for her troubles.

'Don't bother,' sneered Airedale and shoved her towards the stone steps that led down.

She thought suddenly of Mary Kelly, all alone at Miller's Court while Kit sat cooling her heels. She thought of the terrible man bearing down on the woman who was trusting Kit with her life. Kit turned and opened her mouth to shout at Wright that he must find Makepeace, that he must go to Miller's Court, to tell him that the killer would be there and they could get him. It didn't matter anymore, what they knew about her, all that mattered was keeping Mary Jane safe.

Before she got a word out, Airedale's huge open palm slapped into her face, slamming her into a wall and knocking her senseless.

XII

When she came to, she was curled on the cold stone floor. He hadn't even bothered to put her on the pile of straw that passed for a bed in the tiny space. She didn't know how long she'd been out, had no idea how many of her erstwhile colleagues had wandered in to stare at her in disbelief.

She could feel the shape of the revolver pressing into her thigh – he hadn't thought to search her, to take away anything she might use. The truncheon was hanging at her belt, though her helmet was, she presumed, still sitting in lonesome fashion on Wright's desk.

What would he think, her mentor? What would he say? And Makepeace. What would the Inspector say? Do? It occurred to her that she didn't care what anyone thought apart from them.

'Awake are we?' Airedale loomed in front of the bars. 'Ready for some correction?'

'Where's Makepeace? Airedale, I have to speak to Himself, I have to get out of here. You don't understand—'

'I understand that you've been where you shouldn't, been meddling in things you shouldn't have. Don't you know what happens to little girls who get themselves into bad places? Little girls who don't obey the rules? Little girls who wander off the path – they get what's coming to them, that's what.'

He unlocked the cell door, then pulled it closed behind him. He didn't lock it because it didn't matter – her speed was irrelevant when she couldn't get past him. He began removing his tunic and Kit backed up against the farthest wall. 'Little girls who don't follow the rules learn hard lessons, *Katherine.*'

He was so certain of himself, so focused on unbuttoning his trousers, that he just laughed as she cringed away. When she spun back around and sprang at him, he was utterly unprepared. Kit swung the truncheon at the side of his left knee and heard the crack. Airedale went down with a scream, and she leaped over him as he fell. He managed to grab at her ankle and she fell too, striking her elbow on the ground so hard that it went numb. She kicked out and caught his ruddy face with the heel of her boot and heard teeth give way with a satisfying snap.

Kit scrambled to her feet and bolted, up the stairs and burst into the foyer. Wright was still at the desk, still looking perplexed. She shouted at him as she went past – no one tried to stop her – 'Thirteen Miller's Court! The Ripper,' then shouldered her way out through the doors and into the night, every pump of her arms, every pound of her boots on the cobbles a prayer.

Kit didn't wait to hear if there was a rabble of coppers following her, either to give chase or assistance. She flew along the ill-lit streets, desperately trying to recall all the shortcuts she'd ever learned in her time policing Whitechapel. She got turned around twice and had to retrace her steps, sobbing and cursing, words she'd never used herself, but heard so many times from the mouths of the locale's denizens.

Miller's Court was part of the Spitalfields rookery, so dangerous it was double patrolled. It ran off the "wicked quarter mile" of Dorset Street. It was highly populated – people would *hear* an attack, she thought. The voice in her head reminded her it hadn't helped any of the other murdered women. It wasn't an area where people ran towards screams or offered help. They walked quickly the other way to avoid getting themselves into trouble.

The bulk of the Christ Church came into sight and it gave her some kind of hope – she was close. She still didn't know what the hour was. She didn't know how much time she'd lost – she should have stopped to ask before she charged off, she thought, then considered herself an idiot – as if she had any seconds to spare. And if she was too late ... well, then time was irrelevant, wasn't it?

She threw herself to the left into Dorset Street, barely slowing down and almost slipped on the wet paving. She righted herself, kept running until she found the tiny aperture, barely a yard wide, that was the opening of the Miller's Court blind alley.

The space widened as she got through the passage, and saw number 13 on her right. It had its own entrance, Kelly had said, and her common-law husband – no longer so – would be happy to vacate for an evening if Kelly took care of the rental areas. It stretched Kit's meagre reserves, but she'd handed over the outstanding twenty-nine shillings.

Kit slowed as she approached the corner. There were two windows looking out into the court, both had rough hessian sacks hung as curtains and the sight of the orange glow from inside calmed her for a moment – a fire meant warmth and comfort, it meant a home and a hearth. For the briefest breath of a second, Kit thought it would be okay. Then she noticed the corner of one of the windows was broken and a rag was stuffed in the gap, a piece of bleached cloth with dark stains on it.

She reached for the handle and turned it, pushing the door gently inwards.

Kit had never smelled anything like it – the other women had died outside and the scent of their deaths had been somewhat dissipated by that general condition. The air in Mary Jane Kelly's room was thick with the stink of iron and shit and piss. The dancing glow from the fireplace made it seem that what was left of the woman's chest still moved, but Kit knew that was impossible – Mary Jane had been opened up from gullet to groin. There was so much blood that Kit couldn't tell what remained on the body and what had been taken. She could tell that the breasts were gone and the legs spread, and it appeared as if most of her abdomen was scooped out. Her head was turned towards the door and the crater where her face had once been seemed to stare at Kit accusingly. Incongruously, Kelly's clothing was neatly folded on the chair beside her bed. The two rickety tables were mostly bare.

She tried not to breathe too deeply, tried not to swallow. Couldn't force herself to approach the bed, just let her eyes roam around the room, trying to take in every detail she could, everything she might be able to examine in her memory later because she knew her days with the Met were done.

There was clothing burning in the fireplace and she thought it must have come from the empty basket on one of the tables, a sign Kelly had brought her mending to occupy her; the boot prints in blood and dirt; the lack of an obvious struggle which suggested the girl had been rendered unconscious very quickly.

By the time Makepeace, Wright, and six other out-of-breath officers poured through the passage into Miller's Court, she'd seen all she ever wanted to see and taken up position on one of the old barrels that cluttered up the yard.

When her Inspector looked askance at her and asked, 'How did you know?' all she could do was shrug and gesture towards the open door. What could she say, after all? That she had caused this? That she'd risked a woman's life and then lost it after she'd promised not to? He pointed a finger at her and said, 'This isn't over.'

'Never a truer word spoken,' she muttered to his departing back.

He and Wright disappeared into the small room, and their entourage crowded around the entrance, swearing and staring. More than one of them found somewhere to throw up. When a very pale Makepeace returned, and managed to find words, they were, 'Why? Why like *this*? It's not him, is it? Someone – *something* – new?'

Kit shook her head. 'It's him.'

'But . . .'

'He did this because she eluded him for so long. It made him angry and resentful. He could have taken someone else, but she became an obsession simply because he couldn't find her.' Kit stood and rubbed at her arms, which had gone numb out in the cold. 'This became *personal* and he doesn't like being defied.'

She passed her gloved palms over her face, smelling the leather.

Makepeace was caught between watching his officers variously look into the slaughter room, then hurry out, and the sight of Dr Bagster Phillips waddling along the passage from Dorset Street, almost eclipsing the entire space. The doctor's assessing gaze told her he'd heard the news. She was in no mood to be subjected to further interrogation or speculative glances, and stood.

'Where do you think you're going?' demanded Makepeace.

She looked at him. 'You've got your hands full for the rest of the night, I'd imagine. I'm no longer under your control and I'm going home.'

'I have questions you need to answer, Caswell.'

'You know where to find me.' Kit turned and walked away. The men around her stopped briefly what they were doing and watched her, but no one made any move to stop her, not even Abberline as he moved towards the scene with the gait of a condemned man.

They didn't see her the same way, she knew; somehow she'd become a criminal. She wondered if she'd find Mary Kelly's bloody shade waiting beside her bed when she got home.

XIII

Time had never passed like this, she was certain.

Each second was an hour, each hour an eternity, and the day simply stretched on as if it had transformed, somehow become an unfathomable distance. She'd lain on her bed forever it seemed, moving her gaze from the intricacies of the rug, to the painting on the wall, to the wood grain of the wardrobe, to the floral pitcher and bowl on the wash basin, to the embroidered cushion on the chair in the corner.

She did not sleep; she'd not slept in so long but still it would not come. Every so often the bubble around her was punctured by the sound of Louisa screaming, sometimes throwing the lockless door back against the wall in fury and screeching from the hallway, sometimes from elsewhere in the flat. That only stopped when Kit heard Mrs K's soothing voice coaxing her mother away with promises of tea and something to calm her nerves. Kit hoped it was laudanum, a heavy dose, that Louisa would sleep for a very long time and perhaps forget what her daughter had done.

That was the thing, though: Louisa didn't appear to remember *precisely* what Kit had done. She was enraged, she was ashamed, she was utterly certain that her child had brought opprobrium down upon them, but it didn't seem that she recalled what her daughter had actually done. Indeed, it was apparent she'd substituted another sin altogether. As far as Kit could decipher from her mother's rants, Louisa believed Kit had become a fallen woman.

There were more accusations, each more outlandish than the next, but that was the core of it: Louisa believed Kit was a harlot and nothing anyone said could convince her otherwise. Wasn't that why she and Mrs K had gone to the police station? To ask for an investigation? For the police to stop her daughter from doing such terrible things? Hadn't Lucius – dear sweet Lucius, concerned only for his sister's soul – sworn that was what Kit was doing?

Since arriving home in the early hours Kit had not gone to see her brother. She'd heard him through their shared wall, calling for a while, but had not been able to bring herself to answer. She could not bear to look at him and know that his actions, intended to save her, had damned Mary Kelly. She couldn't, she knew, speak to him yet without crying out all the grief building in the pit of her. If she opened her mouth, she would let something awful out, she would push a little of it – oh, just a little! – onto him just to lighten her own burden. She couldn't – wouldn't – speak to him until she could keep all her anger, her guilt, to herself. Until she could lie to him and swear he hadn't played even a tiny part in the tragedy that had reeled itself out last night.

At some point she heard Louisa's snoring begin, the nasal thunder that meant she'd had her "medicine". Soon after there was a tentative knock and it was all Kit could do to drag her attention away from the watercolour of a field of flowers – a gift from the Reverend Caswell. Mrs Kittredge hovered tentatively on the threshold as if unsure she was welcome. Kit cleared her throat, finally found her voice.

'What is it, Mrs K?' She'd not spoken since bidding Makepeace farewell the night before. Night? Morning? Did it matter?

'Katherine,' began the woman, then stopped, moved into the room and shifted the chair beside Kit's bed so she could look directly into the girl's face, as if that was important. 'Kit, I'm . . .'

Kit raised an eyebrow, unsure she was ready for any kind of interaction, but Mrs K wasn't screaming at her, wasn't irrational, wasn't lost in the prison of her own mind. Mrs K wanted to have a conversation, so Kit felt the least she could do was listen.

She sat up, leaning against the pillows, aware she'd not changed out of her uniform – and that it would need to be returned to the station at some point, as would the truncheon, the overcoat and whistle, and the bullseye lantern. She sighed at the thought. The boots lying in a corner, at least, were hers – or rather her father's, the Reverend having had rather small feet and Kit rather large ones.

'Yes, Mrs K?'

'Kit, I am sorry.'

Kit blinked. An apology had not been amongst her expectations.

'I'm so sorry for what we did. I thought it was right, we – your mother had her suspicions, then your brother told us what you were really doing – oh, I know she doesn't know which way's up at the moment but she'll come around – we thought we were looking after you. Only,' she paused, sniffling, 'only when I saw you in that room, in that uniform, so tall and proper, I knew you didn't need saving. I knew you were doing the saving and we'd ruined it. We'd ruined everything.'

She broke down and began to sob. Kit wanted to join her, but tears would solve nothing. She patted Mrs K on the shoulder and made soothing noises, managing a strangled *It's all right*, which caused the woman to rear up.

'It's *not*,' she said forcefully. 'It's not all right! Here's me going to all these women's meetings, listening to calls for the vote and equality, and I go and wreck your future, your steps on a path none of us are allowed to take.'

'I thought you went to church and séances, Mrs K,' said Kit, somewhat bewildered. The idea of the landlady as an advocate for women's rights made Kit think she'd not known her at all. Mrs K looked a little affronted, then abashed.

'Well, I do go to séances, yes, but where do you think we have our suffrage meetings? Where's the safest place in the world? A church. Anyway, what I need to tell you didn't come from going to church or from women's groups, but from the séances. You know I go to chat to my dear old mum?'

Kit didn't, but she nodded anyway. She felt ashamed that she knew so little about the woman who'd spent so much time looking after her mother and brother. It seemed terribly disloyal.

'Well, that poor friend of yours, Mary Jane, I *knew* I knew her from somewhere. From the séances, Kit. They bring in sensitives – mediums who can contact the spirits and the spirits speak through them. Your Mary Jane, she was one of them.'

Kit felt the hairs on the back of her neck stand to attention. Séances – clairvoyants didn't perform for free. It was paid work that didn't involve being drilled up against a wall by a man you barely knew. The kind of work that Mary Kelly, who'd touched Kit's hands and accessed her worst secrets, could do standing on one leg. The kind of work at which the Whitechapel Witches would all take a punt, given the chance. Was that how he found them, this purported Jack?

'Mrs K, did you recognise any of the other women who were killed?

When the papers printed their photos, did you know any of their faces? Might they have been at the séances too, as your mediums?'

Mrs K thought hard and finally nodded as if making a tough decision. 'May well have been, Kit. May well have been at least one of them – sometimes they stank of gin when they arrived and they didn't look like good women, but they were very good mediums. Your Mary Jane gave me the best connection I've had with Mum in years.'

'Do you remember anyone else there, a man showing particular interest in the women?'

Mrs K shook her head. 'Lot of different people, lot of different groups, Kit. I can't think of anyone – anyway, I'm not there to socialise with the living.'

So, perhaps he hadn't been at one of the same séances as Mrs K, but London was a veritable hotbed of people desperately looking for contact with the Other Side. Kit supposed one was bound to stumble across at least one genuine sensitive amongst all the shysters and fakes. And Jack, whoever he was, had certainly been in attendance somewhere he'd seen the power of those Whitechapel women, and he'd *chosen* them for whatever he was trying to do.

'Mrs K,' she said, swinging her feet off the bed, 'I need to go out for a while. Can you keep an eye on the madhouse?'

The landlady straightened and threw back her shoulders; she seemed to regard the task as a chance to redeem herself.

It was late afternoon by the time Kit located Bagster Phillips, after traipsing far and wide. She discovered, only after she'd arrived at Old Montague Street, that Kelly's body had been taken instead to Shoreditch mortuary. When she'd arrived there, the autopsy was well and truly over, and there was only the attendant who told her, for an unreasonably hefty bribe, that Bagster Phillips had been joined by that unbearable snob Dr Bond. While they'd begun proceedings with a good deal of sniping, at the end of their combined labours they seemed to have developed a kinship forged in Mary Kelly's blood and guts. Both were pale and silent when they'd finished picking through the woman's dreadful remains, said the attendant with unhealthy relish.

Kit knew Bond wouldn't have truck with her, but there was a chance Bagster Phillips would. When she at last found him at the Angel and

Crown, he looked as though he'd been doing his best to wipe all memory of the morning's activities from his mind. He peered at her blearily, then gestured drunkenly to the seat beside him. He licked his lips – not in a salacious way – and chewed for a few moments as if his mouth was filled with cotton, then opened his eyes wide and tried to focus. A fat finger waggled at her.

'I always thought there was something different about you, Caswell.'

'Every man is genius with hindsight, Doctor Bagster Phillips,' she said primly, her purse sitting ladylike in her lap, and he grinned.

'I used to think what a pretty boy you were, and lo, here you are, a slightly less pretty girl.' He snorted with laughter. 'I am willing to bet there are several coppers sighing with relief to discover that the young man they were staring at a little too long is, in fact, a damsel.'

'I don't bet PC Airedale's one of them,' she said, and he gave a great bellow of a laugh that almost disguised the fart that followed it.

'Oh dear, pardon me,' he said and waved his hand. Kit wasn't sure if the gas was worse than the smell coming from his mouth as he belched. 'Yes, you certainly took care of that great ape. I'm assuming you had good reason.'

'Doctor Bagster Phillips . . .' she said. 'Doctor Bagster Phillips, did you find anything in Mary Kelly's autopsy?'

He looked terribly sad. 'Poor girl. Poor little girl, didn't deserve that.'

'What did he take?'

'Take?' He looked confused.

'His souvenir, Doctor. He's taken something from all of them, as you well know.'

He shook his head, but then answered, 'The heart. Her poor heart was gone. And the baby.'

Kit felt her stomach heave as it hadn't even when she viewed Kelly's remains. 'She was pregnant?'

He nodded, tears in his rheumy eyes.

'Doctor, the instrument – it wasn't a bayonet, was it? I mean, there was too much – the cuts – I saw . . .'

Slowly, he nodded.

Kit continued, 'Then might it not have been a Liston knife? I've seen you use one when a saw won't do . . .'

Bagster Phillips blustered – the idea that the murderer might be a medical man made him deeply unhappy, she could see – before finally agreeing. 'It could have been. But he's not a doctor, Caswell, he's a butcher, make no mistake about that.'

'Oh, I know, Doctor Bagster Phillips, I know.' She stood, but he stopped her with a meaty hand on her arm. She raised her eyebrows.

'Be careful, Caswell. There's a man out there who really doesn't like women.'

She nodded and patted his shoulder, then left him to his next swig of gin.

Out in the afternoon cold, she glanced at her father's fob watch, which she'd begun wearing since Mary Kelly's demise, in spite of Louisa's protests. She still had time, if she was swift, to go to the shop in Limehouse, to make one final request of Mr Wing. If required, she would tell him his debt would be paid in full for this one last assistance. She wondered if that would be enough.

XIV

There was something she was missing, Kit was sure of it. Something that was in her head, certainly, something she *knew* but couldn't quite grasp the significance of – it was refusing to let itself be noticed. She picked over each tiny morsel of information, no matter how insignificant it seemed – as much to take her mind off the earlier polite but firm rebuff as to find a solution – yet her memory would still not oblige.

After leaving Dr Bagster Phillips to his cups, she'd made her way to the apothecary's shop and found the door locked, with no sign of Mr Wing inside. It took some determined knocking before he appeared and shook his head at her through the window. In the end, when it became obvious she was looking around for something to hurl through the glass, he gave in and opened the door but a sliver, not inviting her in.

Kit was exhausted and chilled to her bones, as if the cold had settled in them and would never go away no matter how many roaring fires she sat in front of or how many warm rugs she wrapped herself in, but she didn't press him, merely asked outright.

'Where is the boy? The youngster who came to me about the woman in Duffield's Yard? The one who brought me the gun?'

He made an exasperated sound and she knew she was very close to the borders of his patience. 'Why do you ask this, Miss Katherine? What could you possibly need to know this for?'

'Because I think he saw the man who killed Elizabeth Stride. I think he came and found me of his own accord – I don't think you sent him at all. I think he found me because he was terrified – too terrified to tell me anything else – but not so scared that he didn't want someone to know.' She held onto the edge of the doorframe so he couldn't close the door without hurting her. 'I think when I saw him last night he made a mistake then covered it up. He said "I saw her" then he changed it to "Saw her body". I think he was saying he saw her being murdered.'

'What an interesting idea, Miss Katherine. Perhaps you should take it to the police.' His voice was flat as was his gaze, but she could tell that he knew what had happened, that he knew she'd lost her position, that everything was different.

She'd surrendered then, left before he could tell her she was no longer welcome to the privilege of a place at the lock-up – and frankly she'd lost enough already. She wasn't prepared to let something else slip from her grasp.

Now, sitting in the parlour as evening closed in outside, her stockinged feet were as close to the fire as she could bear, trying to melt the ice from her very core. Mrs K had thoughtfully provided nips of port and cups of tea and they'd gone some way to helping, but she did wonder if the alcohol hadn't also dimmed her senses. Perhaps that was why she couldn't identify that essential clue.

She was so deep in thought that she didn't hear the knock at the front door, didn't rouse until Mrs K stood poised in the doorway, the shadow of someone looming behind her.

'Katherine? Kit, you've a gentleman caller.'

Mrs K stepped back and Makepeace filled the space. Kit laughed out loud at the idea of her former boss as a gentleman caller. The Inspector held his bowler hat, twisting it around as if it was the best way to keep his hands occupied. Kit was perplexed at his demeanour. He had every right to charge in and interrogate her as if she was some stripe of criminal, in fact she'd been expecting his arrival all day – had half-expected to return from her expedition and find him furious and fuming. Perhaps it was Mrs K's presence that kept his ire in check.

Kit carefully tucked her feet back under her skirts and nodded for Makepeace to enter. Mrs K bustled away, muttering about tea and biscuits. Kit wondered vaguely when the landlady had last set foot in her own kitchen upstairs, or if she'd completely moved down to theirs now.

Makepeace settled in the wingback chair across from Kit and took some time crossing his legs then balancing his hat over his knee. He leaned back against the particularly lumpen cushion and tried to get comfortable. Kit watched with amusement as he wiggled as much as a man well over six feet could be said to do so, and politely tried to beat the item into submission. Finally she took pity and said, 'We usually just throw it on the floor.'

'Thank God for that.' He whipped the thing out from behind him and dropped it beside the chair. 'I will never understand the female insistence upon cushions, Caswell.'

'That makes two of us, sir,' she said, old habits dying hard. 'But I suppose it's not "sir" anymore. It's Mr Makepeace.'

'Edwin, if you prefer,' he offered awkwardly. Kit was amazed that he wasn't angry, more aggressive and demanding. Perhaps the sight of her in a dress, knowing she was *meant* to be wearing it, calmed him down and reinstated his naturally chivalrous behaviour.

'I imagine you're here, Mr Makepeace, to ask some difficult questions.' She played with the edge of the crocheted rug on her lap, tracing the knots and links carefully. 'I'll answer them, of course.'

'Well, that's a relief,' he said dryly, then leaned forward. 'How did you know? How did you know he'd be there, that it would be Kelly?'

And she told everything, from her first meeting with Kelly, to the revelation of witchery among the Whitechapel whores – his face convulsed with disbelief, but she didn't care. She told him about the letter she'd received and the agreement she'd reached with Mary Jane, she told him the horrid end of that partnership and its aftermath even though he already knew. Telling and retelling the tale of her own failure was the very least punishment she could mete out to herself, she decided.

'And you didn't tell me any of this because you thought I'd think you mad, all this rubbish about witches?'

'Don't you now?' She sighed. 'It doesn't matter. I've nothing to hide anymore, nothing to lose. He's got what he wants – Mary always said he only wanted five, that there's magic in the number, like the points of a star; that's what's needed for summoning and making requests. That's what she believed he was doing – that's why he keeps little parts of them for the soul to cling to at least until he'd done what he needed to with that currency.'

'And why this ... Katherine?' He gestured to her clothes, to the uniform that wasn't there. 'Why the disguise?'

She would not share the details of that, the *how* of her double life, about the lock-up or the help from Mr Wing – those secrets weren't hers alone.

'Are you saying, Mr Makepeace, that had I walked into the Leman Street nick in my bustled gown and bonnet, and asked for a job that I'd have been given a respectful hearing? That I wouldn't have been laughed out the door or threatened with a stay in an asylum until I changed my ways and ideas? I have several mouths to support, Mr Makepeace – do you know how far the salary of a milliner's apprentice goes among three people, one of them ill and one increasingly ...'

She did not finish the sentence. 'I did what I needed to. No,' she corrected herself, 'I did what I *wanted* to do.'

'You did what you thought was right.'

'Right? Or convenient? Don't think I don't know how much of this is my fault. If I hadn't been so determined to keep my secrets then this might have been over long ago. I'm very aware that I put myself and my family ahead of the lives of the streetwalkers, because I'm as bad as any man, because I didn't set sufficient store by them. I didn't think they deserved to be safe as much as I did though I didn't say it; I thought they somehow brought the violence on themselves by the very nature of their lives. I judged them less worthy than me and mine, Mr Makepeace, and I will live with that every damned day for the rest of my life.' She pointed a finger at him as he made to contradict her. 'And don't tell you haven't thought the same – that they're worthless, these women. If it wasn't true then you wouldn't be sitting here so calm as you question me, acting as if I've done nothing more than steal a bag of sweeties.

'You don't think they're worth enough to get angry about – you're more infuriated that this man *dared* to defy you and make a mess on your streets, made your men look like idiots, than you're outraged by the loss of these women's lives. Deny it and I'll know you're a liar.'

His lips went white and Kit thought she might have gone too far, but he didn't lose his temper, didn't deny her accusations.

'Tea and biscuits,' announced Mrs K, and entered bearing a tray. She fussed a little, making teaspoons clatter against porcelain saucers as she put the tray down on the small table beside Kit's chair.

'Thank you, Mrs K,' said Kit in a tone that said quite clearly the woman should vacate the room at speed.

As Kit poured the dark brown liquid into a rose-patterned cup, Makepeace's shoulders slumped and he said, 'I heard you.'

'What?'

'I heard you, when Airedale was marching you to the cells. I was in the storeroom behind the front desk and heard you tell Wright to find me. I heard it and I ignored it. I thought *Let that be a lesson to you, little miss, teach you to make a fool of me.*' He looked at the hat perched precariously on his knee.

'How long had you known?' she asked.

'The night after the double event – I came to see how you were. I was on the other side of the street and what should I espy instead of my brightest police constable? A tall woman in a night-gown freezing on her own door-step, watching a whore wander off down Lady's Mantle Court.'

'You knew all that time? You knew and you didn't say anything? You knew and you still listened to me when I told you about the souvenirs?' she said wonderingly.

He shrugged. 'It made sense and I already knew you weren't an idiot. I didn't imagine that a change in your sex would alter that.'

'Thank you,' she said quietly, gratefully.

'But I was annoyed at you. Very much so. When Abberline had you locked up, I didn't intervene. I thought *that'll serve her right.*' He rubbed his face and she heard the rasping of skin against thick bristles that hadn't been shaved in a little too long. 'So when you're apportioning blame, don't forget my share. I'm the one who let them lock you up. I'm the one who let Airedale cart you off – though, I swear, I didn't know he'd hit you – I'm as much at fault for Kelly's death.'

She examined her hands, looking under the nails for specks of dirt, looking anywhere but at him. She was resentful, but knew she had no real right to be – it didn't matter. She'd been the one to live a lie, she'd been the one to take the risk with the other woman's life. It was all on her.

She felt suddenly very tired. She'd not slept since finding Kelly's body; only stared at the ceiling, the door, the walls, hoping Kelly might break through Kit's lack of eldritch sight and appear before her, so that she could tell the woman what had happened, that she'd not been betrayed and left to the darkness.

'I think, Mr Makepeace, that I need to retire.'

He nodded slowly and rose, hesitating until she offered her hand, which he held for too many moments, as if he couldn't find the right words. Kit escorted him to the door and pulled it open just as a small Chinese boy was poised to knock. His eyes went wide at the sight of them and Kit thought he might flee, but he seemed to calm down.

It wasn't the boy she'd sought, but she thought she recognised this one from other times. He pulled an envelope, thick and pearly-grey from his pocket and handed it to her, then ran away without explanation.

'What's that, Miss Caswell?' asked Makepeace.

She smiled and shook it gently. 'Mr Wing the apothecary sends herbs for Lucius, sometimes for Mother's headaches, too. He is very kind.'

Edwin Makepeace nodded and restored his hat to its place and bid her farewell. She watched him lope away, not wishing to close the door too quickly lest it cause him to suspect something was not as she would have him believe.

Back in the parlour she found herself opening a mysterious missive for the second time, but at least she knew who'd sent this one. Inside was a letter and a key.

On a single sheet of thin rice paper, Mr Wing's lovely script told her quite simply that the boy she'd wanted to speak with had been found. He'd been murdered; that the police had no interest in pursuing the crime. He wrote that yes, the boy had seen precisely what she'd thought, but he had no name to give, it was not a commodity in which he trafficked – all he had was the enclosed key, which was to the door in the floor and the door beneath. At the bottom of the page was a map, a miniature artwork in delicate pen-strokes.

Kit felt a pain in her head and spots danced in front of her eyes. Muddy boot prints on the floor of the lock-up, a void on the left side of the right sole. Bloody boot prints on the floor of 13 Miller's Court, an identical imprint. The very thing that had been staring her in the face, hidden in plain sight, one of a hundred ordinary details drifting in her memory.

Kit took a deep breath and steadied herself. She still had her kit, and the gun and the brass knuckles. She'd been surprised when Makepeace hadn't asked for the return of the Met's property. In her room, she pulled an old tweed suit that had been her father's from the back of the wardrobe and dressed carefully. The evening's work did not call for a frock. She laced up her boots, then wrapped a thick scarf around her neck. She slipped into the overcoat, feeling the weight of the revolver still lurking there, then put the knuckles and the truncheon into the opposite pocket so there would be no careless mishaps.

She told Mrs K she was going out and not to worry, although Kit knew the woman would – but she wouldn't stop her either. The landlady stood on the stoop, a stalwart silhouette against the interior lights. Kit's bullseye lantern lit her way down the fog-obscured steps, a thin lonely band of hope piercing the moon dark night.

XV

The lock turned with no more than a whispered *click*. Kit pulled the trap-door open and stared into the dark hole at her feet. She angled the lantern's gaze downwards and made out a metal ladder, brick walls gleaming with moisture and a paved path perhaps nine feet down. The smell wafting upwards told her that this was part of the sewer system. She wrapped the scarf tightly around her mouth and nose; it helped a little.

Tackling the rungs was a fraught exercise as she kept her grip on both the lantern – without it she was lost – and the ladder. She slipped once and almost fell, almost let go of the lamp, but recovered, breathing hard, hang-ing for a few moments by her injured shoulder, which had been healing well until that point.

When she reached the bottom, Kit examined Mr Wing's map in the beam of light. She was thankful she didn't have far to go – the apothecary had considerately marked out the number of paces she needed to cover before turning left, and then right, and then left and left again until she found herself standing before a heavy door, reinforced with rusting studs. The door *beneath*.

Kit tiptoed close and put her ear to the cold surface, felt the slime of it against her cheek. She couldn't hear anything on the other side, but from behind her, back in the tunnels where she'd come from, she thought she heard a splash. A rat. She closed her eyes and shuddered.

She placed the lantern on the paving stones so she could fish around in her pocket for the trapdoor key; when she fitted it into the keyhole she was surprised that it wasn't needed – the door fell open under her touch.

Inside there was a chamber, well-lit by candles set in candelabrum of silver and gold – surely purloined – over which melted wax had spilled. A battered armchair with a fur carriage-rug folded on its seat sat in the middle of a large Persian carpet that had been ill-used. Beside it was a wide table piled with books and vials, pestles and dried ingredients, distorted things in specimen bottles and sharp surgical instruments in an open tooled-leather case, all glinting against the purple velvet lining, catching the reflections of myriad flames.

The room was surprisingly warm, and almost enough incense had been burned to subdue the sewer-stink. At the far wall was an archway hung with a thick purple curtain. Leaving her own bullseye where she'd put it, Kit entered, sliding a hand into the pocket of her overcoat and finding the grip of the revolver, pulling back its hammer so it made a distinct *snick*.

Kit froze, but there was no movement, no one charging out to stop her, and she breathed again, taking a handful of the curtain in front of her and pulling it aside.

A smaller room again, lit as the first one, but empty of all but a low circular altar in the centre, a pentacle drawn on its surface. At each point was a bottle about four inches in height, inside which danced a white-blue light, and in front of each bottle was an unidentifiable rotting lump, but Kit could guess what they had been: voice box, uterus, kidney, finger, heart.

In the centre of it all was a long silver knife and a sad little gobbet of flesh, about three inches in length, like a fat worm; tiny arms, tiny legs, oversized head – it would never have a chance to grow.

Kit swallowed and turned her attention to the man who stood beside this display and smiled at her.

'Hello, PC Caswell.' Andrew Douglas had lost his civilised façade in the time since she'd seen him last. Or perhaps that was just because in this location he'd reverted to what he actually was; here, he did not hide behind a veneer of sophistication. Here, he was not the valued right hand of a rich and famous man. Here, he was a rodent at home with his kin. 'How's your brother?'

Kit cleared her throat but couldn't find words. She should shoot him, she knew. She should just be done with it, but she needed – the witches needed – to know *why*. They deserved for someone to hear bear witness, for some kind of memorial even if it were an ephemeral one of words.

'Cat got your tongue? Come to think of it, if you'd had any power at all I might have taken you and your busy little tongue.' He laughed at his own joke, then shook his head ruefully. 'But you've got nothing, do you? Not even a tiny glimmer. You're no use to me, but you might provide some amusement.'

'Why?' she managed, voice weak, throat ragged. She tried again, 'Why all this? Why those poor women?'

'Poor women, poor women,' he sang like some grim lullaby. 'They made their choices, Katherine – it is Katherine, isn't it? Oh, I read all of your letters to Sir William, quite heart-wrenching the way you described your brother's illness, how he'd stopped walking after your father's demise, how you thought it might be psychological. What a clever girl you are,' he said admiringly. 'I didn't share them with him, obviously, your problems are far too small for the likes of such a great man, but they did provide me with much diversion and I was quite sad when you stopped writing.

'Imagine my surprise when a PC turned up on the doorstep by the same last name. What were the odds of a Katherine Caswell having another brother, a Kit? I was fascinated, so I found those old letters and went to your address. There you were bold as brass in your night-gown, and there she was, the lovely Marie Jeanette in all her slatternish glory. I knew she was the one. And then she went and hid from me, the bitch.'

'Why?' she asked again, hating her pleading tone, hating the weakness and the fear, hating the power she was giving him by letting him know she was afraid, by letting him know she wanted an explanation before all this could end.

'Sir William, that dear man, that great man, is unwell. I've tried everything to help him, every cure, every panacea, every remedy. Everything and nothing has worked.'

Kit saw, at last, a hint of sincerity, a madness tempered by a reason however wrong-headed. 'But you're no doctor, and Sir William is old. He's had strokes – this is a natural progression and deterioration of the body. You cannot stop age.'

He raised his finger as a conductor would a baton, a schoolmaster a cane. 'I may not be a physician, but I am something else, something better, something more puissant. I am a mage. I can summon angels and demons, I have souls to offer in return for Sir William's continued good health for many years to come.'

'You can barely summon the maid to bring tea. If you had any power at all you wouldn't have needed to steal from those wretched women,' Kit said, unable to resist the urge to bait him. 'You stole from them the way you stole from Sir William – his surgical knives, his candlesticks – that's how you repaid him. Those women had so little and you stole that from them.'

'What are their worthless lives compared to his? How many has he saved? Didn't he save me from the streets, from poverty? Didn't he raise me up and make me his closest confidant?' His shout in the confined space made her ears hurt. 'And didn't I know them? Didn't I know what they were when I saw them?'

'You saw them at séances, you fraud. You watched them use their abilities, you didn't divine their secrets. You saw what they openly showed.'

He shook with rage, but seemed to contain himself, before continuing on. 'The first one was hard, I wasn't sure of anything but my mission. It got easier, though. It got so easy I did two in one night, even though you interrupted me.' He gave a proud smile. 'And then the last one, your Mary Jane, she was a delight. That was when I discovered I'd got a taste for it – not just the goal, but for the activity itself! The cut and the slice of it, the colour, Miss Caswell. How is your brother, by the way?'

She was puzzled by his repeated queries then realised his purpose – he wanted to hear Lucius had improved, that he was getting better. That Kit had accepted the deal Douglas had proposed, that Lucius was recovering and that Douglas' power was confirmed – he couldn't have known that Kit had been delayed that night, that she'd not intended to make a bargain with him. 'He's worse. Much worse. The doctor thinks he might die.'

The man flinched as if slapped.

'You are useless, powerless. All of this has been for nothing,' hissed Kit. She watched as the rage welled up again and spilled across his face. He snatched the knife from the altar and threw himself at her just as she managed to bring up the gun, still in her pocket, and fired. There was the smell of gunpowder, of burnt wool, and Douglas staggered as the bullet hit him low on the waist, but he kept coming. The dagger sliced across her chest, opening coat, jacket, shirt and flesh almost to the breastbone, then he drew back and plunged the blade to the hilt into her injured shoulder. She screamed. Douglas laughed and withdrew the weapon, raising it high for another stab.

Kit reeled away, pain searing through her. She stumbled to the altar and her knees buckled, her flailing arms sweeping the glowing bottles to the floor. Douglas howled in fury as each and every one smashed on the stone flags. Kit tried to push herself up, to defend herself, to find the gun she'd dropped back into the depths of her pocket, but she fell to the side, her head landing beside the mass of broken glass and scattered spirits.

She watched as white-blue flashes swirled and rose, spiralling upwards until they coalesced into a single tongue of flame. Douglas made an inarticulate noise, and Kit guessed he hadn't really believed himself. That desperation, madness and misdirected hope had driven him. Well, she thought sleepily, now they both knew better.

She could feel blood pooling under her; her limbs becoming heavy as sin, and she was hypnotised by the blue inferno that was moving closer to her. Then it was on her chest and she felt both heat and frost on the exposed flesh, and then . . . and then it was *in* her. Roaring through her veins, burning her alive, and the voices! Oh, the voices! A chorus of joy and release, freedom and relief, all limned with a dark desire for revenge.

She only recognised one of them: Mary Jane Kelly was chattering away in Kit's skull, marshalling the others, telling them what they must do.

I didn't betray you, thought Kit, *I'm so sorry, Mary Jane, but I didn't give you up.*

And in her head, that rolling lilt of two vales, dulcet tones that sounded like a song as they said *If I didn't know that, do you think I'd be here, you idiot? Now shut up, we're concentrating.*

Kit felt herself lifted, floating up, up, until she hung, cruciform, a foot off the ground, light crackling around her, snapping like a bonfire. In front of her, Andrew Douglas stood, mouth agape, eyes empty of all reason.

He watched as she hovered, as the pulsing flare drew in on itself, concentrated on Kit's chest, then shot out like a ball from a cannon and set him alight. Where the witch-fire had not harmed Kit's skin, it incinerated Douglas, ate him from flesh to bones, until there was only a pile of smoking cinders lying where he had once stood.

Kit, momentarily still suspended, caught sight of a face in the doorway. Makepeace, disbelief and dismay scrawled across his features. Then the moment was gone and Kit dropped like a stone with a resounding thud. Her final thought before she comprehensively passed out was that she should have spoken to Lucius one last time.

XVI

'Well, Kit Caswell, you've certainly gone up in the world.'

It had been almost six weeks to the day since Makepeace – suspicious enough to wait in the cold and follow her to the lock-up – had carried her out of the sewers and delivered her to the tender mercies of Guy's Hospital, where she promptly developed a fever and hung between life and death for several days.

The last time the Inspector had seen her was the morning the fever broke and she set about insisting she be sent home – and made herself thoroughly unpleasant until they discharged her. He then, by Thomas Wright's account, allowed the creative tying up of the Ripper investigation's many loose ends to keep him busy once he knew she was out of danger.

Gruff and fatherly, and seeming to have come to terms with the fact that Kit was a girl, Wright had been a frequent visitor in and out of the hospital, dragging his wife and children along to see her as if she was some kind of circus attraction. Abberline had sent flowers – she didn't know how much he really knew and didn't much care.

'Sir William is very generous,' said Kit, smoothing her dark green silk poplin skirt. Her hair had grown a little and she'd had some colour in the mirror this morning, but even to her own eyes she still looked too thin. She was obediently eating everything Mrs K put in front of her.

'Very generous indeed,' said the Inspector, his gaze roaming over the rich furnishings in the sitting room. The house was the smallest one in the area, not overly grand, but lovely, well appointed, and in the most expensive square in Mayfair, right across the park from Sir William's own home.

Kit was still getting used to having a maid and a footman, but Mrs K revelled in her new element as housekeeper – having happily rented her own home out to a family of nine – and delighted to have people to boss around in her quest to organise everything for Miss Katherine and Master Lucius. Kit had rolled her eyes and threatened to put the woman out if she ever called them that again.

'Very,' she agreed.

Makepeace nodded and sipped the very fine Madeira Mrs K had delivered earlier, then asked, 'Was it by his will or otherwise?'

'More or less by his own accord, although some persuasion was required. He had no desire for his good peers to know that his very own personal secretary had been none other than Jack the Ripper, carving up unfortunates for the purposes of black magic.'

'Would they have believed such outlandish drivel?'

'Doesn't matter, Mr Makepeace. Even the smallest amount of mud makes a mark on a spotless reputation. The moment an accusation was made against Douglas, people would have been brilliant in how much they always *knew* he wasn't quite right.'

'Poor Sir William,' sighed Makepeace.

Kit grinned, then laughed. 'Don't worry too much about the old man, he's become quite fond of Lucius and, for all his grumbling about blackmail, he quite likes me too. The deed to the house is in my name, there is a substantial sum in the bank and Sir William has engaged doctors to look into Lucius' condition.'

'Will he walk again, do you think?'

She shrugged. 'Perhaps, but if not, I'll be able to care for him.'

Makepeace hesitated then asked, 'And your mother?'

There was a long pause before she seemed to answer a question he hadn't asked. 'My father died because he was kind. Almost three years ago he came across a girl in a Limehouse street, the apothecary's granddaughter. She'd been bludgeoned and stabbed – the two men who'd done it were standing over her. My father tried to defend her and the men attacked him, too. They both died watched by people too afraid to help either of them, but happy enough to recount the story afterwards.'

Kit stared out the window into the pretty little garden covered in snow. 'I like to think they weren't alone, then, going into the darkness.' Kit thought of Mary Jane, and Cathy, Elizabeth, Polly and Annie, so isolated in their dying.

'My mother despaired afterwards. You must understand, Inspector, she is not the woman she was – I have to remind myself of that every day. *That* woman did everything to try and keep us together, to keep us fed and clothed and housed. No one wants a clergyman's family after the clergyman is gone.

'When she'd married my father, her own family disowned her – she was better than him, of course, but when a woman marries down she loses all her status, while the man's increases ever so slightly. I found a woman willing to take me as an apprentice – although truth be told, I was the least able milliner-in-training ever to grace her establishment. We struggled along on my wage for a while, but we weren't making ends meet and Lucius' condition didn't make things any easier.

'She went to her family, begged her mother to take her back if only for the sake of the grandchildren. And the woman refused. Wouldn't even offer a basket of food to help tide us over – what kind of impoverished spirit refuses such a basic kindness?' Kit looked at her hands, clasped tightly in front of her. She rose and began to pace the pretty room.

'And so, one night – this was before we moved in with Mrs Kittredge, you understand, in another boarding house less salubrious than our last and less likely to poke into one's business. My mother would kiss us good-night, and when she thought us asleep, she'd pinch her cheeks and carmine her lips, paint kohl about her eyes like a gypsy. She'd loosen her hair and wear the only dress she'd kept from her previous life as a rich woman's daughter, a scarlet ball gown, with black lace and jet beads sewn across it like dark stars.

'I'd hide and watch from the top of the stairs as she walked down to the front door with all the dignity of a Queen and go out into the evening to earn whatever she could to keep us fed, Inspector. Judge as you will, but that was what my mother was willing to do for us.'

'What happened?' asked Makepeace quietly, as if he feared the sound of his voice might break the spell of her story; that she would stop talking and he would cease to be here, in this place where she wove words to conjure another time and place, other people who were not then as they were now.

'She came home late one night, battered and bruised, one ear almost torn off, her dress ripped. They'd cut her, too, there are scars on her belly you'd never wish to see. She survived, but not really. Not up here,' Kit tapped her own temple, then over her heart. 'Nor here. And if that wasn't enough, one of those filthy bastards infected her.'

'Syphilis?'

She nodded. 'She's rotting from the inside out. She's rotting from her brain down to her very core, Inspector. Growing more unstable by the day, and I can't look after her anymore.'

'So she's—'

'Sir William has been very generous – it makes me wonder sometimes if he knew her *before*, but he will not say. I think about what Mary Kelly said about him visiting the girls before he was incapacitated. He's arranged a place for her at a sanatorium near Windsor. Lucius, Mrs K and I visit her once a week, although she still will not speak to me, quite rages when she catches sight of me, so mostly I sit in the foyer and read.' Kit laughed mirthlessly. 'I find it fascinating, don't you, Inspector, that she judges me more harshly for dressing as a man and entering your world than I ever judged her for being a whore?'

He didn't know how to reply, so he changed the subject, 'And all that … magic I saw in you, all that fire – is it gone?'

She answered obliquely. 'It wasn't me, wasn't any power of mine. It was theirs, the witches, I was just an instrument.'

'What will you do now?'

'Oh, there are things to keep me busy, matters to look into,' she said and offered no further explanation.

They sat in silence for a while until Kit smiled and said, 'I don't wish to be rude, Inspector, but it's time for Lucius' physical therapy.'

'Of course.' Makepeace rose and she saw him out the door, brushing close by him and it seemed to paralyse him. He towered over her, staring down. He lifted one large hand and placed it on her shoulder, where he could feel the bandages that still bound her flesh. He opened his mouth to speak, leaning towards her.

'Do not mistake me, Makepeace. I'll be no man's whore.' Kit's lips were tightly compressed into a single angry line. Makepeace blushed and muttered an apology, shrugging on his overcoat and hurrying down the steps.

Kit wondered if she would see him again or not, then decided it probably didn't matter.

She watched him stride along the street until a movement caught her eye. Over by the fence around the private park, the spot where she would have the footman carry Lucius every day when spring came, where she hoped he would walk someday, there stood a woman.

Small with dark brown hair, wearing a forest green dress, a black short jacket over the top and a clean white apron. But she wasn't quite right – her outline shivered and shimmered, hovering between this world and the next. Behind her ephemeral skirts stood a child, holding onto her mother's legs, peeking at Kit as if shy.

Kit wondered at the ghosts, that the child who'd not ever drawn breath would look this way, then she figured Mary Jane could probably imagine her daughter any way she wanted now, could fashion her ectoplasmic flesh as she wished. The other woman smiled, a cocky sort of quirk that said *See? I'm still here. I won.*

Kit returned the grin and raised her hand in greeting, in farewell. Mary Jane picked up the little girl and set her on her hip. She gave Kit a jaunty wave and walked right through the fence into the snow-covered park, fading as she got further away. When she could be seen no more, Kit shook herself and went inside.

There were things to do.

ANGELA SLATTER specialises in dark fantasy and horror. She has won five Aurealis Awards, been a finalist for the World Fantasy Award, and is the first Australian to win a British Fantasy Award. The author of the collections *The Girl with No Hands and Other Tales, Sourdough and Other Stories* and *The Bitterwood Bible* and *Other Recountings*, forthcoming from Jo Fletcher Books is the novel *Vigil* and its sequel *Corpselight*.

vas'tat'ion *n.* (archaic, literary) 1: a renewal or purification of someone or something by the burning away or destruction of evil attributes
or elements; 2: spiritual purgation; 3: devastation; 4: a laying waste.
Origin: Latin *vastation-*, *vastatio*, from *vastatus* (past participle of *vas-
tare* to lay waste, from *vastus* empty, waste) + *-ion-*, *-io -ion*. First known
use: mid-16th century. Synonyms: depredation, desolation, destruction, havoc, ruin, waste, wreckage. Example: *That feeling of absolute
dread you experience when something invisible enters your life . . .*

VASTATION

LISA TUTTLE

ON THE SECOND of October, 1881, a man by the name of Robert Augustus Lowry sat in his house on the outskirts of Poughkeepsie, New York, and felt very comfortable. Although not given to that practice known as 'counting one's blessings', he was keenly aware of his good fortune in life, content with all he had, yet at the same time determined not to waste his inheritance, but to make use of the freedom it had given him to travel, read and think, by giving something back and contributing to the store of universal knowledge. He meant to write a book.

It could not be just *any* book (Lowry held the popular novelists and poets of the day in contempt); it must be a significant work of scholarship. For years, while he read and pondered, he had worried away at the question of the most suitable subject, drawn sometimes to the classics, to the philosophers of antiquity, sometimes to scriptural studies, his inclination shifting with the contents of each new paper or volume he came upon.

On this particular golden afternoon, fortified by an excellent meal of roast pork with a sauce made from apples from his own orchard, Lowry mulled over his latest idea, which concerned the most controversial and difficult book in the Old Testament. He had been making notes about the Book of Job for several years. Now, realising that of note-making and reconsidering there might never be an end, he thought it was time to stop hesitating, and simply write.

It felt good, making that decision. And then, in a moment, everything changed. He became aware that he was not alone. Someone – some *thing* – was in the room with him, a presence like nothing he'd ever encountered was squatting in the corner, radiating evil. As soon as he became aware of it, Robert Lowry was gripped by a feeling of hopeless despair, and as unable to move as if the foul thing held him in its talons and was slowly squeezing the life out of him.

Upstairs, in her room – that oddly-placed chamber with five doors and not a single window – Minnie Lowry woke from her afternoon nap with a start of fear. Terrified, she tumbled out of bed and, without pausing to do up her stays or put on her shoes, rushed out through Emma's room to the landing and down the stairs, along the corridor to the back of the house where she flung open the door to her father's private study, and took in the situation at a glance.

Her father was in his usual chair, but instead of bending over his books or sitting back, relaxed, looking thoughtful, he sat rigidly upright, transfixed with fear, and stared at the hideous thing that squatted on the other side of the room, in a shadowy corner between window and fireplace.

Although she had no name for it, Minnie recognised the evil creature at once. As a small child she had seen it – or another of its kind – crouching half-hidden in the shadows at the edge of the woods that bordered on the family property. It came back to her vividly, how she had stood at the nursery window and looked down at it. Even then, although she could have been no more than three years old, she had recognised in it a greater danger than the pretty flames she was always warned against, or the slobbering, vicious dog she'd seen shot down in the street. And yet, although she *knew* it was evil, she had felt more interest than fear. There was a pane of glass and the whole distance of the backyard between them; she was safe indoors, her brothers nearby, her mother within calling distance, her father downstairs, somehow, by his mere presence, erecting a protective barrier about his family . . . no, she had not been afraid of it *then*; but now, seeing it inside the house, witnessing her father's paralysis, the terror was almost more than she could bear.

She opened her mouth to scream but horror choked her; then, although she wanted to run away, concern for her father propelled her forward, and she flung her arms around him, hiding her face against his chest, blocking the sight of the creature from him with her body.

For long moments he did not move; he was so still that, unable to hear or feel his breath, she feared he had expired. The tears rolled down her face and she continued to clutch him, too frightened to move, even if it killed her, or risk another glance at the awful thing she felt lurking behind, filling the room with the oppressive atmosphere of hopelessness. It was too late. They were doomed. She could only hope her own passing would be quick, and that they would be reunited in Heaven.

She began to pray, hoping the words themselves had a healing, protective power. It was all she could do.

Time passed. She didn't know if it was minutes or hours later when her father's wife came in and found them.

'Robert, dear . . . Minnie! What are *you* doing here? Look at the state of you! Your dress undone, no shoes – what on *earth* . . .?'

Against her will, she was peeled away from her father.

'Go, off to your room.'

'But my father . . .'

'I am here now; I will see to – Robert, dearest, what's the matter?'

He shuddered, his eyes fixed still upon the far corner of the room. Minnie risked a look – and saw nothing there. She gave a deep sigh.

'What are you waiting for? Go at once and put yourself right.' A firm hand propelled her towards the door. Although Minnie resented her treatment – her stepmother seemed to forget she was now a grown woman – she did not protest, but stopped just outside the door, hearing her father begin to speak.

'Oh, my dear, the most dreadful thing – dreadful. Evil come into the house. Pure evil. Emptiness and desolation, all hope lost, there is no hope, no chance of redemption, nothing. Nothing.'

'What are you talking about, Robert? I don't understand. What has happened?'

'A force – I can't explain it, have no idea how it happened – it was just *there*, radiating a power against which there is no protection. At least, I have none. No faith any longer, no hope – it has all been stripped from me. I am lost, Ada, utterly lost. I don't know what to do. There is nothing I *can* do. All is lost.'

'Nothing is lost! Don't be silly, Robert, you've had a bad dream – you ate too much at lunch. Some fresh air might clear your head. Or shall we pray together? Perhaps—'

'You don't understand.'

Minnie burst back into the room. '*I* understand! I saw it!'

'You, too? Oh, poor child. My poor child.' He spoke in a voice drained of feeling, a voice of utter exhaustion.

She shivered and protested. 'It didn't *get* me, Pa! I saw it; I felt what it did to you, what it was trying to do, but – I won't let it win. You can fight it, Pa; you *must* fight, to be yourself again. I know you can! Anyway, it's gone now – see?'

His eyes remained on hers, as if it were too much effort even to turn his gaze to the empty corner, and she saw how awfully the thing's visit had changed him. But she refused to accept that this sad diminution of her beloved father should be permanent.

'Think of it like a bad dream, Pa. You saw something awful – but you were asleep. Now you're awake.'

'I was asleep, but now I am awake,' he repeated. 'Now, I see the world for what it is: an empty, desolate, terrifying waste.'

Tears threatened, but she could not afford weakness, and would not give in to them. 'No! That's what *it* wants. You must fight it, Pa – if you won't fight, we'll have to do it for you.'

'Minnie's right.' For once, the two women stood shoulder to shoulder in common cause. 'You must not give in to morbid thoughts. We're going to get you better again. I think, to begin with, a soothing hot drink . . . a barley cup? I'll massage your temples, and then . . . perhaps a little music? Shall we have Emma play us a tune? Minnie, please go and fetch your sister. Robert, dear, what frightened you was all in your mind. We shall *change* your mind now.'

Although she had learned not to talk about the frightening things she glimpsed occasionally and from a distance in the woods, Minnie had never outgrown her belief in their existence. She could not accept the idea that they 'were all in the mind' – they had existed before she was born and would continue to be whether or not she was there to see them.

Support for this idea had been established when she was ten years old, on a family tour of Europe. Robert Lowry had been abroad twice before, once as a very young man on a *wanderjahr* that had included a visit to the Holy Land, and next on an extended honeymoon with his wife. Now that his youngest children were old enough to appreciate it, he wished to give them all some grounding in great art and high culture.

Minnie had been bored much of the time, trailing through gloomy cathedrals and poorly-lit galleries, being lectured upon religion, history and aesthetics by her father, but once, staring at an oil painting on some religious subject, her skin had prickled with a mixture of fear and delight as she recognised an image of the very same creature that haunted the woodlands near their house: the sly, skulking, thoroughly malevolent little being that no one except she herself seemed capable of seeing.

'What is that, Papa?'

'That is the work of—'

'No, I mean that little animal, there.'

'Some sort of demon.'

'What sort? Where do they live? Are they native to the new world as well?'

'No, no, my dear, you misunderstand.' He smiled indulgently. 'Demons are not *real*. That is merely the artist's conception of an imaginary being.'

'But I—' she checked herself. 'It looks very realistic. As real as that owl.' She consulted the brass plaque for the title of the work. 'Saint Anthony – *he* was a real person. He is in the Bible. And demons, too. Is not the Bible the Word of God – true in every detail?'

She was being deliberately provocative, anticipating her father's reaction. Biblical scholarship was his particular passion, and he was never happier than when in pursuit of knowledge, arguing, discussing, and, above all, *explaining* to those of lesser intellect.

'Come, now, Minnie, you're old enough to understand that there are different kinds of truth, or different ways of approaching it. The stories in the Bible are not necessarily *literally* true. They must be studied in context. Surely you have learned from your reading about symbolism, metaphor and...'

And on and on. Minnie loved her father, but even at the age of ten she had been aware of a flaw in his argument. Although he spoke about different ways of understanding the truth, it was clear that he felt his own method trumped all others; that his version of the truth was the truest. So, she did not argue with him, but neither was she convinced. She would go on believing the evidence of her own eyes, feeling it supported by the work of a long-ago artist who had seen things that her father – his eyes, perhaps, too accustomed to focusing on the printed page – had failed to notice.

A dozen years later, face-to-face with a living demon, he had found the shock to his system too great. Minnie could not understand why he could not accept the evidence of his own eyes. If he had any doubts about his sanity, she could confirm that he was not deluded. She had seen it, too! Why would he not listen to her? Why did the encounter have such a baleful effect on him, but not her? Why did he allow it to oppress him so?

When she quizzed him, he only repeated the same, sad litany: how miserable he felt, how hopeless; how worthless all effort now appeared to his changed mind. He had been in the presence of pure evil, and although he had survived the exposure, it was only as the husk of the man he had been.

None of the home remedies offered as balm by his wife soothed Lowry's spirits in the least: not tea, not tonic, not music, nor visits from well-meaning friends. He could not pray; could no longer bear to read the books that had once provided solace and inspiration. Early on, he spent more than an hour closeted with the minister – Minnie *knew* her stepmother's decision to invite the man was a mistake. The churchman was neither clever nor deep. He had nothing better than platitudes to offer a soul in torment, and Lowry was more adept at quoting scripture, and far more skilled at constructing an argument. His logic could be devastating. Minnie saw the man's face as he emerged from her father's study at the end of their meeting, and she was perhaps the only member of the congregation who was not surprised to find that Sunday's service was conducted by a visitor who informed them that the Reverend Mr Bayles had been taken ill, and had gone away for a rest-cure.

A similar therapy was prescribed for Mr Lowry by their family doctor, who decided that too much thought had strained his nervous system. A change of scene, a vacation with mild physical exercise, healthful food and *no books* was his robust prescription.

The whole family packed up and went away, first to a resort in the Adirondacks, and then to the seaside. But no amount of wholesome, physical exercise in the open air made any difference to Mr Lowry's state of mind, and once winter had set in, they moved to a hotel in Manhattan, where the distraction of art, theatre, concerts and social gatherings might put an end to morbid thoughts, and specialists could be consulted.

It was in the waiting room of a nerve specialist that the breakthrough finally happened – thanks to Minnie falling into conversation with a lady who was waiting for her husband.

The lady was a Mrs Dobson, who turned out to have family in Poughkeepsie, and through them a number of acquaintances in common with the Lowrys. Encouraged by this connection, the motherly lady felt able to address Mr Lowry who had been sitting morose and silent as usual.

'Mr Lowry,' said she, 'I do not wish to distress you further, and I hope you won't find it offensive in me to ask, but there has been a certain amount of gossip and speculation about your illness, and whilst it may be all wrong, nevertheless I have an idea I may know where the problem lies. If you wouldn't mind telling me, in your own words, what happened . . .?'

Mr Lowry's own story never paled in interest for him. Whenever she heard him tell it again, Minnie was alert to every slight change in wording, emphasis and detail, and this time she noticed what she considered a significant alteration:

'It seemed as if some hideous, demonic creature had entered the room and squatted in the corner, giving off malignant, deathly rays . . .'

Seemed as if. Why should her normally precise father use such a phrase? She knew, because he had corrected her own misuse, that one said 'it seemed as if' as a rhetorical flourish, when about to reveal a very different truth, e.g. 'it seemed as if they were doomed to sail on forever, when the lookout spotted land.'

But there was no 'seeming' about his malignant visitor.

She was forced to interrupt. 'Excuse me, please, Father dear – why do you say "it seemed"? There *was* an evil creature in your room – you were not mistaken in your perception. It truly happened, and you are suffering from it still.'

They both stared at her, surprised. For the lady's benefit, Minnie added:

'I was there, too. I saw it – that awful intruder on our family happiness, squatting in the corner – and I felt the evil, although it did not have such a lasting impact on *me*.'

It was a mystery she often puzzled over to herself. Could it be, she wondered, that her childhood sightings of the demon had somehow prepared her, *inoculated* her even, against its ghastly power? Or had the thing come into the house on purpose to discharge its evil – like an adder its venom – into her father's soul, with nothing left to harm her?

It was a topic she wished she could explore, but she had ceased to speak of it after her stepmother accused her of selfishness and attention-seeking by trying to pretend she shared her father's illness.

Now, having spoken, Minnie quailed, expecting to be slapped down. But Mr Lowry only gave a weary sigh and said softly, 'Perhaps . . . perhaps . . . I do not know. I have thought about it so often, and my only conclusion is: *I do not know.* Where did that evil come from? Did it come from without – was it a creature of the Devil, sent to torment me? Or was it a creature from my *own mind,* lying dormant within me, until it was suddenly released and made manifest in the outer world?'

'You love your father very much,' said Mrs Dobson, resting her firm, capable hand upon Minnie's and pressing it warmly. 'You must be a very great help and comfort to him.'

Tears started to the girl's eyes. 'I wish I could help him. I have tried – but I don't know how to save him!'

'No, of course not, dear. How could you, when even the most learned doctors are baffled? But I believe I may have the answer.'

They both stared at her in astonishment as she continued. 'My dear man, from what you have told me, I conclude that you are undergoing a process that may have an outcome far more positive than you could dare imagine. What you are suffering is a state named by the great Swedenborg as *vastation.*'

Mrs Dobson explained that a great philosopher and mystic by the name of Emanuel Swedenborg had himself suffered what Mr Lowry was now going through. Although tremendously painful, it was a necessary stage in a regenerative process leading to rebirth.

'Do not be discouraged, dear sir, for you are being purged, and you will emerge with a new spiritual understanding.'

Mrs Dobson's words – her explanation of what until now he had seen in negative terms – had a galvanic effect upon Mr Lowry. He leaped to his feet, no longer interested in the opinion of another physician. All that mattered to him now was to learn more about the theories of Swedenborg, to follow the slender gleaming ray of hope provided by a chance encounter.

From a bookseller in the city Robert Lowry acquired a copy of *Heaven and Hell* and was directed to the Manhattan headquarters of the

Swedenborg Society where he purchased numerous other publications. At first, following doctors' orders not to over-exert his brain, he scarcely dared to more than nibble at the intellectual content he had acquired, but soon frustration caused him to rebel, and by the end of that week he was spending six to eight hours a day, shut into his room alone with his books, having to be coaxed away from his reading for meals.

Although worried at first that his habits would result in another breakdown, his wife had to admit that her husband had become much more like his old self – even his appetite had improved – and when, at the end of another week, he announced it was time to return home, no one could object.

Only Minnie felt apprehensive about this. She imagined the demon still waiting, invisible but as dangerous as ever, and she approached her father with her concern.

'My dear child,' he said, dropping a kiss on her head. 'You don't understand. *I* did not understand – until now! You remember, I wondered if that demon came from within my own mind, or had some external source? Now, having read Swedenborg, I understand it to have been a creation of my own mind.'

'But how can that be? I saw it, too!'

He grasped her hands, to stop her angry attempt to pull away. 'To say that something was the product of my own mind is not to say that it did not exist. On the contrary. Many things that begin as thoughts in the mind take on a physical reality – books, house, and demons, too. Heaven and Hell are not places located on a map, like Boston or Poughkeepsie, but they *do* exist. People create their own heaven or hell while they are alive, and inhabit their creation after death.'

There was more, far more than she could comprehend, but if her father understood, and Swedenborg's visions made sense of his own experiences, she felt she must take it on faith.

Home again, the Lowrys returned to their usual routines. Emma, quite the young lady now, was in much demand and frequently away visiting her wide circle of friends. Although she had no acknowledged beau, she would undoubtedly soon make her choice and embark on her career as wife and mother, leaving Minnie to grow old in the unenviable position of the last unmarried daughter, someone forever perceived as a child, never allowed to grow up, never to have charge of her own life, although she must take on increasing responsibilities of care for ageing parents.

Minnie did not envy Emma her friends and suitors and invitations; the very thought of such a social whirl exhausted her. After the constant company, the public life of city existence, she found it a great relief to be home again, where she could shut herself away in her own room without having to explain herself to anyone. Her stepmother would still come knocking and rattling at one door or another, with one of her endless demands, but so long as Minnie kept her doors locked and refused to answer, she was safe.

The room that she had taken for her own was the one room in the house with no windows. It had five different doors – most of them opening onto other bedrooms – and it had been used by Minnie's mother as a dressing-room. After her mother's death, Minnie had insisted on having her bed and all her belongings moved into this awkwardly situated chamber. Even after her brothers had moved out to establish their own homes, leaving two bedrooms spare, Minnie preferred to stay where she was.

No one knew the original purpose intended for this space, for the man who had designed the house and ordered it built had died before he could move in, and Mr Lowry had acquired the property cheaply at auction.

When Minnie wanted company she would slip out of her room and go down to her father's study. As long as she was quiet – and she was always quiet – he never minded her company. Engrossed in his reading, he might forget she was there.

She watched him, from her corner, and saw how he'd changed. On the surface, it was as before: he spent hours poring over books, sometimes pausing to gaze into space, lips moving as he formed a response to what he had read. But not only were the books different – they were all the works of Swedenborg and several other, more obscure, mystical thinkers – so was his attitude. Where once he had been calm and reflective, now there was something feverishly driven about him; instead of a leisurely exploration, his reading now seemed a race against the clock, to find the answer before he died.

Minnie had never before given much thought to her father's dying (only the death of her stepmother featured in her musings on the future) but his recent experience had aged him and drained much of his vitality, and although his encounter with Mrs Dobson and the writings of Emanuel Swedenborg had revived his spirit, his health had suffered permanent damage. His hands trembled, he walked with a stoop, and although he ate with renewed appetite, he never managed to replace the weight he had lost.

Winter gave way to spring, and then to summer. By July, everyone was saying it was the hottest summer they'd ever known. At midday, it was too hot to work or think. On Saturday the 15th of July, only Minnie and Mr and Mrs Lowry were at home. Emma was with friends out at the lake, and the maid had been given leave to visit her sister. After a meal of cold ham and potato salad Mr Lowry returned to his study; Minnie and her stepmother cleared and washed the dishes before retiring to their separate rooms.

'Wouldn't you rather lie on the porch, dear?' Mrs Lowry asked, as they mounted the stairs. 'The *chaise longue* is as good as a bed, and I'm sure you'll feel more comfortable with a bit of air circulating . . . I can't think how you stand it, in that box of a room.'

'Please don't worry yourself about me.'

It was true, her room was so hot that on that afternoon it was like being shut into an oven. But even if she was too uncomfortable to sleep, her mind could safely drift, without the need she would feel on the porch to remain vigilant against possible spying eyes.

Through her drowsy stupor an hour later Minnie heard the faint sounds made by her stepmother going downstairs. There was a knock, and the sound of a door opening below, and a muffled mumble of voices. Then— A sickening sound, a crunch, a gasp, a thud . . .

Abruptly she rose as if yanked to her feet, and stood, blinking confusedly as her heart pounded. What was it?

She held her breath and strained to hear more, but silence, as heavy as the heat, had descended upon the house after that brief, incomprehensible disturbance.

Nothing. No more irritating squeak and chatter of her stepmother's voice, nor the lower, always measured tones of her father's.

Then a door closed, slowly and carefully; so quietly she scarcely heard it, only felt something like a settling of the house around her.

Minnie rubbed her face, greasy with perspiration, and went to the jug and washbasin in the corner. When she had washed her face and hands, brushed her hair and sprinkled herself with *eau de cologne*, she put on her shoes and unlocked a door.

It was the door into her parents' bedroom, and for a moment she was puzzled, wondering why she had chosen this exit. Then she stepped forward. The bed was made up, but she could see the impress of her stepmother's body in the coverlet on one side. She went to the vanity table and opened the Chinese lacquered box where her stepmother kept her jewellery. She took out a pair of opal earrings and held them up to the window, watching how the stones flashed fire as they caught the light. Not for the first time, she was tempted to take them for herself. Her stepmother never wore them – 'opals were unlucky' she said, which was also her reason for not giving them away. There would be trouble if she saw them adorning Minnie, and there was certainly no point in taking them if she never dared to wear them – then she would be no better than her stepmother, a miser, dog in the manger – so she shut the box and left the room through the other door.

Downstairs, as she took the turning that would bring her to her father's study, Minnie found her stepmother lying on the floor. Her face was unrecognisable beneath a mask of bloody flesh and bone. Her head had been split open. She was dead.

Minnie sucked in a sharp breath, tasting raw meat and copper, but she did not gag, did not faint. Although she was frightened, her mind seemed to clear and sharpen. Her stepmother had been murdered! That was the noise she had heard – the killing blow. But who had done it? Someone, a stranger, had come into the house. Who? An inmate escaped from the asylum? A robber surprised, caught in the act? Had he fled? Or was the killer still hiding somewhere in the house? Should she retreat to the safety of her locked room, or run outside and scream for help?

She had taken one step back, away from the bloody corpse, when she thought of her father. She remembered the quiet closing of the door. Was the killer in there with him now? She imagined a hideous figure, shaking his blood-dripping weapon in threat, freezing her father into immobility with the horror of it, just as the appearance of the demon had paralysed him last year.

Was she too late? Was her father also dead?

The danger to herself no longer mattered. If there was any chance of saving him, she had to try.

Stepping across her stepmother's corpse, Minnie seized hold of the doorknob and found it tacky with blood. Heart quailing, she nevertheless opened it, and boldly went in.

Her father was sitting behind his desk as usual, but a bloody axe lay across the books and papers before him. When he turned to look at her, his smile was unlike any she had seen before, but she recognised the yellow gleam in his eye. It was the same evil light she had seen – they both had seen – raying from the demon's eyes last year, and it told her everything. Last year, she had been shocked to see that creature had got into the house, and thought there could be no greater horror. But this was worse: she saw it had got into her father.

He leaned forward to take hold of the axe handle, and she knew he meant to kill her.

But her father was an old man, and slow.

Minnie had never moved so fast in her life. She got her hands on the axe and hauled it off the desk, and then she stood, clutching it and glaring at the thing that looked like her father.

He came around the desk and reached to take the axe from her, all the while wearing the same, hideous, mindless smile. She gripped the weapon harder, holding it with both hands, stepped back, and then, when he came after her, she swung.

The blade of the axe sank into his side, through the already blood-spattered cotton of his shirt, and into his flesh, slicing into an area just below his ribcage. With some difficulty, she pulled the weapon free and swung again, this time higher, catching him full in the neck.

When he staggered and fell to his knees, Minnie shifted her grip, hefted the axe with both hands and brought it down on the top of his head, splitting it in two, like a log when you hit it in just the right place.

He was probably dead then, but she struck again: one, two hard blows to his back as he lay prone at her feet, just to be sure.

She threw down the axe and staggered out of the room, just managing not to trip over her stepmother before vomiting on the carpet at the foot of the stairs.

She felt cross with herself, but it couldn't be helped. She would have to clean it up – she couldn't possibly leave it for Maria to find when she came back from visiting her sister; Maria, or Emma, or the police, who would be eager to look for clues to point to the murderer's identity.

The truth would be of no help to her; no one would believe it.

She realised then that she would have to construct a narrative to save herself, a story that would make sense of the two deaths that had taken place in this house. If she overlooked anything, the world would brand her the most notorious murderess of the age, and she would be hanged. She must find a way to lay the blame outside the walls of her home, onto a vanished stranger.

She checked her shoes for bloodstains and removed them before going upstairs to change. Shoes and dress would both have to be destroyed – it was a pity the weather was so hot that a fire would be suspicious, but perhaps she could cut the dress up and disperse the pieces.

It was imperative to think clearly and quickly, to eliminate every bloody clue that could connect her to the deaths, and establish her alibi before anyone came to the house. Upstairs, she stripped off her incriminating clothes, and put on a pair of her father's boots to tromp around the other rooms, emptying drawers at random, scattering items of clothing and books and papers on the floor. She emptied her stepmother's jewellery into a pillowcase, added silverware to make it heavier, and dropped it down the well, feeling a pang for the lost opals.

At last, she retreated to her bedroom, locked every door, and lay down to construct the story of a victim who had quivered and shivered in her undergarments, too frightened by the terrible sounds from outside to move from her hiding place. She thought of taking the axe to the outside of one of her doors, to increase the impression of her own peril, but then she realised this might give rise to questions about why the killer had given up halfway through the job of demolishing her door . . . no, it was better for them to think her life had been spared because the killer never suspected there was anyone – or anything worth taking – behind the locked doors.

She would be horrified, she would faint dead away when they told her what had happened to her parents, and then she would weep and wail for their loss. They would be bound to believe, and to pity her, the poor, orphaned girl that she was now.

Only when she felt she had thought of everything, and worked the story through to its tragic ending, did she allow herself to relax, just a little, and tears came to her eyes as she thought of her father's death. All his studies had been in vain, or too little, too late. The demon had destroyed him in the end.

The question of where it had come from remained unanswered. Whether it had been hatched from his own mind (as he, following Swedenborg, believed), there was no doubt it *had* been inside the body of Robert Lowry when, in self-protection, she had been forced to kill her own dear father.

And where was it now? Where had *it* gone when *he* died?

Lying there in her hot, stifling room, the only living creature in the whole, silent house, Minnie knew she had forgotten something vitally important in her rush to save herself, and she wanted to leap up and rush downstairs before it was too late.

But it was already too late. She felt the great weight land on her chest, and although she could see nothing, she could feel the squat, reptilian body crushing her diaphragm as its hot breath squirted up her nostrils, foetid and putrescent, the odour of damnation.

LISA TUTTLE is the author of numerous short stories, including the International Horror Guild Award-winning 'Closet Dreams', while Volume One of her Collected Supernatural Fiction, *Stranger in the House*, was published by Ash-Tree Press. Her novels from Jo Fletcher Books include *The Silver Bough*, *The Mysteries* and forthcoming the first in the 'Jesperson and Lane' series, *The Curious Affair of the Somnambulist & the Psychic Thief*.

EPILOGUE

WHAT HAVE I done?

Too late now, I realise my mistake!

Words have power.

By stealing these sacred pages and allowing them to be read by one who was not – until you had finished this volume – a true scholar of Horror-ology, I have unwittingly released those damnable words into the world.

Where once I naïvely believed that I could diffuse the malign influence they hold by sharing them with others, instead they have grown and prospered amongst mankind, spreading their evil as each syllable is read and re-read upon the printed page.

By studying the tales recounted within the leaves of this volume, you have not only propagated the malfeasance contained within these words, but you have also attracted the attention of the Librarians.

For this, I am truly sorry.

Can you not already hear their hideous clacking behind the shrill whistle of the evening wind? Can you not already discern their strangely elongated shapes amongst the flickering shadows? Can you not already feel their foetid breath upon your neck as you grasp this book tightly in your hands?

For you, my friend, it is already too late.

They know where you are, and they are coming for *you*.

Amongst the Seekers After Truth there is an ancient riddle – or perhaps it is a curse? – that is often asked of the unwary savant:

What is black and white . . . and red all over?

The answer is, of course, this book . . .

. . . *soaked in your blood.*

TALKING
hORROROLOGY

Read on to find out more about Horrorology, the contributors and the
inspirations behind the anthology

What was the impetus for putting together _Horrorology_?

Stephen Jones: After the success of _A Book of Horrors_, a few years ago I pitched a couple of high-concept anthology ideas to Jo Fletcher at Jo Fletcher Books. She liked them both. So we decided to bring out _Fearie Tales: Stories of the Grimm and Gruesome_ first, in time for the 2013 World Fantasy Convention in Brighton, and then follow it up with _Horrorology: The Lexicon of Fear_.

I like doing these bigger anthologies every couple of years, rather than being on an annual treadmill. It not only makes each of them more of an 'event' book but, because of the more complicated nature of the JFB anthologies (a featured artist, all-original stories etc.), we actually need that amount of time to put them together and make them as classy as possible.

It also doesn't help that I try to get some of the more – shall we say 'established' – authors for these anthologies. These are writers at the top of their game, and consequently they are invariably much in demand. That's another reason why I like the longer lead time – so that we can give the contributors space in their writing schedules to come up with something a little more 'special' . . .

This is the third horror anthology you've published under your own imprint with Stephen Jones as editor – what was your first thought when he proposed _Horrorology_?

Jo Fletcher: How the hell do you spell it? And then, how the hell do you spell it the same way _every time_ . . . and then, we need a _really_ good illustrator to go with that calibre of writing. And then, how the hell am I going to explain this to the acquisition committee?

Whilst no one in the Quercus editorial team has any part in Jo Fletcher Books, and vice versa, I think it's important that within the company we know what each other are doing. I am often surprised – and in a good way – how suggestions and insights can come from the most apparently uninterested people. In this case, Jon Riley, then Editor-in-Chief of Quercus, now Publisher of riverrun, who's an extremely and widely well-read and much-lauded editor, said, 'What a cool idea!' before I'd even started my pitch! So huge thanks to Jon there.

And in fact, once you stop to think about it, *A Lexicon of Fear* is indeed a very cool idea, and it's also much easier to explain to booksellers than some proposals I've seen . . .

What made you want to publish an anthology of this sort?

Jo Fletcher: It's still very hard to publish horror in Britain. The whole genre crashed and burned at the start of the 1990s, after two decades of being able to publish pretty well anything with a haunted house or psycho killer in the description . . . but publishers were so desperate to reap the rewards that editors who knew nothing whatsoever about the history of the genre and what'd gone before were just buying and publishing anything they could get their grubby little hands on – this, by the way, is not specific to horror; name any bandwagon and you won't need me to point out those trying to hitch a ride without understanding the direction it's headed (I'm now going to ditch this analogy before *all* the wheels come off!).

So where were we? Oh yes, why? Well, I'm pleased to see that interest in the genre has been slowly creeping back – we're not talking about Number One best-sellers (well, except for Stephen King, of course, although I think everyone will admit he's paid his dues). What I mean is that we're at that stage where if I bring a horror project into an acquisition meeting, we will all actively consider it, and as I'm not going to bother bringing forward anything but those books I truly believe to be magnificent, we might even agree to take it on.

So I think my task is to start re-introducing horror into the country's literary diet – as one of its five-a-day, along with fantasy, SF, crime, and historical fiction (romantic fiction for desert, obviously!), and what better way to do that than with Stephen Jones, one of the world's most critically acclaimed anthology editors, collecting together some of the world's best writers of short horror fiction, including Clive Barker, who is himself a legend . . .

I think the better question is, *Why wouldn't you?*

*

Did you have a 'wish list' of authors for this anthology?

Stephen Jones: I always have specific authors in mind for any anthology – especially one like this, which was invitation only. I went after a number of 'names' and some we got and others, for various reasons, we didn't. I was also lucky that a couple of the contributors already had finished stories that I could use in the book. This is always the way when you are compiling an anthology. The book changes, grows, as you go along, and it doesn't always end up quite how you imagined it would when you started out.

The other thing with the JFB books is that we have now established something of a 'repertory' group of writers, who I like to mix up between the various projects, while also bringing in different names where and when I can. There is a core of authors that I love to work with because I know that I will get exactly what I want from them for the book. I trust them, and that makes my life easier as an editor. We have a working history. And then there are the newer authors I bring to the project who might be a bit more of a wild card and surprise even me.

It is always more difficult when a writer has to work within a specific set of thematic guidelines, which all the contributors have had to do with my JFB anthologies so far. The good thing is that my concepts tend to be fluid enough that we can usually work something out in the end. I only lost one story from *Horrorology*, and that was because the author decided to sell it to a better-paying market, and I couldn't compete with that. As it is, I still bought it in the end – but as a reprint for my other anthology series, *Best New Horror*!

What was the inspiration for your *Horrorology* tale?

Robert Shearman: I suppose I'm rather bothered by the way some of us get born with a natural talent for something, the unfairness of that – and the worry that the talent is just a genetic anomaly and has really nothing to do with me!

A lot of writers feel the same way, I think – we worry that since we did nothing to deserve it, the talent might fade away. I'm just lucky that I have some sort of ability to put down words on a piece of paper in a certain order that works – just as others have the ability to draw, or play music, or play sports. In a way, having a talent is a curse, because it means you only have the potential to be good – the talent only takes you a little of the way, the rest of it is down to hard graft and regular practice. You feel this responsibility not to let the talent go to waste, and you still know you're squandering it somehow – you're never as good as you ought to be.

I was playing around with this idea, of how finding out you have a special gift is rather like a curse – and I thought what would be truly funny would be if the gift you were born with were not only essentially useless, but blood-curdlingly unpleasant.

I've never liked clowns. No one really likes clowns, do they? I thought it would be a sensationally awkward gift to be born with, to find out what whenever you went to a circus, a clown would always die during their act. There wouldn't be much value to having such a talent, and the more it was practised, the gorier the talent would be – but still, in a strange way, it'd be your talent, it'd define you, and it'd be something you could be secretly proud of. Curse or gift? Aren't they two sides of the same coin? And so my weird tale began!

Michael Marshall Smith: 'Afterlife' arrived in two parts. The first page or two dropped into my head from nowhere, prompted by re-reading *Zen and the Art of Motorcycle Maintenance* for the first time in about thirty years. I had a clear visual image of a man and his life, but no idea What Happened Next. So I set it aside for about two years . . . until I looked at it again – prompted, as so often, by a timely request for a story from Steve – and realised the answer was already there in front of me.

Pat Cadigan: When I chose my word, the weather was cold and so was I. But when I got down to writing it, I had a sudden memory of how I used to freeze to death every summer in Kansas City because of the air-conditioning. I had moved to the area from Massachusetts and the heat was a shock – I'd never lived in a place where you could sweat without moving. I had also never lived in an area where air-conditioning was not a luxury but a necessity. People *died* in the heat without air-conditioning. So the whole thing kinda came together for me – people freezing to death in the depths of summer.

But when I asked myself why this would happen, the answer my subconscious delivered was 'human sacrifice'. (I know, I know; my subconscious needs help but refuses to get any.) And then I remembered what the winters had been like during 1977–80. We had *blizzards*, some of them so bad that there were a few days when I actually couldn't get into work – and I didn't live more than three miles away from my office. So I started looking up old weather data and that was *really* interesting. All of the weather described in 'Chilling' is factual; I only made up the deaths. Then, as I was getting to the end of the story, an old song popped into my head: 'Oh, Susannah'. That gave it a folklore-ish twist, and the whole thing was complete.

Mark Samuels: My tale is a satire on the advance of Internet technology accelerating the decay of complex human reasoning. With the rise of online tools like Twitter, Facebook, etc. etc., one finds, in order to communicate with a mass audience, participants limit their ideas to slogans, advertising, sound-bites, and the dictates of peer pressure. Moreover, in order to com-municate – other than very briefly at the level of a truncated mass shouting match! – civilly, interactions within the system *require* certain shared and often unexamined philosophical and political assumptions. 'Decay' also satirises the current fad of believing that human level sentience is a simply a matter of achieving, in a machine, either a high enough degree of brute computational power and/or the requisite algorithmic programming.

Joanne Harris: I wrote 'Faceless' while I was staying alone in an old par-sonage in Oxford. It was snowing; there was no Internet or phone line; the house was enormous, ancient and (I thought) visibly haunted. What else could I do?

Muriel Gray: Everyone's idea of horror is different. It occurred to me while watching some soul-scouring reality TV show that to some young people the idea of not existing on social media is a kind of death. Perhaps worse than death. To this new generation, demons, monsters and witches would not be night terrors haunting their dreams, but simply points of interest to include in selfies. Creatures that would win 'likes'. Their real deep-rooted terror is to be invisible, ignored, forgotten. What a different variety of fear this is to the darkened attic windows of abandoned Gothic houses that frightened me as a youth. Add this to the notion of a non-gender specific witch, minding its own business, never bent on vengeance unless pushed, and 'Forgotten' was born.

Kim Newman: I think they're all worn on the sleeve, for a change – I was thinking of pretty much everything that was happening in France in the late 1890s, and the way French history and culture fed into the gruesome type of theatre known as *Grand Guignol*, and mapped that onto more recent trends in explicit horror.

It's part of a cycle I've been writing called 'Angels of Music', which will turn up as a book in the near future – and that's a gloss on *Charlie's Angels* and *The Phantom of the Opera*, playing with the adventuresses of 19th and 20th century fiction. I've done stories riffing on Stoker, Stevenson and Doyle, so this time I looked to French creators like Gaston Leroux, Louis Feuillade, Alfred Jarry and Oscar Méténier for source material.

My first trio of angels was Christine Daae (from *The Phantom of the Opera*), Irene Adler (from Conan Doyle) and Trilby (from George du Maurier) . . . but this story features Kate Reed (from Bram Stoker, very loosely), Clara Watson (from Octave Mirbeau and the *Grand Guignol* adaptation of *The Torture Garden*) and Yuki Kashina (from the *Lady Snowblood* films).

Having used well-known characters earlier, I wanted to go with less familiar folks this time – Kate, whom I've been developing in my *Anno Dracula* and *Diogenes Club* stories, gets a Paris holiday and is very much the lead this time round. I listened to a lot of Offenbach while and watched a lot of video nasties writing the piece.

The Angels of Music will return in *Phantom Ladies Over Paris*.

Ramsey Campbell: As many of my tales do, 'Nightmare' originated in an everyday setting that suddenly took on a darker aspect, at least in my head. The setting was a bunch of recently built streets – a suburb off the Wirral Way, a nature trail we often walk along. The notion of being lost in a mundane suburb that begins to prove worse than unhelpful occurred to me, and I took some of the elements the place included, not least the lost pet posters, a common sight these days. In the writing the tale left behind some of the developments I'd meant to include, and there may be enough of them to make up a separate story in time.

Reggie Oliver: I have always wanted to write something about the 1960s, in particular the dark side of its glamour: the rapacious greed of its hedonism, the male exploitation of sexual liberation.

I was a young teenager in that decade living in London and found it all thrilling. One film that superbly captures that era in all its glitter and seediness is Antonioni's *Blow Up*. The image of the young and then beautiful David Hemmings as the photographer in that film standing over the prone body of one of his models, pointing his camera down at her, as if raping her with it, was a starting point . . . That coupled with pictures of David Hemmings towards the end of his life, paunchy, unglamorous, disappointed, an Adonis no longer . . .

Angela Slatter: Well, mine had a bit of a convoluted beginning: I was writing the story under another title for another publisher and when I got to the end I thought, 'It doesn't *precisely* fit.' Stephen Jones wrote to me in the meantime, with the *Horrorology* pitch and I thought, 'It does *precisely* fit there.' So the novella was re-titled 'Ripper' and went to a new home (rest assured, the other publisher has been furnished with an equally lovely novella . . . of course, when I say 'lovely', I mean 'creepy').

The inspiration was, fairly obviously, the Jack the Ripper murders. As a policeman's child with deep, dark interests this was naturally the sort of historical event that caught my attention (and the Yorkshire Ripper later on). I'd read Kim Newman's 'Red Reign' as a teenager and I think there's an element of *homage* in 'Ripper'. There are so many theories about this serial killer, and there've been so many stories about him/her, it was hard to find my way to adding to the literature – or rather feeling I had an idea that would do justice to everything that's gone before. I *think* I got it right.

Lisa Tuttle: Many years ago, reading Leon Edel's biography of Henry James, I was struck by his description of something that happened to the writer's father – also named Henry James. Here's the relevant passage:

'One day, toward the end of May 1844, the elder Henry James ate a good meal and remained at the table after his wife and boys had left it. The afternoon was chilly and there was a fire in the grate. He gazed contentedly into the embers 'feeling only the exhilaration incident to a good digestion'. Relaxed, his mind skirting a variety of thoughts, he suddenly experienced a day-nightmare. It seemed to him that there was an invisible shape squatting in the room 'raying out from his foetid personality influences fatal to life'. A deathly presence, thus, unseen had stalked from his mind into the house.' (from *Henry James: The Untried Years 1843-1870* by Leon Edel, 1953).

These days, something like that would probably be defined as a nervous breakdown, and doctors in those days took a similar attitude, telling James he had overworked his brain and needed to rest. But James felt it was something else, and attempted to figure out if the evil creature he had seen had come from his own mind or from another realm, eventually finding an answer that worked for him in the writings of Emmanuel Swedenborg.

When Stephen Jones asked me if I'd like to contribute to his lexigraphical anthology, the word that came immediately to my mind was 'Vastation' – the Swedenborgian term that Henry James Sr. gave to the above-described experience. I was pretty sure nobody else would have beaten me to that word – and I was right.

Who have been your favourite horror authors over the years?

Jo Fletcher: Gosh, that's an impossible question, because it changes from day to day as names I've temporarily forgotten edge back up to the surface . . . I've always preferred 'quiet horror' to 'splatter' (which isn't to say that there isn't some very visceral horror writing out there which I think is completely brilliant) . . . I suppose the first horror story I ever read for myself was 'The Snow Queen', because my grandfather had this beautiful edition of his fairy tales illustrated by Edmund Dulac, and I always thought the pictures were as much a part of the experience as the stories . . . And the other book my grandfather used to read to me was a great tome of myths and legends of the world, also beautifully illustrated, and I particularly remember the eagle, pecking out Prometheus' liver, stomach, intestines, and so on, only for them to re-grow in time for the bird's dinner the following day . . . I'm all for nurturing the avian population, as you know, but there are limits. Those ancient gods were not just about turning into flora or fauna to have their way with any pretty young thing that happened along; they did a fine line in eternal punishment and retribution too . . .

And then of course one moves seamlessly on to M.R. James, Elizabeth Gaskell, Sheridan Le Fanu, Algernon Blackwood and Mary Shelley and their ilk, not forgetting Keats, and Milton, and Blake, and Dante, and then we're into the 20th century, and the wonderful Edith Nesbit and Edith

Wharton, Rudyard Kipling – there's a Kipling story about a man trapped in a great horseshoe-shaped arena, where the people all live in coffin-shaped and -sized holes in the sides, but he cannot get out, because of the shifting sands . . . I had nightmares for months afterwards, and I have never been able to read it again, just in case . . . and of course H.P. Lovecraft led me to August Derleth and all the Arkham House writers, and thence to the young pretenders, like Ramsey Campbell and then of course, Charles L. Grant, the master of quiet horror, and I'm not even a quarter of the way through the first shelf of a *very* substantial bookcase and I am missing out so many astonishingly wonderful names, like Manly Wade Wellman and Karl Edward Wagner, and then there's the even younger Young Turks . . . [voice fades away and three days later fades back in] . . . and Lisa Morton and Robert Shearman and Tom Fletcher and Nancy Holder and Alison Littlewood and Kim Wilkins and Angela Slatter . . .

Can you remember the first story you read that made you think 'I want to write!'?

Robert Shearman: Oddly enough, it wasn't so much a specific story, as a specific environment. My father owned a lot of books – enough that he built his own library as an extension to the house. As an infant, a treat for me would be to go in there and look at all those books, and wish I could add to their number. I didn't really care what those books would be about – so long as they had my name on the spine.

When I was five years old I used to take down encyclopaedias and copy out entries (about anything, really anything, it was almost random), fold over the page so that it was a little like a book, and write a name and title on the cover. I was a plagiarist back then. And because for work my father collected foreign language dictionaries, I'd then translate those so-called books I'd pretended to write into French, Dutch, Swedish, Finnish – anything I could lay my hands on. (Of course, I had no idea about conjugations and declensions or that sort of thing – I wasn't translating anything for real, just looking up all the words and replacing them with a foreign equivalent – but it meant I could turn the very same book into multiple editions! And it gave me an interest that stood me in good stead when I did become a translator, for a little and wholly unsuccessful while, in my late teens.)

It took me years to realise the greater pleasure with my father's books would have been to try reading the things. Who knew?

Michael Marshall Smith: The very first stories that interested me in the idea of writing fiction were the 'Of Adventure' series written by Enid Blyton, which I loved when I was a kid. I remember starting something along those lines when I was about twelve, but quickly running out of steam. The book that really pushed me over the edge was *The Talisman*, by Stephen King and Peter Straub. A friend of mine badgered me into reading it – I'd read nothing by King or Straub at the time, and very little 'horror' of any kind – and before I'd even finished the book I knew this was the kind of thing I wanted to do with my life.

Pat Cadigan: I'm afraid not. I'm one of those people who always knew what she wanted to do; in my case, it was write. I was pounding away on my mother's old Underwood typewriter when I was three years old. However, I can tell you the books that really drove me to get serious: Judith Merrill's *The Year's Best S-F* anthologies. I found them in the public library – my mother used to let me take books out of the adult library on her library card and Judith Merrill's science fiction anthologies took my breath away. My ambition was to write well enough to be selected for one of them. I wish someone would bring them all back into print; the few I have are very tattered paperbacks.

Mark Samuels: I can't recall that there was a single story that made me determined to become a dedicated writer. I do remember certain tales that impressed me in my early teens, mainly the Sherlock Holmes series of detection adventures and macabre tales by Poe and Lovecraft. Back in the 1980s, it was a case of undergoing something like an apprenticeship within the fanzines and honing one's craft. I garnered a large number of (very justified) rejection slips at the time. It was during a later period, in the mid-1990s, that my reading in all forms of literature expanded dramatically, and my own efforts began to improve. Though my first published story was in 1988, I don't believe I considered actually self-identifying primarily as a writer, even of the very obscure and almost 'underground' type I am now, until quite recently.

Joanne Harris: Ray Bradbury's short story 'The Smile'.

Muriel Gray: In common with most of my contemporaries, I used to read *The Pan Book of Horror Stories* beneath the bed covers with a torch at night. This was such a common pursuit it must have been the law. It's hard to pick out a single story from that cornucopia of delights, but I longed to be able to invent dark worlds as elegantly as my horror idols from that early beginning. Saki's 'Sredni Vashtar' and Ambrose Bierce's 'The Damned Thing' both appear in a diary list I kept age eleven of 'Things I Like', so they must have made an early impact. M.R. James was my hero from early teens. That hasn't changed.

Kim Newman: 'The Sea Raiders' by H.G. Wells. It's the one about killer jellyfish.

Ramsey Campbell: I can't identify just one, I'm afraid. I was reading from an unnervingly early age – Hans Christian Andersen and George Mac-Donald before I was five, Edith Wharton and M.R. James (both in *Fifty Years of Ghost Stories*) by the age of six, H.P. Lovecraft's 'The Colour Out of Space' at seven . . .

All these must have spurred me in their different ways, but as far as I can see the first thing based on a recognisable source that I wrote (when I was around seven) was the start of a science fiction novel called *Dogs in the Stratosphere* and mercifully unfinished – lost as well. It derived from Clifford Simak's *City*, then a favourite novel of mine, but he should in no way be blamed for my grisly imitation.

Reggie Oliver: Oh, undoubtedly it was Sherlock Holmes, but I couldn't say which one. Possibly *The Hound of the Baskervilles*, which was the first novel I ever read to myself. Conan Doyle's horror tales too – 'The Leather Funnel' for example – were equally an influence. My first attempts at writing were nearly all imitations of Doyle in his horror or detective story modes.

Angela Slatter: That's really awfully hard. Maybe *The Wolves of Willoughby Chase* by Joan Aiken? Or perhaps *A Wrinkle in Time* by Madeleine L'Engle? I read a lot of M.R. James' ghost stories as a child in various anthologies, so perhaps something by him. I do remember reading 'The Tower' by Marghanita Laski in high school and being seized by the idea that maybe it was something I *could* do – the desire to write and the idea that I could write were definitely two separate moments.

Lisa Tuttle: Well, no – because I can't actually remember a time when I didn't want to write, as well as read, stories. So the inspiration probably came even before I could read, from one of the children's books my parents read to me, or even from the pictures I had to interpret to myself, lacking the ability to read the words that would have explained them.

Is horror a sort of natural home for you or do you lean more towards another part of speculative fiction?

Robert Shearman: I think I can't stop myself tipping towards horror. I've just got that sort of imagination. For years I thought I was really a comedy writer – it was my bread and butter for such a long time, I wrote a couple of dozen comic plays for the theatre and the radio before I even thought to write horror prose – but when I read them back, I realise the jokes I tell are so black, and the situations so strange and absurd, that it's really horror by another name.

Comedy and horror are so close to each other anyway – in both, the writer is trying to shock the audience into giving an audible response. And my sense of humour has always been of the grisly kind – it just leaks into everything.

Michael Marshall Smith: Horror is the home I keep coming back to, after time spent wandering around other types of fiction. It's what first started me writing, and I think it's the broadest church of all the genres – a flavour you can add, as much as a type of story.

Pat Cadigan: Now, that's a funny thing. Back in the day, the field of fantastic literature wasn't as stratified as it is now. *Everything* was science fiction – Heinlein, Tolkein, *Gormenghast*, *Frankenstein*, *Dracula* – they were *all* in the science fiction section of the public library (I should mention this is the US public library I'm talking about; we were too poor to buy books so I used to denude the SF shelves in the public library on a regular basis).

In 1980, it was my great good fortune to take Robert Bloch (*Psycho*) to dinner when we were both at a conference in Florida. I was an attendee and I'd just made my first professional sale. I had met him a few years earlier at an SF convention in Kansas City and I wrote to him and asked if I could take him to dinner. He accepted – and what a dinner we had! Afterwards, we stayed up talking until almost 5:00 a.m. It's an experience I treasure. But one of the many things that became clear to me over our hours of conversation: Robert Bloch considered himself a science fiction *fan* – and a science fiction *writer*. Because it was all science fiction. And it was like that in the Judith Merrill anthologies. Her best science fiction of the year included hard SF, contemporary fantasy, horror, and what today we would call 'slipstream' – like 'The Jewbird' by Bernard Malamud, and a very witty story by John Cheever (I've forgotten the title) about how the dinosaurs really became extinct; spoiler: after too many cocktail parties, they died of ennui.

So to actually answer the question: fiction with a fantastic element is my natural habitat. When I start a story, it tells me whether it's science fiction, fantasy, or horror, and I just go with that. But I can also write to order, and I am as much at home in a rocket ship as I am in a haunted house or a magic shop no one else can see or anywhere else.

Mark Samuels: I don't sit down at my laptop thinking 'now to write another horror tale (heh, heh, heh!)'. I think my imagination tends to be stimulated and to operate along certain thematic lines and that the sense of the profound mystery behind existence itself is what really fires my imagination into life.

Joanne Harris: I write all kinds of things. My first novel was a horror story, but I like to explore all areas of speculative fiction, including fantasy, sci-fi and magical realism.

Muriel Gray: Horror is my first love, passion and absolute natural home, but Science Fiction is another passion and has always tempted. I have a half-finished SF young adult Western set on a very hostile planet, full of monsters, fighting star ships and half-formed things. But it's gathering dust in some deep buried file, mostly because it's absolute pants.

I'm also keen on comedy and the book I'm currently working on is a comedy horror. So it will never sell. Everyone hates those. Everyone. I don't care, and you can't make me stop.

Kim Newman: As a critic, I spend a lot of time putting books and films into genre boxes, but as a writer I tend to try to escape from them. I think I write 'Kim Newman stories' rather than horror or science fiction or whatever – though I have used titles like 'Another Fish Story' and *An English Ghost Story* to signify my attempts at staying neatly inside the box while trying to do things that interest me with the forms – but that's a good thing, since no one else is going to write them, really.

Ramsey Campbell: I'm guessing you already know the answer. Let me quote myself from elsewhere:

I'm Ramsey Campbell. I write horror.

That's how I introduce myself at readings and on panels, and I should have thought it was straightforward enough to be uncontentious. Perhaps not, because my saying so at a British Fantasy Convention offended a splattery writer, apparently for presuming to claim a name rather than because he found my fiction insufficiently horrible for his taste. Nevertheless I'll continue to announce myself that way, in conversation too if the opportunity arises.

I quite enjoy being told that people don't like horror, which they don't read (a situation that prompts me to ponder how they can know). Sometimes they even tell me that they don't like the sort of thing I write, although they haven't read it. On occasion they approach me to let me know as much. Admittedly the sort of fun this affords is limited, and I think there's a better reason for me to keep up the image. I believe I'm in a minority of writers who say that they write horror.

Some of those who made their name with it seem eager to show they've moved on. Some might even like to convince us that they never entered the field, and seek to erase all traces of their presence as they flee the scene of the crime. I won't be doing either. Perhaps I was lucky to encounter the classics of the genre first – anything that found its way between hard covers and into the public library – but I've never faltered in my conviction that horror is a branch of literature, however much of it lets that tradition down. I started writing horror in an attempt to pay back some of the pleasure the field has given me, and I haven't by any means finished. I don't expect to choose to, ever.

I'll just add that when Liverpool John Moores University gave me an Honorary Fellowship for (their phrase) 'outstanding services to literature', I said at the beginning of my speech that I would like to accept the honour on behalf of my field as well.

Reggie Oliver: Yes, though I have sometimes chafed at the term 'horror' simply because some people (mostly literary snobs) have such limited expectations of it. By it they tend to mean a lot of blood and sordid sex, and physical torment. And while I don't entirely reject that side, I do think there's a lot more to it than that.

I like the term that Charles Williams used for his 'speculative fiction': 'spiritual shockers'. If I could be seen as a writer of 'spiritual shockers' I'd be happy.

Angela Slatter: It does seem to be . . . or at least I've washed up here. I started out in fairy tales (actually, I started out writing chick lit, but don't tell anyone), and I really feel that fairy and folk tales are the ancestors of horror. Think about it: your mother sends you off to starve in the forest; your father wants to marry you; you are forced to wear red-hot iron shoes and dance yourself to death; you're punished for being vain by being given a pair of dancing shoes you can't take off so you ask someone to cut off your feet to save you . . . I rest my case.

The darkness has always been more interesting to me as a source of tales.

Lisa Tuttle: Although I am not entirely easy with calling myself a 'horror writer', I have always been drawn to the weird, the strange and the supernatural in fiction. That is certainly my natural territory.

Even though when I first began getting published in the 1970s I was identified as a 'science fiction writer', most of my stories (and they were all short stories then; it took a long time for me to feel ready to write a novel) would probably be better identified as horror or fantasy. But SF was the dominant genre then; there were few markets for weird and supernatural short stories.

What makes Clive Barker the perfect illustrator for *Horrorology*?

Stephen Jones: With each of the JFB anthologies we start out asking ourselves who would be the best artist to work on the project. That will also give me a clue as an editor as to how the book is going to come together. I have also worked as a designer all my life, so I try to be very hands-on when it comes to the look of my books, and for the most part I think that has worked very well.

To be honest, my initial suggestion to Jo Fletcher was that we should use H.R. Giger. A number of people were surprised that he was still alive and, in fact, he sadly died while the book was being compiled. It was Jo who actually suggested Clive. I had wanted a story by him anyway, and she thought that he would be a perfect fit as an artist as well. I agreed. We made an approach, and he accepted, and that was it.

The funny thing was that as the anthology developed I realised that it was becoming a kind of homage to Clive's classic *Books of Blood*. This led me to add the 'wrap-around' material, putting the book in context just as Clive had done with his first set of collections. In fact, I even managed to slip a little 'tribute' into the opening section. So, having Clive contribute the dust-jacket illustration and interior illustrations, along with an original short story, seemed somewhat appropriate.

Obviously, Clive and I have worked together on various projects since the mid-1980s, so we had a bit of fun with the bio at the back of the book as well . . .

You're offered the chance to visit the Library of the Damned – do you accept?

Stephen Jones: Hmm . . . given what happens to our narrator in the 'wrap-around' material, I'm not so sure. But then again, who could pass up the opportunity to look at all those lost and forbidden books that have been hidden away from all but a select few for centuries? No matter how horrific the ultimate consequences are . . .

The Library of the Damned material also allowed me to pay tribute to the work of H.P. Lovecraft and Clark Ashton Smith, which is never a bad thing so far as I am concerned.

Robert Shearman: There'll be books there, yes? Lots and lots of books? How could I ever refuse?

I have a weird relationship with horror, inasmuch as that, although I enjoy writing it, I'm very easily frightened by it. Not the horrors of my own imagination, which are easy and funny and safe in my head, but the horrors of other people's. I can only watch horror movies at home, because I'm too afraid to see them in public – I know I'll put my hand in front of my eyes and squeak, and that never looks good.

But horror in book form is another matter – I go to them wanting to be unnerved, wanting to feel my imagination is being twisted and expanded. That's the great joy of good horror, the way it seems to refresh the entire world. Library of the Damned? I'd never want to leave!

Clive Barker: Without hesitation.

Michael Marshall Smith: Yes, obviously. How could you not?

Pat Cadigan: Absolutely! I've probably got the library card in my wallet. I hope they've got my books, or at least some of the anthologies I have stories in. Where is it, anyway? Can I get there by public transportation or will I have to take a cab?

Is the Library of the Damned supposed to be scary or something? *Please.* I kicked terminal cancer's arse *and* I've been married three times.

Mark Samuels: I doubt it.

Joanne Harris: Of course. Is there tea?

Muriel Gray: Not only would I accept the chance to visit the Library of the Damned, I would demand a membership card and spend the majority of the day there at a table I'd claim most aggressively as my own. It sounds like Heaven for those interested in Hell. Even without wifi.

Kim Newman: I am fond of libraries . . . though I let more invitations slide than take them up these days.

Ramsey Campbell: If it contains books, by all means.

Reggie Oliver: Oh yes. I'm with the African/Roman dramatist Terence on this. '*Homo sum, humani nihil a me alienum puto.*' 'I am a human being I count nothing human alien to me' – even 'damned' humanity.

Angela Slatter: Is there cake? Or doughnuts? And coffee, good coffee . . . actually that would be the absolute embodiment of damned: gluten-free cake, stale doughnuts and cold instant coffee. And probably a very strict librarian, shushing you every time you complained.

Lisa Tuttle: Well, I'd probably want to check it out on the Internet first, find out what people were saying on TripAdvisor and so on. I'd need to give it some thought.

Jo Fletcher: Damn straight!

The future of horror is . . .?

Stephen Jones: To be honest, I fear for the future of horror. Oh, there's no lack of self-published, print-on-demand, ebook-only horror – the market is literally swamped with it. But that's not going to support the future of horror, despite what some people may think.

We need properly *paying* markets – we need professional publishing imprints to include horror on their lists and to pay a fair sum for the fiction they use, otherwise there will be no professional horror writers in five years' time. Just part-time authors, writing whenever they can between a full-time job because they can't afford to live any other way.

Without the support of professional publishers and editors, writers are never going to learn about style, construction, spelling, punctuation, and all the other things that will help their work stand out from the rest. No matter how long you've been published, you always need a second opinion from somebody who knows what they are doing. With *Horrorology* I not only had Jo, but Nicola Budd was my editor on the project as well. And thank god they were both there for me – they caught numerous things that I had missed or hadn't thought about that ultimately made the book better in my opinion.

And if authors can't earn a decent living from their work, then eventually most of them are going to go off and do something else. And then where will horror – and all the other literary genres – find its new stars? How will writers learn their craft, and develop, and become the best-sellers of the future? These are the questions that worry me as I see how dramatically the horror genre – and publishing in general – has changed in just the past few years.

But I guess my biggest concern is that we are losing the readership. I go to conventions now where people don't care about reading in the genre any longer. Oh, they like to dress up as characters, play games, or watch film and TV adaptations, but they just are not interested in going back and reading the source material (let alone anything classic or new that they may be unfamiliar with). They don't seem to realise that there would be no *Game of Thrones* TV show or tie-ins without the hard work that George R.R. Martin put into his original novels. The same is also true for so many other popular franchises that are based on literary works.

If successive generations stop reading novels and short stories then, eventually, there will be no new ideas and all we will be left with are remakes of remakes because nobody knows anything better. I've gone on record as describing this as the 'Morlocks vs. Eloi Syndrome' – and if you don't know what that is a reference to, then the genre is already in more trouble than even I realised . . .!

Robert Shearman: We live in a world now where we're almost numbed to the idea of global catastrophe, where you can turn on the computer and catch videos of atrocities. I love vampires and werewolves and ghosts, but partly because they now seem so likeable and so quaint – there's a wonderful and terribly moving nostalgia to them.

I think horror's future is more an acknowledgement that we are barraged by insanity on all sides – that there is a growing dissonance between the way we expect people to behave and the way they really do. In all horror, old or new, there's nothing I find as unnerving as the realisation that life has just gone a little askew and nothing makes sense any longer. I think we're living in the world of the uncanny, and all we writers can do is try to keep up.

Michael Marshall Smith: The same as the past. Good stories, told well. Anything else is a fad that will pass.

Pat Cadigan: The future of horror is alive and well. Who doesn't love a good scary story? Only party-poopers.

Mark Samuels: One usually gets two types of responses to this.

Here goes: The first is along the lines of a request (very often, and most vocally, from old white males themselves) that greater inclusiveness is the future, that a higher proportion of female and minority writers must be afforded greater exposure. Personally, I think true equality consists of treating everyone on the same artistic basis, not a quota basis, and the final criterion for acceptance should be the actual quality of the fiction submitted, not gender, not ethnicity, not disability and not any other factor. What matters is the imagination and the skill of an author in telling a tale. Nothing else. I certainly do not subscribe to the view that individual old white men are, for any reason, more intrinsically capable of writing quality horror fiction than individuals drawn from any other category in society. But the idea that extrinsic political considerations be the benchmark for judging a work of fictional composition is, I contend, a species of patronisation.

The second common response is along different lines. Horror has entrenched itself into the movies and the vast majority of people no longer read books anyway. Successful (I mean highly *commercially* successful) horror authors had either better write a novel that can be turned into a Hollywood blockbuster film or else produce a body of work that can be utilised as a movie franchise. It's not a vision that inspires me in the slightest. The other thing to bear in mind, and it was a staple view in the 1990s and the 2000s – but, it seems has finally, and mercifully, died off – is that there will be no return to the likes of the 'horror boom' of the 1970s and 1980s in publishing. The decline of literacy has advanced to such a degree that the days of such cycles in publishing are over. The end was in sight when conglomerates took over all the smaller publishing houses that used to proliferate. Now the small press, with one or two notable exceptions, is all that remains for those who might once have been mid-list mass market authors of horror story collections (not anthologies) or novels that are not the size of a brick.

My own view is this: writers will continue, in the future, to work in this continuum of fictional composition (parts of which have been labelled 'horror' or 'weird' etc. for quite some decades now) as they have always done. No single author, no matter how masterful, is the summation of that continuum. And the label itself certainly isn't important except for outside factors not connected with literary artistry, like commercial marketing. Ideally, the impetus for the author to engage in that continuum should come from within, and not from without.

Joanne Harris: Inside us all, awaiting its chance to break out again through the pitiful veils of rationality and reassurance we like to drape around ourselves . . .

Muriel Gray: The future of horror is more horror. As much of it as we can get. To me it is the very highest of literary genres, which is why so many of the greatest writers who ever lived have at some time dabbled in the supernatural. Those who cannot imagine an unseen world are probably not looking at the real one closely enough.

Kim Newman: Clive Barker stamping on a human face forever?

Ramsey Campbell: As vital as ever, I'm quite sure. Whenever the field is declared dead (and indeed, at other times as well) it produces new talents.

Reggie Oliver: Exceptionally dark and exceptionally bright, a sort of 'divine darkness', as St John of the Cross would have called it, especially when placed in the hands of Stephen Jones, Clive Barker, or in fact any and all of the contributors to *Horrorology*. I really think this is a great age for horror, because of its exceptional variety and inventiveness.

Angela Slatter: It's Lisa L. Hannett, Helen Marshall, Damien Angelica Walters, Gemma Files, Mercedes Murdock Yardley; it's Robert Shearman and Rio Youers, Mark Morris and Johnny Mains, Kaaron Warren and Margo Lanagan . . . it's all the folk who come out to play after dark.

Lisa Tuttle: Even if I knew, I wouldn't be allowed to tell!

Jo Fletcher: Slow and steady, and most importantly, of very high quality. After all, people still love being scared – as long as they know they can turn the light back on at the end of the story . . .

* * *

ACKNOWLEDGEMENTS

I would like to thank Jo Fletcher, Nicola Budd, Clive Barker, Mark Allan Miller, Anne Riley, Mandy Slater, Dorothy Lumley, and all the authors for their help and support.

Photo credit: Stephen Jones and Clive Barker, 1989. Copyright © Peter Coleborn.

Stephen Jones and **Clive Barker** have been working together since they were first introduced to each other by their mutual friend Ramsey Campbell in the 1980s. In 1985, Clive's short story 'The Forbidden' (the basis for his successful *Candyman* movie franchise) was first published in *Fantasy Tales* #14, co-edited by Steve and David A. Sutton. Six years later, Steve compiled *Clive Barker's Shadows in Eden*, the first critical study of the author's work. After working as the Unit Publicist on the films *Hellraiser* (1987) and *Nightbreed* (1990), both scripted and directed by Clive, Steve published the official illustrated guides *The Hellraiser Chronicles* and *Clive Barker's The Nightbreed Chronicles*. In 1997, Steve wrote *Clive Barker's A-Z of Horror*, based on the BBC TV series of the same name. Since those early collaborations up to the present volume, Clive has also been a regular contributor to anthologies edited by Steve.

A
BOOK
of
HORRORS

Edited by
STEPHEN JONES

DON'T TURN OUT THE LIGHTS, BUT DO OPEN THE COVER . . . IF YOU DARE

Stephen Jones, Britain's most acclaimed horror editor, has gathered together masters of the macabre from across the world in this cornucopia of classic chills and modern menaces. Within these pages you will discover the most successful and exciting writers of horror and dark fantasy today, with a spine-chilling selection of stories displaying the full diversity of the genre, from classic pulp style to more contemporary psychological tales, to cutting-edge terror fiction that will leave you uneasily looking over your shoulder, or in the wardrobe, or under the bed...

Jo Fletcher
BOOKS

FEARIE TALES

Stories of the Grimm and Gruesome

Edited by Stephen Jones
Illustrated by Alan Lee

Two hundred years ago two brothers, Jacob and Wilhelm, collected together a large selection of folk and fairy tales and published them as Kinder- und Hausmärchen (Children's and Household Tales). So successful was the first collection of 88 stories that they kept adding more to subsequent editions. Since then, the tales of the Brothers Grimm have been translated into upwards of a hundred different languages and are known and loved throughout the world.

Now award-winning editor Stephen Jones has tasked some of the brightest and best horror writers in Britain, America and Europe with reinterpreting some of the traditional Hausmärchen, putting a decidedly darker spin on the classic stories.

Jo Fletcher
BOOKS

Curious Warnings
The Great Ghost Stories of
M.R. JAMES
150TH ANNIVERSARY EDITION

Edited with an Afterword by

STEPHEN JONES

Illustrated by

LES EDWARDS

Montague Rhodes James - M. R. James - was an English academic and provost of King's College and Eton. He started writing ghost stories to entertain his friends... one hundred and fifty years after his birth he is now revered as the father of the modern English ghost story.

This gorgeous hardback collection contains all thirty-five of M.R. James's highly acclaimed ghost stories, including the classics: 'Oh Whistle, and I'll Come to You, My Lad' and 'Canon Alberic's Scrapbook'. As well as a foreword by Clark Ashton Smith and an extended Afterword by Stephen Jones the book is gloriously illustrated by award-winning artist Les Edwards, who has provided a frontispiece and a dozen full-page illustrations, as well as many small pictures throughout the text.

Jo Fletcher
BOOKS

VIGIL

ANGELA SLATTER

Verity Fassbinder has her feet in two worlds

The daughter of one human and one Weyrd parent, she has very little power herself, but does claim unusual strength - and the ability to walk between us and the other - as a couple of her talents. As such a rarity, she is charged with keeping the peace between both races, and ensuring the Weyrd remain hidden from us.

But now Sirens are dying, illegal wine made from the tears of human children is for sale - and in the hands of those Weyrd who hold with the old ways - and someone has released an unknown and terrifyingly destructive force on the streets of Brisbane.

And Verity must investigate - or risk ancient forces carving our world apart.

Jo Fletcher
BOOKS

· THE · CURIOUS · AFFAIR · OF ·

SOMNAMBULIST
AND THE
PSYCHIC THIEF

Lisa Tuttle

Jesperson and Lane, at your service

For several years Miss Lane was companion, amanuensis, collaborator and friend to the lady known only as Miss X - until she discovered that Miss X was actually a fraud. Now she works with Mr Jasper Jesperson as a consulting detective, but the cases are not as plentiful as they might be - until a case that reaches across the entirety of London lands in their laps.

It concerns a somnambulist, the disappearance of several mediums, and a cat . . . the links with the cat are negligible, but there is only one team that can investigate the seemingly supernatural disappearances of the psychics and defy the nefarious purpose behind them.

Jo Fletcher
BOOKS

THE
HIDDEN
PEOPLE

ALISON
LITTLEWOOD

IN HALFOAK, TRAGEDY IS ONLY
HALF-A-STEP AWAY . . .

Pretty Lizzie Higgs is gone, burned to dead on her own
hearth - but was she really a changeling, as her husband
insists? Albie Mirralls met his cousin only once, in 1851,
within the grand glass arches of the Crystal Palace, but
unable to countenance the rumours that surround her
murder, he leaves his young wife in London and travels
to Halfoak, a village steeped in superstition.

Albie begins to look into Lizzie's death, but in this place
where the old tales hold sway and the 'Hidden People'
supposedly roam, answers are slippery and further
tragedy is just a step away . . .

Jo Fletcher
BOOKS